The Girl from Penny Lane

Kitty stood on the edge of the kerb, contemplating the length of Penny Lane. As she did so a figure came cycling slowly along Greenbank Road, stopping at each lamp post as he reached it. The lamplighter was doing his rounds. If I don't get up me courage an' start a-knockin', the Lord above knows what I'll do tonight, Kitty reminded herself stoutly. Git a move on then, kid!

Obedient to her own command, Kitty crossed the road and began to walk along the pavement. Immediately it struck her that these neat little suburban houses had no great flights of steps under which she might hide herself for the night, nor could she even begin to think about a return to Rodney Street until she'd had a few hours rest.

So you've got no choice, Kitty Drinkwater, she told herself firmly. It's find the girl from Penny Lane or get took up for a vagrant and chucked into the work'ouse. So start, Kitty, or git back to that park afore the gates is locked an' barred.

Katie Flynn has lived in the North-West for thirty-two years and during that time has seen many changes in Liverpool, especially around the docks and in the city centre. A compulsive writer, she started with short stories, articles and radio talks when her children were small. As they grew up she turned to writing novels under several names, and has enjoyed great success.

Also by Katie Flynn
and available from Mandarin

A Liverpool Lass

KATIE FLYNN
The Girl from Penny Lane

Mandarin

A Mandarin Paperback
THE GIRL FROM PENNY LANE

First published in Great Britain 1993
by William Heinemann Ltd
This edition published 1994
by Mandarin Paperbacks
an imprint of Reed Consumer Books Ltd
Michelin House, 81 Fulham Road, London sw3 6rb
and Auckland, Melbourne, Singapore and Toronto

Reprinted 1994 (three times)

ISBN 0 7493 1348 X
A CIP catalogue record for this title
is available from the British Library

Printed and bound in Great Britain by
BPC Paperbacks Ltd
A member of
The British Printing Company Ltd

For Tim and Sylvia Turner,
who introduced me to the Rock.

Acknowledgements

My thanks go once again to the late Richard Brown, whose wonderful stories have helped me to build up a picture of Liverpool some seventy years ago, and whose experiences 'on the tramp' as a youngster have been freely adapted to enrich my tale. Thanks also to the staff of the Local History section of the Central Libraries on William Brown Street, and to the café on the top floor, for feeding me when reading got me down!

In addition, thanks to Rosie Hague and her mother, Lily Evans, who introduced me to *Her Benny*, by Silas Hocking (essential reading for all Liverpudlians), and last but not least a big thank you to Terry Billing of Norwich, who was kind enough to lend me, gratis, a keyboard for my word processor when I found myself in his area, with a book to write and no keyboard to type it on.

Chapter One

1924

'Kitty Drinkwater, ain't you the idlest kid ever to come out o' Paradise Court? Didn't I tell ye an hour since to take them trimmin's over to the milliner for me? Might just as well save me breath. Now will you put that handful o' rubbish down and git over there right this minute, afore I catch you one across the side o' your lug!'

Kitty guiltily lay down on the doorstep the three fragments of broken pottery she had been holding and got to her feet. Trust Ma, she thought crossly, to interrupt the only winning streak she'd had for days and days ... she'd lost her five hoarded cherry stones the previous day to Humpy Alley, who had amazing luck, and she could scarcely remember the last time she'd actually owned an olly; for weeks now she'd been forced to borrow other people's for the odd game, which meant anything you won was theirs, and made playing pointless, almost.

'All right, Mam, if the stuff's ready I'll git a-going,' she said as soothingly as she could. Sary Drinkwater's temper was legendary, not only amongst her large brood of neglected children but amongst the neighbours, too. Little Etty O'Mara, who had been playing with Kitty and Ellen Fosdyke, stumbled to her feet as Kitty did and prepared for flight. Etty knew full well that Sary, with drink inside her, could fetch you a thump which would knock you halfway into next week whether you were her kid or not, and Etty was

1

too little and weak to risk that sort of violence.

'Well? If you're just a-going, why ain't you here, takin' the stuff off of me?'

'You put it down on the step, an' I'll fetch it,' Kitty said diplomatically. 'I wasn't born yesterday, Mam, I's not comin' too near, not I!'

'Nasty, sly little slut,' her ungrateful parent mumbled, eyeing her first-born broodingly through slitted lids and clenching her fists in a horribly workmanlike way. 'You'll come 'ere when I sez or . . .'

She swayed and clutched the doorpost. Inside herself, Kitty chuckled. Sunshine was the enemy of the morning after, she reminded herself gleefully. Mam had been down at the Black Dog on the corner of Vauxhall Road until the early hours, she wouldn't come into the bright afternoon willingly. 'Where's the box to go, Mam?' Kitty asked. She could tell her mother's head must be paining her something shocking, what with the drink and the close work which making the trimmings entailed. 'Which milliner do you mean? Is it Miss Hughes on Upper Freddy?'

Sary made another threatening gesture with her fist but it was weaker than the first. She's yaller as a wax candle, Kitty thought gratefully. She ain't going to belt me one, not now she ain't. If only I can get her to bring the box out onto the step . . .

'You know bloody well I only works for Miss Hughes, now,' Sary Drinkwater said thickly. She put a wavering hand to her brow and half-closed her eyes, but Kitty could see she was still watching with spiteful intensity through her swollen lids. 'Oh Gawd, me 'ead's splittin'. Come 'ere, Kit, or . . .'

'Put the box on the step, Mam,' Kitty coaxed softly. 'I aren't going to let you tek a swipe at me, you don't know your own strength an' that's the truth! If you give me a broken arm I ain't likely to get that box delivered this side o' Christmas, am I? Put the box on the step and I'll be over to Upper Frederick Street and back again afore you've had a chance to miss me.'

'Me own child ... ungrateful .... never a word but she's wicked as the devil ... what've I done to deserve ...'

Sary's muttering retreated as she began to go back into the house behind her. Kitty waited. If she got within a couple of feet of the door and her mother was hiding behind it she'd not escape, but if she stood well back and bided her time ...

A small figure appeared in the doorway. Kitty's sister Betty stood there, both arms wrapped round a large cardboard box. Like all Sary Drinkwater's children she was barefoot and dirty, but she wore a proper dress and not a man's shirt with a piece of orange rope round the waist, as Kitty did, and her fair curls were tied back from her face with a piece of once-white ribbon. She was an appealing child, round-faced, healthy-looking, but now her blue eyes were saucered with apprehension and her small mouth drooped pathetically. She kept glancing behind her as she came out onto the step, a clear warning to Kitty that her mother was still lurking. 'Ere you are, our Kit,' she said. 'For Miss Hughes.'

'Righto, Bet, fetch it over here,' Kitty said briskly. 'Did Mam give you a penny for me tram fare?'

A muffled roar from behind the door was answer enough – not that Kitty had the slightest expectation of having to do anything other than lug the box, on foot, half across the city. And for nothing, too, she knew. If Mam had made one of the other kids go it would have been a farthing for a gob-stopper or a couple of liquorice sticks, but if she sent Kitty ...

3

'You're the eldest,' she would say briefly, if Kitty ever questioned her treatment. 'You owes it to us.'

Once, Kitty had felt forced to point out that though she was indeed the eldest, Arny and Bob, the twins, were a mere eleven months younger than she, and both bigger and stronger. Her ears had rung for days from the resultant pounce and pounding, so that was one point she had not laboured. It was useless expecting fairness from Mam, and Pa, when he was home, was worse. The other kids got ha'pennies, sweets, even hugs. All Kitty got was abuse. Pa even grudged her food, wouldn't have her sitting near them when he brought in a paper of chips or a hot pie. She was forced to lurk in the back kitchen, a noisesome hole with no fireplace and a damp earth floor, waiting for a brother or sister to have pity on her and sneak her a mouthful or two.

Sometimes Kitty indulged in a beautiful fantasy – that she was not Mam's eldest daughter at all but a changeling of some sort, which was why Mam treated her not like her own flesh and blood but more like a slave, or an enemy, even. She would look at her reflection in a window pane, seeing not the tangled mop of red-brown hair tied back with a bootlace nor the man's shirt which reached to her knees and was all the dress her mother bothered to provide. Instead, her mind's eye saw white skin, coppery curls, a pretty dress . . . and shoes on her bare and dirty feet. After all, Mrs O'Rourke, who had lived only two doors away from the Drinkwater's, though her home was as different from theirs as it could be, had once hinted that there was something special about Kitty, but she wouldn't go the whole hog and say what that something was. Mrs O'Rourke had been a nurse in her young days and had gone abroad with Florence

Nightingale to nurse wounded soldiers, so she should know.

Kitty and Mrs O'Rourke had first become friends when the older woman had found Kitty in the Court, weeping bitterly over a cabbage. Kitty had been small and the cabbage was large, so lugging it home from the Great Nelson Street market, where she had stolen it from a busy stallholder, had been a task which had taken her most of the short winter afternoon. So when her mother had snatched the cabbage from her arms, snarled at her for being out late and slammed the rickety door in her face, it had seemed like the end of the world to the young Kitty.

She had cast herself down on the dirty flagstones and not only sobbed but railed against fate, too – and railing against fate, when you are seven years old and don't have much experience of life to call upon, consisted, in Kitty's case at least, of using the worst words at your disposal at the top of your tear-choked voice.

'Bloody, bloody, bloody-bloody-bloody cabbages,' she shrieked. 'Lazy, sluttish, greedy, idle cabbages! Stinkin', rotten, bastard cabbages!'

In her heart, she half-hoped her mother would come out again, even if she only battered her for swearing and then took her inside, but Sary did not reappear; the stained and crooked wooden door with a hole where the handle should have been remained closed.

After she had cried all her tears away and was at the sad, hiccuping, snuffling stage, a quiet voice spoke to her from out of the increasing dusk. 'Now what do we have here? Well, if it isn't little Kitty Drinkwater, a-lyin' on the flags an' bitin' great chunks out of 'em, very like! Sit up, lovie, an' tell me what's caused you grief.'

Kitty sat up, knuckled her eyes and looked around her. Mrs O'Rourke was standing on her neatly whitened doorstep looking down at Kitty. She was wearing a blue serge coat with shiny buttons over what looked like a navy wool skirt and she had sensible lace-up shoes on her feet. Her thick grey hair was neatly parted in the middle and drawn back behind her ears and she wore a tiny pair of spectacles perched on her fat little nose. Behind the spectacles twinkled a pair of shrewd grey eyes.

'Well, darlin'?' she said now in her soft, Irish voice. 'What's caused you grief? Is it hurt you are? Knocked your knee?'

'Mam shut me out; she snatched me cabbage an' then banged the door in me face,' Kitty said, the words bringing her tears to the surface again. 'It was 'eavy, that c-cabbage, it m-med me late, it waren't my fault!'

'Shut out, are ye? Did you give de door a bit of a knock, then? Or a bit of a shove?'

Kitty shook her head. She found herself reluctant to describe the conflicting emotions which made her accept her dismissal, since it would also entail admitting that if she did go indoors she would probably be in more trouble, though for what she could not be certain. She knew, without understanding why, that the mere sight of her could put Sary in a rage and though, by and large, she accepted this unwelcome fact and did her best to keep out of her mother's way when she was in a mood, she was still baffled by the violence which could descend on her head simply because Sary had forgotten to buy the bread, or even because a younger brother or sister had been difficult.

'No, ye wouldn't, of course,' Mrs O'Rourke said, having given the suggestion of Kitty knocking the

6

door some thought. 'Well, how would ye like to 'ave tea with me, chuck? There's soda bread, sardines an' a fruit cake for afters. 'Ow about it?'

Kitty scrambled to her feet, all thoughts of unfairness and grief forgotten. The food sounded weird and wonderful, but what she valued most was the invitation. To get beyond that whited doorstep and to see the wonders within! It was rumoured that not only did Mrs O'Rourke's house have all its floorboards still intact, it had carpets as well, and linoleum in the kitchen to cover the bricks. And there were embroidered squares on the chair-backs so your greasy head didn't mark her covers and pictures on the walls, to say nothing of refinements such as wallpaper and a sideboard with polish on.

And now Mrs O'Rourke had opened her front door – a wonder in itself, painted a lovely deep green with the panels picked out in cream and the doorhandle and door knocker not only present, but made of well-polished brass – and was ushering Kitty inside.

Kitty stopped on the doormat to stare. All the rumours were true, in fact they weren't the half of it! A broad mantelpiece supported a ticking clock, some beautiful ornaments, and two vases each containing three pink roses. There was marvellous carpet on the floor, a very pale creamy brown colour with wreaths of pink and red roses scattered over it. Because it was summer there was no fire in the grate, but where in winter flames would blossom now Mrs O'Rourke had a big blue vase filled with bulrushes.

Kitty's eyes travelled slowly over the wonders. White net curtains across the lower half of the window panes, and a red baize curtain by the front door though this was pulled back in deference to the warmth of the July day. And the chairs! They had pictures on the seats and backs and the couch had half-a-dozen cushions thrown casually down upon it, whilst against one wall was a little bookcase crammed with books, and against another a dresser with gleaming china – all roses and arbors – laid out carefully to best advantage. Against the third stood a small upright piano made of some reddish coloured wood, with a picture above it of a wistful lady leaning on a sun-dial with a sheet of music in one hand and her mouth open, so you guessed she was singing.

'Sit down, chuck, while I put the kettle on,' Mrs O'Rourke said hospitably. 'It's on the hob in the back kitchen, so I shan't be two minutes. Can you read?'

Kitty had attended school sporadically for two years and could read better than most children of her age but she nodded rather doubtfully. 'I can read from readin' books,' she said. 'Them Rainbow Readers . . . stuff like that.'

'If you can read them you can read anything,' Mrs O'Rourke assured her. 'Take a look at the book on the little table by the fire – it's what they calls a magazine – it's got pictures of the King and Queen in there it has.'

Kitty sat down, suddenly conscious of the state of her clothes and the smell of them. All she wore was a shirt, but it had never been washed – never been off her back since her mother had slung it at her a couple of months earlier. She had seen Mrs O'Rourke going to and from the hospital where she worked and was sure her hostess changed her clothes, probably as frequently as once a month! But she would be very careful with the magazine . . . she put out a grubby hand to pick it up, then pulled it back. She would look with her eyes, there was no need for hands to be involved; that way the magazine would stay clean.

And fortunately Mrs O'Rourke was as quick as she had promised, so she had only looked at the shiny cover of the magazine, wondering which of the people illustrated thereon were the King and Queen since everyone was dressed, so far as she could see, in perfectly ordinary clothes with not a crown nor a coronet in sight, when Mrs O'Rourke wheeled a trolley into the room. It held a teapot under a knitted cosy, two white china cups, two plates and the promised food. Kitty wouldn't have known that the object was a trolley – she thought it looked a bit like a miniature tram in fact – except that Mrs O'Rourke referred to it as such. Sitting herself heavily down on the sofa she leaned forward and took the cosy off the teapot.

'A trolley's a deal lighter than a tray, to be sure,' she observed, tapping the side of the round white teapot approvingly. 'And it'll hold more . . . do you like tea, chuck, or would you rather have a cup of milk?'

Kitty had never tasted milk, so the choice was agonising. She screwed up her face, praying for guidance – this chance might never come again – which would she prefer?

'You'd like the milk,' Mrs O'Rourke said, deciding for her. 'Better for you . . . put some flesh on those bones.' She poured herself a cup of tea, then poured milk for Kitty. The jug was small and white with a frill round the rim, and the cups proved to have a full-blown rose on either side. She handed a cup of milk to Kitty and Kitty tasted it. It was lovely, though somehow unexpected – she had thought it would be thicker, had not imagined it would slide down so easily, quenching thirst.

'Now . . . here's some buttered soda bread and a

9

sardine . . . you squash the sardine flat on the bread, see, like this, with a speck or two of salt. I'm rare fond of sardines so I am.'

Kitty decided after a mouthful that she, too, was rare fond of sardines. She wished she could have a little sardine squashed up on a piece of soda bread every day of the week – and then Mrs O'Rourke cut the cake.

That cake was the nicest thing Kitty had ever tasted or ever hoped to taste, for that matter. Mrs O'Rourke, handing her a crumbling slice, explained that the fruit was in fact sultanas, currants and mixed peel and not fades from the market, as she had at first supposed. It was made with eggs and flour and milk, butter and dried fruit, and it was moistened, as Mrs O'Rourke put it, with brown sugar . . . it was a prince, nay a king, amongst cakes.

And while she ate, filling her starved and empty belly, Mrs O'Rourke filled her achingly lonely mind.

'Your Mam give you a clat round th'ear, is that right?'

Nod, nod, went Kitty's head as her mouth dealt with mashed sardine and soda bread.

'For bein' home late, is that it?'

'I brung 'er a big cabbage,' Kitty said thickly. 'She bawled at me an' slammed the door in me face.'

'And you don't know why, eh, queen? Because she ain't so rough with the other kids – that about the size of it?'

Nod, nod, *nod*, went Kitty's head again, emphasising that it was very much the size of it.

'Ah. Well, you's different, queen. Always has been, always will be. There's nowt wrong wi' being different mind, but your Mam had a rare bad time givin' birth to you. It's often that way wi' a first child. And . . . I don't know if you knew, you was born th' wrong side o' the blanket, which sometimes meks a woman more fond an' sometimes meks her uncommon grudging.'

Kitty swallowed her mouthful, cleared her throat, and said what was in her heart.

'Was it my fault, that I was born the wrong way round, like? Was it suffin' I did?'

Mrs O'Rourke took a sup of her tea and wagged her head at Kitty. Her grey eyes looked kindly, as though she really did sympathise.

'No, chuck, it were more . . . but ne'er mind that. You've got an 'ard cross to bear, that's for sure, but it's nothin' you done, it's more what you are . . . can you understand that?'

Kitty nodded again, not because she understood – she had not the faintest idea what Mrs O'Rourke was talking about – but because she wanted to please this wonderful warm, motherly woman who had taken her in and been kind to her.

'You do?' Mrs O'Rourke looked doubtful, then smiled. 'Oh well, tell you what, chuck, you come an' see me when things get too much for you, and we'll 'ave a nice cuppa an' a nice chin-wag. 'Ow about that, eh?'

And Kitty, full of delicious food and with a white milk-moustache round her upper lip, agreed with starry eyes that she would come and see Mrs O'Rourke often. And by the time she left, her small belly as hard and full as a new-laid egg and her mind warmed from the attention and kindness she had received, she was almost reconciled to her lot. It no longer seemed so important that her mother hated her and her father despised her. Indeed, over the days that followed she somehow managed to convince herself that what Mrs O'Rourke had actually said to her, what she had really meant, was that Kitty was not a Drinkwater at all, but someone different. Someone finer, more intelligent and sensitive than any Drinkwater could possibly be.

However, right now, with the round hat-box clasped in her arms, it was hard to remember that first meeting and the ones that had followed without also remembering where Mrs O'Rourke was now.

Dead. And it had been Kitty who had found her.

Walking as fast as she could, which was not particularly fast as the box was both heavy and awkward, Kitty cast her mind back to that December more than two years ago, when she and Mrs O'Rourke had had their last tea together. It had been a cold, miserable day: with Christmas only days away and Hector Drinkwater home from sea and nasty-drunk most of the time Kitty had been outside her house more than she had been in, so the sight of Mrs O'Rourke gesturing to her in her doorway had been more than usually welcome.

'I bought's a pair of bloaters,' Mrs O'Rourke said, when she had closed the door safely behind Kitty. Sary Drinkwater had early shown belligerent fury that her daughter should be asked in to a neighbour's house, so by unspoken consent the visits had become a secret between the two of them, with Mrs O'Rourke beckoning from her window and Kitty, like as not, sneaking in under cover of darkness. 'And I made one of those treacle tarts you like.'

Ecstatically, after their tea, the two of them talked: about books, because Mrs O'Rourke had joined Kitty and herself up at the big library over on William Brown Street; about sewing and knitting, because Mrs O'Rourke was teaching Kitty to do both; and about Father Riordan, because Kitty went to Mass

12

with Mrs O'Rourke if she could get away, a couple of times a month.

Kitty had been reading *Her Benny* and wanted to discuss it with her friend, whilst Mrs O'Rourke was rather anxious to discuss the recent disappearance, from the shop shelves, of tins of red salmon. Between the two of them their tongues had never stopped until, at close to midnight, Kitty decided it would be safe to go home.

She kissed Mrs O'Rourke goodnight, said she'd come round again before Christmas and sneaked into her own home. By moonlight, she joined her small sisters and the twins in the fusty little back bedroom, diving into the big pile of rags which constituted their bed. She had slept soundly with a full stomach and a happy mind, for Christmas meant a present from Mrs O'Rourke and Kitty had saved some pennies to buy her friend a gift in return. She intended to shop for it in the morning.

But next day the knife-grinder, meeting Kitty as she hurried off on an errand for her mother, told her he'd not been able to get an answer from Mrs O'Rourke's place and he had a pair of scissors for her, well-sharpened, and would Kitty like to take them and hand them over when her friend was in?

'Well, she's in today,' Kitty said. 'She don't go out much, mornings, an' she said last night she'd be workin' on her knittin', today.'

You couldn't peer through Mrs O'Rourke's windows because of the net curtains, but the door wasn't locked. Kitty went in, worried that her friend might be ill, and found her, dead and cold, sitting in her fireside chair with the jumper she had been knitting still in her lap.

Relatives who had never bothered with her in life

came to the hooley after the funeral. Father Riordan preached a lovely sermon and everyone cried, even if only Kitty meant it. The lovely, clean house which Mrs O'Rourke had worked so hard to keep decent was let to a young married couple, and within a couple of years the man lost his job, the girl had two babies, and the floorboards came up to light a fire during a hard winter. The house, Kitty knew without ever setting foot in it, would be very similar to the Drinkwater establishment soon. And she averted her eyes from it as she passed and planned how, one day, she would run away and find her real parents, the Duke and Duchess, or Prince and Princess, and live happily ever after.

But Mrs O'Rourke had died more than two years ago, and Kitty had grown resigned to the loss of her friend. She still went to the library and borrowed books, but she had to hide them well or her mother would have sold them. She had never told Sary, or any other member of the family, about her ability with a needle, for if her mother knew she would force Kitty to help with the trimmings. Life was hard enough, Kitty concluded, without taking on more unpaid and unappreciated work. When Sary could catch her she made Kitty light fires, chop wood, cook whatever food was available and keep an eye on the kids. Kitty had no desire to add sewing to the long list.

So now, peering over the top of the box as she crossed the Scotland Road to make sure there was no traffic about to mow her down, Kitty considered her lot. Twelve years old, thin as a lath and generally dirty and unattractive, she had almost no chance of a job, yet work would be her only escape from Paradise Court. She was happy enough in school, mixing with other kids and finding the work well within her

14

capabilities, but there were always those embarrassing occasions when a parent was summoned to come to the school, or an outing was planned, or a group photograph taken. It went without saying that Mr and Mrs Drinkwater would not turn up and would not cough up, either. Whilst Mrs O'Rourke was alive she had slipped Kitty oddments of money for errands run or small tasks performed, but now she was dead it was steal or go without, and though Kitty was by no means averse to a spot of thievery, she knew that her friend had disapproved and did her best to stay on the straight and narrow. Besides, though her brothers stole and her father brought things home from sea which Kitty doubted he had acquired honestly, she knew without any doubt that if she was *caught* pinching, her parents would kill her. Not half kill, but finish her off once and for all.

Any excuse, in fact. Kitty's left eardrum had been perforated when her father had punched her in the side of the head, she had had ribs fractured and a broken wrist after an encounter with her mother when drunk, and her skinny arms were always black and blue from the automatic, almost casual, blows which were the result, it seemed, of a parental eye lighting upon her.

One day I'll go, she told herself now, clutching the increasingly heavy box of trimmings. One day I'll just up and off, and they won't even pretend to be sorry!

But right now she was on her way to Upper Frederick Street, where the small milliner's shop run by Miss Hughes and Miss Morton was situated. The two spinster ladies ran a very successful small business and they would give Kitty the money for the trimmings in a small brown envelope, a new bundle of ribbon and lace for embroidering and finishing, and, if she was lucky, a piece of cake, an apple or even, as had happened on one momentous occasion, a meat and potato pie.

Kitty never thought about the money in the envelope because it had no significance for her. Her father's allotment was paid to her mother monthly, she believed, and so far as Kitty could make out the extra earned from the needlework enabled Sary Drinkwater to lift her elbow more frequently than she would otherwise have done. That was its only significance for Kitty, though her mother frequently told friends and neighbours that without her earnings the kids would have starved. Kitty, getting by on the scraps her mother allowed her and the odds and ends she picked up, usually made herself scarce when the family were having their evening dinner, the only significant meal of the day. What was the point in getting too near her mother's strong right arm just in the hope of a chunk of bread and a cup of weak tea? She could go in late and get anything left over, then go to bed.

Not that she would be able to do that today, because she would have the money and a new bundle of trimmings to take back for Sary to work on. So she would have to go straight home today . . . but she would be safe enough, this time. She had noticed that she was always safe when she had been performing an errand for her mother, so perhaps she should regard that as payment enough.

On a tram the journey between Paradise Court and Upper Frederick Street would have been long and slightly tedious but perfectly possible. On foot it was as long as a route march. Kitty went right the way along the Scotland Road, never noticing or caring as it became first Byrom Street and then the Old Haymarket. Trams passed her, ringing their bells, but since she had no pennies for her fare they, too, meant nothing but an added hazard should she want to cross the road. Pedestrians dodged the small girl with the big box – some smiled, others frowned – but no one offered to give her a hand and indeed, had they done so Kitty would have been highly suspicious. The box might look like nothing much but the trimmings were worth a lot of money, she wouldn't hand them to anyone, not she.

On Old Haymarket the trams were lined up, nose to tail, waiting for departure time. Kitty glanced at them, but continued doggedly to walk, dodging the people hurrying for their homegoing trams. She had set off at a good pace, but it was late afternoon by now and women, shopping in the centre of the city, were turning their steps homeward in order to cook a hot meal for husbands and children. At least, so Kitty enviously surmised, for thanks to Mrs O'Rourke she knew what mothers were supposed to do, even though her own parent seemed to remain largely ignorant of her duties. Along Whitechapel she went, past the sailors' home, into Paradise Street, and finally, when she had traversed Cleveland Square with its big houses and leafy trees, she dived left into Upper Frederick Street at last and knew she was almost halfway through her journey – for once she had handed over the box she would be given another and would begin the weary trek back.

Unfortunately, Upper Frederick Street was a very boring thoroughfare for someone of Kitty's age. Warehouses, public houses and tradesmen's properties jostled down either side of the road, with never a shop window to please the eye. Until you got to the milliner's shop, of course.

Miss Hughes and Miss Morton had a lovely window, Kitty considered. Two or three wax heads with disdainful expressions displayed the most expensive hats, and the rest were laid out tastefully on swatches of material or beside a vase of artificial flowers. In spring, Miss Morton, who was the artistic one, always put a china hen and a clutch of china chicks amongst the hats. In summer, it was a bucket and spade and a cleverly constructed sandcastle made of cardboard, and in winter a Christmas tree dominated the window, all decorated with tinsel and toys. Kitty, who knew about the seaside only from books, stopped to look in the window and envy those children lucky enough to possess buckets, spades and sandcastles. She rather liked the hats, too – the big straw one with artificial poppies round the crown, the fluffy, feathery one, the one which had a brim so wide that Kitty doubted whether the wearer would know if it rained or shone – and anyway, looking in the window gave her a breather, which she needed before going inside.

She did take a look through the half-glazed door, though, because she knew that the Misses Hughes and Morton much preferred her to enter the shop to transact her business when they were not busy with customers. A severe-looking lady was at the counter, paying for a purchase, but as soon as she had left, with a rustle of unfashionably long skirts and a fearful glance at the blue sky overhead, as though she spent her life expecting a downpour, Kitty nipped inside and heaved her box up onto the counter.

'Trimmings from Miz Drinkwater,' she said breathlessly: the counter was high and the box heavy. 'An' can I tek the nex' lot, please?'

Miss Hughes, who had been serving the severe-looking lady, had gone into the back of the shop as

18

soon as her customer left, but a plain and spotty girl, not a lot older than Kitty herself, moved forward to take the box from her. 'Drinkwater,' she said heavily. 'Wait on, I'll git the new lot.'

She was about to disappear in her turn when the shop door rattled. Kitty turned automatically as it opened, intending to give just a quick glance behind her – and instead of glancing, stared. The newcomer was the most beautiful young lady she had ever imagined. Thick, softly shining red-gold hair was coiled into a bun at the nape of her neck, her skin was white and clear and her eyes large and violet blue. She wore a beautiful navy blue dress which fitted her slender figure to perfection and a little jacket made of the same material. She went towards the counter and the girl who had been talking to Kitty turned automatically towards her.

'Yes, miss?'

'Miss Hughes is making a hat for my sister to wear at a wedding. It's white, with a wide blue ribbon – I wondered . . .'

The spotty one nodded violently, turned without a word and went to the door behind her, opening it to reveal the beginnings of a flight of stairs.

'Miss 'Ughes!' she shouted up the stairs. 'It's the gairl from Penny Lane, she's called for th' weddin' 'at!'

A voice shouted a muffled reply which evidently made sense to the spotty one. She turned back to her customer.

'She says it's ready, Miss. I'll jest go up an' fetch it down for you.'

She disappeared and the beautiful young lady said, apparently to herself, 'The girl from Penny Lane, indeed! What sauce!'

Kitty nodded earnestly and the movement caught the young lady's eye. She swung round, looking properly at Kitty for the first time.

'Oh! I'm sorry, I didn't see you there – are you being served or did I push in ahead of you?'

'S'orlright,' Kitty said. 'I ain't a customer, I's brung work in.'

The young lady nodded.

'I see. Well, if the hat's ready I shan't be long, since Nellie – that's my sister – paid the first instalment, and there's only one shilling and sixpence owing, which I've got in my purse.'

'I'm fetchin' trimmings,' Kitty confided, delighted that this pretty, beautifully dressed young lady was disposed to chat. 'Me Mam makes 'em for Miss 'Ughes an' Miss Morton. They sends plain ribbons an' she 'broiders 'em, an' stitches lace an' makes button-'oles an' all sorts.'

'She must be very clever with her needle,' the young lady said. 'My sister can sew, but I'm not very good. Can you embroider?'

'Well, I can, me friend taught me, but I wouldn't tell me Mam,' Kitty confessed. 'She'd make me do it all, else. 'Sides, don't suppose I could do all them fancy stitches an' that.'

'You should practise,' Kitty's new friend said kindly. 'Then, one day, you'll be able to help your mother, perhaps in the evenings, when you are home from your job of work. Fine needlework is always useful.'

At this point someone began descending the stairs heavily. Miss Hughes, who was carrying a huge, wide-brimmed hat with great reverence, began to speak almost as soon as she appeared in view.

'Miss Larkin! I thought it must be you when my niece said . . . dear Sophia remembered you had been staying with Mrs Gallagher in Penny Lane, but that is really no excuse, as I told her, for rudeness! But there, she's my elder sister's only child and is new to our work, though determined to do well, quite determined, and as I said to Miss Morton, better to keep it in the family, with so many valuable materials, to say nothing of all the new lines we're beginning to stock . . .' She held the hat out to her customer. 'Now what do you think? Will it not make madam quite the best-dressed lady at the wedding?'

'It's beautiful,' the girl said, eyeing the hat admiringly. 'I have the rest of the money here, and thank you very much, Miss Hughes, I'm sure my sister will be delighted with your work.'

'I hope so, I hope so indeed. And should your employer ever desire something a little special, a little out of the ordinary, and should you feel able to recommend us, I should be most grateful . . . you would not regret such a recommendation, you may be sure.'

'My employer has been ill and rarely leaves the house,' the girl said sadly. 'If you could put the hat in a box, Miss Hughes, and let me have a receipt . . .'

'Of course, of course,' Miss Hughes said. She frowned slightly at Kitty, who was leaning against the counter and drinking in every word. 'Yes? What do you want, my dear?'

'Me Mam's money,' Kitty said promptly. 'An' the new trimmin's.'

'Ah, yes, you're the Drinkwater child,' Miss Hughes said. 'When I finish with this lady I'll call Sophia; she's fetching the box and your Mama's wages.' She turned back to the girl, gave her a practised smile and then dived under the counter, reappearing with her hands full of white tissue paper. 'Now, I'll just wrap the hat up for you.'

Kitty watched, fascinated, as the hat was swathed expertly in the tissue paper and plunged into the depths of a handsome hat-box only just big enough to contain it. Then the box was tied up with string and pink sealing wax and the string formed into a neat carrying handle.

'There you are!' Miss Hughes said triumphantly, handing the beautiful, light parcel over to her customer. 'Good afternoon, Miss. Convey my respects to Mrs Gallagher.'

'Good afternoon,' echoed the girl. She then turned to Kitty and gave her the most brilliant and beautiful smile. 'Good afternoon, Miss Drinkwater, and thank you for your company.'

Politeness costs nothing, Mrs O'Rourke used to say, and *Good manners are a sign of good breeding*. So Kitty smiled and gave a little bob and said, 'Same to you, Miss, I'm sure,' and then watched as the beautiful young lady, the hatbox swinging from one hand, left the shop, closing the door gently behind her.

'Well, well,' Miss Hughes said vaguely, as Kitty turned reluctantly back to the counter. 'Where were we . . . ah Sophia!'

There was a faint hail from up above, then a thundering of heavy feet descending the stairs which made Miss Hughes's earlier progress sound positively fairylike.

'Ere we are, Aunt,' Sophia said, thumping down the last stairs. She had a box in her arms which looked, to Kitty's despairing eyes, even bigger and heavier than the one she had just delivered. 'Trimmin's for Mrs Drinkwater an' the money for the last lot.' She waved a small brown envelope, then put it down on top of the box. 'Miss Morton's just mekin' a cuppa. She says if you go up now, I can go up later.'

'Ah, tea,' Miss Hughes said, half-closing her eyes and smiling fondly at her niece. She turned to Kitty. 'Here you are, child. Carry them carefully, there are a lot of expensive materials in there. How far have you to go?'

'Paradise Court, off Burlington Street,' Kitty said. She usually put the envelope containing the money inside the box, but decided that it might be safer slipped down inside the neck of her shirt-dress, where it would lodge against the rope which spanned her middle. 'It's a helluva walk.'

Miss Hughes's eyebrows rose almost into her thinning grey hair but the fat Sophia giggled. Kitty gave her a cold glance. You could see that Sophia hadn't done much walking, not with a belly on her like a woman six months gone! She would have liked to tell Sophia so, but prudence demanded that her good manners remain with her for a little longer. Miss Hughes usually came up with something.

And today was no exception.

'Burlington Street! That must be several miles ... but of course it's on a direct tram route.'

'I walked,' Kitty said bluntly. 'Me Mam don't 'ave no gelt to spare for leccy-rides.'

'You *walked*?' Miss Hughes stared at Kitty for a moment as though doubting her own ears, then she gave a quick little nod and reached under the counter. 'Well, here's a penny, catch a tram home. And – wait a moment.'

Whilst she was gone, labouring up the stairs, Sophia came and leaned over the counter the better to see Kitty, apparently, for presently she remarked, 'Where's your boots?'

'Ain't got none,' Kitty said at once. 'Me feet's 'ard, I don't need no boots in summer.'

23

'And in winter?'

Kitty shrugged.

'None in winter, either? Nor clogs? And that ain't a dress, it's a man's old shirt. You aren't 'alf dirty, an' all.'

'I might 'ave boots, next winter,' Kitty said, ignoring the slur on her apparel and her cleanliness. There was little she could say, since her dress was indeed a shirt and she knew herself to be very dirty. Curiosity getting the better of her, however, she added, 'What's it like up there, above the shop? What does you do? Are you learnin' to mek 'ats? Ow d'you get a job like that, eh?'

But Sophia, whilst apparently thinking her own nosiness justified, drew back in offended astonishment at Kitty's questions.

'That's none of your business,' she said sharply. 'You need brains and a good 'pearance to work in a nice shop like this. And boots.'

Kitty had filled her lungs for a quick – and insulting – retort when Miss Hughes came thumping down the stairs again. She had a thick slice of bread and jam in one hand and a tin mug of milk in the other. She put them down on the counter, breathing hard.

'Lord, but it's hot,' she remarked. 'Drink that, child, then eat the butty as you go. You want to get home before dusk.'

Kitty was thirsty and drank the milk at a draught, with murmured thanks, but had only just sunk her teeth into the bread when the shop door opened once more and Miss Hughes made violent shooing motions and began to brush the crumbs Kitty was making off the counter. She drew herself up and smiled brightly across the top of Kitty's head whilst hissing, 'Off with you!' under her breath.

Kitty glanced at the handsome old lady with crimped grey hair, and at her companion, a stringy girl in her twenties, and then made for the door, with the bread and jam resting on top of the enormous box. She would get herself to the tram stop with all possible speed and eat her food in comfort once she was there.

She might not have caught a tram from here before, but she had often wished she could, watching enviously as the huge Oceanics whisked by full of rich people. That girl, the one from Penny Lane, would undoubtedly have caught a tram, lucky thing, and would be home by now. But Kitty was lucky too, with a penny in her hand for a ride and food to eat.

Kitty reached the tram stop just after a vehicle had picked up the waiting passengers, so she put her box down on the pavement, sat on top of it, and began to eat the bread and jam. Presently one or two other people came up, and Kitty thought gleefully that the tram would soon be here and then she could get rid of the heavy box. She felt no curiosity over the contents; trimmings were trimmings, after all, but for the first time in her life she wondered just how much money her mother was paid for all that close work. After all, if the girl from Penny Lane was right, when she left home she would have a vested interest in how much one could earn for sewing work.

The envelope, however, was comfortably wedged against her ribs; to get it out and start trying to open it, or even to feel for the size of the coins in front of the people gathered at the stop would be a silly sort of thing to do. Instead, she finished off her bread and jam with deep contentment, wiped her sticky hands on the dusty pavement and got to her feet just as the tram came whooshing down upon them.

'Move along there,' the conductor shouted jovially.

'Want an 'and wi' that thumpin' great box, chuck?'

'Sounds as if 'e's 'ad a skinful, dinnertime,' someone behind Kitty muttered as the conductor heaved the box aboard, but Kitty was just grateful for the man's strong hand, and watched him stow the trimmings under the seat, wishing everyone was as kind. This was turning out to be a really good day, despite the long and tiring walk.

The tram was full and at every stop there seemed to be people jostling to get aboard, so it took longer than Kitty had anticipated to reach the Black Dog on the corner of Vauxhall Road and Burlington Street, but they got there at last and Kitty climbed down, hoping that someone who knew her was watching. It was not every day that she caught a tram. The conductor handed her down her box, Kitty shifted its weight onto her hip, and the Oceanic trundled off with its load whilst Kitty began the short walk home.

Halfway down the street, however, she remembered her curiosity over the contents of the little brown envelope. She slid her hand across her front. There were coins, she could feel them pressing into her ribs, but she thought she could feel a sort of rustling, too. Did that mean paper money? Good lor', there might be a ten shilling note inside the scruffy little envelope! Mam never opened it in front of her, just snatched it and shoved it into her own capacious bosom, but ... oh, she would simply have to get it out and see whether she could discover the contents without actually unsealing the flap.

Kitty looked around her. She was fast approaching a shop she hated because of the smell. A fishmongers, with white trays holding crabs and lobsters whilst the fish nestled in beds of ice. Down the side was an entry, where fishboxes, buzzing with bluebottles, awaited collection. It wasn't a very pleasant place, what with the smell and the flies, but it struck Kitty that if she went down the strong smelling little back alley, at least she wasn't likely to be disturbed. So, still lugging her heavy burden, Kitty stole past the fishboxes, past the big black delivery bicycle propped against the wall with the fishmonger's name in white letters across the wrought iron basket on the front, and down to where the back of someone's privy formed a conveniently private place to examine the envelope. She put the box down and delved into the front of her shirt, but she had scarcely got her fingers round the fascinating envelope when someone's shadow fell across her. Startled, she looked up.

Two boys stood there, grinning at her. One of them wore the filthy, stained apron of a fishmonger's apprentice, the other had a very large checked cap pulled down over one eye and pieces of string tied round his trouser-bottoms. Oh 'eck, Kitty thought, dismayed, I didn't oughter be down here and them's the lad what guts the fish and the lad what delivers. Now I'm in trouble!

She took her hand out of her shirt front and went to pick up the box of trimmings but one of the boys, the one with the string round his trouser-bottoms, put a foot down on the top, only just missing her fingers.

'No you don't, gal! Wharra you got in there, eh?'

'Nothing! Well, only ribbons an' that, for ladies' 'ats,' Kitty said nervously. They were large, well-nurtured boys of fourteen or fifteen, a clack from either of them would hurt! 'Me box is that 'eavy, I stopped for a bit of a rest.'

'Ribbins? What's de user dat?' The delivery boy went to turn away but the other stood his ground. It struck Kitty for the first time that they might rob her – thank heaven she hadn't pulled the envelope out of her shirt, for money could always be spent but what use would a couple of lads have for a box of unworked trimmings?

'Got any gelt? Dey pay you for what you brung 'em?'

Kitty cursed the perspicacity of fishmongers' apprentices; the other turned back immediately, his narrow face menacing. He brushed impatiently at a bluebottle which seemed to have followed his rich smell down the entry.

'That's ri', dey pay for t'ings like dat! Where's de cash?'

'They pay me Mam, not me,' Kitty quavered. 'I's jest to fetch an' carry. Come on, let me go 'ome.'

The delivery boy would have let her go, she was sure of it, but the other was altogether a nastier proposition. He stared at her hard for a moment, then bent and picked up the box.

'Tell you what, you go 'ome an' tell your Ma that she can 'ave 'er ribbins back for a coupla bob. 'Ow about dat?'

'She'll kill me,' Kitty said fearfully. 'She will, she'll kill me. She ain't overfond, me Mam. Come on, fellers, gi's me box back.'

'Where's your money, then?'

'I ain't got none,' Kitty squeaked desperately. 'I 'ad a penny what the shop lady give me, but I caught a tram, the box is that 'eavy. C'mon, gi's me box.'

'No money, no box,' the apprentice said. 'And jest in case you've gorrit in mind to tattle . . .'

He put a hand into the long pocket in front of his filthy apron and pulled out a knife, a huge thing, sharp, wicked. He stepped forward, and whilst his companion tucked the box under his arm in a very final sort of way, pressed the knife against Kitty's throat, so hard that she dared not even swallow, convinced that any movement would send the razor-edge deep into her flesh.

'Understand, chuck?' his whisper was more frightening than a shout or a cuff would have been. 'One word from you, jest one word, an' your Mam'll find you up dis entry tomorrer wi' your t'rottle cut from ear to ear. An' don't t'ink you can escape from me, 'cos I'll git you, I swear on the face o' God.'

Kitty, rigid with terror, said nothing. She could feel perspiration running down the sides of her face but she was deathly cold. He would kill her and get pleasure from it, she was sure. She could do nothing to save the trimmings, but if she said she'd come back later with the money perhaps . . .

'Off wit' you!'

A hand grabbed her shoulder and twisted her out of the corner into which she had shrunk as a pin twists a winkle from its shell. A violent push sent her staggering up the entry, and as she regained her equilibrium she simply flew, her feet scarcely touching the slippery, smelly cobbles.

Out on Burlington Street, with people about her, she dared not glance back. That knife – and the threat that went with it – had been all too real. She kept her head down, dodging passers-by, heading hopelessly for Paradise Court. She reached it and then shrank back, suddenly realising what a fix she was in.

If she went in without the trimmings her mother would kill her, even if she handed over the money. And would she be allowed to explain what had happened, how she could get the box back if she took a couple of bob to pay the boys' blackmail demand? Her hand stole down across her shirt-front once more. She still had the money, but because she had lost the trimmings the money would mean nothing to Mam, who would have to pay it all back, and more, probably, to Miss Hughes to make up for the missing work.

Caught on the horns of a horrible dilemma, Kitty stood there, gazing into the tiny, cobbled court. If only Mrs O'Rourke had still been alive, she might have helped Kitty to explain her predicament to her mother before the blows began to fall. But she was not. This problem was Kitty's and Kitty's alone.

Tears began to form, to fill Kitty's eyes, to trickle down her cheeks. Oh, God, what was she to do? She realised, suddenly, that if she took two shillings back to those boys they would think that she had a source of income and would probably give her back a few ribbons and demand more money. What was more, they had made no arrangements for the handing over of the cash, she could scarcely walk into the fishmonger's shop, hand over money and expect to receive her box of trimmings in return! She could hang around the entry, she supposed doubtfully, then knew she would never dare. The boy with the knife was mad, he would probably take her money and then slit her throat, she never wanted to go down that entry again as long as she lived.

But what was her alternative, really? If she ran away then they would have the scuffers after her because she'd stolen money. If she went indoors without the trimmings then she was as good as dead. She wondered about going back to Miss Hughes's shop and explaining, offering to run errands for a hundred years, if only Miss Hughes would replace the trimmings and say nowt to Mam. But the shop would be closed, it would be dusk soon, there was no hope there.

Kitty sat down, with her back to the side of the wine merchant's shop, and began to sob.

Chapter Two

Lilac Larkin, with the new hat for her sister Nellie nestling in its tissue wrappings, had to catch two trams to get back to Penny Lane, so she decided, since the afternoon was sunny, to walk the first part of the way. She would enjoy the exercise and besides, she needed time to think.

The truth was, despite appearances, Lilac was not comfortably settled in a nice job with an employer to look after her. Not any more. She had said nothing to Miss Hughes, but her entire life had just been thrown into turmoil and she was still none too sure what course to take. Because for the first time in her working life Lilac was about to become unemployed. It was a bad time to job-hunt, too. Although the first Labour government was in power, and the British Empire Exhibition had been opened at some place called Wembley, up London, and everyone said that could mean more jobs, as yet there was little to show for either event.

And though Lilac had been a valued member of the household as personal maid to Mrs Matteson, a doctor's wife, she was otherwise untrained. Indeed, she had been there ever since she had started work and had fancied herself settled there until such time as she might meet Mr Right and marry him. In fact several Mr Rights had come into her life, only to be spurned at the last minute. And then a couple of months earlier Mrs Matteson had had a stroke, and after nursing her back to a semblance of health her husband had decided that his best course would be to take her out of the city and into the countryside, to the small village of Scarisbrick, just outside Southport. There, she might be near her sister, Lady Blanche Elcott, yet far from the noise, grime and strain of living in a large city like Liverpool. But the house to which the Mattesons would move was small, too small to allow them to employ a lady's maid, and besides, Mrs Matteson would be living quietly and in a very different style to that which she had enjoyed in the city.

'A little gardening, a little sea-bathing when we're in Southport, perhaps – for her health, you know – and gentle visits to her sister will be all the excitement she either needs or wants,' Dr Matteson told Lilac gently. 'We will give you an excellent reference, I'm sure you know that my dear, but it would be quite impossible for my wife to employ a personal maid in such circumstances. For though I hope to help the local man out when he's overstretched, I shall no longer have a practice of my own.'

Lilac quite understood, of course she did, and had hurried round to Nellie's comfortable little house in Penny Lane to ask her adopted sister's advice. For though Nellie was a mere thirteen years older, she had considered Lilac as her own particular responsibility ever since Lilac had been found on the doorstep of the Culler Orphan Asylum, where Nellie had been living since her parents' death when she was not much more than five.

When told that Lilac was about to lose her job Nellie was a brick as usual, and had suggested that Lilac should move in with them. She knew, however, that having had financial independence for so long,

Lilac would not be happy without a job of some sort. 'Think about it, and decide what you'd most like to do,' she had urged. 'Something tells me you won't want to stay in domestic service, not with anyone other than your dear Mrs Matteson. There's plenty of other jobs – you could nurse, like I did – but you must make up your own mind, Li, love. And there's no hurry, you're lucky there. So give it some thought and then we'll talk again.'

So Lilac, sauntering along and swinging the hat-box idly in the bright afternoon sunshine, had plenty to think about. What did she really want to do? Nellie was right, domestic service, or skivvying as the unkind called it, had only been bearable because the Mattesons had treated her more like a daughter than an employee. But nursing did not appeal to her; now that the war was no more than a memory nurses did not have interesting soldier-patients, so you were likelier to end up slaving for a crabby hospital sister on a women's ward than meeting a handsome man who would offer you his hand, heart and fortune. And shop assistants were notoriously underpaid and over-worked. You were on your feet all day, she had heard, and could be sacked immediately if a customer complained. And customers were always complaining, it was their natures. During the war, Lilac remembered, it had been perfectly possible for women to do all sorts of things – they had driven trams, dug ditches, managed offices, delivered the post, even – but now the choice was limited once more.

What about working in an office, then? Lilac asked herself. She could not type, but she had neat writing and a good grasp of arithmetic. She could probably do bookkeeping work of some sort, though with such a large number of unemployed men in Liverpool, it was not easy for a girl to get a job which a man, who had probably fought for his country, could do as well or better.

As she walked, Lilac glanced in at the windows of the offices she was passing. Solicitors, accountants, surveyors, insurance companies, they all employed some women. She could see them poring over ledgers, carrying cups of tea between the desks, sitting beside bad-tempered old men taking dictation. The offices, from out in the sunshine at least, looked fusty, dusty and traplike. No, she did not think she would want to become an office worker.

What about making something, then? Hats sprang to mind, having just visited Miss Hughes's establishment. That might be quite fun, except that she had never enjoyed sewing, and even inventing a confection with a wide brim, on which she would balance a positive greengrocery of artificial cherries, plums and hazelnuts, would mean stitching the fruit into place. The materials were lovely, though – would she not enjoy working with tulle and straw, felt and feathers?

But then she remembered that most milliners employed at most one girl, and decided against that, too. Lilac enjoyed the company of girls her own age and, truth to tell, had begun to fret a little even at the Mattesons once they cut their staff down as the doctor began to see fewer and fewer patients. Polly, who was Lilac's particular friend, had gone, and the fat cook and bright Liza. The woman who came and scrubbed twice a week was a taciturn creature with a large family and very little conversation and Mrs O'Malley, who described herself as a good plain cook, might have been good and was certainly plain but did not excel in the kitchen. Lilac, who enjoyed her food, had begun to quite look forward to the moment when the doctor would come roaring down to the basement, a broken tooth in one hand and one of Mrs O'Malley's scones in the other. But it hadn't happened and now Mrs O'Malley was looking for another situation and had probably been promised a good reference, which meant someone else would soon be tackling her hard pastry, overcooked meats and soggy vegetables.

A sweet-faced girl in a grey coat and matching hat, pushing a heavy pram and holding the hand of a small and sticky boy, approached along the pavement. Should I be a nursery-maid? Or perhaps a governess? wondered Lilac idly, rather admiring the uniform. Except that governesses had quite gone out, the rich were sending their children to school just as the poor did, although to far superior establishments, of course. And although everyone knows babies are lovely, I think I'll admire them from a distance rather than get really involved with them, Lilac decided. Being an honorary aunt was one thing but changing napkins, mopping up puddles, soothing the fractious, smacking the naughty ones and buying chocolates for the good – Lilac's ideas of bringing up rich children were hazy to say the least – appealed to her no more than domestic service, now that she considered it seriously. After all, in the nature of things she would marry one day and have kids of her own; there was no sense in having all the work and none of the pleasure, which was how being a nanny struck her. And marriage, so far as Lilac was concerned, was something for the future, not entirely out of sight but quite far off. A number of ardent young men dancing attendance on her was fine, but actually settling down with one of them seemed like the end of the story. Lilac felt she wanted a good deal more fun before she settled for a tiny house, a husband and a number of noses to wipe.

But marriage was beginning to seem more attractive, ever since her path had crossed that of Alan Blake. She had met him whilst waiting on a party in a smart house in Huskisson Street. He had been one of the guests, a tall, handsome young man in naval uniform, who told her that he was First Officer aboard a liner, the *Lady Mortimer*, plying between Liverpool and New York.

'May I have the next dance?' he enquired presently, smiling down at her. 'I'm sure you dance divinely.'

'Dance? Me? I'm *waitressing*,' Lilac had told him. 'You'd get me dismissed without a character, and I enjoy these evening jobs. They pay quite well, too.'

'Come out into the corridor,' the young officer had said, his light blue eyes dancing. 'Come on, if we just nip through the baize doors . . .'

She went, not because she took him seriously but because she had a trayful of empty glasses to return to the kitchen. But he took the tray from her, stood it on the floor and swept her into a modern waltz, though she was sure the music was playing something quite different.

In his arms, leaning back to look up at him, laughing, protesting, she had seen the light eyes darken as his mouth drew nearer her own – and had broken free, recaptured her tray and made for the kitchen once more. But back in the ballroom he had lain in wait.

'Meet me afterwards?' he had begged. 'I'm on leave for a couple of days and this is my aunt's house so you'll know where to find me. I'm Alan Blake, First Officer on my ship and a pillar of respectability, I assure you. Ask anyone, I never seduce beautiful girls – not unless they ask me to! But if we meet when

37

you finish work we'll talk about a proper evening out. We could have supper at that big hotel down by the waterfront – they have marvellous oysters – or I'll hire a car and drive you to New Brighton, just ask, beautiful lady . . . what's your name, by the way?'

'Umm, I'm Lilac Larkin,' Lilac murmured. 'And by the time I'm finished here you'll be tucked up in your bed. We have to wash and clear, you know.'

He nodded, the merry eyes still holding her own.

'Right. Ask, Lilac Larkin, and whatever you want shall be yours! What about tomorrow night? After you finish work? Only I sail on the tide the day after that.'

'I've got to go and see my sister tomorrow night,' Lilac said, trying to sound casual. She would have loved to agree, but something told her that if she didn't want to be thought of as a pushover, an easy conquest, she had best play a little hard to get. 'Still, if you're in the Pool regularly . . .'

'Oh, Lilac, those are beautiful words, words of hope! Where d'you live?'

She laughed, shrugging.

'You'll forget, but for the next couple of weeks I'm at the Mattesons' house, on Rodney Street. After that I'm not certain where I'll be, though 39 Penny Lane will always find me. It's my sister's address.'

He nodded, scribbling in a tiny pocket-book.

'Right. I'll drop you a line and we'll paint the town red when next I'm here.' He squeezed her hand. 'Don't forget,' he commanded. 'Alan Blake of the *Lady Mortimer*. I shan't forget you, Lilac!'

But as she hadn't seen the young officer since that night, Lilac, reaching the tram terminus on the Old Haymarket, dismissed Alan Blake from her mind. He would probably forget all about her, never get in touch, but at least she'd enjoyed their brief acquaintance and it had made her see that there could be a future for her which did not include either skivvying or marrying a bank clerk.

She scanned the line of trams and there was the one she wanted, waiting. The driver was leaning against the door chatting to another driver and smoking a cigarette. Lilac jumped aboard, settled herself on the slatted wooden seat and decided to tell Nellie she simply couldn't make up her mind. No need to mention Alan, definitely a ship that passed in the night. Nellie always knew what was best for her, anyway. Why, by now she might well have a dozen schemes to put forward. So Lilac pushed the hatbox under the seat, drew her money out of her pocket, and sorted out her fare. Then, with the tram under way, she simply gave herself up to the pleasure of a free and sunny afternoon and let her future take care of itself.

'I'm anxious that you get the right sort of job this time,' Nellie said later, when the two of them were settled in the kitchen preparing a meal together. 'Stuart has always said you were wasted in domestic service, and I do think he's right. You know you're welcome to move in with us, but even then you'd want a job of some sort, Li, my love, because you're used to a bit of independence ... unless you've decided to make marriage your career and take on Art, or one of your other admirers?'

'I'm not going to marry anyone, yet,' Lilac said firmly. 'I like Art all right but I reckon we've known each other for too long, we're more like brother and sister than anything else. And banking's awfully boring when you come to think and anyway, he couldn't afford to marry me for years and years, and I want some fun before I die!'

'Well, you aren't yet nineteen, I suppose, and I didn't settle down until I was a good deal older than that,' Nellie admitted. The two women were in the kitchen, Lilac shelling peas into a large zinc saucepan whilst Nellie, enveloped in a huge white apron and with a smudge of flour on her nose, made the pastry for a steak and kidney pudding. 'It's just that you're so pretty, Lilac love, and I do worry about you.'

'You're very pretty yourself,' Lilac said gently. Nellie had a fine-boned and delicate face, she looked a real lady, Lilac always thought, with her grey eyes, light brown hair and very white skin. Lilac knew her own red-gold hair and deep blue eyes were instantly striking, instantly memorable, but she thought, with rare humility, that perhaps it was Nellie's face which stayed in the mind the longer, whilst Nellie's loving, giving character could be read in the sweet line of her mouth, her straight and honest glance.

'That's very sweet of you, Lilac dear,' Nellie said, twinkling. 'But no one could accuse me of prettiness right now, especially carrying all before me as I do.' She stroked a hand down her stomach, distended by the child within. 'Still, I do feel fit and well, so perhaps I don't mind being hideously fat. And Stu's as excited as a kid at the thought of being a father.'

'And I can't wait to be an honorary aunt,' Lilac said. She ran a finger down the last pod, popping the peas into the pan with a rattle like gunfire. 'So what do you advise, dear Nell? Another job in service, or a complete change? Only I don't know whether I could stand starting at the bottom again, as a kitchen maid.'

'You wouldn't have to, chuck,' Nellie said at once.

'You've had a first-class training, any fine lady would be glad to employ you. Go down to the employment agency in Clarence Street and see what they've got to offer. But personally, I don't think you're going to find another Mrs Matteson, and perhaps it might be better to get right away from that type of job from the start.'

'I suppose I could give the agency a try,' Lilac said reluctantly. 'The only thing is, being a lady's maid and companion is all I know, and I've often thought it would be fun to work for a younger lady, with more interest in fashion. It's a pity Stuart's salary doesn't run to a lady's maid, dearest Nell, or you could employ me and we could all be happy.'

'I'd hate to have a maid, it would make me feel useless, although Stuart's doing awfully well,' Nellie said. She was lining a large earthenware pudding basin with pastry, working quickly and methodically, as was her wont. Having completed the task she took the steak and kidney which she had already cooked and tipped it into the basin, then topped it with a circle of pastry, nipped it together, tied a clean piece of cloth over the top and went over to the stove. She lowered the basin into the pan of water already boiling over the gas, then went back to the sink and rinsed her floury hands. She picked up a striped towel and began to dry them, moving slowly across the kitchen as she did so, her glance abstracted. Lilac, who knew the older girl better than most, was instantly alert.

'Nell? What is it?'

'What do you mean?'

'Something's happened,' Lilac said positively. 'Something you aren't too sure I'll be pleased about. I can read you like a book, our Nellie!'

'Oh, Li, you're right, I've been meaning to talk

to you for weeks, only ... then Mrs Matteson was
taken ill, and Stu said it wasn't likely to happen for
a bit anyway ...'

'Nell, you aren't frightened of telling me your news,
surely? Don't say that something bad's happened? Tell
me at once, before I invent some awful sorrow for us
and make us both needlessly miserable.'

Nellie smiled but shook her head.

'No indeed, not an awful sorrow at all, just an
upset. Li, love, Stuart's been offered an excellent job
with very good prospects.'

'An upset? But Nell, that's marvellous news! I
always knew he was undervalued, now ...'

'Now he's been offered the chief crime reporter's
job with the *London Evening Telegraph*,' Nellie said. 'But
it will mean moving down to London, you see, and we
hadn't meant to do that until you were settled.'

Lilac shook her head sadly at her sister's worried
frown. 'You mean you didn't intend to go *ever*?' she
said with mock incredulity. 'Because I may never
settle, not in the sense you mean. Nellie, I'm going
on nineteen years of age; when you were that old
you were taking care of me, earning your living in
miserable circumstances at the Culler, working in
your spare time ... you weren't much older than
that when you went off to France to nurse the soldiers,
risking your life every day, working your fingers to the
bone, and happy to be doing both. Why, compared
to you I've had no life at all, yet! I've got all sorts to
do before I "settle down" as you call it, so you and
Stuart mustn't think twice, he's got to take this new
job – think of the baby, chuck.'

'We do think of the baby, of course, and of Stu's
future,' Nellie admitted. 'This is a lovely house, so
new and modern, and we've been awfully happy here,

but we'd both like a garden and Stu says we won't live right in London but in the suburbs, so we can have a bit of space around us. Why, Stu wants me to learn to drive a motor car, Li, so that the baby and I will have some independence whilst he's at work!'

'Cor!' Lilac said inelegantly. 'Nell, you're a lucky lass, you are indeed. And why shouldn't I get a job in London, eh? I'm told there's plenty of jobs down there.'

'And leave . . . all your friends?' Nellie said tactfully. 'You wouldn't want to do that, chuck! You've a good many admirers, not just Art O'Brien, and when I saw Polly last she said she had helped out waiting on some party or other where you were much admired by ever such a handsome young man. I know you're sensible, but handsome young men at posh parties don't always mean well by young girls. Of course I don't know who he was, he might have been someone you knew from school, but it wasn't Art, Polly said; she knows Art.'

'Oh, Nell, that young officer was only being polite, and he was fun, not dangerous or anything. Anyway, I've more sense than to be taken in. I wouldn't meet him, after. He says he'll write, though I daresay he won't. But you're still hoping I'll settle for Art O'Brien, aren't you? Well, you can forget it, same as Art can! We was pals as kids, I don't deny it, and we had some fun together, but now he's a ploddin' young bank clerk an' I can do better'n *that*.'

'How you drop your fancy accent when Art's name is mentioned,' Nellie said teasingly. 'You go broad scouse, chuck! But Art's a good lad and a good friend to us all, so I can't help hoping. This officer of yours is probably a good lad as well, but as Stu said when we were discussing Art . . .'

'I don't want to hear Stu's opinion of Art, not one bit I don't,' Lilac said crossly. 'I've told Art a hundred times I'm not gettin' tied up yet and I'm prepared to tell him the same a hundred more. And now I'd better go or Mrs Matteson will wonder what's happened to me.'

'Oh Lilac, love, don't go off in a huff just because I mentioned Art – and anyway you can scarcely call it mentioning him to say it *wasn't* Art you were with at the posh party! There's no need to be horrid about him either, queen, because he's been a good friend to all of us, not just you. But I understand how you feel – you want to make up your own mind who you'll marry, you don't want us deciding for you, and you want to have a choice, even if you decide – sorry, sorry, I nearly put me foot in it again! So sit down and I'll make our tea and we'll have it early, before Stu gets home, so's you won't be leaving Mrs Matteson alone for too long.'

'She won't be alone, exactly,' Lilac admitted. She had taken her jacket off the hook behind the back door but now she hung it up again, then walked over to the pantry and got out a loaf of bread and some butter. 'All right, I'm silly to be huffy with you, dearest. I'll stay to tea, I won't be missed for a bit. Shall I slice this loaf and butter it?'

'Please. And I'll tell you what, why don't you get a job for now and then come and stay with us in London once we're settled? Then, if you like it, you can try for work down there.'

'I might,' Lilac said, slicing bread. 'Nell, this move . . .'

'I know what you're going to say. Is it for ever, that's what you're thinking, isn't it? No, love, of course it isn't, but Stu knows it's important for him

44

to work on a London paper as well as a provincial. He's been a foreign correspondent, but never on the staff of a big daily. As for staying away, I don't think either of us could settle far from the Pool for long. Our life is here, all my relatives, you ... but Stuart needs the experience, needs to get away for a bit. Then he can put in for Mr Mullins' job when the old feller retires, and get to be editor, which is what he's aiming for, eventually. So his plan is to get the necessary experience in London in order to be able to apply to the *Post* or the *Echo* when a first-rate job comes up here.'

'I can see that,' Lilac said, buttering bread. 'So there really wouldn't be much point in me moving to London, would there?'

Nellie pressed a fist into the small of her back and then sat down in one of the fireside chairs.

'That's better – I've been on me feet all day, just about! You're a shrewd one, our Lilac, that's just what Stu said. No point in her settling down there and us moving back, he said. Better let her get on with her own life. Because I won't deny that when he first told me I said I wanted to take you with us or I didn't want to go.'

'Oh Nell, you are kind,' Lilac said. 'But I've got to stand on me own two feet, Stuart's right about that, at least, and as you say, all my friends are here. I'll visit you, though ... come to think of it, if I get a job in a shop or a factory I'll get set holidays, won't I? Domestics get half a day here and a day there, and though the Mattesons were very good they still expected me to take a holiday when they did, even if it wasn't very convenient. So I'll start looking in the next few days. All right?'

'I suppose so. When will the Mattesons be moving out to Southport, then?'

'Within a month,' Lilac said rather guardedly. 'When are you going to London, Nell – the truth, now!'

'We-ell, Stuart's going in a fortnight,' Nellie admitted, pink-cheeked. 'I said I wouldn't go until you were settled, love, but it does go against the grain to stay here when he leaves, so if you really can manage, I'll go when Stu does.'

'Of course I can manage,' Lilac said stoutly, though her heart sank a little. 'But that means you won't have the baby before you go!'

'No. My little lad or lass will be born in London, though he or she will be Lancashire through and through, 'cos Stu and me are both Liverpool born and bred.'

'I shan't see it until I can get down to London to stay with you, then,' Lilac observed rather sadly. 'Still, these things happen and must be faced. I'll get on a train and come down as soon as I possibly can, just to take a peep. After all, he's me only nephew.'

'Or niece,' Nellie observed, heaving herself out of the chair. 'You're as bad as Stu, he always talks as if I'm bound to have a boy. But for my part, I think a girl is likelier. Boys lie high, this one . . .'

'Oh? Who says?'

'Everyone says,' Nellie insisted. She walked over to the pantry and began to lay the table for the main meal of the day, always taken in the evening when Stuart was home. 'Girls lie low, like this one, and boys lie high. Wait and see if I'm not right, anyway.'

'I don't have much choice,' Lilac pointed out. 'Shall I put the kettle on now, our Nellie? That steak and kidney pudding isn't for tea tonight, is it? Because

46

meat puds take hours to cook and I've got to get back before Mrs Matteson's bedtime.'

'No, it's for tomorrow. Tonight it's casseroled mutton – can't you smell it, cooking away with thyme and rosemary and nice little new potatoes – with apple pie and custard for afters. You feeling hungry already, then?'

'I am. But I do love steak and kidney pudding,' Lilac confessed. 'Can I come back to tea tomorrow, our Nell?'

Nellie pretended to consider, head tilted, whilst her eyes twinkled at the thought of Lilac actually asking for an invitation to tea instead of just announcing that she would be attending the meal.

'We-ell, the mayor will be poppin' in, and Stu said he'd asked Lord Liverpool, being as how steak and kidney's his favourite pudding too, but I daresay there'll be room at the table for a littl'un. Yes, our Li, you come along. When you pull the kettle over the flame, just stand the pot to warm, would you?'

Lilac complied and the two girls began the final preparations for the meal, bustling round Nellie's neat, modern kitchen. Lilac, even as she bustled, found herself looking wistfully round her. She had known some very happy moments in this room – indeed, in this house. It didn't belong to Stuart and Nellie, of course, only the rich owned their homes, everyone else rented, but they had rented it when they married two years earlier, and Lilac had helped to hang the dark red damask curtains in the sitting room, had gone with Nellie to choose the square of pink carpet, had picked the wallpaper for the little front bedroom where she slept when she stayed over, and had varnished the chest of drawers and the small wardrobe which Stuart had bought at Paddy's Market

47

and carted home on a coal wagon, or so he claimed when the stuff arrived.

'What'll happen to the house, Nell?' Lilac asked at last, when the table was laid, the tea made and the bread and butter tastefully arranged on Nellie's best china cake plate. 'Who'll have it, d'you suppose?'

'Well, Stu and me were wondering whether you'd like to have a couple of friends in and share it,' Nellie said hesitantly, astonishing Lilac totally. 'Working girls sometimes share houses and flats in London, Stuart said, so if you and a friend or two want to take over the rent – it isn't expensive, not between three or four.'

'Oo-ooh!' Lilac squeaked. 'I never thought of doing that, but it's a really clever idea, our Nell! Surely we could afford it, if we got enough of us? Why, Polly left the Mattesons two months ago, she's working in a factory, and Liza's in Lewis's, selling wedding gowns, and then there's Blanche who was at school with me – 'member Blanche, she was the one with bright red hair? – and there must be heaps of girls who leave the Culler and don't stay in domestic service, even if they start out there.'

'We've got the three bedrooms, so if two of you shared the double and you had one each in the singles, that would be four of you sharing the rent,' Nellie said. Lilac could see how enthusiasm and excitement were lighting Nellie from within, taking the anxiety out of her expression and curving her mouth into a happy and hopeful smile. So Nellie was not really as easy in her mind at the thought of leaving me to my own devices as she pretends, Lilac thought. Their lives had been too closely interwoven for too long for either to contemplate losing the other without a good deal of pain. Lilac felt a warm glow at the realisation that even now, with her own husband and a baby on the way, Nellie still thought a lot of her adopted sister. She's been mother and father to me for too long to let me go my own way and not worry a bit, Lilac told herself, and was happy that it was so.

'Then there's the sitting room, and the little room Stu calls his study . . . you could have a couple more of you downstairs if you wanted,' Nellie went on, still planning how Lilac could best manage when she and Stuart had left the city. 'It 'ud take a weight off me mind, our Lilac, if I thought you were with pals.'

'I'll have a word, tomorrow,' Lilac promised. 'Oh, but would the landlord mind? I mean with you and Stu living here he knows everything'll be seen to and done right, but with a parcel of girls . . .'

'Stuart's already had a word with Mr Ellis,' Nellie said. She went a little pink. 'Truth is, Stuart said he'd still keep it in his name and see to things . . . we're bound to want to come back one day so you could say you were keeping the house warm for us. And it'll be nice for us to have somewhere to stay when we pop back for a day or so, just to see how you're getting on, like. So when we come back Stu says he'll tackle anything you can't manage.'

'Nellie, love, if you're thinking about climbing ladders and carting loads you don't want to worry about that sort of thing, not if we get Polly, Liza, Blanche and me all living here. I don't want to sound swelled-headed, but there'll be fellers queuein' up to give us a hand, four girls living alone, to say nothing of Polly's young man, who won't be far off. Not that we'd need help, not after having been in service, because we've all done our share of lifting and carrying.'

'Yes, I suppose you're right,' Nellie admitted, 'I got pretty strong nursing, I suppose I'm inclined to forget the cans of hot water and the buckets of coal you heave up and down stairs without a second thought when you work in a private house.'

'That's it. Water up, slops down, empty chamber pots, fill ewers, get a laden breakfast tray from the basement to the furthest bedroom on the first floor and don't spill a crumb or a drop,' Lilac said wryly. 'Then there's coal for the bedroom fires, carrying down the ash-cans . . . domestic service may not be everyone's cup of tea, but it keeps your muscles in trim.'

'Well then, I shan't need to worry about you at all,' Nellie said cheerfully. 'Is that Stuart's key I hear in the lock? Mash the tea, our Lilac!'

After weeping dolorously for ten minutes or so, Kitty scrubbed her eyes dry with the backs of her hands, blew her nose into her fingers, and scrambled to her feet. Kitty Drinkwater, you've bin a-tellin' yourself these past two years that you'd leave, one of these 'ere days, she told herself fiercely. Well, now's your chanst, girl! If you poke the gelt through the 'ole in the door when they're all asleep, with a note to say what 'appened and who took the trimmin's, then probably Mam won't set the scuffers on to you. What's more, since you'll be far away by then, she won't be able to mek you go back to get 'em yourself. Kitty had no illusions about her mother; if there was a choice between never seeing her trimmings again or having her daughter's throat slit from ear to ear but regaining her property, she was sure Sary would have plumped for her trimmings without a thought.

Unfortunately, however, she didn't have a stub of pencil or a chalk on her, which made the writing of a note difficult, to say the least. And she was too near to Paradise Court; at any moment her mother or a brother or sister might stumble out to see what was taking her so long – at the thought of the explanations, the blows, Kitty turned pale all over. Best clear off until the early hours, then return with the note written on the envelope. If she wandered down the Scottie, she was almost bound to see a friend who might lend her a writing implement of some description, particularly if she looked in on Paddy's Market. They stayed open late and someone there, a stallholder or a customer even, might have the necessary pencil or chalk.

Despite the lateness of the hour it was still not dark and the air, after the sunny day, was warm and pleasant. Kitty began walking rather gloomily along the pavement despite this, but very soon the good humour of the women shopping and the men lounging in front of the pubs lifted her spirits and she began to look about her and take more notice.

Scotland Road was a wide thoroughfare, and most of the shops didn't close until very late, so that goods and lights spilled in a prodigal fashion out across the pavement. Shopkeepers shouted their wares, housewives shouted back, bargains were struck and baskets piled. Kitty was not usually out so late, since Sary tended to shout the kids to bed early in order that she could go off out, and the brightness and intensity of this side of the city's night-life intrigued her. Who'd 'a thought it, she marvelled, all these folk wanderin' the streets when us is abed! Oh, there's Wally Mick – wonder if 'e's got a pencil on 'im?

Wally Mick was in school with Kitty and lived a bit further along the court but since he was older than she they rarely exchanged more than the most casual of greetings. But Wally Mick's sister Dora was one of Kitty's cronies, which meant that they were on quite good terms, since Wally Mick was a fond brother and Kitty had long admired his kindness to his sister as well as his fair, cheeky face. Asked for the loan of a pencil, however, Wally Mick could not help. He had no pencil right now, he was helping the greengrocer. But later, when the shop closed, he would get given any fades that were going besides a bob for his pains.

'Waddyer want wi a pencil?' he asked rather plaintively, rubbing a filthy hand across his spiky fair hair. Kitty thought it was Wally's yellow head and round blue eyes which had got him his job – he looked so trustable, somehow. 'Most kids is after a plum or a handful o' cherries, which I can manage, now an' then.'

'I want to write a note; just a little one,' Kitty said persuasively. 'I only want to *borrer* it, it ain't for keeps.'

She had noticed that the greengrocer, a strapping fellow with bright ginger hair, had a well-sharpened pencil tucked behind one ear. Now she directed her gaze meaningfully at the older man.

'That's for addin' up wiv,' Wally Mick said doubtfully. ''E can't borrer you that one. 'Ere, wait on.'

He disappeared into the darkness of the small shop at the back of the mounds of fruit and vegetables and came back a moment later, breathing rather heavily, with a tiny, blunt stump of pencil.

'Bring it back,' he muttered, pushing it into her hand. 'Don't be long, either; we shuts in 'alf an hour.'

'I will, and thanks, Wally,' Kitty said fervently. 'You're a pal, you are. Dora's real lucky, wish our twins was like you.'

'Oh, Arny an' Bob's awright,' Wally Mick said awkwardly. 'They's only kids, an' your mam's a real frightener.'

52

'I knows it,' Kitty agreed fervently. 'I'll bring the pencil back awright, you see.'

She would have returned it under any circumstances, but the thought that Wally Mick might act as messenger and put the envelope through the door for her was an attractive one. On the other hand, there was money in the envelope and Wally might be less trustable than his round blue eyes and yellow hair seemed to suggest.

Considering the problem, Kitty found a quiet corner by a knife-grinder's cart and settled herself, back to the wall, knees up. She spread out the envelope, pondering deeply. There wasn't a great deal of room – what should she say for the best? Sitting there, it was suddenly not quite so easy to explain, but she must do her best or have to contend with the police on her trail as well as the other dangers of the streets.

After five minutes of fruitless wondering she began.

Mam. No point in trying for a pleasanter tone when your pencil was old and blunt and your paper just a small and dirty envelope. *Mam. Here is the muney from the Hat Lady. Them boys at Harraps Fish stowl the Trimmens off me. Kitty Drin*

At this point she ran out of envelope and pencil simultaneously, the one being filled with her uneven writing, the other now reduced to the scatching of bare wood.

Still. It was readable, even in the flickering light of the gas lamps, and it said what needed saying. As for the half signature, if anyone knew her name it should be her mother, so that was all right. She had said nothing about her future plans, but why should she? Sary Drinkwater would not care, she would say good riddance to bad rubbish, until she next needed an errand running or a head to clack. And by then,

Kitty thought gleefully, scrambling to her feet and shaking her head to clear it of the desire to sleep which kept creeping insidiously over her, by then I'll be far, far away!

Chapter Three

Deciding to run away was all very well, but when, in the early hours of the morning, Kitty crept cautiously back to Paradise Court, number eight looked almost inviting. Darkness and quiet brought their own beauty to a place singularly lacking in attraction, and the moon, high in the clear night sky, even managed to make the house look as though it might possibly be more comfortable than a cold doorstep.

Kitty knew well that this was an illusion, but just for a moment she toyed with the idea of stealing silently up the two filthy steps and pushing open the creaky wooden door with the missing panel, through which the naughtier of the neighbours' children watched the Punch and Judy fights, rows and beatings in which Sary and Hector Drinkwater specialised. Facing Kitty then as she stepped through the doorway would be the Drop, a gaping hole in the floorboards into which generations of tenants had tipped the ash from their fires. It was really dangerous now that Sary was in the habit of ripping up floorboards whenever her need for a fire became urgent, because an unwary step could mean death by choking as you sank over your head in ash five or six feet deep.

But Kitty, used to the Drop though rightly terrified of it, would walk carefully round the sinister, coffin-shaped hole and up the shallow wooden stairs. At the top she would turn right into the slit-like room where the children slept on old newspapers, rags and anything else they could scratch together. Although it was a balmy night, Kitty thought wistfully of that heaped-up bed. In sleep there were no animosities, no tale-bearing, no snatching. They would all cuddle up close, like puppies in a pet-shop window, and for a few hours the illusion of loving togetherness would envelop them all, even Kitty.

But then morning would come, and discovery. She would have to tell her story ... her flesh crept at the thought ... and take whatever punishment her mother meted out. And it was bound to be something dreadful, really bad, for a girl who had lost a whole box of trimmings.

Once, Sary in one of her real furies had threatened to hang Kitty with a length of orange-box rope from the top bannister, cutting her loose before she was quite strangled so that she might drop into the ash below and die of asphyxiation. Kitty had fled the house then – she had been only seven – and taken refuge under Houghton Bridge by the Leeds & Liverpool Canal. She had been driven back on the second night by a tramp who had coveted her bed and threatened to drown her if she didn't git, an' quick. Kitty had been as much frightened by his hissing, bubbling voice, the result, someone told her later, of being gassed in the trenches, as by his threats. She had stumbled off home, sobbing drearily, but when she went downstairs next morning her mother had been too preoccupied with the fact that she wanted some coal nicking from the railway depot to even comment on her absence, let alone ask where she had been.

Might that happen again, perhaps? Might it be safe to join her brothers and sisters in their warm and smelly nest? But she knew it was no good, not really. The small Kitty had annoyed Sary by some tiny misdeed; she had not lost a fortune in trimmings. And that first time Kitty had been away almost two days and nights . . . perhaps if I'm away for a week this time, Kitty told herself hopefully, turning away. Or a fortnight, or a month . . .

But it was silly to start regretting anything or planning to come back. Once I'm gone I'm gone, Kitty told herself grimly. She crossed the Court, climbed the steps and applied an eye to the hole in the door. Darkness. Nothing stirred, nobody creaked up or down the stairs. Nobody snored in the front room, which meant that Sary had got herself up the stairs and into bed. She must have decided that Kitty would be a while, having to walk such a distance so heavily burdened.

Kitty raised the envelope to push it through the hole, then hesitated. If she tore the envelope just a little, perhaps she might abstract a coin or two, just to see her on her way? After all, Sary owed her a good deal one way and another, even if you only judged what she would have had to pay a neighbour's child to trek right across the city for her trimmings. She don't even feed me, not like she feeds the others, Kitty reminded herself. She glanced across at Mrs O'Rourke's house. In her mind's eye she could see the elderly woman with her head tilted thoughtfully as she gave the matter her full attention. Then she smiled at Kitty and nodded slowly. *Aye, lass,* she seemed to be saying, *you're owed it a dozen times over; no harm to pay yourself a few pence for your trouble.*

Trembling a bit, Kitty turned her back on the door and sat down on the step. She put a finger under the flap and opened the envelope, just a tiddy bit. Then she opened it a bit further. Coins, big ones.

57

Two half-crowns, round and silver and heavy, then notes. Nothing smaller.

Oh 'eck, Kitty thought, dismayed. She turned, in her mind, to Mrs O'Rourke's benign shade. Wharrer we goin' to do me old pal? There ain't no kick, not even a bob, only the 'alf dollar. Can I tek so much? But I's scared to 'ave no gelt at all and that's gospel truth.

In her mind's eye, Mrs O'Rourke thought, then nodded, so Kitty put the half-crown into her lap and turned her attention to the envelope. She had torn so carefully that it had parted right along the fold. With a bit of luck, Mam would snatch it up from the floor, rip it open, and not even notice anyone had been before her. As for the sum within, it was a fortune, so surely she would not bother her head about a missing half-crown? Indeed, from what her mother had let drop from time to time, her payments did vary and she was often at a loss to understand why.

Kitty stood up and put her hand, with the envelope clasped between her fingers, through the hole. With the skill born of long practice she lobbed the envelope gently to the right, heard it clunk softly down on the odds and ends of materials which Sary thriftily saved to use on the trimmings, and then, with the half-crown rapidly growing warm in the palm of her hand, she gave one last, valedictory glance at her home and set off at a determined trot in the direction of Houghton Bridge.

The canal might not be very far from home, the bridge might not offer much shelter in case of rain or prowling policemen on their beats, but at least it was somewhere definite to stay until morning. Another night, when she had more strength in her legs, she might make her way up to Exchange Station and try to kip down in the subway which ran from Pall Mall to St Paul's Square, but for now the bridge would have to do.

Padding barefoot along the pavement she passed the Black Dog, where her mother liked to drink of an evening. It gaped blankly at her, doors and windows locked and barred, deserted for once by the revellers who usually crowded the benches and spilled out onto the pavement. She crossed Vauxhall Road, strangely quiet without the hum and clank of trams or the clatter of horse-drawn carts, the thunder of motorized vehicles. Only the moon looked down on the shiny tram lines and the open-air swimming baths and the looming bulk of the Tate & Lyle sugar refinery beyond the strong curve of the girders of Houghton Bridge. Only the moon looks down on me, Kitty thought, as she climbed nimbly around the side of the bridge and dropped down onto the canal path below. And let's hope the moon tells no tales, because I don't want no humping great scuffer disturbin' what's left of the night for me!

After enjoying the beautiful mutton and the lovely apple pie, Nellie and Stuart insisted on walking Lilac as far as her tram stop because exercise was good for Nellie in her condition and Stuart said he had been working in the office all day and would be glad to stretch his legs.

'I'm perfectly all right to walk up to Ullet Road on a sunny evening in July,' Lilac said, touched by their kindness but not wanting to put them out. 'Honest, our Nell, when you move I won't be fussed over like this.'

'When we move you'll be living on Penny Lane and probably working nearby, and even if you aren't you won't be visiting much after dark,' Nellie pointed out. 'And you'll have Polly and Liza and whoever else you get to share to keep you company. Besides, though this isn't a rough area, you get strange people in the parks sometimes. They're lonely for a girl to walk through as dusk is falling.'

'I could catch the tram up on Smithdown, instead of coming to the Ullet-Croxteth circus,' Lilac pointed out. 'Then I needn't go through the parks at all.'

They were walking three abreast, arms linked, with Lilac, feeling very loved, in the middle. Stuart unlinked himself for a moment in order to wag a reproving finger at the younger girl, whilst the dark eyes in his thin, brown face sparkled with amusement. Lilac had once fancied herself in love with Stuart and even now, knowing how he and Nellie felt about each other, she was perhaps fonder of him than she should have been. But if he knew it he never made her feel uncomfortable or guilty, and he treated her just right, with a mixture of affection and teasing, so she pushed to the back of her mind the knowledge that Stuart still meant more to her – a bit more – than a brother-in-law should, and behaved naturally towards him.

'Will you be grateful, young woman!' Stuart said now with mock severity. 'We're not going to admit twice in one evening that we need the exercise, nor how much we like walking in the park, so let's just get on and enjoy our little excursion. And don't forget, we shall expect a letter every other day and a postcard in between, just to reassure our Nell that you haven't been sucked down the plughole whilst having a bath, or pecked to death by a parrot escaped from the Sefton Park aviary.'

'Or got dragged down by an octopus on the lake,' Nellie contributed. 'Really, young people these days – you just don't know what they'll do next.'

They were walking down Greenbank Lane, Lilac trying to peer through the screening trees and bushes at the big houses on the left-hand side of the road, whilst Nellie gazed dreamily out over the fields and trees to the right.

'I don't suppose we'll ever live anywhere nicer than this, not even if we do move into the country, and just think, if we'd still been here, living at 39 Penny Lane, our littl'un might have gone to that school,' Nellie remarked as they drew level with Greenbank School in its beautiful wooded grounds. 'Imagine a kid having all that wonderful space to wander in! Why, it's as big as Sefton Park, very near.'

'Might be bigger,' Lilac said, peering through the hedge. 'Well, when I marry my millionaire, Nell, I'll pay for your tiddler to come back here and get his education – isn't that a fair offer?'

'By the time you marry a millionaire I'll be one in my own right,' Stuart said. 'And by the time young Gallagher is thinking about school we'll be back here anyway, I'm sure.'

'Or cleaning out Buckingham Palace for yourselves,' Lilac said. 'Ouch, Nellie, don't pinch!'

'Stop gabbling you two and step out,' Stuart advised. 'Come on, Nellie love, you know what it said in the book about exercise, the more you take the easier the birth will be. Besides, we've got to prove to all those soft southerners that Liverpool lasses make the best little mothers in Britain. Left right, left right!'

He unlinked arms once more and began to walk with a ridiculous goose-step, lifting his knees to hip level with every step and swinging his arms so vigorously that Nellie and Lilac fell back to give him room.

'Come *on*, girls!' Stuart adjured them. 'Follow my example and use your whole body when you walk. March like little soldiers – come on, show me what you're made of!'

'If we walked like that we'd show you our bloomers,' Nellie grumbled. 'And if you had young Gallagher kicking and squirming inside you, you'd take things a bit easy too. So stop fooling about, Stuart, and take my arm. Lilac's coming to tea tomorrow, as well, so we'll be able to discuss our plans for this house-sharing business then.'

'Oh. Right. I'll consider myself cut down to size,' Stuart said. He put his arm round Nellie and gave her a squeeze. Nellie squeaked, then squeezed back and Lilac, watching, felt a curious little stab of something very like envy twisting in her breast.

But I don't want to marry and settle down, she reminded herself as they began to cross the park. I want some fun before I start letting some young man order me about. Time enough for all that, and certainly there's nothing I'd like less than to have my figure ruined by some wretched baby!

But later, when she was aboard her tram and turning to wave, she watched the two figures strolling slowly back the way they had come, Nellie's head very close to Stuart's strong shoulder, his arm comfortingly round her thickening waist, and the curious little stab of envy pricked her once more.

They were going far away, and they were going together. But she, Lilac, would stay here growing older, all by herself, with only her friends for company, with no lover to warm her.

The conductor shouted to someone to hurry up

please, the bell ting-tinged and the tram lurched into motion. Lilac noticed someone who had been standing some yards from the stop suddenly decide to jump aboard; she saw him leap, heard the conductor shout, and then a tall figure was pushing its way between the seats and slumping into the one beside her.

'Art! What on earth are you doing here?'

'Doin'? Catchin' the tram, our Lilac, same's you.'

Art grinned affectionately down at her. He was tall and husky, with bright brown hair which fell in a cowlick across his forehead, a broad, almost simple grin and a pair of shrewd brown eyes. He would probably have been the first to say that his face was undistinguished and his figure too chunky, but even if she didn't want to marry him Lilac still had a soft spot for her old playmate and smiled back at him whilst shaking her head sorrowfully.

'Catching the tram indeed! Well I know that, puddin'-head! But I've been to supper with the Gallaghers; what are you doing in Penny Lane?'

Art chuckled and put an arm along the back of the seat. Lilac edged forward a bit; she did not want to be cuddled in a public service vehicle!

'This isn't Penny Lane, Miss know-it-all, this is Ullet Road. Do you remember Tippy Huggett?'

'No. Should I?'

'Oh, queen, you must remember Tippy! He was the feller who got turned out of the Rotunda for making spit-balls. Don't you remember, we were all kicked out by the commissionaire – you said . . .'

'Oh *him*,' Lilac said hastily. The tram was crowded, she did not want the other passengers to hear all about her misspent youth. 'What about him?'

'He's lodging on Ullet Road; he's working for

63

William Griffiths & Son, the tailors in South John Street. Doing well for himself is Tippy.'

'I can just imagine him sitting cross-legged on the floor, but I can't imagine him using a needle and thread,' Lilac observed. 'He was a right devil was Tippy.'

'So was I,' Art said regretfully. 'So was you, queen! Fact is, we all have to change as we grow up or we'd starve. But Tippy doesn't sit cross-legged – whatever give you that idea? – he's in the showroom. He shows patterns and takes measurements; he was always kind o' neat, wouldn't you say?'

'Ye-es,' Lilac agreed. She remembered Tippy as a small, aggressive boy with sores round his mouth and hair which looked as though mice had nibbled it. 'Smartened himself up a bit, has he?'

'Haven't we all?' Art said reproachfully. 'I call to mind the day you fell on your face in Mersey-mud an' Stuart chucked you in the bath . . .'

'Don't keep getting so *personal*,' Lilac snapped, 'or you can move to another seat! Kids are always mucky. So anyway, Tippy lodges in Ullet Road and you were visiting him and just happened . . .'

'Don't get swelled-headed,' Art advised kindly. 'I just happened to walk down to the tram stop and saw you get aboard, I nearly didn't bother to come on as well, I meant to walk, only . . .'

'You thought you might as well ride,' Lilac said sarcastically. 'Oh well, if you're getting off at my stop you can walk me up to Rodney Street if you like.'

'And give you a kiss and a cuddle on the doorstep?'

'No!' snapped Lilac, all too conscious of listening ears. She moved pointedly further along the slatted wooden seat. 'I've got my good name to consider, Art O'Brien.'

'Aw, c'mon, Lilac love, don't get all starched up wi' me, you knew I were only joking!'

But Lilac settled primly back in her seat and gazed out at the summer dusk and the hissing gas lamps on a level with the top deck. I won't marry till I'm good and ready, she told herself crossly. And when I do it won't be a bank clerk with a worn suit and cracked black shoes. That smart young ship's officer, he's more my style! I could see he liked me, and he came of a rich family, that house was full of good stuff.

Then she thought about Nellie and her Stuart, who would be happy, she was sure, on a desert island sharing their last coconut between them. But she was different, she did so like her creature comforts, pretty dresses, money in her pocket, warm fires in winter and iced drinks in summer! She would find it very hard to settle for anything less than the sort of life she had grown to enjoy with the Mattesons. She doubted that she could be happy with anyone who didn't have money and some sort of position, and Art really wasn't cut out even for clerking in a bank. He's rough, she told herself virtuously, and I'm not. Not now. And I won't end up like Mrs O'Brien or the other women in Coronation Court – overworked, always hungry, fighting a losing battle against the filth, the vermin, their menfolk.

Yet Nellie, whose life had been considerably harder than Lilac's, would have followed Stuart to hell and back, barefoot. Lilac knew it as surely as she knew she drew breath.

I'm made of weaker stuff, she thought sadly as the tram rumbled on. Even if I thought I loved . . .

someone . . . which I don't, I couldn't marry just for love. I'm not strong, like Nellie.

It was a curiously humbling thought.

Kitty woke when the sun came up the next day. She had found a patch of long grass by the canal and since the night seemed fine and likely to remain so, she had curled up amongst the soft blades, not bothering with the dubious shelter of the bridge.

Now she sat up, knuckled her eyes, and looked about her. A horse the size of an elephant was coming along the path towards her, towing a canal boat. It was a brightly painted boat with elaborate pictures all over it, and it towed in its turn another boat, the second one heavily laden with timber. There was a scruffy lad of about Kitty's age balanced on the timber, steering with a long pole-like rudder, a little girl in a blue cotton dress was watering the big earthenware pots of tomatoes set out on the roof of the first boat, and a good smell of bacon cooking came wafting over the water to Kitty's suddenly interested nose.

The boy spotted her and raised a hand.

'Marnin,' lass, an' a gradely one at that,' he observed, in what Kitty considered a thick country accent. 'Sleepin' rough, art tha? I see thee in thy nest, earlier.'

'Oh, I only come 'ere till me mam cools off,' Kitty said hastily. 'I'll go 'ome to get me butties.' But she fell into step beside the first boat, her nose pointing towards the bacon as though given the chance it would have leaped the gap and helped itself, if only to the rich and delicious smell.

'We'm 'avin' bacon,' the little girl chimed in. She picked up a thick sandwich from the cabin roof and waved it in a friendly sort of way towards Kitty. She was a pretty child of six or seven, with curly fair hair and blue eyes. 'Tis only t'best for us, eh, Cally?'

'That's right,' the boy agreed. 'On a Sat'day, any-road.'

'I'll likely get bacon too, when I goes 'ome,' Kitty lied manfully. She swallowed. 'Yours smells a treat,' she added.

The little girl looked back at the boat containing her brother. He obviously interpreted her glance for he said, 'Go on, 'en.' He turned to Kitty. 'Wanna bite?'

'I can't tek your grub,' Kitty began, but the little girl carefully put her watering can down on the roof of the
boat, picked up her sandwich and held it out.

'Oh, I can't . . .' Kitty began, then the smell reached her and she was lost. Her hand stretched out of its own volition, her grubby fingers sank deep into fresh-baked bread, and the sandwich was in her mouth, her teeth feeling first the softness of the loaf, then the delicious, greasy crispness of well-fried streaky bacon.

'S'orlright, innit?' said the little girl. 'I'll git another from me mother, don't fret yoursel'.'

'Thanks,' Kitty gasped. The bread and the bacon had already disappeared, were already nothing but a happy memory. 'Thanks a lot.'

She slowed her pace, wistfully watching as the small group moved further along the canal and entered the patch of shadow under Houghton Bridge. The horse's huge round hindquarters gleamed with grooming, its head was up, its step long and comfortable. The first boat was clean and homelike, the second sensible and properly packed so that the horse might not have to drag an uneven load. How enviable were the lives of those two children! Bacon sarnies, a horse to ride, a boat to steer – and a warm and comfortable Mam, who not only handed out bacon sarnies to small daughters, but would hand out a second, it appeared, and no awkward questions asked!

She stood and watched until the boats had disappeared behind the bulk of the Tate & Lyle warehouses, then walked along to Houghton Bridge, swung herself back on to the road, and considered the morning.

It was still very early. The sun, a red ball occasionally glimpsed between the buildings, seemed to promise another fine day. How lovely it would have been had she been asked aboard the canal boat, given a job, and more bacon sarnies, told she might stay with them! But things like that only happened in stories, in real life you were likelier to get thumps than kisses, so she'd better start moving. Sary never got up till noon, especially when she'd had a skinful the previous night, but the eleven-year-old twins Arnold and Robert – known as Arny and Bob to their friends – were often abroad far earlier and had been known to visit the canal for the purpose of either nicking off the boats or fishing in the turgid water with a bit of string and a bent pin.

'All they'll catch will be colds in the head,' Mrs O'Rourke used to say when Kitty explained why her brothers were somehow never expected to work as she did. 'They'll grow up bad, those two.'

Kitty thought they were pretty bad already, but you couldn't altogether blame them. Sary didn't much like any girls, but she did adore the twins, so they got their own way with everything, waxed fat on their own thieving and Sary's sporadic generosity, and never gave a thought to the sister who had pretty well brought them up, save to tell tales of her to their mother whenever the opportunity arose.

So where'll I go, then? Kitty asked herself, looking

round the early-morning street, already beginning to bustle as the night-shift got ready to leave the factories and the day-shift began to stream in. What'll I do today? By 'eck, that sarny were good – I wouldn't mind another one jest like that! And I've got the 'alf dollar an' all – I could get me some grub to set me up for the day.

It was strange to know that the day was her own, and whether it was the unexpected kindness of the boat-people or the comfortable fullness engendered by the bacon sarny, Kitty was beginning to feel that her life was on the up-and-up, that there was hope for her, a future, even. Other girls left home and prospered! Boys, too – did not her favourite book, *Her Benny*, tell the story of two Liverpool kids from the slums who made it to better things? The uncomfortable thought that little Nellie, the book's heroine, had died and gone to heaven before real good fortune came to Benny was easily dealt with; Benny was the eldest, as she was, so she was bound, like Benny, to be all right, to make her fortune, and to live happily ever after.

But not, of course, if the twins found her and told Sary, nor if either Sary or her father came across her. All they would consider would be how many bones they should break before tossing her remains into the River Mersey for the fishes to nibble. They'd brand her a thief no matter that she'd handed over the money and told them where the trimmings were to be found. Oh well.

She was walking along the pavement when a woman drew level with her. As she did so she glanced down at Kitty, sniffed suspiciously and produced from her handbag an embroidered hanky, which she pressed defensively to her nose. She also increased her speed, plainly eager to get past the younger girl as quickly as possible.

Reckon I niff a bit, Kitty thought unconcernedly, for was she not always dirty and unkempt? She glanced down at her stained and filthy shirt, then looked again. Oh dear Lor', she thought, look at them 'ands!

They were not only black, they were striped, where the bacon fat had run down. Kitty guessed that her chin was probably fatty too, and she remembered that at home, unless her mother was up betimes and chased her out, she usually did her best, without soap or a flannel, to wash her face and hands under the pump shared by all the houses in the Court. And if you wanted anything, you were more likely to get it if you were at least clean.

There's the deserving poor, someone had said to Mrs O'Rourke in Kitty's hearing, and there's the squalid, idle drunkards and wife-beaters. Charity isn't any use to the latter, they abuse it or drink it; the former hate being the recipients of it but at least use it to escape from the poverty trap. So if she wanted help from anyone, Kitty reasoned, she had better set about becoming deserving poor right away.

Kitty returned to the canal. She knelt on the bank and rubbed at her hands and arms until they were pink and only lightly smeared, then she doused her face and rubbed that too. And finally, because it was a lovely morning and the sun was shining on the water – and also because her nits were itching her something cruel as they wandered across her scalp – she ducked her whole head in the canal and held it there for two or three lung-bursting minutes, then sat back, gulping air and squeezing water, dirt and even one or two nits out of her tangled locks.

She sat on the canal bank until she was pretty well dry, though her hair would probably stay dampish for a while yet, then climbed over the bridge once more and looked cautiously about her. No one so much as glanced at her. A passing scuffer, with his helmet in one hand to let the sun warm his curly dark hair, did not even see her, though he trod on her little toe with his great clumping black boots. Kitty said a few things under her breath, but continued to walk – or rather, limp – along Vauxhall Road, heading away from home, leaving the richly stinking tannery, the coal wharves and the small, familiar streets behind. She could feel the half-crown, wrapped in a bit of rag, nestling near her roped-in waist, comfortingly solid againt her bony ribs. It represented food, safety, hope. Public houses were still locked and barred but drowsy, blowsy women wrapped in big aprons were emerging from them to scrub steps and brush pavements, to shout curses at horses who left piles of steaming manure too near their doorsteps and to hail the milkman as his dozy steed dragged the milkcart up and down the small streets.

Kitty didn't know many eating places, but everyone knew Paddy's Market, and she did consider going there. They sold marvellous, mouth-watering food and it was cheap, too, and though she would not be able to afford even a second-hand dress she might beg or nick one, explaining – or not, of course – how she wanted to be the deserving poor and not the idle and feckless. But you could meet anyone in Paddy's, the twins nicked all sorts from the stalls, and kids of all shapes and sizes hung about it, including half Kitty's classmates, so it simply wasn't safe. No, she would have to get a lot further from home before she stopped to eat again.

But if there was one thing Kitty was used to, it was being hungry and not being fed. So it was with the bright optimism still burning within her that she began the trek to another part of the city, somewhere where the name Drinkwater wouldn't have people clutching their baskets and covering their pockets.

I'll make me fortune, she told herself, peering interestedly into shop windows as she passed. I'll run messages and carry shopping, I'll scrub doorsteps and hold horses, but I'll keep meself a deal better'n me mam ever did.

And with that thought to hold on to – and it wasn't so very much to attain, after all – Kitty plodded on through the bright morning.

Kitty had lived in the city all her short life. She knew the streets, the canal, the gas works, the factories and the tannery, the rice and flour mills, the various railway lines and stations, the smells and the sounds of it all. But her Liverpool consisted of a smelly, crowded mile to mile and a half at the most. When she ran errands for her mother, making her way to Paddy's Market to fetch rags or to the fruit market on Great Nelson Street, she was still more or less in her own territory. But when she went to and from the millinery shop on Upper Frederick Street, sneaked down to nick ends of timber from the yard opposite St Anne's on Rose Place, hung around outside the Free Library on William Brown Street, too scared to go in yet longing for the books which Mrs O'Rourke used to borrow for her, she was in Indian country, a stranger in a strange land.

So, padding along the dusty summer streets and wishing that the water-cart would come along and spray her hot, aching feet, it was not so very long before Kitty began to feel herself safe from the entire Drinkwater clan. Her father was a stoker on a merchant ship which plied across the Atlantic, taking goods to the United States of America. It was a long journey and so Hector Drinkwater was away more than he was home, for which fact Kitty was frequently devoutly thankful. She knew he was a seaman of course, that Liverpool was a great port, but since she was a far cry from being a favourite child she had never been taken down to the docks to view her father's ship from afar, nor lifted down onto the muddy sand at low tide to play with other kids in the rich, sticky mess.

Yet in a way the sea was in her blood, for the wind which blows nine days out of ten over the city was sweetened with salt, as well as with the oily, tarry, fishy smells from the docks. Kitty had breathed in the smell all her life and, indeed, knew no other.

So when she had passed, with a half-wistful glance, the end of Upper Parly, as the kids called it, she turned left along Park Lane, where those great, swaying land-ships, the trams, thundered along sounding their warning bells, and then she turned right into Beckwith Street, with the smell of the sea stronger than ever here and a strange excitement mounting in her. It was an ugly little road, too. She passed a huge building which announced that it was Heaps Flour Mills, then a shipyard, only by now the street had begun to call itself Carpenters' Row; no wonder, thought Kitty, appreciatively sniffing the smells of sawdust, tar and engine oil, a great many carpenters must be employed to make huge ships!

She emerged from Carpenters' Row on to Chaloner

Street – and saw the overhead railway for the first time. It scared her when the train came rattling and chugging along, but then she saw the docks, and her attention was caught and held.

Ships! Water, lots of it, and when she skirted Wapping Basin and began to cross the swing bridge which looked just exactly like another piece of road – if she hadn't been able to read she would never have known it was a bridge at all – she found the sea! Wide and blue today, with the buildings on the opposite bank shimmering in a heat-haze and looking very far away, but undoubtedly the great ocean she had read about, which divided Liverpool first from Ireland and then from the United States of America, though she was not quite certain how this division worked.

A girl of about her own age was playing hopscotch with another girl on the wide dockside. Kitty approached them.

'Hey, is that the sea?' she asked, sure of a confirmatory nod. But instead, two shaggy heads shook.

'Nah, chuck, that's the Mairsey,' the smaller of the girls assured her. 'Ain't you never seen it afore? Biggest river in the 'ole wairld, me da says.'

'Oh!' Kitty said. She had lost face, but the girls didn't seem to care at all. The taller one threw her piece of slate into the crudely chalked squares and began to hop. Kitty watched for a minute, then ambled on. She had found a fish and chip shop on Chaloner Street, squeezed between the Great Western Railway goods station and a small tobacconist shop, and still had the paper which had held the chips, though she had eaten the contents hungrily within moments of handing over her half-crown and watching sadly as it was reduced to two shillings, a threepenny joe and two pennies.

She'd had a drink of water just before accosting the two girls, because there was a drinking fountain at the side of the road, so she was comfortable enough in herself. And now she began to wonder if she might find employment of some sort amongst the ships which thronged the docks, or perhaps someone needing an errand run. For in fact Kitty, a gregarious little soul, was beginning to find the loneliness of her wandering almost as trying as the fear of being picked up by the police or the dread of dying of starvation: fates which, she well knew, did befall unwanted children.

But the afternoon was wearing on and fascinating though the dockside was to one as new to it as Kitty, it was patently no place for a skinny, barefoot girl. Mostly she was ignored, but now and then someone spoke to her – not always in English, either – and a strong sense of self-preservation warned her that the men who called out to her and cajoled her with sweets to come and talk to them meant her no good and might well be as dangerous as an encounter with Sary or Hector Drinkwater.

So she abandoned the docks and wandered back into the city proper once more, this time into a better area where the houses were big and very clean and the pavements wide and well-swept.

She glanced up at the road sign nearest her. *Rodney Street*, it read.

Kitty walked on. A great many of the houses had brass plates on the door; she stopped to read one. *Dr G.B. Matteson. Member of the Royal College of Surgeons.* Wondering vaguely what the wording meant, Kitty continued. But she was getting tired and Rodney Street did not seem like the kind of place where she might find a fried fish shop, nor one of the delightful cocoa rooms where a cooked dinner might be had for sixpence – not that she intended to waste her substance on cooked dinners, of course, when chips were available for so much less. Besides, it was evening and she really ought to be finding a nice warm nook for the night, not wandering gormlessly on with no thought for the future.

So she turned and began to retrace her steps.

Chapter Four

Lilac had settled Mrs Matteson tenderly in bed, put a glass of iced water within easy reach, arranged a light shawl comfortably round the older woman's shoulders, and gone downstairs to the kitchen to fetch up Mrs Matteson's tray, on which there should already be a light and tempting supper. Since she was going to the house in Penny Lane for a meal she wanted to get her work over so that she could change her print gown and flat shoes for something a trifle more fashionable, but she would never have dreamed of hurrying her mistress. Nevertheless, she entered the kitchen hoping devoutly that the evening meal was prepared.

The plain cook, stomping about her domain, gave Lilac a nasty glare as she entered the room; Mrs O'Malley had found another place and the dislike Lilac felt for her was now seen to be mutual. She had already prepared two plates of food, one for the mistress and one for Dr Matteson, and when Lilac looked at the unappetising helpings she felt a cold rage envelop her. The woman had cut the cold mutton into chunks and scarcely warmed the cabbage, whilst the potatoes, small, new, toothsome, had been boiled to a miserable mush. She had made a thick, solid-looking gravy and the mint sauce, which should have been sweet and green with the well-minced herb, was last week's, so it was brown as a cup of milkless tea. She had used one of the best plates, it was true, but there was a smear of gravy across the gold-rimmed edge and she hadn't bothered to match up the knife and fork: the knife had a heavy pearl handle and the fork had embossed ivy leaves on its silver surface. Bullied by Lilac into at least a semblance of caring, she had put a rose in the silver vase on the tray, but the rose was half-dead and heavily infested with greenfly and the vase had smears of plate polish down one side.

'This is disgraceful,' Lilac said shortly, not bothering to hide her annoyance. 'Mrs Matteson is an invalid, cook; we are supposed to tempt her appetite. Do you remember what the doctor told you when he first employed you?'

'He never told me no jumped up orphing from a 'sylum 'ud be 'titled to order me about,' the cook muttered rudely. 'Tek it or leave it, Miss.'

'Mrs Matteson will leave it, because it's badly cooked and stale-looking,' Lilac said firmly. 'Get the bread and butter out, please. I'll make her a few sandwiches – if you haven't ruined the rest of the food in the pantry, that is.'

The cook snorted; her big, work-roughened hands went behind her to untie her apron.

'Do it yourself,' she snapped. 'I'm orf.'

'You aren't due to leave for another hour and a half,' Lilac said. 'What do you think Dr Matteson will say when he sees what you've prepared for him and his wife?'

The cook continued to shed her apron, then snatched her coat off the back of a chair where it had plainly been hung ready for her departure.

'Don't care what the 'ell 'e finks,' she said. 'I've got a new place waitin' for me, unlike some. I'm orf now and I won't be back. Put tharrin your pipe an' smoke it, you snotty bitch.'

Lilac, fairly trembling with rage, cleared the tray of the greasy, rapidly cooling food and threw the dying rose into the bin. Then she watched as the older woman struggled into her coat and jammed a felt hat down over her greasy hair.

'So you don't even intend to work out your week! Well, good riddance to bad rubbish is what the Mattesons will think,' she said to the cook's back as the woman headed for the kitchen door. 'Now that you've gone, and your nasty, lazy habits with you, perhaps I can get my poor mistress a meal that's halfway decent for once.'

Mrs O'Malley did not deign to reply but sniffed scornfully, then slammed the kitchen door resoundingly behind her, just as Lilac filled her lungs for another blast of truthful abuse. Seeing that she would be talking to herself, Lilac began to scrabble round, preparing a tray from scratch since there was nothing whatsoever left to hand once the original plateful had been consigned to the bin.

As she worked, she wished she could have got word to Nellie, to say she would be late. She guessed Nellie wouldn't start the meal without her and poor Stuart would be hungry as a lion by the time she had finished here. The Mattesons knew that she had to find a new place and had told her, with all their usual sympathy and understanding, that she might have as much time off as she wished provided Mrs Matteson was never left alone, but tonight she had the cook's job to do as well as her own and was bound to be very late indeed arriving at Penny Lane.

However, wishing was not much use and working hard was likelier to shorten Stuart's wait. So she ran into the back garden and found a beautiful white rosebud, just unfurling. She picked it, put it in the silver vase which she had already wiped clean and polished with a duster, then she went into the pantry. Looking round her, she realised that cook had been steadily using up all the available food and not bothering to spend the housekeeping money she was given to stock up again. A very small pat of butter, a tin of sardines in oil and another of ham in jelly, together with a heel of bread met Lilac's eye. The bread was stale, she could see that at a glance, and Mrs Matteson did not care for ham. She opened the meat safe, expecting to find the rest of the mutton reposing therein, but it was empty. What cook had done with the mangled remains of the joint she could not imagine, but it was nowhere to be seen.

Still, they say, necessity is the mother of invention. Lilac cut two thin slices of bread and toasted them, mashed the sardines with a little vinegar, salt and pepper, and spread the resultant savoury paste on the toast. Then she covered the fish with thin slices of tomato and ran into the garden again to pick some parsley, which she chopped and scattered over the food. She lit the gas-grill and slid the toast under it, then got a bottle of white wine out of the sideboard in the dining room and poured her mistress a modest half-glass. She deserves something to help that down, though it'll be tastier than the muck cook had prepared, she told herself grimly, putting the hot food onto a warmed and clean plate and setting it carefully on the tray, with matching cutlery beside it and the glass of wine beside that.

Upstairs, Mrs Matteson's eyes brightened at the sight of the tray.

'Looks – n-nice,' she said hesitantly. 'Pretty. Ooh, wine!'

'Her speech is improving,' Dr Matteson had said

to Lilac earlier in the day. 'With peace and quiet and no worries, and with me on hand all day, she'll make a complete recovery, I'm sure of it.'

Now, Lilac arranged Mrs Matteson's pillows so that she was sitting upright, cut the hot toast into small squares, and sat down beside the bed.

'The doctor won't be long, now,' she said cheerfully. 'You eat up, Mrs Matteson, and think how pleased he'll be to see a clean plate when he gets back!'

'Umm,' Mrs Matteson said. She picked up the wine glass, her hand shaking, and carried it to her lips. She drank, then replaced the glass. A smile curved her lips. 'Nice,' she said again.

'Yes, it's a good wine I believe,' Lilac said. She had never tasted wine, but she knew what Dr Matteson would have said. 'Can you manage the toast?'

'Umm. Oo-oh, sard . . . sa . . .'

'That's right, sardines. Do you like them?'

'Mmm!' A vigorous nod of the head accompanied the hum. 'N- nice.'

Lilac sat by the bed, watching for the first sign of tiredness, for the fork to drop from Mrs Matteson's thin, nervous hand, but all went well. Apparently sardines on toast were a treat to someone who habitually tackled a heavy cooked dinner at night – particularly heavy lately, since Mrs O'Malley believed in sending up large helpings as a method of disguising her inability to present palatable food. And presently Lilac hurried down the stairs with an empty tray, and carried up the only dessert she could find: a helping of raspberries, sugared and topped with thick cream.

Coffee followed that and Lilac tried very hard not to think how time was flying by, nor how late Dr Matteson was. Indeed, when his step sounded on the stair she did her best to stand up casually, as though she had all the time in the world.

'Evening, doctor. As you're late, should I bring your meal up on a tray? Then you can sit with Mrs Matteson whilst you eat. Your wife has only just finished!'

'Excellent,' Dr Matteson said heartily. 'Many thanks Lilac – what has cook prepared for us tonight, then?'

'Nothing. She's done a bunk,' Lilac said briefly. 'Good riddance, I say. The pantry's bare, but I can do you toasted ham sandwiches with mustard, and there are raspberries and cream to follow.'

'*Toasted* sandwiches? Why not plain old bread sandwiches?' Dr Matteson said, tiredly sitting down in the chair Lilac had just vacated. 'Anything will do, my dear . . . and I'll have a glass of wine, too.'

'The bread's stale,' Lilac said. 'It toasts fine, though. Shan't be a tick, sir.'

But she was, of course. The doctor didn't need a rose on his tray but Lilac knew he would like a clean tray-cloth and she had to make up fresh mustard. The tin of ham was easily opened and despite Lilac's suspicion of tinned meat, proved to be fresh enough. But by the time she had found another tomato and sliced that as a garnish on the side of the plate, poured the wine, changed her mind and put the bottle on the tray, sugared the raspberries . . . goodness, it's going to be dark before I get there, Lilac told herself, dismayed at the way time was flying.

As soon as the meal was served she hurried up to her room. She changed with great rapidity into a light green skirt and white blouse and donned a pair of neat black shoes with a medium heel. She brushed her hair, coiled it round her hand and wedged it on top of her head with a number of hairpins, snatched up her jacket and headed for the attic stairs.

On the first floor, she remembered the tray. Damn! She fetched it, the doctor having cleaned both his plates and emptied the bottle, and hurried down the two flights of stairs into the basement kitchen. And though it wasn't her job to wash up she had best do it rather than have the poor doctor go down later to make his wife's hot milk and find the kitchen in disarray. The washing up was done at speed, Lilac snatching crocks in and out of the water and slapping them on the dresser without pausing for breath. When it was done she looked round the kitchen, decided it would have to do, and headed for the front door, making a lightning decision as she went.

She would go to Nellie's by cab!

She descended the steps and stood on the pavement, looking about her. There was a cab rank outside the Philharmonic Hall and it wasn't far to the Philly, she would simply turn to her left and walk up Rodney Street until she reached the crossroads, then turn right along Hardman Street, past the School for the Blind and St Mary's Church and there you were, with the bulk of the Philly to your right and cabs lined up against the pavement waiting for fares.

But she was in luck. She had scarcely walked more than ten yards on her way when a cab came towards her with its flag up; cruising for fares, no doubt, possibly having just dropped someone off further up Rodney Street. As she stepped into the cab, having told him Nellie's address, she heard a shout. She looked round, the vehicle already on the move, and saw a skinny child waving at her from the pavement.

Puzzled, the glanced about, because the child

couldn't possibly be waving to her, she didn't know the girl. The street was empty though, so perhaps the kid just thought she recognised Lilac. Or was her skirt caught in the door? It had happened, Lilac knew, and could result in a nasty mark on a precious garment. She checked, but her skirt was all in the cab with her and very nice it looked, spread out on the cracked red leather seat. And presently, as the cab made its way towards Penny Lane, she forgot about the child and began to think about the steak and kidney pudding she would presently enjoy, and Nellie's wonderful lemon chiffon pie which would follow. How odd it is that this evening I'll be eating a much better meal than the Mattesons, who are very rich compared to Nellie and me, she thought. What a topsy-turvy world it is – money can't always buy you the best. And she decided to get Nellie some really good chocolates as a thank-you present, to eat on the journey down to the snooty south of England.

Kitty had walked up as far as Leece Street and bought herself an enormous bowl of pea and ham soup and a wedge of bread at the refreshment rooms opposite St Luke's Church. Considerably heartened by this repast, she bought two blackjacks for a farthing from Thomas Henry's, a very superior sort of provisions shop, and decided to save the sticky sweets for the long watches of her second night under the stars. Not knowing quite where to go, she then returned to Rodney Street. It was quiet, the lamplighter had not yet been along and the sky was a peaceful greenish blue, deepening to red-gold along the western horizon. No one was about, so she found a house with deep steps, under which was a dry, cave-like hidey-hole. She clambered into it and stared out down the street.

A door opened somewhere, then shut with a sharp snap. High-heeled shoes clack-clacketed down steps and along the pavement. A woman, quite young, Kitty decided drowsily. Wonder what she's doin' out at this hour, when everyone else seems to be settled indoors?

The woman came into view. Only it wasn't a woman, it was a girl and a very pretty one, too. With renewed interest, because the pretty girl looked somehow familiar, Kitty eased herself out of her hiding place and stood up, then her heart gave a great bound in her skinny chest.

It was her! The girl from Penny Lane! And she was walking swiftly and confidently along the pavement, any moment she would be on a level with Kitty!

She'll help me, Kitty thought unhesitatingly. She will, she's a real lady, Mrs O'Rourke said real ladies were always willing to help. I'll 'splain about me mam and the trimmin's and all that, she'll tell me what to do and where to go.

She moved hesitantly forward just as a car came past and the girl gestured to the driver, who pulled over and stopped by the kerb. Kitty waited; she would speak to the girl from Penny Lane just as soon as the cab had driven on. How lucky it was that she had chosen a Rodney Street doorstep for her bed! But it seemed her luck had run out, for the girl from Penny Lane said something to the cab driver, then opened the door of his vehicle and jumped inside. Kitty ran forward, waving, calling, desperate that her one hope of help should not disappear. In fact she pursued the cab all the way down Rodney Street, turned the corner onto Hardman Street at such speed that she burnt the side of her bare foot, and saw with real dismay that the driver was accelerating and would presently outstrip her.

Kitty ran on, but she knew it was useless, and presently, sobbing with effort and with a hand to the stitch in her side, she slowed to an amble and then a walk. She would never catch up, not if she ran and ran, and even if she'd had the money to get into a taxi herself and shout 'Follow that motor!' she would never have the nerve. Why, for all she knew, Penny Lane might be miles and miles away.

She had been shuffling along the pavement, intermittently sobbing and hiccuping, whilst tears spilled down her cheeks, but now she stopped short and stared sightlessly at the building ahead of her. Penny Lane! Her new friend was the girl from Penny Lane, they had said so in the milliner's shop. So all Kitty had to do to find her friend was to find Penny Lane!

'Lilac! Well, our kid, you had us well worried!' Stuart gave his young sister-in-law a friendly hug and drew her into the small, square hallway. 'My lady-wife was all for calling out the scuffers to search for your body, but I told her you were probably working late and would arrive in time for the meal if we hung on a bit.'

'Oh Stu, you didn't wait supper for me? I couldn't help it, honest . . . that wretched cook I told you about left without warning and I was landed with gettin' Mrs Matteson her tea and cookin' for the doctor . . . *how* I wished you were on the telephone, so I could have let you know I was going to be late.'

'We'll be on the telephone in London, since I'll need to be in contact with the newspaper,' Stuart said. 'So there'll be no excuse for not getting in touch, young lady. Come on, let's get sat down now you are here.'

'I'll just put me jacket on the stand,' Lilac said, wriggling out of her short coat. 'Ooh, I've been thinking of steak and kidney pudding all the way . . . I caught a cab, you know, like a proper lady!'

Stuart looked down at the vivid little face so near his own and remembered the first time he had met Lilac. A skinny, scruffy kid she'd been, covered with mud and stinking like . . . like the Mersey at low tide, which was where the mud had come from. He'd made her take a bath in the old tin tub before her aunt's fire and had been astonished, when she emerged from the water, to find she had a mass of red-gold curls and very white skin as well as a pair of dazzlingly blue eyes. She'd been a regular little brick then, for all Nellie mourned her selfishness and quick temper, and she was a regular little brick now, though she did still tend to see life strictly with a view to her own best interests. But Nellie was all she had in the world, apart from a few friends her own age and a good many ardent young men, and Lilac had stressed that she would cope happily with life alone to make it possible for Nellie to go down to London with a clear conscience. Stuart was well aware that, had Lilac bemoaned her fate, said she'd pine for Nellie, his wife would have felt guilty and unhappy about putting her husband before the girl she had treated more like a daughter than an adopted sister, and would have been unsettled and unhappy in their new home as a result.

'You are a lady, chuck,' Stuart said now, throwing open the kitchen door and smiling across at his wife, standing by the table enveloped in a huge white apron, whilst the steam made her hair curl in tiny tendrils around her face and turned her cheeks scarlet. 'Here she is, Nell darling, as safe as houses and as pretty as a picture.'

Lilac walked into the room and kissed Nellie's hot cheek, then turned back to Stuart, her blue eyes dancing with innocent flirtatiousness.

'Oh Stuart, I wish I were a lady, for if I were I'd do all sorts of exciting things, but there's no gainsaying that I'm just me.' She turned to her sister. 'Nellie, love, I'm sorry I worried you, but it wasn't my fault I was late, honest to God.'

'It never is, honest to God,' Nellie said drily, ladling the steaming pudding onto three plates. 'Tell us what happened; is Mrs Matteson all right?'

'Fine, now. Better for that wretch of a cook leaving without warning just at dinner time,' Lilac said. 'That was why I was late, I had to get some decent food and Mrs O'Malley, the awful cook, had left us with a bare pantry, so it took a while. Shall I put the spuds round whilst you do the greens, Nell?'

'You sit yourself down and be a guest for once,' Stuart ordered her. 'She hasn't told you how she got here, Nell. What a girl she is!'

'I came by cab,' Lilac said proudly, when Nellie looked an enquiry across the table. 'I was so desperate to reach your steak pudding, our Nell, that I didn't grudge the money one bit. And it were a good drive, too. I enjoyed it, though right at the start I thought I'd caught me skirt in the door of the taxi, which could easily have spoiled it.'

'There you are; eat up,' Nellie ordered, pulling her own chair up to the table and picking up her knife and fork. 'What made you think you'd caught your skirt in the door, chuck?'

'I can't remember . . . yes I can, it was a little girl,

a real street arab, standing by the kerb screeching something at me and waving. And then when the cab started to move she ran behind for a few steps, so I thought she must have wanted to warn me I'd trapped my skirt. Only I hadn't.'

'I see,' Nellie said placidly. Stuart, eating, grinned to himself. He did love feminine logic, and anyway he was feeling supremely happy. The two women he loved best in the world – he was very fond of Lilac even when she was acting like any other pretty, empty-headed youngster – were sitting at his table, his wife was expecting a baby, and they were about to move south to a well-paid job. Furthermore, he had always wanted to work in London because the city fascinated him.

But thinking about the baby made him think about something else, something he would rather have forgotten. When he had asked Nellie to marry him she had told him that long ago, when she had been little more than a child herself, she had borne an illegitimate son to another man. He had been shattered, astonished, hurt. Nellie had always seemed perfect to him, a delicately beautiful, sensitive girl whose main aim in life had been to guard the child Lilac against all ills and to strain every nerve to bring back health and happiness to the wounded soldiers in her charge – for Nellie had been nursing when they had first met as adults. He had been so sure of her innocence, too, and for a couple of days he had kept away from her, feeling betrayed and cheated.

But it had not lasted: Stuart was too fairminded not to see the double-standards he was applying to Nellie's unwelcome and unexpected revelation. He had had a good few experiences himself, and he had not got the excuse of youth and innocence, either.

A pretty Parisienne, a warmhearted brunette from Bootle, a blonde and bubbly girl-reporter covering the same story as he in France, had all shared his bed at one time or another and he had instigated the relationship in each instance. Yet even knowing that he had no right to expect Nellie to be different, he still felt, irrationally, that he had been cheated. If only she had talked more about the affair, explained . . .

Apologised, you mean, Stuart said crossly to himself. After what that girl suffered during the war, surely you aren't still of the opinion that women are in some way different to men? That your little flings are to be tolerated with a smile whilst her one fall from grace must be frowned upon as a deeply immoral act? You know Nellie, you know she's a sweet, giving person. She must have thought she was in love with the chap . . . she never said what happened about the baby . . . Oh but it's different, I can't bear it, she's mine, all mine, I've got her present and her future in my loving hands and the truth is I want her past, too!

'Stu? What a grim expression!' Lilac smiled at him, breaking into his train of thought, bringing him abruptly back to the present, to the cosy kitchen, the untouched food on his plate. 'If you don't want your dinner, I know someone who does!'

'Don't say you're still hungry, our Lilac!' Nellie exclaimed. 'Better start your meal, Stu love, or the poor, hungry orphan will be whipping it off your plate and on to her own!'

'I am, I am,' Stuart said, hastily beginning to eat. 'Nellie, you're the queen of cooks,' he added through a full mouth. 'This is prime! I can't blame the kid for wanting seconds.'

'There's a bit more pudding left, and some veggies, if you'd like them, Lilac,' Nellie said. 'Pass your plate, queen.'

Lilac laughed but shook her head.

'Couldn't, I'm stuffed fuller'n a Christmas turkey,' she declared. 'And did someone say it was lemon chiffon for afters?'

'Someone did. And now since Stu's come out of his brown study and started to eat I'll fetch it through. It's on the marble slab in the pantry, keeping cool.'

Nellie got up to fetch the dessert whilst Lilac cleared the table and Stuart, conscience-stricken, ate as fast as he could. He was just thankful that no one had offered him a penny for his thoughts though, because a guilty blush might have led Nellie to make a pretty shrewd guess as to why his face had seemed grim.

'All done, love?' Nellie said as he pushed back his plate. 'Lemon chiffon? Or would you rather have cheese and biscuits?'

She always asked, almost always provided a dessert, though she knew Stuart invariably chose cheese. His wishes, he knew, came first with her, she studied to please him in everything, never really considered herself at all. So why could not he, in his turn, be more generous over the only action of hers which he could not entirely understand and condone? This evening, to make up for his unkind thoughts, Stuart eyed the lemon chiffon appreciatively and said he would try some, thank you, dear.

'You can have cheese afterwards,' Nellie said, twinkling at him. 'A chiffon is ever so light.'

I wonder if he was dark or fair, her first fellow, Stuart's mind wondered perversely as he began to eat the delicious, lemony dessert. Or he might have been grey haired, or a red-head ... he could even have been bald, with a great white beard!

'Go on, Nell, you're eating for two, remember,' Lilac remarked. 'Take the last bit of chiffon, it'll make young Gallagher grow up big and strong!'

Stuart finished off his dessert and reached for the cheese. What on earth was the matter with him tonight? What did it matter if her lover – even thinking the word was like a knife twisting in his guts – was dark or fair, grey or bald? He was past, perhaps dead, certainly out of both sight and mind. Or out of Nellie's mind, anyway. So why should the bloke, whoever he was, persist in entering Stuart's thoughts on the least possible excuse, to plague and irritate?

'Biscuits, love?'

Nellie held out the small, round tin. Stuart selected two, cut himself a wedge of his favourite cheese and watched the two girls as they bustled round clearing the table, for they were later than usual and Lilac would have to be walked to the tram stop soon or she would miss the last one.

As he ate, it occurred to him that there might be a rather nasty secondary reason for his sudden preoccupation with Nellie's past. The obvious reason was her pregnancy, because every time he looked at her he could not help remembering that this was not the first time her stomach had slowly swelled and ripened with a child. He thought guiltily that the secondary reason might easily be that with Nellie's pregnancy pulling her out of shape and making her tired and pale, he was noticing Lilac's ripe young beauty more than ever before – and perhaps as a result was very conscious of the fact that Lilac still had an almost childish affection for him, which took the form, often, of friendly flirtatiousness.

If it wasn't for Nellie . . . he found himself thinking, and was appalled at his own shallowness. He loved his wife deeply, devotedly, and he loved Lilac as one loves one's wife's pretty little sister. He harboured no carnal desire for the younger girl either, despite her lovely looks; he was simply intrigued by the sneaking suspicion that, should he make advances, Lilac would fall into his hands like a ripe plum.

'Finished, dearest? Then pass your plate and go and read the paper whilst Li and I wash up and have a good gossip.'

Nellie gave him her sweetest smile and Stuart, muttering that he really ought to help, left the room, clutching the evening paper and feeling a complete cad.

Well, he had looked himself squarely in the face and he didn't much like what he had seen. A man who could not bring himself to forgive his wife for a long-dead, girlhood love-affair, yet admitted to a prurient interest in her pretty younger sister. What sort of a fellow was he, for goodness sake? He sat down in the basket chair by the window and opened the paper. He would never think about Nellie's past again, what did it matter, it was over, finished! Though one day, when they were both much older and wiser, he might just ask her . . .

Nellie set down her teacup and eased her aching back, then stood up. Stuart must be roused from his newspaper so that he and she might walk Lilac to the tram, and Lilac must be brought indoors and put into her coat, because at present she was gossiping over the back wall to Ena Evans, next door.

Nellie sighed and began to walk slowly across the kitchen. Having a baby was a tiring business, her legs hurt, her back ached and now even her mind was uncomfortable, because she knew her dear Stuart as well as she knew herself, and she had known as soon as she saw the expression on his face at supper-time, that he was thinking about Davy again.

Not that he knew about Davy, he just knew he wasn't her first lover, that this baby would be her second child. He had sworn it didn't matter, wouldn't affect their love, and it hadn't, not at first. Not until she told him she was expecting his child and she saw how his first joy had been tempered by the thought, *she's done it all before.*

It was a pity, really, that they had both agreed never to mention the matter again, because some things, Nellie believed, needed discussion before complete understanding could result. She had never told Stuart that Davy was married, and happily at that, to a girl called Bethan from the little village of Moelfre in Anglesey. Never told him that Bethan's eldest child, Richart, was the baby to whom she, Nellie, had given birth on that chilly March day in 1915. Not that anyone had known she was the child's mother. Bethan, believing Davy dead, had longed for a child and Nellie had known she could not give Richart a tenth of what would be his as Bethan's boy. So they had padded Bethan with cushions, and covered Nellie with voluminous aprons and a cloak, and Richart had stayed in Moelfre where he was totally accepted as Bethan's son. Even Davy, who had been posted as missing but who had in fact been picked up by a passing ship and was in rude health, thought the boy was his and Bethan's. Conceived on his last leave, born in his absence ... Davy was sure that Richart was the best thing that had ever happened to him.

So though Nellie could have told Stuart that her child's father was a married man and to the best of her knowledge alive and kicking, she could never tell him who that father was nor that the child was living with his father and that father's legal wife on the Isle of Anglesey. It was not her secret to tell and she and Bethan had vowed silence. To break that vow would have been unforgivable.

So perhaps not mentioning it ever again was the best idea, after all. If only Stuart could have put it right out of his mind, pretended it had never happened. Nellie did just that, most of the time. There was no point in dwelling on it; what can't be cured must be endured, her Aunt Ada used to say. Well, it was true and she was doing her very best to endure, but when she saw Stuart looking at her as though she was somehow evil ... well, it was hard.

I needn't have told him anything, she reminded herself sometimes. I could have kept it to myself, same as I have with everyone else. But everyone has their own set of rules, and Nellie's rules said that you didn't hold back, not with someone as important to you as Stuart was to her. She could not be totally frank and tell him everything, because it wasn't just her secret, but she'd done her best. Besides, if he had wanted to back out, not to marry her, he'd had his chance, and he'd not taken it. So why should he keep dwelling on it now, when she needed his love and support as never before?

Nellie was Liverpool born and bred. In the poverty-stricken court off the Scotland Road where she had been born, the air she had breathed for the first twenty years of her existence had held the whiff of Mersey mud and the rolling fog which came in from the Irish Sea, and was dyed yellow and sulphurous by the fumes from the factories. She had travelled to France during the war and been kept going by the accents of her home city all around her, as Liverpool girls clung together and did their best to save lives. The city was her home and she loved it; when the war ended she had come home and vowed never to leave again. But that was before Stuart had been offered a job in London, of course. A wife must support her man; she had agreed unhesitatingly to go with him. Far from home she would go, far from friends, far from Lilac, too, who was more than a sister, dearer than any friend.

But she would do it all, for Stuart. She would even consent to her child being born in the soft south, picking up heaven knows what horrible habits and accents and affectations amongst those effete Londoners who had never eaten scouse or conny onny butties, wouldn't know a stirring cart if it ran over their feet, and probably thought a scuffer was a doormat.

And how did Stuart treat this selfless devotion to duty, this denial of her natural wish to be in her own place, to bear her child amongst friends? Why, with grim glances, a downturned mouth, a secret grudging of her one dreadful mistake – she had loved too well, and as it turned out, very unwisely. Was she to suffer for it for the rest of her days?

She had crossed the little hallway and now saw Stuart asleep in his chair. Her heart, hardened by what she imagined Stuart had been thinking, softened at the sight of him. Brown curly hair flopping over his forehead, the worry lines smoothed out, mouth open, dark eyes closed . . . he did work hard, poor Stu, and anyway she supposed that he was right; it was wicked to make a baby with a man before you married, she had done it and suffered the consequences. Perhaps she should take Stuart's disapproval on board, along with all the rest – her guilt over leaving Richart, lying to Davy's parents, deceiving her relatives and friends.

She moved softly across the room, her simple dress rustling over its petticoat. Stuart stirred and opened his eyes. For a moment he stared up at her, looking puzzled, then his eyes lit up with the most loving and tender glance.

'Nell! I was dreaming . . . such a nice dream . . .'

'Stu, we've got to walk our Lilac to the tram now, but when we get home, I want to talk.'

He frowned. Not crossly, but as though she had puzzled him.

'We talk all the time, sweetheart,' he said gently. 'What's different about talking later this evening?'

'I want to talk about – about what you were thinking, at supper tonight. Thinking so hard, love, that you forgot to eat.'

'Oh.' He looked stricken, then guilty. 'Nell, I try not to even let it cross my mind, I try to tell myself it never happened. But . . .'

'I know. I'm the same in a way. We'll talk about it though; right?'

He smiled, nodding a bit, and then rubbed his eyes like a child.

'Right,' he said.

Lilac climbed to the top deck of the tram and took the vacant front seat. Then she turned round to wave to Nellie and Stuart, already setting off for home.

Lucky them! So happy together, so ... so *complete*, somehow. Small, slender Nell – slender from the back, anyhow – walking with her arm round tall, dark Stuart's waist, whilst his arm encircled her and their heads drew close. They were made for each other, Lilac decided, fishing in her handbag for her fare. Absolutely made for each other. The two of them would face the move, the new job, the strangeness of London, and come out happily smiling, glad to be together. Perhaps it would even be a relief to them not to have Lilac forever on their doorstep, forever popping in for a meal or a chat.

But she didn't believe the last bit, not really. She knew herself to be loved and valued. So she smiled sunnily at the conductor when he came round, and presently, when Suzie, who had worked with her a year or so earlier, climbed up to the top deck, she hailed her to come and share her seat and they gossiped all the way back to Rodney Street.

Despite her resolve to find Penny Lane, Kitty speedily realised that it was not practicable to set off tonight. She had no idea where it was and though the commercial streets would still be buzzing with people for some time yet, the quieter, residential streets were not. It would be hard to find someone to give her directions once she got out of the main city, and she had a feeling that Penny Lane was a residential district which at this time of night would be deserted save for the odd householder returning from the pub or walking a dog. Accordingly, she made her way round the backs of the houses, searching for a gap in the hedge or a wall she could climb, and sure enough soon found one.

Long ago she had learned to climb walls, using

her bare toes with great cunning to find every tiny crack in the brickwork, and throwing any garment available over the broken glass set into wall-tops by provident householders. Lacking a jacket or even a pair of knickers to throw over the broken glass, she now resigned herself to scratches at best and a few deep cuts at worst, but luckily the householder she chose was either less canny or more trusting than his fellows, for the wall was merely topped by a single piece of barbed wire. Kitty got over without a mark on her and dropped down into the garden as quietly and lightly as a cat.

Once there, she looked consideringly round her. Rows of vegetables and some fruit bushes met her eyes, with a patch of lawn beyond and the house itself beyond that. Up against the back door there were dustbins – she could dig about in them – and a door in the wall which was swinging open. It's their privy, Kitty thought, pleased with her own perspicacity. She had heard that grand houses had their privies indoors and had only half-believed it, which was as well since she could now see with her own eyes that it had been a lie. She stole up the garden, a shadow amongst shadows, and sneaked into the privy. It was a proper flush one, a real lavvy, not a stinking enamelled bowl with a wooden seat on top shared by all thirty people in one of the courts off Upper Burlington Street. Kitty enthroned herself, used the lavvy as nature had intended, found a neat little box of toilet paper and used some for the proper purpose and stuck the rest down the front of her shirt in case she needed paper some time. She might want to send another note. Then she climbed down, not daring to pull the porcelain pear hanging from its chain in case she woke the whole house, and set off to explore.

There was a coal house, but it was summer so there wasn't much in it and anyway she had no need of coal: you could neither eat it nor sleep under it. There was a garden shed, however, and though she could not see much through the tiny, dusty window she thought it might be worth investigating. She was right. The door was locked but the key was still in it. Carelessness brought its own punishment, Kitty thought smugly, nipping inside and pinching two wonderfully warm sacks, which had once held seed potatoes and would very soon hold Kitty Drinkwater. She found a lovely big ball of string but took only a few yards, since it was a bulky thing and would be difficult, she imagined, to either use or sell. She was terribly tempted by a little fork, the sort of fork some people used in their window-boxes, but decided against it. I can always come back another night, she told herself, conveniently forgetting that she was bound for Penny Lane, and in any case she could scarcely make her fortune by prigging forks from garden sheds.

Having decided that the shed held nothing else of interest, Kitty abandoned it, not bothering to shut or lock the door again since if she tried it would probably squeak and bring someone down on her. But she did get herself a long, satisfying drink from the rainwater barrel – she thought the water tasted interestingly different and imagined that the householders probably preferred it to the dull stuff which came out of pumps – and also took a duster which someone must have forgotten to take in off the line earlier in the evening. I can wash me face wi' that, Kitty thought, stowing it down her shirt-front.

Next was the vegetable patch. In the dark it was difficult to differentiate between what was edible and what was not, but Kitty went back for the little fork, dug up a root of potatoes with it, and ate them raw, though after the first two she washed the rest in the water butt because the grit got in her teeth. Then she dug up another root for breakfast and found that the pea-pods were full, so she picked a score or so, flitting busily up and down the rows, thoroughly enjoying herself. Finally, she filled her shirt-front – already bulging, and most certainly not with Kitty – and set off for the wall once more.

She was tired now, but still managed the climb all right, avoided the barbed wire, and was about to drop down into the entry when something made her glance to her right. Someone was standing there, very still, against the wall. Someone big and dark, almost invisible save for the whiteness of face and hands.

A scuffer! A bobby, a busy, a bloomin' peeler, a policeman! Kitty had heard them called all sorts, but right now she didn't care what this one was called, she just wanted him to clear off. Heart thumping so loudly that she feared he might hear it, Kitty peered cautiously towards the man. She didn't think he had seen her because his face was in profile, but she dared not move and draw his attention . . . she could never get off the wall and run faster than he, not with her shirt full of her ill-gotten gains.

After a few seconds, though, she wondered why he was standing so still – and, what was more, facing the wall. Then she heard a gentle swishing sound and understood his choice of this dark and private entry. In the darkness, Kitty grinned. Even scuffers were human, he'd been taken short and was having a widdle, so it wouldn't be all that long before he took himself off and left her to make her escape.

And she was right. A few more moments passed whilst Kitty kept her head down and scarcely breathed and the policeman attended to his trouser buttons. Then, with majestic tread, the officer of the law walked slowly down the entry, turned left and disappeared. As relieved as the policeman, Kitty nipped down off the wall, slid along close to the bricks until she reached the pavement, then peered cautiously out. Nothing. Not even a broad back. The policeman had gone on his way and she, Kitty Drinkwater, could find her nice warm nook and settle down for the night.

Back on Rodney Street she identified her chosen doorstep easily, for the lamplighter had been and the soft glow of the gas made identification simple. She spread out her sacks, one to lie on, one to pull over her in lieu of a blanket, arranged her booty right at the back, where the cement wall divided her steps from next door's, and lay down. She ate a few peas, not deigning to take them out of the pods but crunching down the whole works with an eager appetite. They were sweet and young and sweetness was something that Kitty frequently craved. Then she pulled the second sack over her shoulders. Within five minutes her breathing had deepened; Kitty slept.

Chapter Five

Kitty had thought it would be easy to find Penny Lane, but she had reckoned without the city dweller's reluctance to stray far from his roots.

'If it ain't on a leccy route, queen, I won't know it,' a tram-driver said, when asked which way she should go.

'Penny Lane? Sure an' haven't I hord folk mention it over 'n over? But whether tes out Aigburth way, or over to Bootle, or a bit past Everton, that I couldn't tell ye, love,' said a knife-grinder, stopping his hissing, sparking machine to answer her query.

And what was more, because she was alone and more than a little afraid, she found she did not fancy moving far from her doorstep home in Rodney Street. During the day it was far too busy a spot for her, since the house above it was inhabited by a number of doctors, who appeared to have divided the whole house into consulting rooms. Caretakers, a very old man and his very old wife, lived in the basement in decrepit squalor, but they were both deaf and half-blind and never knew they had another tenant who slept each night under the front steps and always picked up her bed and walked by sunrise.

After a couple of weeks of searching the streets within half a day's tramp of Rodney Street, Kitty began to lose heart. Just what would she say when she caught up with the girl from Penny Lane anyway? Kitty looked down at herself, at her shirt, which no longer even looked like a shirt but more like a filthy scrap of rag, at her limbs, stained to a rich brown with outdoor living and dirt. She carried a sack over one shoulder with all her worldly possessions in and would have defended it, had anyone tried to snatch it, to the death. She had given up on her hair though she still attacked her little visitors by dipping her head into the water barrel from time to time. Givin' me nits a swimmin' lesson, she always thought as she ducked her hair and rubbed vigorously, though she was wryly aware that though she might lose a few in the water the rest would cling on and survive. The nit nurse had a painful steel comb, paraffin, and other smelly, efficient douches; water alone could never do the trick.

Thinking about the nit nurse made her think about school, and that made her wonder what she would do come September, when school started again and the dreaded attendance officers would be out, scouring the streets for kids sagging off school. She liked school all right, but the teachers would take one look at her and realise something had happened ... even Sary would have sniffed and found her some sort of dress for school had she seen the state of Kitty's present garment.

Although nothing would have persuaded Kitty to go home, she was in a quandary over what she should do. She was beginning to think she would never find Penny Lane and even if she did, she doubted that she would dare approach the girl, not in her present state. But how to get herself cleaned up and respectable she could not think; she dared not return to the canal, it was too near the Court. Yet despite the fact that she was dirty, nit-ridden and sometimes very lonely, and would soon be indecent, for her shirt was falling apart, she felt surprisingly well, and hunger, her constant companion in the old days, had been routed by the vegetables and odds and ends of food which she nicked each night from the gardens and dustbins of the rich.

So going home was out of the question – she still shuddered at the thought of the violence and abuse which would greet her if she tried – yet Penny Lane had come to seem an insubstantial dream, somewhere to think wistfully about, but not a place which a girl like her would ever actually visit. And time was passing. In a few days – she had lost track of time – the school holidays would be over and the authorities would undoubtedly find her and either put her into the workhouse or force her to return home.

If only I was clean, Kitty yearned. A clean, well-dressed child could do all sorts and no one would ask where they were going or what they were doing, but a filthy little street arab was everyone's enemy, from the school truant officer to the scuffer on the beat.

And then, when she was beginning to lose heart and to think about going back to Upper Burly and throwing herself on someone's mercy, she had a stroke of luck. Sack on shoulder, she was trying a new direction, a way she had not gone before. She decided to try going in a straight line instead of wandering randomly, and eventually she struck Lark Lane and, crossing it, Linnet Lane. Lark Lane was busy, with a great many shops and businesses, but Linnet Lane was quite different. The houses on her left as she walked were huge and set so far back from the road that she could only make them out by peering, and even the houses on her right were substantial, with nice big gardens and motor cars standing in their driveways.

Then she reached another intersection, Park Lane, and when she looked to her left now, she could see a public park, an absolutely huge one, and what she thought must be several miles of grass and gravel walks, hundreds of trees and, in the distance, what looked like water . . . a canal? A river? A lake? She knew it could not be the sea, but it was worth investigating. So Kitty set off across the park and was soon in a daze of pleasure over its many attractions.

She found a half moon of cages, each one containing various species of rare and exotic birds. Children's nannies, in navy coats and heavy shoes, with their small charges in high perambulators or running alongside, sat and gossiped around the gravel sweep, and called to the children not to run on the gravel or they'd fall and skin their knees and then what would Mamma say? Kitty stayed close to the cages and eyed the children with interest but without envy. What a quantity of fussy clothing they wore, considering the warmth of the day! And although they were fat and well fed, with lovely clean pinafores and dresses, how the nannies nagged at them!

'Master Reginald, don't tease the pretty parrot!'

'Miss Dora, you'll feel the weight of my hand if you spit; little ladies do not spit!'

Kitty, who had just spent an absorbing ten minutes teasing the parrots, and who did not grudge the beakful of skin one of them had endeavoured to gouge out of the back of her hand, smiled with secret sympathy at the would-be parrot teaser, slouching back to his minder with hanging head, but then she began to notice that she was the object of attention from several of the nannies. They were looking at her oddly and she realised that she was very out of place in this beautiful park where the children of the rich came to feed the birds, row on the water and play ball on the soft, green grass. However, just as she was about to turn tail and continue her search, a stop-me-and-buy-one came trundling along one of the walks, and the attention of the nannies was immediately diverted. Almost with one voice, the children demanded ices and the nannies, equally with one voice, reminded their charges that tea would be spoilt – and pretty dresses and trousers ruined – should they be allowed such a treat at this hour.

The stop-me-and-buy-one winked at Kitty, then began to shout his wares. Kitty, like a moth to a flame, drew nearer. The stop-me-and-buy-one leaned over and lifted the lid off his chilled container. The most glorious smell wafted out. The lad – for he was little more – picked up a metal scoop and began to pile the rich yellow ice-cream into a large cone until it looked like the picture of a pyramid in Kitty's school primer.

'Want one, luv?' he said enticingly. 'Only 'alfpenny to you, queen.'

'I 'aven't . . .' Kitty began, but picked up at once on the tiny shake of the head he gave, and the warning glance in his rather watery eyes. 'Oh, thanks,' she said instead, holding out a filthy paw gripped into a fist, as though her closed fingers held the money owing.

'Master George, little gentlemen don't ever hit ladies. If you do that again . . .'

A nanny had been kicked in the shins for her refusal to part with pennies for an ice-cream, Kitty realised. She grinned, taking the cone from the lad and conveying it slowly and with maximum effect to her mouth. The afternoon was hot, however, and the ice-cream was already beginning to melt so she shot out her tongue and swiped an all-encompassing lick at the sweet, slithery mountain of frozen cream.

'*She's* got one and she's only a guttersnipe,' whined George. 'Georgie's hot, Nan, Georgie wanna nice-cweam!'

'If you call names you'll get nothing,' the nanny in question said quickly. 'Come along, Master George, time you wasn't here.'

'You said guttersnipe,' Master George said sulkily. 'You said it was a rum thing when little gutter-snipes. . .'

'That's enough,' the nanny said sharply, her spade-shaped face reddening. 'Speak when you're spoken to, Master George.'

'Mamma often lets Philly and me have ices when we've been good,' a tot in a pink cotton dress, with a butterfly bow in her curls, said persuasively to her nanny. 'Sometimes when it's hot she comes up to the nursery and gives us pennies so's we can run down when we hear the man's tinkle-bell.'

'Very well, Miss Rose, you may have a cone this once, but only because it's so very hot. Yes, Master Philip, you may have one too, and since you're the gentleman you may take the pennies, and go and buy two cones . . .'

It started a rout, of course.

'Ices, ices,' rose the babbling cry. '*She's* got one ... everyone gets an ice but me!' Nannies fished in pockets, in handbags, down the side of perambulators and presently the stop-me-and-buy-one, with his leather bag full of pennies, prepared to ride on, giving his big black bicycle a shove off, accompanied by another wink at Kitty.

But Kitty, seeing what amounted to the first real friendliness she had known since she left home about to disappear, forsook the aviary, crammed the rest of the best food she had ever tasted into her mouth, and followed.

'Oy, mister,' she said, desperately trotting. 'D'you know where Penny Lane is? I come along Park Lane an' Linnet Lane ... is it near, eh?'

'Oh, aye, everyone knows Penny Lane, chuck; it's only t'other side of the park,' the lad said. 'Know Greenbank, do you?'

'No, I don't know anything much round 'ere,' Kitty admitted, padding along on her hard, bare feet but rather regretting the gravel, nevertheless. 'I'm from Upper Burly, meself.'

'Oh aye? I'm from Coltart Road; Colly, we call it. Let's think ... Upper Burly ... eh, queen, you're a long way from 'ome! So far's I recall, that's the far side o' the Scottie, ain't it?'

'That's right. But I've got a friend lives in Penny Lane, I never been there though. Nice, is it?'

'Yeah, nice 'ouses,' the lad said. 'Foller me, I'll put you on the right road. 'Cep' I'll 'ave to stop off at the cricket ground if there's a game goin' on.'

So for the rest of that hot afternoon Kitty followed the stop-me-and-buy-one and they chatted of this and that and Kitty admitted she'd run away from home and told the lad why. But she gave him a false name – Kathleen Legatt – and told him her da was on the ferries. It wasn't that she didn't trust him, exactly. More that she trusted no one. And with Penny Lane no longer a dream but about to become reality she had no desire to feel a hand on her shoulder and hear a constable's voice saying, 'Hello-ello-ello!' in the time-honoured fashion.

The roundabout route taken by the stop-me-and-buy-one meant that day was fading gently into dusk by the time Penny Lane actually came into view.

Kitty's new friend, who had been pedalling slower and slower, came to a halt and pointed at the road opposite.

'There y'are, chuck! Want the last of me ice-cream?'

Kitty accepted the cone eagerly, then looked doubtfully down the road which the stop-me-and-buy-one had indicated. It was longer than she had imagined, and much smarter, though the houses seemed to be mostly terraced or semi-detached. But now she had arrived she began to wonder how she would ever get up the nerve to knock on one door, let alone dozens and dozens, always assuming she did not strike lucky at once. And if she did, what was she to say?

'It's gettin' late,' she said pensively. 'A bit late for callin', would you say?' The lad chuckled and began to push his heavy old bicycle away from the kerb. 'Don't purrit off, love,' he advised kindly. 'Tomorrer's a long way off an' you've walked your feet down to the ankles I shouldn't wonder, jes' to get 'ere. A friend's a friend, no marrer what time o'night you turns up, so she'll tek you in. Cheerio, Kat'leen, an' good luck!'

'Bye, and thanks,' Kitty said earnestly. 'Thanks for everyt'ing. You're a real pal, you are.' But he had gone, with one last wave, pedalling tiredly away, his whole body drooping with fatigue.

Kitty stood on the edge of the kerb, contemplating the length of Penny Lane. As she did so a figure came cycling slowly along Greenbank Road, stopping at each lamp post as he reached it. The lamplighter was doing his rounds. If I don't get up me courage an' start a-knockin', the Lord above knows what I'll do tonight, Kitty reminded herself stoutly. Git a move on then, kid!

Obedient to her own command, Kitty crossed the road and began to walk along the pavement.

Immediately it struck her that these neat little suburban houses had no great flights of steps under which she might hide herself for the night, nor could she even begin to think about a return to Rodney Street until she'd had a few hours rest.

So you've got no choice, Kitty Drinkwater, she told herself firmly. It's find the girl from Penny Lane or get took up for a vagrant and chucked into the work'ouse. So start, Kitty, or git back to that park afore the gates is locked an' barred.

Lilac heard the bad news about the house only a matter of days before Nellie and Stuart left for their new home in London. She had been given a day off because Mr Matteson had hired a car to drive himself and his wife up to their cottage in Scarisbrick to choose curtains and carpets, so she had come round to help Nellie with her packing.

In fact she was full of her own plans as that very morning Polly had confirmed that if the house in Penny Lane was really to be theirs, she had a fourth girl eager to join Lilac, herself and Liza.

'Marie's little sister 'ad twins two days ago; Marie's Mam thinks it'ud be better if Marie moved out, though she'll still want a bit of money from 'er, especially now,' Polly had said. 'But wi' four of us rent-sharin' . . . .'

Stuart had told the landlord of Number 39 that he had passed on the property to respectable relatives, who would pay the rent as promptly as he and Nellie had done, but unfortunately, whilst discussing the hand-over, the landlord suddenly realised that his new tenants were four young girls. As soon as he did so, his whole demeanour towards Stuart changed.

'I'm a God-fearin' Cat'olic, and dere's no bawdy 'ouse bein' run in any of *my* properties,' he exclaimed angrily. Although Stuart did his very best to reassure the man that the girls were decent, hardworking young women who would not dream of entertaining young men on his premises even during daylight hours, he simply tightened his self-righteous, rat-trap mouth and shook his head.

'Dey isn't comin' 'ere, Mr Gallagher,' he repeated with parrot-like obstinacy and a complete disregard for every word his tenant had uttered. 'What would de priest say to me, allowin' such a carry-on?'

'I'm that sorry, queen,' Stuart said, when he let Lilac in and took her through to the kitchen where Nellie was wrapping china in newspaper and placing it in tea-chests. 'I did my best to explain but there was no hope of his even listening properly once he found you were under fifty. He's an old fool, but it is his house.'

'Well, I suppose it was too good to be true; anyway, the house is a long way from my new job,' Lilac admitted. She was to start work at the bag and sack factory in Bridgewater Street the following Monday, and had consoled herself for having to put up with what would, she believed, turn out to be a boring and repetitive job with the thought that at least she was to have a little house to run and friends to share it with. She was bitterly disappointed over Stuart's news, but did not intend to let Stuart and Nellie believe they had let her down. 'Polly and Liza are both keen, though, so perhaps we'll find somewhere else, even if it's not as nice.'

'Try for a good neighbourhood, love,' Nellie urged. 'Oh dear, if I'd known . . . but there are decent little rooms to let round here, I suppose you could get one of them.'

'Look, we'll be all right,' Lilac assured her. 'Don't worry, our Nell, it's not good for the baby when you worry, and anyway Mrs Matteson will let me stay on in Rodney Street till the end of the month so there's no hurry. I'll let you know as soon as I find somewhere and it will be somewhere respectable, honest to God. I won't go back to the courts, even if I'm offered.'

'Most of the people in the courts are grand: clean and hardworking,' Nellie said quickly, guiltily. Lilac knew that Nell tried very hard not to be ashamed of her background. 'But there's the bugs . . . you'd not want to tackle them, chuck, having been away from it for a bit. Aunt Ada used to say it was one long battle . . . oh do try for a nice little place.'

Lilac nodded rather impatiently. She could remember summers in the Court when all the cleaning in the world could not entirely get rid of the fat grey bugs which came out of the walls and made themselves at home, fastening on to your flesh so nimbly that you scarcely noticed until they had sucked your blood and gone, leaving the swollen, itchy spots which were their trademark. And then there were the fleas, hopping ceiling-high on their long legs, driving you mad if they got a hold. And the nits which bred in your hair, and cockroaches and rats . . . She would have to be very desperate indeed to take that lot on again!

'Honest to God, our Nell, I wouldn't dream of living somewhere which wasn't clean and decent,' Lilac said, shaking her head sadly at her sister's lack of faith. She picked up Nellie's best teapot and began to swathe it in newspaper. 'There's respectable houses letting rooms, you know, as well as slum-dwellings. Polly and I will share one room between us and Liza will probably get Marie to share another, now that Marie's sister's had the twins.'

Overcrowding in the courts was always a problem. With rents high, even for property which should have been condemned and torn down years ago, people tended to double up when children were born or times were hard, and most houses in the city tenements contained three generations – grandparents, parents and children, often with a widowed cousin and her family thrown in.

'Aye, I know you're sensible. But what am I doing, letting you wrap up me teapot, which will be on the go until the removal men come and after?' Nellie took the pot from Lilac and unwrapped it, then looked round the room, already cleared of everything but the furniture. 'Honest to God, me mind's going, I swear it. Don't say I've been and gone and packed all me cups and saucers away?'

'I'll get the kettle out,' Lilac said tactfully. 'You root for the cups; don't bother with saucers for heaven's sake, our Nell.'

She could see that Nellie was disturbed at having to leave her without lodgings, but apart from promising to be careful in her choice, there was very little she could do about it. She guessed that Nellie would want to take a look at whatever she chose, but since she would be leaving the city in forty-eight hours, there was no chance of that.

'Bless you, chuck. Lor', I'm tired ... if I sit down for a moment, can you make a brew and take a cup through to Stuart? He's packing the books in his study, that'll take him most of the day I reckon.'

Two days later Lilac came over on the tram, walked through Sefton Park in a drizzling rain, and watched rather mournfully as Nellie and Stuart saw the removal van off with all their worldly possessions aboard.

'We've got a cab coming,' Nellie gulped. She had been crying for hours if you could judge by her red eyes and swollen nose. 'Can you come with us to Lime Street, our Lilac? Wave us off, like?'

'Of course I will,' Lilac said gently. 'Cheer up, Nellie love, you're not going to the ends of the earth, flower!'

'And I'm going with you,' Stuart said, putting his arm round Nellie's bulging waist. 'Poor old lady, she's been up half the night with backache and indigestion and now this!'

'Why indigestion?' Lilac said, hoping to lighten the mood. 'I always thought you'd a digestion like an ostrich!'

'I f-fancied p-pears and custard. We had 'em for supper, only I didn't f-fancy them then,' Nellie stammered tearfully. 'So when I c-couldn't sleep I came down and ate 'em cold, acourse. It must'a been around two o'clock in the morning and they sat on me chest and kept trying to get out . . . oh, Stu, I don't want to go! Can't we change our minds?'

'If you're unhappy we'll come back,' Stuart said soothingly. Lilac saw his thin, brown fingers cross behind his back and smiled to herself. 'Don't worry, queen, just give it a go, eh? For me and the littl'un.'

Nellie's tear-garbled reply was lost as a taxi-cab screeched to a halt beside them.

'Gallagher? For Lime Street? 'Op in then, or you won't mek it afore your train leaves.'

This galvanised Nellie into action. She seized her lightest case and heaved it on the step beside the driver, watched whilst Stuart put the rest of their luggage on top, then climbed awkwardly into the cab.

'Come on, our Li,' she urged. She looked happier, to Lilac's relief. 'You heard what the driver said, we've no time to lose.'

It's odd the way Nellie blows hot and cold now, Lilac thought to herself. Once, she was so calm and sensible but now everything upsets her and she doesn't like anything for long. I suppose it's all part of having a baby, though . . . fancying pears and custard at two o'clock in the morning indeed!

'Move over, love,' Stuart said, getting in beside them. 'I'll drop you a line in a couple of days, Lilac, to tell you how we've settled in. Where's the string bag? It's got our carry-out in it, and the flask.'

'It's on my lap,' Nellie said. 'Have you got my knitting, Stu? I might as well knit – better than sitting on the train staring out of the window and feeling miserable.'

'I've got *everything*,' Stuart said forcefully. 'Every hand-hemmed handkerchief, every nappy, every safety pin, every . . . oh my God!'

'What?'

'We left the kitchen sink! I bet you never thought to pack that, our Nell!'

And Nellie laughed and slapped Stuart and Lilac laughed and hugged him, and the three of them tried not to look out through the window at the city speeding by, the city which two of them were to leave and one was to find a lonely place, without her Nellie.

Kitty knocked half-a-dozen doors that first evening without success and the woman in the last house she tried set the dog on her. To be sure it was a very small dog, but it had sharp white teeth and when they buried themselves in Kitty's ankle they hurt, and she kicked out so that the dog went sailing back up the garden path.

'I'll 'ave the law on you, kickin' me little Mitzi,' the old woman who had set her dog on Kitty shrieked as her pet, uttering an undoglike scream, sailed backwards towards the front door. 'Oh, you dirty little slut, knockin' doors in the dark an' kickin' me only friend!'

Kitty felt guilty; it was getting dark and she supposed the old woman had a right to be wary, but even so the bite hurt. Her ankle was throbbing something awful and she could feel tears only just behind her eyes. 'Sorry missus,' she called. 'But the dawg's gorra lump out of me ankle, honest to God.'

'Clear orf, clear orf,' the octogenarian shrieked, shaking a tiny fist as wrinkled and brown as an old walnut. 'There's a copper lives down the road a ways, get outa here or I'll set the law on you!'

'Well, I reckon the girl from Penny Lane don't live there, any road,' Kitty mumbled to herself as she set off along the pavement once more. 'She wouldn't ha' looked so purty an' 'appy if she'd lived wi' an old witch like that 'un. So what'll I try next?'

She eyed the nearby houses uneasily, for she had seen several curtains twitch during the fracas and though she suspected that the old woman was lying, policemen, she supposed, lived in ordinary houses when they weren't hounding homeless children. It had not occurred to her before but she'd be in real trouble if she knocked a door and a scuffer answered it! It was dark now, seeming even darker than it really was because of the streetlamps with their circles of hazy gold and it was time she settled for the night because although she'd had two ice-creams and there was half a cabbage in her sack, she really ought to have a drink and something solid inside her, or sleep would be courted in vain. She looked hopefully up and down the road but there were no dustbins standing out and she found, suddenly, that she was far too tired to think about climbing walls and prigging herself a meal.

What was more, she had remembered the palm house.

Earlier, in Sefton Park, she had noticed the palm house admiringly, not consciously considering it as a place to sleep. But now, *in extremis*, she was pretty sure that she could kip down on one of the benches, with her sacks around her and the cabbage to gnaw on until she fell asleep. If she chose a west facing seat, what was more, she would not be woken by the sun in her eyes.

The park was locked, of course, but railings, though not easy, were meant to be conquered. With the aid of her sacks and her rope-belt, Kitty was over the railings and back inside the park in seconds. She found she was very disorientated by the darkness, and by the fact that she had not entered the park the way she had left it, but after scouting around for a bit her eyes grew accustomed to the lack of light and she began to recognise landmarks. She remembered that the palm house was surrounded by trees and had a flagstaff nearby, and in a remarkably short space of time she was there, selecting her bench, spreading her sacks, and curling up. She thought about the cabbage, but since she was resting her head on it and had got comfortable she thought she would save it for breakfast. Besides, all the walking and the excitement had tired her out. Within five minutes of settling down on the bench Kitty was sleeping the sleep of the totally exhausted.

She woke when someone coughed nearby. It was a deep, rasping cough and whoever had coughed also rustled. Kitty pulled her sack up a bit higher and shivered. Who was it? Some old tramp, waiting to murder her in her bed for the half cabbage? Or a park attendant, patrolling the grounds, eager to throw out any kid who might have planted themselves on a bench by the palm house? Grown wise in the ways of sleeping rough though, Kitty did not sit up, she merely kept as still as she could, opened her eyes wide, and stared around her.

Nothing. No one. Only the trees, their branches moving slightly in the wind, and the palm house behind her, its glass still reflecting warmth from the day's sunshine. And the bench beneath her.

Someone cleared their throat, sighed and rustled again.

Whoever it is, they've settled down for a sleep so they probably don't know I'm 'ere, Kitty told herself thankfully. Now all I've gorra do is wake up first, in the morning. And with this comforting thought she closed her eyes again and immediately plunged into a lively dream in which she was playing cricket with a cone for a bat whilst the stop-me-and-buy-one bowled at her with a cabbage and Mitzi rushed around yapping and biting ankles.

She woke the second time to broad daylight. During the night she had managed to roll onto her stomach so the first thing she saw were the wooden slats of the seat on which she lay. The second thing she should have seen, of course, was the ground beneath the seat, but instead, between the seat and the ground, she saw a pale face topped by rough, hay-coloured hair.

Whoever had coughed during the night was now curled up asleep under her bench, with old newspapers below and above, which was why he had rustled as well as coughed. It was a lad, age uncertain, temper equally so, for Kitty knew lads were only men not yet grown and as likely to clout as pass the time of day with the likes of her.

Very gently, so as not to disturb the sleeper, Kitty moved a bit, so she could see how much lad there was under the seat and judge his dangerousness, for she saw lads, all lads, as the enemy. Mostly the lads who lived rough were bigger than her, stronger than her and very much nastier than her; they could make mincemeat of her if she crossed them so she tried very hard to steer clear. This one was quite tall, taller than she, and bony. But having looked long and hard at his sleeping face, Kitty decided he did not look dangerous. His eyes were closed of course so she did not know how the expression in them might change if he woke and caught her staring, but he had a mouth which looked as though it smiled a lot and an unlined, though exceedingly dirty, brow.

However, there was no sense in courting trouble. Kitty sat up and started to get off the seat, to go through the preparations for the day ahead – and then stopped short, staring.

The palm house was surrounded by gravel, then trees, and then miles and miles of glorious grass. But if she had not remembered this from the day before she would never have known, for now the grass was invisible beneath a smooth, soft blanket of white mist, which twisted and swayed between the tree-trunks and even sent a few tentative smoky tendrils curling across the gravel, whilst the sun, suddenly appearing between the trees, dyed the top layer of mist goldy-red, turned the trees' tall trunks to glowing flame, and gilded the edge of every leaf, every tiny twig.

Kitty knew very little about natural beauty, but she recognised this sunrise as beauty unparalleled and gave it the attention it deserved – an open-mouthed, wide-eyed attention which not even her desire to be gone before the lad woke could break. So she was still sitting there, with unexplained and unwanted tears suddenly filling her eyes and blurring her vision, when a voice behind her exclaimed: 'Christ A'mighty, ain't that suffin? Wharrer sight, eh?'

Kitty turned. The boy had crawled out from under the seat and was kneeling on the gravel, staring as she was at the mist, the sunrise, the edges of the grass gradually coming into view, every blade topped by a diamond drop.

'Yeah, it's pretty,' she said inadequately, having glanced round and made sure it was she that the lad was addressing. 'I never seen the sun come up in the country, afore, though I've read about it in books.'

'I 'ave, but not so . . . oh, I dunno.' The lad heaved a deep sigh and then looked properly at Kitty for the first time. 'So you read books, does you? What've you read?'

'Lot's an' lots,' Kitty said promptly. 'Well, one a week since I was seven, an' I'm twelve now.'

'Get on! I'm fourteen, but I reckon I ain't read many more'n you. What's your name, kiddo?'

'What's it to you?' Kitty said immediately, poised for flight. Talking about reading was one thing, dis-cussing names another. But then she remembered she hadn't yet put her belongings into the sack and looked uneasily at her companion. Suppose he decided to nick her stuff? He was older, taller, stronger, but somehow, she decided, as he grinned down at her, she didn't think he had theft in mind. And the cabbage on which her head had rested all night didn't look all that appetising, either.

'Fierce, ain't you? What've you done, eh? If you've nicked that scrawny cabbage, chuck, I can't think anyone's gonna fight you for it, an' sacks are mostly give away. So why not be civil, eh? No 'arm in it, surely?'

He had a pleasant voice with a smile at the back of it. Kitty didn't know why she thought that, she just knew she did. She looked at him properly, harder. He was tall and bony, as she had surmised even through the newspapers, but he was a lot cleaner than she was and his shirt and trousers, though by no means new, were respectable. She found that she liked his face, from the broad brow to the deep blue eyes with laughter creases already forming, to the straight nose and the curled, amused mouth. And when he smiled she saw he still had all his teeth, a rarity amongst the courts where hunger took its toll of teeth and gums as well as of muscles and skin. Smiling back, Kitty was glad she had all her teeth, too, though it wasn't something that had ever occurred to her before. But she wished her hair was like his – the soft, hay-coloured locks were overlaid with gold where the sun had caught them. It was roughly cut, hacked, really, so that it stood up at the back in a series of ridges and peaks, but you could see his hair was clean, not greasy and nit-ridden.

'Seen all you want? Well, I'm Johnny an' as I said I'm nigh on fourteen. Been on the road since I were ten. Who're you when you're at 'ome?'

'I'm Kitty, I'm twelve, like I said. On the road? Wha's that mean?'

He laughed, then stood up and pulled a bag out from under the bench. 'Means I don't stay nowhere long,' he said laconically. 'Might as well 'ave a bite afore the place wakes up. Like bread 'n cheese, does you?'

'Oo-oh, *yes*!' Kitty breathed as he produced half a loaf and a thick heel of cheese from the depths of his bag. 'I'm rare hungry – all I 'ad yesterday was an ice-cream an' a bite o' cabbage.'

'Right. An' I've a ragin' thirst on me – got a bottle?'

'No ... but I got a tin.' Kitty delved into her own sack and produced an empty corned beef tin. 'I drinks outer this, mostly.'

'That's grand, better'n a bottle. Why didn't I think o' that?' Johnny looked at her tin with such respect that Kitty felt the first faint stirrings of pride in her thin little bosom. Something she had was worth envy ... and now he was dividing the bread and cheese! Her mouth watered so hard that she had to keep swallowing.

'Here. Start on that, chuck, whiles I fetch us some water. There's a drinkin' fountain at the back o' this palm 'ouse.'

He handed her the bread and cheese, the bread folded over so that it formed a sandwich. Kitty took a deep breath and a big bite. It was marvellous, the best food she had ever tasted, better even than the stop-me-and-buy-one's ice-cream. But she went slowly, knowing how easy it was to get the cramps in your bread-basket if you bolted food after a long period without anything, and the boy was back with the water before she was halfway through her sandwich.

123

'There y'are! Tek a drink, then a bite. 'Elps it down, like.'

Kitty was having no difficulty in getting it down, but obeyed his injunction and realised that it made the food go further, filled you up more. She said so, and Johnny smiled.

'Oh aye, you gets to know all the tricks when you're on the road. Don't meet many lasses sleepin' rough, though. What 'appened?'

'Me Mam sent me on an errand, but I were robbed and I dustn't go 'ome,' Kitty said briefly. 'She'd kill me, them trimmin's was worth prob'ly a 'undred shillin's.' It was the biggest sum she could think of, too huge to contemplate. 'She'll owe the milliner, see? Oh aye, she'd kill me awright if she got 'er 'ands on me; she's tried afore.'

Johnny nodded, chomping his bread and cheese.

'I believe you! My ole man tried that, so I 'it 'im over the 'ead with me gran's walkin' stick an' lit out. Ain't never been 'ome since.'

'Where's you from?' Kitty said thickly, through bread and cheese.

'Burly, that's what we call . . .'

'Well, knock me down, ain't that the strangest thing! Upper Burlington Street . . . we call it Burly, too!'

Johnny, bread and cheese halfway to his mouth, stopped to stare.

'No! Well I'll be 'anged . . . whereabouts?'

'Paradise Court, that's the second entry on the –'

'We was nex'-door-neighbours, Kit, as good as! I were from Elysium Court, right by you. Elly and Parry, we called 'em. Wha's your last name, then?'

'Drinkwater; me mam's Sary and me da's 'Ector an' there's the twins, Arny an' Bob, and Betty, Eth,

Mo . . . she's Maureen really . . . an' Phyllis.'

'The kids'll all be younger'n me,' Johnny said dismissing them. 'I'm Johnny Moneymor, we was from Londonderry, way back.'

'Oh ah,' Kitty said. Talk of Irish antecedents was common in the courts, though no one ever seemed able to tell you what Ireland was like since they had either left as nippers or never been there at all. 'I once 'eard me da say 'e 'ailed from Connemara. But I's from Liverpool, an' proud of it.'

She didn't quite know what made her say it, she only knew that, as the words left her mouth, they were true.

'Me an' all,' Johnny said contentedly. 'I allus comes back, teks a look and goes again. One o' these days I'll sail from Liverpool Docks aboard a big ole transatlantic liner, an' come 'ome wi' a pocketful o' cash an' a heap o' good things. An' I'll go on deck an' look up at the Liver birds sittin' broodin' over the Mersey, an' know I'm 'ome.'

'I will an' all,' Kitty decided. 'I'll sail from the Docks, jus' like you, Johnny.'

'No way. Lads only,' Johnny said, gazing dreamily into the distance. 'No wimmin aboard.'

'Yes they is!' Kitty contradicted. 'Or I'll put on trowsis an' pertend I'm a lad. I'll go, you wait an' see.'

Johnny chuckled and reached out a long arm. He rumpled her filthy hair, then sat up straight and looked at her very seriously.

'Guess you will. Ever 'eard of the public baths, chuck?'

'Sure. But I don't 'ave no gelt,' Kitty admitted, knowing at once what he meant. 'I's filthy, I know it.'

125

'Well, what about a dip in the Scaldy?'

Every kid living within a mile of the Leeds & Liverpool Canal knew all about the Scaldy, though it was mainly the boys who bathed in it. It was a section of the canal near the Chisenhale Street Bridge where the big sugar refinery, Tate & Lyle, pumped quantities of hot water they no longer needed into the canal, turning it into a paradise for the local lads. So now, though Kitty knew exactly what he was suggesting, she looked at him doubtfully.

'Me? But it's only lads what swims there, an' besides, me brothers might see me.'

'Oh aye, I forgot. Do they go there at night, then?'

'At *night*? No, course they don't!'

'Then we will, you an' me. I'll snitch a bit o' soap an' we'll get us a penny or two so's you can do your 'air wi' paraffin. I'll nick a dress off a washin' line. Eh, queen, your own fam'ly won't know you!'

'Oh, I don't know,' Kitty quavered. 'I can't swim, Johnny. Kids get drownded in the Scaldy.'

'Not if they're wi' me they don't,' Johnny assured her stoutly. 'I swim like a fish, I'll see you right, Kitty. Only you'll be picked up an' sent to the work'ouse when summer ends, you know that, doncher, unless you cleans up a bit. Wharrer you been livin' on?'

'Cabbages, spuds, stuff outer dustbins,' Kitty muttered, hanging her head. 'I done awright, honest.'

'Well, wi' me you'll do better,' Johnny assured her. 'Are you game, Kit? Want to come on the tramp? I gets through a lorra books, you can 'ave 'em after me, an' you'll eat well, I promise you that, an' you'll sleep soft.'

'I dunno,' Kitty said, terribly tempted. Not only had she missed her friends and familiar surroundings, she had missed the fictional life she plunged into every time she opened a book. 'I come to Penny Lane to 'unt for me friend . . . I only tried six or seven 'ouses so far.'

'Oh ah? An' what'll your friend do for you that I can't, eh?'

Kitty looked at Johnny's sun-tanned face and gilded hair, at the deep blue, laughing eyes. He was the best thing that had ever happened to her, he knew what it was all about, he would help her, see her right – hadn't he said so just now? Beautiful and kind the girl from Penny Lane might be, but she wouldn't want Kitty trailing round after her, being an embarrassment, Kitty acknowledged that now. So she smiled back at Johnny and jumped to her feet, slinging her sack over her shoulder as she did so.

'She won't do nothin', Johnny Moneymor,' she said, and laughed with pleasure at her own sudden certainty. 'Fancy me, swimmin' in the Scaldy when everyone else is tucked up in bed! Lead on, I'll tag along o' you!'

It was one thing to talk gaily at sun-up in Sefton Park about swimming in the Scaldy, Kitty realised later, but quite another to set off through the dark streets, with the gas lamps' hiss the only sound, heading towards home. Every foot of the way, once she got onto home territory, she expected to see a Drinkwater hiding behind a tram-stop, or in a doorway, or under the dark arch of a bridge. But she knew in her heart that she was safe enough. The pubs were long closed, no matter how bad the twins might be they wouldn't be roaming the streets at two or three in the morning, and even when Da was at his worst and wickedest, even when Sary was roaring, hitting drunk, they'd not stray far from the Court at this hour. So Kitty padded along beside Johnny, carrying her precious new dress in her sack with a cracked pair of boots slung by their laces round her neck.

'You'll need boots, on the tramp,' Johnny had said, but she didn't believe him; they felt hateful on her feet after weeks of toe-wriggling freedom, and anyway she only ever wore boots in school, because the teachers got nasty if you didn't.

'Not far now, chuck,' Johnny murmured into her ear. 'Want me to carry them boots?'

'No, I'm awright,' Kitty said quietly. 'They ain't heavy, not like a coupla cabbages.'

They were heavier than most cabbages and her neck was tired, but she wouldn't have admitted it for the world. She wanted Johnny to think her strong as himself and as keen on the adventure ahead.

'Here we are,' Johnny said at last. Even in the dark the canal waters shone, reflecting the starry night sky. 'Put your clo'es under the bridge, chuck, an' foller me.'

Kitty didn't have many clothes to take off, in fact only her shirt and her rope. She threw both articles down and tiptoed after Johnny, who had stripped off his own shirt and trousers, shed his boots and socks, and was poised on the edge.

'See the steam?' he asked her as she drew alongside. 'Eh, it'll be lovely an' warm – I can't wait!'

He was in, plopping quietly into the water, then holding out a hand to Kitty. 'See, I'm standin' so you won't get your face wet. C'mon!'

Kitty took a deep breath and joined him. She was smaller than he, the water came halfway up her chest, but it was quite hot and when Johnny handed her a small square of some sort of red, strong-smelling

128

soap, she began to rub it all over her torso with real enthusiasm. It would be so good, so very good, to be clean! Mrs O'Rourke had insisted that before she ate, Kitty should have a good wash. Once or twice, in winter, she had got the tin bath down, filled it with saucepans of steaming water heated on the fire, and handed Kitty the soap with instructions to 'Have a good splash now, child, but don't you be forgettin' to use that soap!' Sary rarely bothered with washing her children but when she did it was under the tap in the yard and she held you there, letting the icy water batter you until you could escape. No pleasure there, only Sary's fingermarks bruising your arms for weeks afterwards, and red slap marks all over you where she'd beaten you into some sort of submission.

'Sit on the bank an' wash your other 'alf,' Johnny told her above the splashing. 'Go on . . . I'll parry your 'air.'

He had very nearly been caught nicking the paraffin, had been forced to pay for it, in the end.

'Why doncher go to the Disinfection Office on Burly, they'll do 'er free, there,' the man in the hardware store had suggested rather too loudly, when Johnny had whispered something to him. 'She your sister? Tek 'er there, they'll see to 'er all right an' tight.'

Johnny knew she wouldn't go back to Burly though, not during daylight hours, so the paraffin it had to be. And after he had rubbed the stuff into her scalp until she would have screamed had anyone else done it, and then helped her by holding her head – but not her face – under water to a slow count of five hundred, she thought her hated visitors might really have swum their last this time.

After that, they played, frolicking in the warm and soapy water, admiring the slow whitening of

Kitty's limbs, the dark, clean masses of her hair.

'It's real thick,' Johnny said at one point. 'Your 'air, I mean. An' curly, I reckon. It'll be nice when it's dry.'

'I wish I was a water baby or a mermaid,' Kitty said wistfully as Johnny tried to teach her to swim. She had read about Tom the water baby at school. 'Oh . . . I can stay up, I can swim!'

It didn't last long, but it was a start. 'Five strokes . . . it'll be ten next time you 'ave a go,' Johnny said. 'Race you to the bank . . . walkin', not swimmin'.'

They stayed in the water until dawn began to turn the sky to pearl, then Johnny helped her out and they ran races along the towpath until they were dry, lacking towels of any description.

'Now put the dress on,' Johnny said at last. 'An' the boots. Wish I could ha' got you stockin's, but there, at least you've gorra pair o' boots.'

Kitty had been longing to put the dress on all day, but Johnny had been firm. A clean dress could only be worn by a clean person, he explained, so she had waited. But now the moment had arrived, and in the first milky grey of dawn, she slid the dress down over her head and Johnny did up the buttons at the back.

Kitty looked down at herself. It was a blue and white checked dress, gingham she thought the material was called, and though a little long, it fitted well. She turned to face Johnny, half-expecting some masculine rudeness, but Johnny looked at her slowly and carefully, walking all round her as though her appearance was truly of interest to him.

'You look real good, real pretty,' he said at last. 'Tomorrer I'll git a blue ribbing for your 'air. Put the boots on an' we'll go along to Mrs Bridge's eating place, down by the Albert Dock. She starts at six, it must be near on that now, and she does a lovely lentil an' spud broth. An' you get 'alf a loaf with it, as well as a mug o' tea.'

The two of them wandered slowly down to the docks, Kitty in her new boots as well as her new dress, which was a good reason for their lack of speed. The boots felt strangely heavy and unnatural, but Johnny assured her she would come to appreciate them, in time.

Mrs Bridge had a tiny wooden shack with three tables and twelve chairs, but she gave the youngsters two large plates of her broth for tuppence and sent them to sit by the water to eat since all her chairs were taken.

'Bring back me plates,' she warned them, but comfortably, with a smile. 'Who's your little pal, Johnny?'

'She's Kitty; she's a good kid,' Johnny said proprietorially, as though he had known Kitty for years, if not actually raised her personally. 'We're off on the tramp later today.'

'Oh ah? Where you thinkin' of headin' for, this time?'

'This time we're headin' for Wales,' Johnny said. 'Ain't that right, our Kitty?'

Kitty thrilled to the casual possessiveness in his tone.

'That's right, Johnny,' she echoed. 'We're headin' for Wales!'

Chapter Six

With Nellie and Stuart gone and the Mattesons about to depart, Lilac began to be very dependent on her friends. But Polly was courting, Liza had an evening job serving behind the counter in a fish and chip shop on St James Street, and visiting Marie Springfield meant cramming into her cramped little house and 'minding' the kids whilst Marie's Mam and her sisters went down to their local pub. What was more Ella, the sister who had just given birth to twins, had a rather dubious reputation – she 'walked' Norfolk Street of an evening, folk said – so Lilac was uneasily aware that Nellie would disapprove of too close a friendship with the Springfields.

She had found lodgings, though she did not think she cared for them much. It was a once-smart house in Great Nelson Street, handy, the landlady said, for the library, the art gallery, St George's Hall, and other such refined places of culture. But it was also near Lime Street – Lilac could hear the trains arriving and departing from her lonely room – which made her think wistfully of Nellie.

She had not heard from the handsome Alan Blake, what was more. It was all very well telling herself that she'd not expected to hear, but it did not do much for her self-confidence. It was the first time that any man had virtually stood her up, and to make matters worse Art, who had always danced attendance on her, suddenly seemed to have found better things to do with his time. Had someone been advising him that she would never fall into his arms if he hung about her, but might do so if he withdrew a little, Lilac wondered indignantly. Well, if so, he would presently get a big surprise, for she was doing well enough without him. As for Alan ... if he walked up to her in the street she would pretend she couldn't tell him from Adam, which would teach him a lesson, him and his posh relatives and his big transatlantic liner!

Work was far more absorbing than she had expected, however, and far harder, too. Lilac, who had done extremely well at school and was generally thought of as bright and able, was horrified at the difficulty she encountered in managing her machine. She was afraid of pushing the sacking too far in case the needle went through her finger, the smell of the raw material made her sneeze and her eyes seemed to run constantly. She told herself she was not mechanically minded, but no one else thought twice about taking their machine to pieces when something went wrong and putting it together again so that it worked. Also, the other girls in her room worked at twice the speed and seemed to her to be entirely fearless, and the supervisor, a harsh-faced, tight-mouthed harridan called Mrs Loose, took an instant dislike to her newest employee.

'It ain't your fault you're a bit slow, queen,' Bertha Harris, the loud-mouthed, short-skirted girl on the next machine told Lilac. 'You need to start young at dis job – do as I do, folly me an' you won't go far wrong!'

Lilac was used to broad Liverpudlian but she often found Bertha almost impossible to follow, since Bertha's use of slang was entirely individual. Words, Bertha said once in all seriousness, meant whatever she told them to mean ... shades of Humpty Dumpty in *Alice Through the Looking Glass*, Lilac thought, grinning to herself. 'When I use a word it means just what I choose it to mean – neither more nor less.' But she kept the quotation to herself, having already discovered that though the girls in her room could all read, more or less, it was only with great effort and never for pleasure. Books are a closed book to them, Lilac concluded, chuckling inwardly. But they were kind enough, particularly Bertha, and it was through her that Lilac discovered everyone on her assembly line was at least a year younger than her and sometimes more: Bertha herself, talking her strange blend of scouse, pseudo-American slang, Cockney rhyming slang and anything else she could lay tongue to, forever at jazz concerts and dances, bringing home sailors in at least three different shades, astonished Lilac by admitting to being 'Seventeen, come next March.'

'They're friendly and nice, but they're awfully rough,' she told Polly, who grinned and said it was a far cry from the Mattesons and admitted that in the Ellison Fancy Pickle factory, where she worked – and wept as well, since they pickled a lot of onions – the staff on the shop floor were all either young girls still wet behind the ears or old shawlies who had been doing the work forever.

So after Lilac's first week's work, when she had sat in the dying sunlight in her small room and written a cheery letter to Nellie, heated herself up a tin of soup on her small gas-ring, and washed out her cotton stockings and her second-best blouse, she decided to give herself a bit of a treat. She could not go and see Nellie yet because she had not been with the firm long enough to take a day or two off, and though Mrs Matteson and the doctor had urged her to go up to Scarisbrick to see them she thought it was too soon, but it would be rather fun to go round to Coronation Court and see Art's family – his sister Etty had been a friend – and find out at the same time just where Art had got to.

Not that I'm interested in Art's whereabouts, Lilac reminded herself, choosing a light and summery cotton print to wear, for the autumn day was warm and sunny. Since it was Sunday she got some white gloves out of her long drawer and pulled them on. She had a rather nice blue hat which went with the summery dress so she stabbed that in place with a couple of hat-pins and decided on the spur of the moment to go to morning service at St Anne's on Cazneau Street, the church she had attended with Nellie and Aunt Ada when they had lived on Scotland Road. Whilst she was working for the Mattesons she had gone to church with them, but now she could please herself and it would be rather nice to go back, see her friends. After the service I'll maybe go round to the Corry, she planned busily, and after that I'll buy myself a meal at Miss Harriet Young's Dining Room on the Scottie, and after that ... oh, after that can take care of itself!

The service was a bit of a shock to Lilac, after several years of attending the very much smarter church on Rodney Street with the Mattesons. She had forgotten how shabby everything was, including the congregation, and how small. Even the East window, at which she had gazed in awe as a child whilst singing hymns at the top of her voice, seemed smaller and duller, the jewel colours that she remembered paler and less striking.

And though there were several people she recognised, they all seemed to belong to her aunt's generation. The vicar was a younger man than the Revd Charlesworth, with a deep, actor's voice and a great thatch of brown hair in place of Revd Charlesworth's shining pate. He was very polite to Lilac, shaking her hand outside in the porch and telling her it was nice to see a new face in the congregation, but she had not enjoyed the rather sanctimonious delivery of his sermon, every word accompanied by upturned eyes and pious glances, so she murmured something conventional and eased her hand out of his damp clasp as soon as it was polite to do so.

The O'Briens were Catholics, so they would go to Mass, not morning service. Of course, Lilac thought to herself, as she left Cazneau Street, crossed into Rose Place and began to stroll slowly down towards the main road, it's quite possible that I might meet ... someone ... once I reach the Scottie. She turned into Scotland Road, glancing into shop windows as she walked. It was equally possible that the Catholic service might end at the same time as that at St Anne's, so if she continued to walk at her present pace she might presently find herself overtaken by, well, by anyone who happened to have attended St Anthony's that morning.

If I do hear familiar footsteps I won't look round, I'll pretend to be absorbed in the beautiful hats in Miss Denny's, or the gold chains and diamond rings displayed in Murphy's the jewellers, she decided. She by-passed Jim's Fried Fish, which reeked of last night's trading, and the Market Inn, redolent of stale beer and worse, and began to walk a little faster. She could hear people coming along the pavement, she would walk past Young's Dining Room, idly, then stop a little further on and turn back, as though she'd not quite made up her mind where to eat.

She strolled on and presently heard footsteps following her; she was almost sure she knew who made them. She turned to stare fixedly into the nearest window, pretending absorption, her whole attention really focused on the maker of the footsteps, now about to overhaul her, to pass . . .

'Well, if it isn't our Lilac!' The young man stopped in front of her, gently taking her hands in his. 'What are you doing on the Scottie on a Sunday morning, chuck? Not shoppin', that's for sure!'

'Art!' Lilac said with a well-simulated start of surprise, 'Fancy seeing you – I was sure you'd be in the middle of Mass, or off with your pals for a day at New Brighton!'

'Just come out of St Anthony's,' Art said. 'So? What are you doin' here, our Lilac?'

'Attending church, same as you,' Lilac said demurely. 'No point in trailing all the way back to Rodney Street, and anyway, I only went there because the Mattesons expected us to do so. I thought I might pop into the Court, see how everyone is, only it's quite late and the shop windows are fascinating . . .'

'Particularly that one,' Art said. There was a laugh behind the words, almost, Lilac thought indignantly, as if he didn't believe she had been happily window-shopping, with never a thought for where she was!

'Yes, I've always been . . .' her voice trailed away and she could feel the heat start to burn in her cheeks.

'Fascinated by death?' Art said, too smoothly. 'J. Whitaker & Sons, Undertakers . . . that was the window you were starin' in, I believe?'

Lilac began to giggle. Trust her to make a fool of herself and trust Art to rub her nose in it!

'Was I? I was still thinking about the hats up the road ... not that I wear hats more than I have to. I like to feel the wind in my hair so I thought I'd walk along the river later, down by the pierhead.'

'Well, I'll come along with you a ways,' Art said.

Lilac, glancing sideways at him, saw that he was looking his best in a dark suit and white shirt, with a panama hat in one hand. He really is rather nice-looking, she thought, with a tiny frisson of excitement chasing up and down her spine, then she reminded herself that this was the Art she had known all her life and the excitement died.

'All right. Who's at home today, Art? Your mam and da?'

Art shrugged. 'Dunno; haven't been back meself yet. I'm lodging in Ullet Road now, with Tippy Huggett; remember, you met me there a few weeks back when I'd been round to take a look at the room.'

'Oh ... then. Yes, I remember.' Lilac, who had assumed Art had been lurking in order to be with her, felt more than a little crestfallen. So he really had been visiting in Ullet Road! 'Well, are you goin' back to the Corry now?'

'Eventually. I have to take me old woman her money or she'd never last the week,' Art said cheerfully. 'But how about a spot of grub first? We could go to one of the canny houses if you like, cheap and cheerful.'

There were a number of small eating houses in the courts, places where the woman of the house was a better than average cook and could earn herself a few pennies by selling the delicious stews and soups which she had been making for her kids and the rest of her family for years, ekeing out

138

a mutton bone with every available vegetable and seasoning the food with pot herbs, grown in half a beer barrel in her back yard or even in a window box.

'I was going to treat meself to a chump chop, potatoes and gravy at Harriet Young's,' Lilac said wistfully. 'They do a lovely steamed pudding too, with candied peel and sultanas. But if a canny house suits you better . . .'

Art took her arm. His hand was warm and firm on her bare skin and she was aware of him towering over her as they set off again, back the way she had just come. I've always liked tall men; what a pity it's only Art, she thought, moving a little closer to him. Eh, but it was good to see him again, good to be chatting easily to her old friend!

'Young's it is! I were pullin' your leg over the canny house, our Lilac, I wouldn't take you somewhere low. I reckon that with Nellie gone you're longing for decent, home-cooked grub, aren't you? But Tippy an' me works wonders when we get goin' of an evenin', wi' a frying pan and a couple of eggs, a few rashers, some cold spuds . . . oh aye, we eat better'n we ever did at home.'

Lilac bit back the words, 'Of course you do,' remembering that Art had never grumbled over his mother's total lack of domestic ability. She glanced up at him though and saw that he was grinning down at her.

'Go on, flower, say it! Me mam's no cook . . . still an' all, we survived, the six of us, so now we've gorra learn to feed ourselves. Here we are!'

He ushered her into the dining room and they chose a quiet table against the wall. Art, with an air of authority, ordered clear soup, chops and steamed pudding for two, then sat back and regarded her with deep pleasure.

'You look a treat, Lilac,' he said after a moment. 'Makin' bags an' sacks suits you.'

'It doesn't,' Lilac said, 'but it's a job. Like the bank is, I suppose.'

Art chuckled.

'It can't be as dull as the bank, queen,' he objected. 'Eh, but there's times . . . still, no point grumblin'. It's the means to an end. Ah, here comes our food.'

The meal was simple but well-cooked and satisfying, and rather to her own surprise, Lilac found Art amusing and even exciting company. He really was handsome, when he smiled you saw his nice white teeth and he smiled often. Lilac became aware that several girls of about her own age kept glancing enviously across at their table and the waitress was putty in his hands, bringing them a cupful of pieces of ice when Art told her the water was warm, coming over a couple of times to make sure everything was all right . . . Lilac knew the signs, it was clear that women liked her companion. And he talked naturally, easily, telling her all the latest gossip in the Court – who was going steady with whom, who had jobs, who was wearing charity clogs – and all the gossip in the bank, too. Lilac made him laugh with her factory experiences and all was going swimmingly when Art took her completely by surprise.

'Don't know if Nellie mentioned it, queen, but I've been offered the chance of a job with Deacon's, over the water in Birkenhead.'

'Birkenhead? That one-eyed town?' Lilac said rudely. 'No point in vegetating there, Art, when you could be here, where the action is!'

'Birkenhead's a big town and it's quite an important job,' Art said equably. 'It 'ud mean a rise in pay and they've agreed to a living-out allowance. I could afford a house of me own – a small one.'

'Really? But you could go across every day, on the ferry. Lots of men do, if they work in the shipyards.'

'True. But since I've moved out of the Corry anyway, I might as well go the whole hog and cross the water.'

'I suppose you could, though I don't see the point,' Lilac said doubtfully. Why was it that she couldn't feel entirely comfortable about Art moving away from Liverpool, even though it was only to Birkenhead which you could see, just about, from Bridgewater Street? 'I suppose Birkenhead may be all right, in its way. Only you'd miss the cinemas and theatres and things, wouldn't you? And the shops and the concerts.'

'No, because if I wanted a night out which Birkenhead couldn't provide, I'd come over on the ferry,' Art said logically. 'It's not a one-way thing, the ferry, queen. Besides, it's like Stu was saying, you've got to look to the future. A feller's career *is* his future – and his wife's, for that matter.'

'Oh, you talked it over with Stu, did you? But he's wed, with a kid on the way, if you were married it would be different, I could understand you wanting to go.' Lilac waited whilst the waitress cleared their plates and put the desserts in front of them, then dug her spoon into the plump and creamy steamed pudding. 'Ooh, I do love a duff, and this one's prime! But since you aren't married, I don't see why you can't stay here.'

'No-oo, I'm not married yet, I grant you, but I'll be married one day, and I've gorra look to that day, or me

141

wife won't get the best of everything, and that's what I want for her.' Art put his own pudding spoon down and leaned across the table. He took hold of Lilac's chin in a firm but gentle hand, tilting it so that she had to look up at him. His face was ardent, his eyes glowed with an expression which Lilac recognised, with some embarrassment, as strong and emotional affection. 'Lilac, as soon as I'm settled in the job, I'm goin' to ask you to move over to Birkenhead and take a chance on me.'

Lilac's mouth was full of steamed pudding and she was jolly sure she had custard round her mouth. What was more, Art's proposal – if you could call it that – had come out at full blast just when one of those silences which fall on an assembled company had occurred. All round her, Lilac saw heads turn, attention fix on her face.

And she had a mouthful of pudding and custard round her mouth. She knew she was scarlet with embarrassment, looking a fool, feeling a worse one. She sat back, pulling away from Art's imprisoning hand, swallowed her mouthful and then, defiantly, spooned more pudding into her mouth and swallowed that, too, before she spoke.

'I'm not moving anywhere,' she said crossly. 'Not with you, Art O'Brien. Haven't I said it enough times?'

'I've not asked you yet, Lilac,' Art said quietly. Lilac, sneaking a look at him, saw that he was red as a turkey-cock, with sweat beading his brow. 'So I'd best not bother, eh? Is that what you mean?'

Lilac stared down at her plate. He was being perfectly horrible today, he had quite spoiled the nicest meal she'd had all week, he'd embarrassed her in front of a great many people and now all she wanted to do was get away from him and have a good cry somewhere quiet, because her lovely day had turned sour on her. Suddenly, she was not at all sure that she wanted to see Art go right away from her, never come calling, never jump aboard an Oceanic when she was already sitting on the slatted wooden seat. Hadn't the sight of him warmed her heart, lightened the darkest day for her? But why did he have to rush everything? Why couldn't he accept that she wasn't ready for marrying or committing, that all she wanted for a year or two was to have some fun before she settled down?

'Well, queen? If you don't want to take a chance on me, then I might as well be off – to Birkenhead or wherever. But if you've still got an open mind, mebbe we could gerron a bus and go to New Brighton, play the pinball machines, paddle in the sea, act like a coupla pals for a bit.'

Lilac looked at him, seeing him waveringly through the hot tears which filled her eyes. Why oh why did she have to answer him now? Why couldn't she just say New Brighton sounded fun and hadn't they better pay the bill and get aboard a bus? But, still convinced that everyone in the dining room was waiting for her reply, she spoke stiffly, as to a stranger.

'Me mind's made up, so no point in pretendin'. You'd best go to Birkenhead and forget me.'

He went white. She had never seen Art's face, or anyone else's for that matter, drain of colour so completely.

'Me, forget you? Queen, I'll never do that. But don't worry, I shan't stay 'ere an' pester you. I'll go.'

He shot back his chair. He'd taken his jacket off whilst they ate, now he put it on again, wildly, with half the collar tucked in and his tie awry. He jerked some money out of his pocket and threw it down on the table. It was quite a lot of money and some of it missed and fell on the floor, rolled and tinkled and fell.

There would still have been time. She could have got to her feet, said she was sorry, caught hold of him ... but she did none of those things. Scarlet-faced, longing to crawl away somewhere and hide, with the waitress coming across the room looking concerned and all the other customers staring at them, Lilac got down on her knees and began to try to pick up the money.

'Oh Art, honest to God, what a way to behave! Give us a hand, can't you? Don't just stand there!'

Even then all might have been well. If only Art had helped her, or made some joking remark! But instead his words were bitter, a reproach flung at her head with intent to wound.

'Oh, so I'm good enough to grovel on the floor and give you an 'and, but not good enough to marry! That's right, our Lilac, first things first, you get the money – that's what counts, isn't it? That's what you're after, at the end o' the day ... a feller wi' cash an' a posh accent, who can buy the sorta clothes you want to show off in! I 'ope you find 'im, queen, because I'm not just goin' to Birken'ead, I'm goin' a lot furder dan dat!'

She had not heard his speech turn so broad since they were kids together, and perhaps his words stung all the more for being spoken in the white-hot heat of anger.

Lilac sobbed once, then shouted, 'Go, then! For God's sake go and be done with it!' and saw, through her tears, Art's figure actually heading at a run towards the door.

She sat back on her heels, then stood up, slowly,

the money in her hot hand. She crashed it down on to the white tablecloth and picked up her gloves, then headed for the door. The waitress called after her that the bill hadn't come to as much as the gentleman had left, but Lilac ignored her. She was quite literally shaking, partly with temper, for Art had made her look a prize fool, and partly with distress, for she knew she had behaved very badly and had hurt not only herself, but Art as well.

The door was still swinging from Art's violent exit, so she slid through the doorway and into the sunny street. She looked to the right, then to the left. A good number of people thronged the pavement, men, women, children, but of Art there was no sign.

Lilac hesitated. Should she go to the Corry? To Ullet Road? Where would he go, where would he run? Because he would be feeling really bad, as bad as Lilac felt, and she realised that she felt absolutely horrible, as though . . . oh as though she had lost something very precious, something she really valued, and she shouldn't feel like that, not over Art, because he was simply a friend from her past who had proved that he wanted to be more than a friend. And she wasn't ready for that yet – would never be ready so far as Art was concerned. Would she?

Lilac shook herself and set off along the pavement. Perhaps he had gone to the Corry – should she go along and take a look? But she would never have the courage to go up to Art's old home, not with her eyes all red and her nose the same, very likely. Art's mum was a proper horror, she'd be real pleased to see Lilac, whom she despised and disliked, so down.

But Art was miserable, and so was she; she really ought to try to make amends. She wanted to meet him somewhere quiet and private, where she could apologise nicely without half the world staring, and explain to Art . . . explain that if only he'd spoken quieter, or when her mouth wasn't full of pudding . . . not that her answer would have been different . . .

Oh Gawd, it was no use. They'd meet up in a few days . . . she'd go to his bank on Exchange Flags and ask for him, she'd hang around outside until he came out . . . how could she have behaved so badly to one of her oldest friends? Even if she didn't want to marry him – well not yet, anyway, not right here and now!

Lilac was walking without either knowing or caring where she was going, but the autumn sunshine warmed her and presently she began to feel a little better. They had both been fools, both been unkind. Art should apologise too, there were faults on both sides. And he hadn't taken into account that she had just started a strange job, was living in strange lodgings, that her little family, Nellie, Stuart and the as-yet unborn baby, had moved down south, leaving her to her own devices.

If only . . . if only she hadn't been *quite* so hasty! If only she'd been a little more polite – if it had been anyone but Art she would have thought about his feelings, done her best to let him down gently. Why oh why had she been so thoughtless?

She stumbled along the pavement, indifferent for once to the shops, the passing crowds. It was Sunday, so there wasn't much traffic; she crossed over a couple of side roads, then the main road, then simply walked, whilst inside her mind raged round and round the problem. By the time she came to herself, however, and found she had reached the pierhead, her anger was directed less at herself and more at Art.

She had planned a lovely day and Art had ruined

it. She'd not asked him to propose marriage in front of a roomful of people, and she'd every right to say no, anyway. Why should she marry anyone, she wouldn't be nineteen for another eight weeks . . . Art was selfish and pushy and he'd made her look a fool, it was that she couldn't forgive. But when a voice hailed her, when a hand caught hers, she knew a moment of total delight, of relief so great that her knees went weak. He had found her – they would be friends again, the sunshine had meaning, the blue sky smiled on her!

'Well, if it isn't Miss Lilac! Where have you been? I've searched for you; I wrote but you never answered.'

It was Alan Blake, looking incredibly handsome, incredibly debonair, with his naval cap tilted over one eye and his eyes sparkling with admiration for Lilac in her prettiest summer dress with the little blue hat pinned on to her piled-up, red-gold hair!

Just for a moment Lilac's unreliable heart sank like a stone, then it rallied a little. Here was someone who would appreciate her, someone who would understand!

'Well, Mr Blake! I thought you'd forgotten all about me!'

'You're unforgettable, Lilac. You were unforgettable in a black dress with a little white cap and apron, but in blue you're a vision the heavenly hosts couldn't forget! Where are you bound? For the ferry? How about giving me your arm whilst we talk, then we can stroll down to the dock, see what's going on . . . have you eaten?'

'Yes . . . but it was ages ago,' Lilac said quickly. Unhappiness had given her an enormous appetite, she now realised. She could have sat down to clear soup, mutton chops and steamed pudding again and eaten the whole lot with relish. 'Where were *you* going, Mr Blake?'

'Call me Alan, please. I've every intention of calling you Lilac; it's such a beautiful name, so appropriate – your colouring is as fresh and striking as a lilac bloom in spring! I wasn't going anywhere in particular so I can accompany you on a walk, or a ride, or for a meal. Oh, I'm delighted to have found you again, I never thought I would!'

'If you'd written . . .' Lilac said, but she sounded indulgent rather than angry, even to her own ears. 'Why didn't you write, Alan?'

'My dearest girl, I did! I wrote from New York, as soon as we arrived, then again a couple of days later. When we docked here I went straight round to 39 Penny Lane and a woman I'd never seen before answered the door!'

'Oh dear, you can't trust anyone! She promised faithfully to forward any letters,' mourned Lilac. 'What did your letter say, Alan?'

'Well, I described the voyage and New York, then I suggested we meet at the pierhead at three on Saturday afternoon – a week ago yesterday, that was. So when I saw you strolling along I thought maybe you'd mistaken the day and the date; my handwriting leaves a lot to be desired but you didn't look as though you expected to meet anyone . . .' He put his arm round her waist and gave her a squeeze. Lilac drew back, but not very far. It was so good to be admired by someone, especially someone as nice-looking as Alan, and what was more he had a successful career, a big house, rich relatives . . .

'So what would you like to do, Lilac? Let's celebrate our meeting up like this – was it entirely by chance?'

'It was,' Lilac admitted. 'I won't say I'd forgotten you entirely, but you most certainly weren't on my mind. In fact, I was thinking about someone else altogether.'

He nodded, then took her hand and tucked it into his arm.

'Naturally, a beautiful girl like you has a great many admirers, but I'm out to prove . . . well, let's say I'm out to prove that we can enjoy one another's company. I'll hire a cab and we'll go off into the country, to a nice little village I know. There's a woman who does splendid cream teas in her cottage garden; it runs down to the river, and after we've eaten we could hire a boat and go for a row, or walk in the woods, or just stroll through the village, watching the sun set over the hills. What do you say?'

Lilac pretended to consider, but there was no competition, not really. She could go back to her room, boil an egg in her kettle to make herself a meal and cup of tea at the same time, read her copy of *Woman Magazine* which she already knew from cover to cover, mend a hole in her stocking, and go to bed early.

Or she could get into a cab and go off to the country with a handsome young man who was jingling money in his pocket, and have a high old time!

'Come on, Lilac, take pity on me! It's a lovely sunny afternoon, but I've no one to share it with unless you come out to tea with me. Is there anywhere you'd prefer? I only suggested the country and a cream tea because it's such a lovely afternoon.'

'Well, I've some mending to do, and a friend will be coming in later . . . oh, all right, I'll come,' Lilac said, having quite a job even to imitate reluctance.

'But I start work at seven tomorrow morning so I've got to be in by ten.'

'Trust me, Cinderella! Hey, cabbie!'

'Well? Whaddya think?'

Kitty looked at herself in the lid of the biscuit tin which Johnny had produced from somewhere and a slow smile spread across her face. She looked ... well, different. Respectable. Pretty, even. Her cotton dress was neat and clean and Johnny had found a white belt and a pair of almost white plimsolls, much better than the boots which had been so heavy she'd developed painful blisters.

The previous day he had borrowed some garden shears from a man cutting a hedge. He had told her to keep very still – she hadn't screamed, even when she felt the metal against the nape of her neck – and he had scrunched cleanly through her curls, chopping away with the shears and a look of great concentration on his face until, apparently satisfied, he stood back.

'There y'are!' he had said triumphantly. 'Lorra girls 'ud give their eye-teeth to 'ave this new-fangled bobbed 'air, you've got it for nowt. What d'you think?'

She had felt cautiously up her neck ... up and up ... to the ends of her hair which now felt like a prickly garden hedge. Her hands came round to the front.

'Me lug'oles show,' she remarked, not sure whether she was voicing a complaint or making a comment.

'Tha's right. You've gorra wash 'em now, queen.'

'Ye-es ...' She felt across her forehead. 'Ooh, it's all bristly, like a bloody sweep's brush!'

'It sticks out a bit, 'cos it's new-cut,' Johnny

150

said quickly. 'It'll soften down after a few washes. Jest you see.'

A few washes? Kitty was about to exclaim that she couldn't wait years for soft hair when it occurred to her to wonder if Johnny meant she would be washing her hair regular, like say once a month. She opened her mouth to ask him, then closed it again. No point in courting trouble, better to demand a mirror.

'Gi's me shears, den, lad, if you've done,' the hedge clipper said as Johnny lowered the shears down onto the pavement. 'Well, if I ha' knowed why you wanted 'em . . .'

'Yeah, but she looks awright, don't she?' Johnny said, handing the shears back. 'There's a lorra girls 'ud give their right 'ands for nice bobbed 'air, like what our Kitty's got.'

'Mmm,' the man said a shade doubtfully. 'Oh well, I ain't never come to tairms wi' fashions; mebbe you're right.'

So now, staring critically into the shiny tin-lid, Kitty smiled to herself. Johnny might not be a skilled hairdresser – well, he wasn't – but he'd done as good a job as he could. And there was no doubt about it, she looked better. Cleaner. And she did look just like the flappers who queued outside the cinemas and dance halls on a Saturday night. Last Saturday she and Johnny had been in Edge Lane, quite near the Brayton Dance Hall, and they had both remarked on the numbers of crop-headed girls in very short silky dresses hanging around outside waiting for it to open.

'Well? Whaddya think?' Johnny said again, though Kitty guessed that he'd have a pretty shrewd idea of her feelings just from looking at her face.

'It's real nice, Johnny,' she said at last. 'You're right, it's neater an' cleaner an' . . . an' everything.'

'Glad you like it,' Johnny said. 'Then we'll go tomorrer. Awright wi' you? So this arvy we've gorra get our stuff together.'

'What stuff? We don't want me old clo'es, do we?' Kitty said. 'But I've got me sack an' me tins an' that.'

'Kitty, why did I decide to tek you with me, eh?'

'I dunno, Johnny,' Kitty said humbly. She had frequently asked herself the same question. 'Why did you?'

'Because you read, you like books. An' when you're holed up in an 'aystack an' the rain's comin' down like stair-rods you need somethin' quiet to do, which ain't mischief. See?'

'You mean we oughter nick some books?' Kitty said doubtfully. She had always used the free library, but you had to take the books back regular, you couldn't just borrow them for months on end. 'Where'd you do that, Johnny?'

'Nick *books*? Don't ever let me 'ear you say that agin,' Johnny said impressively. 'Ain't you never 'eard of second'and books? Old 'uns? They ain't pricy, an' what's more to the point, if you looks at it right the 'ole country's a liberry. Cos the book you buy for a penny or two in Liverpool you can swop for other books in Crosby, or Southport, or Wales, even. 'Sides, books is . . . oh, they's special, see? We'll buy 'em, like toffs.'

'Awright, Johnny,' Kitty agreed. She, too, thought books were special but she had never queried the supply of tatty old romance and adventure tales which Johnny fished out of his old brown sack. 'What wiv?'

'Money, acourse. Is there anythin' you can do to earn?'

'Prig some flowers an' sell 'em at street corners? Or

I could carry shopping. The shawlies will be shoppin' for Sunday up an' down Byrom an' the Scottie any time.'

'Nah, you ain't strong enough for that, yet,' Johnny said. 'And you'd be bound to meet one o' your fambly. Best get some flowers, though in the country there's flowers to pick for nothin'!'

'You mean you don't 'ave to nick 'em from a garden?'

'That's right. Still, we ain't in the country yet. Go off, then, an' meet me 'ere tonight with some money. We'll get the books first thing in the mornin', then slide off.'

Kitty nodded. They were under a quiet bridge on the canal, with the light already fading and the water the colour of pewter. It was a good tramp to the flowers she had in mind, but well worth it to buy the books Johnny talked of. She just hoped she would get a say in what they bought; Johnny's taste ran to bloodthirsty adventure right now, though he'd read most of the children's classics which Mrs O'Rourke had nurtured Kitty on. But Fenimore Cooper could pall when you'd read ten of them on the trot, as Kitty had.

'Awright? See you later.'

Johnny raised a hand and was gone, swallowed up by the dusk. Kitty, with a sigh, shouldered her nicking sack, took off her plimsolls and slung them round her neck by their laces and set off too, for the long walk to Rodney Street.

Art had made all his arrangements. He'd even got himself lodgings in a pleasant suburb of Birkenhead. He'd explained to his parents that the money would be better and that, should he be unable to visit, he would send his share of family expenses home by post.

I'll keep on helping until I have responsibilities of me own, he would have said, once. Until I've me own wife and kids to take care of. Once that happens, I'll need all the money I earn for them.

But he didn't bother to so much as mention it, since he knew, now, that he wouldn't be marrying. Not now, not ever. He'd known some decent girls in his time, some beautiful, some plain, some full of bounce and go. But he'd only ever been in love with one of them and that was Lilac Larkin. He'd loved her since he was seven, when she'd come to Charlie's wedding in Coronation Court in her pink silk dress with its matching ribbon.

She'd been full of courage, even then. He'd teased her and she'd thumped him, kicked his shins with her little black boots, sworn at him . . . he chuckled at the memory. A right tartar, young Lilac. Oh God, what had happened to her to change her so completely? She had become a single-minded little snob, so eager to climb the ladder of social success that old friendships meant nothing to her. Yet how would he go on, without even the hope that one day she'd turn to him?

He was walking down Scotland Road, trying to convince himself that he was making the right move. He and Lilac had had their row weeks ago and she'd not contacted him, given no sign. If only Nellie and Stuart had still been in Penny Lane he could have engineered an accidental-on-purpose meeting but as it was he only knew she was working in Bridgewater Street, at the bag and sack factory. He'd considered hanging about there, but she'd know. He couldn't bear her to know how he ached for her, how he longed to creep round there and beg her to remain his friend for old time's sake, even if she couldn't abide the thought of a closer relationship.

He reached Miss Harriet Young's ill-fated Dining Room. If only he hadn't been such a fool as to put into words what his heart had been saying for the last year at least! Stuart had warned him, but he'd taken not a bit of notice.

'Our Lilac's young and getting her independence for the first time,' Stuart had cautioned. 'Don't try to tie her down before she's ready. If you wait, Art old friend, she'll turn to you. But let her sow a few wild oats first, eh?'

'I thought it was fellers who sowed wild oats,' Art had protested. 'Young ladies aren't like that!'

Stuart chuckled.

'Who said our Lilac was a young lady? She's a modern Miss, a flapper, an ambitious kid ... call her what you like, she isn't going to fit into that old out-dated mould! Take my advice – which you asked for, remember – and let her have her fling.'

But he hadn't, because the job in Birkenhead had seemed such an ideal opportunity, and he was *sure* she'd come down the Scottie hunting for him, sure she'd wanted to see him. And then they'd fought, hurt each other, parted. And she'd not sought him out nor he her, because damn it, even a feller fathoms deep in love has some pride. And now he was leaving, walking up and down the Scottie saying goodbye to the old places, the old ways – his old life, really. And hoping, really hoping, that presently he'd see a red-gold head weaving its way through the crowd ahead of him, or feel a soft little hand catch at his arm, hear her voice with the liquid bubble of laughter in it which he loved so well.

Art walked on. I'll give it five more minutes . . . ten . . .

Chapter Seven

It must have been the cock crowing in the farmyard which woke Kitty. At any rate, something had. But she was wise to country ways now and did not pop her head out of the cosy nest she and Johnny had made last night in the farmer's haystack. Instead, like a dormouse, she curled neatly round, taking care not to knock against Johnny, and began, very, very carefully, to shift the loose hay which they had pulled in after themselves when they went to bed . . . not much, just enough to see through.

They had chosen their stack and made their nest in darkness, which was probably why they hadn't realised quite how near the farmhouse was. Now, through the screen of stalks, Kitty could see the low, grey house, the outbuildings with lichen patching their roofs, the cushions of moss and stonecrop where the slates were cracked and broken. An old farm, she saw approvingly, but inhabited. A cock had crowed, it was clearing its throat for another burst, and she could see a kennel, the black and white sheepdog within raising a head for a moment to listen, before settling down once more, chin on paws.

Kitty, with infinite caution, cleared a slightly better window for herself and gently insinuated her head into the hole she had made. Looking sideways this time, she could see the beautiful countryside, spread out before her like a living map. There was something different about this scene though, something unexpected. Living rough, on the road, she had already learned a lot, and one thing which was important was to know as much as possible about the countryside through which you were passing. Such knowledge, Johnny had impressed upon her, would never be wasted; not in the long run it wouldn't. Accordingly, Kitty looked round her carefully. Above the farmhouse were the humped shoulders of the Berwyn Hills, and below the farmhouse was a fertile valley. Sheep grazed there, and cattle. The road which snaked along at the foot of the hills was, according to Johnny, the road to London – imagine that! The hedges, which yesterday had been bright with autumn's passing, looked colder this morning, as though the first breath of winter had touched them . . . of course! What was different was the frost! Sparkling white in the first rays of the sun, already disappearing from the tops of the wind-bent trees, crisping the last of their burden of brilliant leaves, the first frost of winter had painted the valley, touched even the mighty hills with its crystal breath.

Kitty sat back to think about this newest development. Winter was serious. Johnny said so, and he knew everything. They couldn't sleep rough once winter came, he said. Well, not every night, anyroad. They would have to look for shelter when the weather was particularly bitter and farmers, mean as their meanest guard-dogs, would lock their barns and fire off their blunderbusses at anyone trying to steal a night's shelter in wintertime, when they wanted every last wisp of hay, every stored turnip or mangold, for their own stock.

Yet, looking out on the white and gold, it was difficult to believe that this actually heralded winter.

Or that, if it did, winter could be so unwelcome. No mozzies, Kitty thought gratefully, rubbing a faded mosquito bite on her arm. No milk turned sour in the heat, no pushing through breast-high bracken abuzz with bluebottles all attacking you as if they had a personal grudge against kids, no spending half a day soaking in a tepid river pool, trying to get rid of the fleas which had infested the last barn.

Beside her, Johnny stirred and woke. He put a hand out and touched her arm. Kitty turned and slid back into their nest. She put her face close to his, loving the feel of his breath on her cheek, the warmth of him so close.

'There's a frost; an' the farm'ouse ain't more'n thirty foot away,' she hissed. 'The dog's awake, but no smoke from the chimbley yet.'

'A frost! Well, we ain't too far from 'ome, but we needn't go back yet awhile. Pity we overslep', but we was awful late gettin' 'ere. Best burrow through.'

Kitty rolled onto her stomach and inched her way back to her spy-hole. There was still no sign of movement from the farm but in the red-gold light of the rising sun the windows stared blankly at her. She concluded that the farmer, as well as his wife and six children if he had them, could all be just the other side of those brilliantly reflective panes and she would never know. And Johnny wouldn't take chances, or only calculated ones.

'Aye. Someone's bound to be about soon; I'll go first.'

In the dusky dimness of the big stack she found her carrying bag and looped its rope round her ankle. Then she began to burrow, digging her way through the hard-packed hay like a little mole. It occurred to neither of them that they were also as destructive as moles – that farmers had a good reason for not wanting nests made in the middle of their haystacks, since animals like their hay handled as little as possible – and if it had, it wouldn't have affected their actions. They had to sleep somewhere, after all, they had their own way to make just like the moles, the farmyard rats and the farmers themselves.

Light began to filter in as Kitty's scrabbling hands neared the outside of the stack. Behind her, she knew, Johnny would be filling in. They might sleep here again in a night or two – nothing was likelier, in fact – so they wanted no gaping holes to announce their recent occupation.

She reached daylight and cautiously began to pull the final plugs of hay inwards. She was facing out onto gentler country now, the road and the soft meadows with their bleating occupants spread out below her. Lying here, she could see on the further side of the road a pond, willow trees, a great many hazels and alders and then the beginnings of moorland, with more sheep and a couple of ponies grazing on the thin grass amongst the gorse bushes.

'All clear, Kit?'

That was Johnny, gently nudging up close behind her.

'Aye, norra soul for miles. Out we go?'

'Out we go!'

At this point, speed was essential. The last thing you wanted was to be caught half in and half out of a haystack. Kitty wound herself into a tight ball, pulled the last of the hay to one side and then launched herself. It was a fair drop but she landed easily, like a cat, and turned to see Johnny already out and repairing the stack behind him before dropping lightfooted down beside her. His face was still pink from the warmth of their nest and his hair tousled, but the sleep was beginning to clear from his eyes, leaving them bright and alert.

'Lead on, chuck,' Johnny said. 'Them hazels will do.'

They made for the hazel clump; once in its shelter Johnny leaned against a young tree and grinned at her.

'Well, what d'you say to some brekfuss?'

'I'm 'ungry enough to eat an 'oss,' Kitty agreed. 'What've we got?'

Johnny shrugged dismissively. He must know as well as Kitty did that their carrying bags were more or less empty.

'We'll go to the farm. Clean me up!'

It wasn't easy. They had both managed to pick up a good deal of their bedding, but Kitty worked away, clearing Johnny from head to toe of the evidence. Then he did the same for her, remarking as he tousled her hair until hay-dust and hayseed flew that she could 'do with another 'aircut, an' the sooner the better if 'e'd gorra get the 'ay out of it often!'

'I's no wuss'n you,' Kitty protested. 'Wash your face!'

They both washed, the water, cat-iced round the edges, making them catch their breaths with the coldness of it. Kitty was only glad that Johnny hadn't decided they should bath – he was a demon for cleanliness and insisted that they wash as often as water came their way.

'You right? C'mon, then.'

Back to the farmhouse now, along the driveway, innocence in their shining faces, their neat persons. Not a strand of hay, not a seed. Two children who could have spent the night respectably in a proper bed, asking to buy some milk – Kitty knew Johnny's

161

ways by now — and then finding they didn't have enough money, but would work for it . . . they were on their way somewhere . . .

The dog barked at them and shot out, but it was chained. It was a typical Welsh sheepdog, black and white fur muddy, narrow head buzzing, Kitty thought resentfully, with an urgent wish to sink its white and pointed teeth into a kid's leg. No matter if the kid was clean and fresh-faced, the dog knew where they'd spent the night. Thank God it can't tell anyone, Kitty thought devoutly as the dog lunged at them. Thank God it's tied up an' all!

Johnny knocked confidently on the leaning wooden door. His knock echoed hollowly, as though the room beyond was empty. But it wasn't, they could hear someone moving slowly across the room. Shuffle shuffle, pause, shuffle shuffle.

The door creaked a little ajar. Kitty could only see a large, open-pored nose and one deep-set, suspicious dark eye. The owner of the eye said something in Welsh; it sounded unfriendly.

'Sorry, we don't speak the lingo, but we're 'aving a walkin' 'oliday in Wales,' Johnny said, with just the right mixture of friendliness and deference. 'We was wonderin' if you'd sell us some milk? We're that dry, me an' me sister.'

The door opened a bit further. The man who stood there was enormous, he couldn't stand upright in the doorway but had to do a sort of semi-crouch. He looked slightly mad to Kitty, and she drew back a little, wondering how Johnny could stand there bold as brass and talk to the great, unkempt giant before them.

'Or per'aps you could let us 'ave a drink o' water, if you ain't got milk,' Johnny continued. For the first time in their acquaintance, Kitty heard uncertainty in Johnny's dulcet tones. People usually answered him, if only to lunge forward, clack him round the lug, and slam the door in his face with a shout of 'Git out, you nasty young beggar!' But this man did nothing, he just continued to look at them. It occurred to Kitty that perhaps he spoke no English, in which case they really were stumped.

'Water? A drink? Do you speak English?'

The same thought had obviously occurred to Johnny, for he spoke slowly and with great care.

The big man frowned, then nodded slowly.

'I speak English,' he said slowly. 'Also Welsh. You want some milk?'

'Yes, please. We've got . . .' Johnny fumbled in his pocket, then turned to Kitty, his expression puzzled. 'Kitty, did you take the purse when we left that cottage this morning?'

Kitty prepared to patter out her usual story of lost money but the man shook his head at them.

'Not pay. You work? You would help Maldwyn?'

'Oh, what a good idea,' Johnny said, as though he'd not just been about to suggest it. 'I'd never ha' thought o' that! Yes, Mr Maldwyn, we'll work for our milk, my sister an' me. What's to be done?'

The huge man closed his eyes for a brief moment and a spasm of pain crossed the great, craggy face. Looking harder at him, Kitty saw that one of his huge feet was insecurely wrapped in rough bandages, and that he was not resting his weight on it. She had moved back when he and Johnny started talking but now she moved forward again. She pointed.

'Wha's the matter wi' your foot?'

The giant Maldwyn glanced down.

'Crushed. Caught in tractor . . . pain iss ferry bad.'

Kitty sucked in her breath but Johnny immediately ducked under the man's arm and entered the kitchen.

'Kit, get some water,' he said. His eyes were bright. Kitty could see that he was pleased by a development which meant they could be useful. 'Sit you down, Mr Maldwyn, whiles we see what we can do.'

'Milk cowss,' the man said in a faint voice. He sank heavily onto the chair which Johnny had pushed forward. It was an old basketwork one and slumped sideways under his weight, but you could tell by the legs, Kitty thought, that it had been slumping sideways, without breaking, for many a year. 'Let Patch off 'er kennel; give 'er to drink.'

'Right. Only we'll do something about that foot first,' Johnny said authoritatively. 'You need a doctor, mister!'

The man took no notice. Kitty jerked Johnny's arm. 'Johnny, 'e's passed out! What'll us do?'

'Get them bandages off,' Johnny said. 'Put the kettle ... oh, no use, the fire's out. Light the fire, Kit. There were chips by the barn door, I seed a big pile. Then 'eat some water.'

Long experience had shown Kitty that if you were given an order you obeyed it at once or took the consequences – which were generally unpleasant – so she rushed across the yard and got an armful of kindling from the barn, then laid it carefully on top of the still-warm ashes in the open stove. She found matches and lit the fire, then since Johnny was unwrapping the strips of torn up sheeting with almost womanish care and gentleness, she went to the back door and stared ruminatively at the dog.

Poor thing! It was growling and scowling, but its water-container was empty and it looked desperately wild. Kitty tried to pick up the empty tin to refill it, but the dog snarled warningly and made a pass at her hand, so she went across the yard to the well she had noticed and staggered back with the half-full bucket which had been standing waiting. She tipped water into the tin and the dog drank deeply, then stood back. Kitty inched forward. The dog was watching her keenly, its bright, light eyes fixed on her face. She went nearer still.

'D'you wanna be unchained?' she asked softly. 'If so, you gorra let me get near!'

The dog moved its front paws in a little dance on the spot. Its long, filthy plume of a tail moved slowly from left to right. It cocked its head and gave a tiny whine.

Kitty knelt.

'Come 'ere, Patch,' she said. 'Come to Kitty, there's a good gal!'

The name was probably the password, she thought afterwards, but at the time she was just so relieved that the dog's animosity seemed to be lessening that she didn't stop to wonder why.

'Patchie, Patchie, Patch,' Kitty crooned in her softest tones. 'Come to Kit, there's a lovely gal then.'

And the dog came. On her belly, slowly, she slid forward until her trembling head was resting on Kitty's bare knee. And Kitty unclipped the rusty chain and fondled the dog and then led it indoors.

'Dog's off the chain,' she said nonchalantly. 'Wonder what 'e gives it for its grub?'

Maldwyn was still out for the count, it appeared. Johnny looked up, shrugged, and returned to his work. He had got all the bandages off save for the last layer, which was black with blood and stuck into place.

'Dunno. Find it something . . . that there's got

food in.' He pointed to a cupboard, door ajar. 'I'd best soak this off. Bring some water over.'

Kitty found an enamel bowl and half filled it with water. The fire was taking hold so she pulled the kettle over the flame. Behind her, Maldwyn gave a deep groan and Johnny gasped at the same moment. Quickly, Kitty returned to his side.

'What is it? Are you . . . oh, Johnny!'

To say that the foot was crushed was no more than the truth. The poor, mangled thing lay there, the toes blue, the flesh torn so that she could see the white of bone and sinew.

'How the blazes 'as 'e stuck it?' Johnny whispered. 'Kitty, I'll stay 'ere, you'd best go to the next farm, fast, an' tell 'em to send for a doctor.'

'Which way's the next farm?' Kitty asked practically. 'Can I take the dog? Then they'll know it's awright.'

'Good idea. Look, give it a bit o' bread an' 'ave some yourself, to eat on the way,' Johnny ordered. He was never at a loss, Kitty thought admiringly. 'See if there's cheese . . . only this weren't done yesterday, 'e's been badly for a coupla days, I reckon.'

Kitty, rooting, found a huge cheese and cut three bits off, one for each of them. Maldwyn, who had regained consciousness, was still not up to bread and cheese. He lay in the chair, sickly white, and now and again he sucked in his breath and let it out in a low moan. Even to Kitty's inexperienced eyes he looked in great pain.

'Got it? Then off wi' you. No, 'ang on, let's see what Maldwyn says.'

But Maldwyn wasn't able to understand what they were asking. He would stare at them for a moment and then slowly close his eyes; never a word passed his lips whilst they made tea in his pot, fetched a stool for his foot and propped it up with a cushion which Kitty found in the front parlour.

'Oh, well,' Johnny said resignedly when they had asked Maldwyn in every way they knew whether Kitty should turn right or left outside the farm gate. 'Best get on, Kit. Tell 'em 'e's mortal bad an' they'd best 'urry. I dussen't do owt more'n we done awready.'

Kitty set off. The driveway down to the road was long and the hedges overgrown, but the gate swung smoothly enough on its hinges and she had the dog on her length of rope trotting beside her. She and the dog had shared the bread and cheese, which seemed to give Patch the idea that they were friends. Kitty, who had longed for a dog without any expectation of even knowing one, got enormous satisfaction from the dog's mere presence and when, after walking at least two miles, they came to a neat grey farmhouse with geese strutting in the yard and a man with a full bucket in each hand crossing the road towards them she had no hesitation in hailing him.

'Mister, I've come from the farm up the road a ways; Maldwyn's in a spot o' trouble . . .'

The man stopped walking and set his buckets down, then smiled at her. 'Mornin', lass. What you doin' wi Maldwyn's Patch, then?'

Kitty hadn't realised she had been afraid of the sort of reception she might get until the man was so matter of fact and friendly. Then she had to fight to stop her voice wobbling as she told her story.

'So me brother Johnny's there now, an' me an' Patch come for 'elp,' she ended. 'We think 'e's real badly, mister. 'Is foot's 'orrible, raw an' 'orrible.'

The man picked up his buckets again and motioned her to open the gate. 'Right, I got you,' he said briskly.

'Don't take no notice of them old geese, just stay close. Get the missus I will, she wass a nurse before we wed.' A young man in a worn cap and labouring clothes came out of the byre carrying a long pitchfork and Kitty's new friend raised his voice to a bellow. 'Eifion, get in the motor an' go for a doctor; Maldwyn Efans 'as 'ad a nasty accident. Like to lose 'is foot, by the sound.'

The young man propped his pitchfork against a wall and turned away without a word; presently Kitty heard the roar of an engine and a motor car came round the corner of the building. The young man raised a hand to them, roared something in Welsh, and was gone up the drive. Kitty's companion turned to her and stuck out a hand.

'Dewi Jones,' he said. 'Bronwen'll come . . . stay you here.'

'I'm Kitty and me brother's Johnny,' Kitty supplied. 'I'd best start back, mebbe.'

Dewi Jones shook his head.

'No, wait on. I'll fetch out the trap, see, and we'll be at Maldwyn's place in a trice.'

He disappeared into the farmhouse. Kitty sat down on the bench alongside the door and waited, with Patch sitting beside her, leaning against her knee. The geese, which had rushed forward as soon as they saw her but had retreated again when their master shouted at them, began sidling towards her once more, round bright eyes fixed on her face, big orange beaks agape with hisses.

But Kitty was no soft city-dweller, not now, not after three months of country living. Besides, she had Patch. She waited until the leading bird was no more than a foot away, then she leaned forward and slapped it decisively across the chops. The gander, thoroughly thrown off balance, weaved for a moment, then came on again, so Kitty mentally targeted the heart area and kicked out with both feet. She got it right in the middle of its soft, bulging breast with sufficient force to send it staggering, and counted the black bruise from its beak as nothing when the gander, after a long and doubtful look at her, suddenly turned tail and waddled off, taking his numerous wives with him.

'There y'are, queen,' Kitty told Patch, who was watching the geese retreat with great interest. 'A clack over the bloody lug works wonders, whether it's a feller or a goose!'

'I told him to call for me when his ship comes in, and he said he would, and it's this very evening,' Lilac said, feeding a length of material expertly into the hungry maw of her machine and turning it to form the bottom of the sack. 'So if you want to take a look at him, Bertha, now's your chance!'

'I bet 'e's 'andsome,' Bertha said wistfully, zipping round a completed sack and throwing it on to the pile. 'You're ever so pretty, chuck, the prettiest gal in the room.'

'We're all pretty,' Lilac said. ' And we're all different. But Alan *is* handsome, only . . .'

'Only what, chuck?'

Lilac shrugged and zipped her own sack out of the machine, snatching up another piece of material and feeding it in almost in the same movement. In the months which had elapsed since she had started here she had finally become as quick and expert as any other girl in the room and, when she thought about it, was proud of the fact.

'Only I'm not sure I want to marry anyone, or even go steady with anyone! Believe it or not, Bertha, I like me bit of independence and anyway, I've only known Alan a couple of months.'

'A couple of months!' The girl on Lilac's other side, a short, broad-faced girl with slavic cheekbones and slanting, dark eyes, laughed. 'Why, that's a lifetime for someone like our Bertha! You mek it sound like a couple of minutes, queen!'

'Don't tease, Lily,' Lilac said. She had a special fondness for Lily, whose parentage – Liverpool mum and Chinese dad – always made her think of her friend Polly. 'It isn't long; not for me. I'd known Art O'Brien for years, not weeks . . . and I still couldn't make up me mind to marry him!'

'I t'ink it's a pity you didn't,' Doreen muttered. Doreen was dark of hair and eye, bewitchingly pretty, and easily the most spiteful of the twenty-four girls in the sewing room. 'Per'aps we'd of 'ad some peace if you'd gone on goin' steady wi' that O'Brien feller.'

'There wasn't any point, not if he wanted to marry and I didn't,' Lilac said. 'Besides, we were just a couple of kids. It wasn't a – a proper relationship, not like with Alan.'

''Cept you don't want to marry Alan, either, by all accounts,' Lily pointed out. Her machine whined and clattered slowly to a halt. Lily swore colourfully and reached for a new reel of the coarse brown thread. 'Damn, it snapped. I reckon we lose more time re-threadin' these bloody things . . .'

'I might want to marry him,' Lilac said defensively. 'Anyway, I'm going down to London at Christmas to see me sister Nellie and the new baby. Perhaps I'll make up me mind then.'

'Aye, and when you see the lickle gal – what's 'er name? Elizabeth, that's it – you'll see dere's a'vantages to famblies.'

'I know there are, Bertha,' Lilac sighed. She still missed Nellie fiercely, though they wrote a couple of times a week and she rang the small house in Balham at least once a month. 'I expect I'll marry one of these days . . . I just wish . . .'

'What, luv?'

'Don't arst 'er,' Doreen cut in. 'She'll tell you all over again 'ow she can't mek up 'er mind . . . jest don't arst!'

The other girls laughed and Lilac, smiling ruefully, continued with her work. The nicest thing about making sacks and bags, she had concluded weeks back, was that they didn't need a lot of concentration. You could let your mind wander where it willed whilst your hands and your body continued to feed the machine, see to it when it stuck, repair it when it failed and fetch it fresh material when it ran out. All in all, apart from the fact that you were run off your feet half the time and standing all day, it wasn't such a bad job.

'Want more material, Lilac?'

Stubby the warehouseman, only he should rightly have been called a warehouselad since he was no more than five foot tall and only in his teens, came thundering into the room, arms full of sacking. Everyone knew he was sweet on Lilac so there were covert grins, but Lilac just smiled and said she could do with a yard or two, and after he'd left relapsed into her thoughts once again.

Christmas wasn't very far off. Another ten days and it would be upon them. Alan would be home for a couple of days but she wouldn't be able to see him since she was going down to London to visit Nell and Stuart. And Elizabeth, of course. Nellie's letters were full to bursting of Elizabeth, telling Lilac the exact colour of her hair, the brightness of her eyes, the way she smiled.

She would miss Alan, of course. Christmas was a time for friendship, for being with the people you love . . .

Art. She'd not seen hide nor hair of him since that stupid, worrying quarrel. She hadn't *meant* any of the things she'd said and she was sure he hadn't meant the things he'd said, either. Only . . . bad and silly things had got said, feelings had been hurt . . . she'd gone back to the Court a couple of weeks ago, but though she'd seen Mrs O'Brien she hadn't liked to ask. The old devil had looked so sly, like a cat with the cream.

Christmas was a time for making up. She couldn't remember who had said that, but she was sure someone had. So why not make up with Art? Oh, she was going out with Alan, some people might even say she was going steady, but this wasn't about that sort of thing at all, this was about friendship, about love, not about . . .

Love? Did you say love? Oh, but I didn't mean *that* kind of love, Lilac reminded herself hastily, I meant the comfortable sort of love your have for a feller you've known all your life, the feeling that you want to be with him, that nothing you say or do can be wrong, that, together, you could go anywhere, do anything.

Lilac's machine coughed, grunted, stopped. Lilac stared into space. Love? What *was* love, exactly? Wasn't it the exciting, fizzing sort of feeling you got when a handsome young man paid you compliments, taught you to dance the Charleston, kissed you in the queue to get into the Gaiety cinema on Scotland Road or squeezed you in the back-row doubles at the

Smithdown Picture Playhouse? Yes, that was love; it had to be, it was what all the girls talked about, dreamed about – wasn't it?

'Li, yon bugger's stopped! Wake up, queen!'

Hastily, Lilac took the crumpled piece of material out of her machine, straightened it, rethreaded the needle and set it going again.

So if she was right and that was love, what was this dull, gnawing ache? Was it because some part of her simply needed to see Art, to be forgiven by him, to hear his voice?

'Lilac Larkin, that last bloody sack's got no neck, you've sewed clean acrost it! Oh my lor', the gairl's asleep an' dreamin' so she is!'

Lilac frowned and took the sack Mrs Loose was holding out to her. She saw, guiltily, that she had indeed sewn round all four sides. She held it up, then slung it onto the floor at her feet.

'I'll unpick it,' she said wearily, words she had not had to use for weeks and weeks. 'Sorry, Mrs Loose, it won't happen again.'

She could go purposefully into Deacon's Bank, not just wander in and out as she had done half-a-dozen times over the past weeks. She could go in and ask for Art O'Brien, get his address, go over to Birkenhead and see him, tell him she was awful sorry and would he please be friends again?

With the thought, an enormous rush of warmth and comfort engulfed her. The ache, which had been so persistent lately that it had become almost a part of her, miraculously lessened. She zipped the latest length of material into her machine, watched it as it became a sack, zipped it out and threw it on the pile. What a fool she'd been, standing on her dignity, telling herself that it didn't really matter, that if Art cared he'd come to her, not wait for her to come to him. Now that her mind was made up, now that she had decided she would go to any lengths, she felt quite different – warm, hopeful, cheerful even.

It no longer worried her that Art might think less of her for the gesture. Christmas is a time for forgiveness, she reminded herself. I'll take him a present, tell him about Nellie's baby, ask him if he'd like to come down to London with me to see the Gallaghers!

Christmas, which had seemed only moments ago to be rather a hollow mockery, was suddenly decked with bells and bright with holly.

On the Saturday before Christmas, Lilac put on her nicest dress, a fashionable blue shift with a lace collar, and her best silk stockings. She wore her new black court shoes and her camel-hair coat with the black astrakhan collar and cuffs. She had the sweetest hat, also made of black astrakhan, which perched on her newly cut hair and made her look very fetching indeed.

'Miss Dashing Twenties herself!' another lodger remarked as she met Lilac on the stairs. 'Who are you off to impress, Miss Larkin?'

'An old friend who won't be a bit impressed, Miss Dodman,' Lilac told her. 'Old friends don't care much about clothes, but I want to look as if I've tried.'

'Old man friend or old lady friend?' Miss Dodman said with a twinkle. She was in her thirties and therefore, to Lilac, old as the hills, but she was smart, friendly and efficient. She worked in the big library on William Brown Street and she and Lilac often chatted in the kitchen or waiting outside the one bathroom. Miss Dodman frequently told Lilac that with her looks and education she could do better for herself than a factory job. Lilac was sure she was right, but reluctant to chance her luck – unemployment was still rife and a good few of her friends were out of work. So she decided she would ride out the bad times in the factory since no matter what else went by the board, it seemed that sacks and bags would always be needed. She would try for a different, more interesting job when things began to look up.

'Man, actually,' Lilac said. 'See you later, Miss Dodman.'

'Good luck,' Miss Dodman called as Lilac ran swiftly down the rest of the stairs and across the narrow hall. 'Have a nice day, dear.'

Lilac, making her way down Lord Nelson Street, smiled at the well-muffled passers-by, and enjoyed the sting of the cold on her cheeks, for despite the sunshine it was an extremely cold day. She turned left into Lime Street, scarcely giving the station more than a passing glance as she did so. Next week she would be catching a train from Lime Street to go to Nellie and Stu, to meet her adopted niece for the first time, to see the house in Balham, the park where Nellie walked, the trams and trains and theatres, cinemas and dance halls, all the excitements of the capital city. Yet none of it thrilled her as the prospect of meeting Art again did; she could have danced every step of the way to the ferry, except that a tram heading for the pierhead drew up beside her and it seemed downright daft not to jump aboard, climb the stair and sit on the upper deck with the wind making her eyes run whilst the sun warmed her nose into rosiness. From her lofty perch she saw Liverpool go by, the crowds shopping, the windows dressed for the holiday. At the pierhead she got down and went over to the quayside. A ferry was steaming in, people aboard lining the rail. They would be coming over for Christmas shopping – what a day they had for it, too! A pale blue sky, the brilliance of a wintry sun, the city clear of fog and sparkling like a diamond in the chilly, exhilarating salt wind. But she wouldn't change places with the shoppers, not for a million pounds she wouldn't – she was going to see Art and tell him she was sorry!

The young man she had approached in the bank in Liverpool had not been exactly helpful, though.

'Arthur O'Brien? Oh aye . . . he left.'

'I know. I wondered if you could tell me where he'd gone.'

'Hmm . . . was it Chester? I seem to remember some talk about Chester.'

'I think it was Birkenhead, actually,' Lilac said patiently. 'I wondered if you could give me the address of your branch in Birkenhead.'

'Certainly. It's on Hamilton Square; you can't miss it. Big building, on your right as you come up from the ferry.'

She had known all along that she'd have to beard Art in his den, so to speak, but she was disappointed that the young man hadn't made any comment at all about Art's house or his circumstances. Still, he was probably jealous.

People were jostling aboard the ferry now, so Lilac joined them. She found a place by the rail easily, the ferry being comparatively empty now that all the Liverpool-bound shoppers had abandoned ship, and settled to enjoy the short voyage. In the old days she would have explored every inch of the vessel, but now an older and wiser Lilac just stood by the rail, enjoying the motion, the buffeting wind, and the prospect of Birkenhead getting nearer and nearer.

They docked. Lilac and the other passengers disembarked and Lilac set off uphill, first along Woodside, then up Hamilton Street and into the Square itself.

She saw the bank at once, just where the young man had said. It was a big building though nowhere near as big as the building in Exchange Flags where Art had worked. She went through the revolving doors, her heart hammering so hard in her breast that she thought people must be able to hear it, and came out into the bank, all mahogany and hushed voices, dim lighting, respectability. So near, so near!

There were several young men behind the big counter. She went over to the nearest – she had seen at a glance that Art was not one of them – and spoke before she lost her courage. 'Excuse me, might I see Mr O'Brien, please? On a personal matter.'

The young man looked up and smiled dazedly; I knew this hat suited me, Lilac thought absently, and I wasn't wrong.

'Mr O'Brien? I don't think we have anyone of that name here this morning, Miss. If you'll wait a moment . . .'

He left, with several backward glances. Blue always was my colour, Lilac thought, trying not to sparkle too obviously.

There were small conferences and confabulations going on behind the counter. Young men with their heads together, then an older man . . . Lilac began to feel uneasy. She glanced around her, but this was Deacon's Bank, all right, she hadn't made a mistake. Perhaps this was Art's morning off, perhaps they could give her his address so she could visit him at home.

The young man came back with the older one behind him. The older man smiled at her.

'Good morning, Miss. I'm afraid Mr O'Brien has left the bank's employ; he wasn't here very long, which is why Mr Rumbold was unable to help you.'

'Left? *Left*? But he was so pleased ... it was promotion ... he even rented a house ...' Lilac stammered. 'Is he still living here, do you know? Could you possibly give me his address so that ...'

The elderly man stepped forward. He looked a little hot and bothered, a little embarrassed. I hope to God he doesn't think I'm in trouble and trying to find Art to hand him the baby, Lilac thought, horrified. She leaned forward earnestly.

'Look, I'm awfully sorry, I didn't realise Mr O'Brien had left. The truth is we were at school together and I'm getting married in the spring. I would like him to attend my wedding, and since I happened to be in Birkenhead this morning – my fiancé is meeting me here, we're going to buy the ring – I thought I'd just pop in and tell Mr O'Brien to keep the fifteenth of March free. But I could always write, if you'd pass the letter on.'

Two brows miraculously cleared of their troubled frowns; they *did* think I was going to accuse Art of something awful, Lilac thought with a good deal of indignation. But the older man was shaking his head regretfully.

'I only wish we could help you, Miss, but the fact is, Mr O'Brien didn't leave to go to another bank or another branch. He decided he wasn't cut out for a business life and he joined the Merchant Navy. I believe he's assistant purser on one of the big liners, though I wouldn't swear to it. I'm afraid it would be difficult, if not impossible, for us to forward a letter in the circumstances. I suppose you don't know his parents' address, or . . .'

'Oh yes, of course, I know the O'Briens well, but since I no longer live in the city myself I'd not thought of contacting them,' Lilac lied, with a dreadful heaviness descending on her so that it was difficult even to get the words out. 'I'm so sorry to have troubled you. When we've chosen the ring my fiancé and I had better get a cab and go visiting! Thank you for your time.'

She left. Outside, the sun still shone, people still bustled about getting the last of their holiday shopping done. Lilac went and sat down in the Square garden. She felt as though the ground had been cut from under her feet, as though she had fallen heavily, jarring every bone in her body, bruising herself in the process. What should she do now? He didn't live here any more, hadn't lived here for months by the sound of it.

She got to her feet after a few moments thought, however, and headed for the quayside once more.

Right! The time for silliness and holding back was past. She was going to Coronation Court and she was going to find out where Art was and what he was doing if it killed her! Blow her pride, blow her best clothes, blow everything. Let his mother gloat, his sisters sneer; she had an apology to make!

Chapter Eight

Kitty heard the cock begin to crow and got out of bed. She no longer saw the bed as the height of luxury, a thing to be regarded with awe. Now it was just her bed, with blankets to be washed once a month and a pillow whose coarse white cotton slip had to be changed weekly.

In the winter, of course, she had snuggled down each night almost unable to believe her luck. But with summer's arrival she had grown accustomed – accustomed to so many things! A roof over her head, food in her stomach daily, definite jobs to do, tasks to perform.

Johnny was away for a few days though, so right now she should be down in the kitchen, getting on. Maldwyn had explained that he wanted someone to go over to Dublin in Ireland to buy Irish cattle for fattening. Johnny had said he would go when Maldwyn had explained that he could accompany Mr Dewi Jones and his son Eifion and Mr Meirion Davies from further up the valley. Maldwyn would have gone himself, once, but his foot was far from right. He couldn't put weight on it. Kitty doubted that he ever would, and though he got around on his sticks there were a great many things that he still couldn't tackle, might never be able to do again.

Maldwyn was unmarried, so the doctor had asked Mrs Bronwen Jones from up the road if she would come in every couple of days to dress the foot. She did it for three weeks, then asked Johnny if he and Kitty intended to stay.

'For if 'tis so, I might as well show you 'ow to do the dressings, see?' she said. 'No point in me coming 'ere every other day when you and the little girl is on the spot, like.'

So until the foot healed, Johnny and Kitty did the dressings between them, and Maldwyn never grumbled, never cried out, even though there were times when Kitty was sure they must have hurt him.

After Christmas Maldwyn told them he didn't know what he'd have done without them, and said he would pay them a wage for the work they did. They had been sitting round the kitchen table, having finished off a joint of mutton between them, with potatoes from the straw-stacked pile in the back yard and some winter greens, cut with the frost still on them. Johnny looked slowly round the table, then let his gaze stray further, to the fire-bright kitchen, the range with the kettle hissing away on the hob, the doors open so that the warmth of the blaze might offset the cold outside. Snow had fallen for the first time since they arrived, and though it wasn't much of a fall it had laid, spreading a thin white blanket over the countryside, topping the Berwyns with ice which hid the dead bracken and heather.

'You're keepin' us,' Johnny pointed out, bringing his attention back to Maldwyn and the offer of a wage once more. 'We've gorra roof over our 'eads. That'll do us, over winter!'

Maldwyn shook his great, shaggy head. I really must have a go at his hair with the scissors, Kitty thought with some relish. She always offered to cut Johnny's hair but he did his own, squinting into a polished tin-lid and a window-pane to do the back. But Maldwyn's thatch would really present a challenge!

'No, I'll pay you something . . . a share, like. Save it up. A labourer is worthy of his hire as it says in the Good Book.'

Maldwyn was a chapel-goer and a deeply religious man, but his religion was a private thing. He never tried to persuade either child to do more than help him to the chapel door, and had told the minister in no uncertain terms that both Johnny and Kitty were devout Catholics and not to be swayed from their faith. Kitty, whose idea of religion was hazy and consisted mainly of the threats her mother had voiced . . . if you do so-and-so Father O'Hare will 'alf kill ye . . . was happy to go along with whatever Maldwyn said, but Johnny occasionally looked thoughtful.

He had looked thoughtful over being paid, too.

'Does that mean we can stay all winter?' he said finally. 'We'd work 'ard, eh Kit?'

'Ever so 'ard,' Kitty agreed, gazing hopefully from one face to the other. The thought of facing that snow, with no roof, no bed, no bright fire, was as painful to her as the thought of living once again with the Drinkwaters in Paradise Court would have been.

'Stay till you want to go, like,' Maldwyn said. 'No chick nor child of me own do I have . . . stay and welcome.'

They had been glad to agree and now whenever Maldwyn got money for his stock or for the milk from his four placid Friesian cows, Johnny and Kitty got some money too, and Johnny put it in an old tobacco tin and hid it somewhere. Kitty didn't ask where and Johnny never told her, but she guessed it would be outside. Maldwyn was kind and their friend, but he was not young. You never knew, Johnny said darkly, and continued to save all their wages in his old tobacco tin.

Whilst she thought about the past months, Kitty had been splashing her face with water and wriggling into her clothes. If Johnny had been here she would have washed longer and brushed her hair harder, but since he wasn't she skimped a bit, salving her conscience with the recollection that since her first task that morning would be to muck out the byre, she would have to wash again anyway after that.

Presently she padded downstairs and put the kettle on. Maldwyn was a hard and honest worker even with his injured foot, but it took him a while to get dressed; as soon as he was able after the accident he had dispensed even with Johnny's assistance. What he did like, however, was a big mug of tea so that he could take a drink as he struggled into his thick homespun shirts and practical working trousers. Accordingly, every morning Kitty went downstairs, riddled the fire and took out the ashes, filled the kettle and made the tea. She carried the big mugful up to Maldwyn's room, banged on the door and put the tea down by the bed. Then she went over to the window and drew back the curtains, letting in the sunlight, or a view of the slanting silver rain, or even of snowy pastures. Maldwyn always sat up and greeted her and gave her his shy, awkward smile.

'Feels like a king I does,' he invariably remarked. 'Nice it is to be waited on now and again!'

He did the same this morning, picking the mug up with both hands and tilting it blissfully to his mouth, his eyes smiling at her over the rim.

'Managing without Johnny, are you?' he asked presently, as Kitty, having admired a brilliantly sunny

August day, made for the doorway once more. 'Eh, I used to enjoy going to Dublin in the old days.'

'I'm muckin' out first, so if you're down before I come back in, don't forget I'll be hungry enough for two,' Kitty said with a grin. 'I don't mind doin' Johnny's chores, so long as I get to eat 'is grub!'

Maldwyn laughed.

'You eat plenty on your own account,' he said. 'A couple more rashers will go in the pan though, since you've said.'

Kitty, skipping downstairs, smiled to herself. There were men who wouldn't want to cook the breakfast whilst a bit of a girl mucked out, but Maldwyn wasn't like that. He'd done everything for himself since his old mother had died ten years back, and was only worried that he might be overtaxing his workers when his lameness made a job impossible. But he managed most things. He could swing a scythe with the best, not that he needed to do so. The local farmers hired harvesters, tractors, anything they might need between them, and then they went from farm to farm come harvest time, helping with the entire crop. As for sheep-dipping, shearing, taking the beasts to market, Maldwyn and Patch between them did wonders. Patch would bring the sheep right to Maldwyn's knee, who with his great size and strength and his sticks could get even a reluctant ram into the dip, or wedge him under one arm whilst wielding the clippers with the other hand.

But he needed the children. Not just for the things they could do without a second thought which would have taken Maldwyn hours, not for the dressing of his foot, which had finished weeks ago anyway. He needs us now, Kitty thought, because he has grown used to us. His previous solitude had been forced upon him but once he got to know Kitty and Johnny he found he was able to tell them all sorts of things – his private worries were shared, his anxieties, his pleasures, even.

Kitty, who had always been garrulous herself, with the Liverpudlian's liking for discussing, in intimate detail, everything which happened to her and her friends, could well understand his desire for conversation. To sit down of an evening in front of the range and talk over the quality of the wool he had cut last autumn and the price he expected to get next back-end, to muse over the advisability or otherwise of letting Patch have a litter of pups, to wonder aloud whether a flock of geese would not be a good idea, or possibly whether they should set the broody hen on a clutch of duck eggs, so that they could have ducks on the pond, was good and necessary to both her and Maldwyn.

The only real problem which had arisen had been books. In towns and cities there were always shops which sold old books, and libraries which would lend, but in the heart of the country books were not available and Johnny needed books. He said he was educating himself for a fine future, but Kitty, who had the books after him, thought he read mainly for entertainment and love of reading.

Then Maldwyn wanted some cattle cake and Eifion Jones offered to take him into Corwen the next time he went. Johnny went along to give Maldwyn a hand – it was in the early days when their friend was not so well-used to his sticks – and came back positively glowing.

'There's a liberry, queen,' he gasped as soon as he was over the threshold, thrusting a pile of books into her arms. 'Maldwyn joined . . . it's a free library . . . and said I could tek 'is share. They've got all sorts, *and* there's an old bookshop. I picked up a copy of

Bleak House for a penny; it's got no cover, but all the words is there!'

'Oh, Johnny!' Kitty said, almost as excited as he. She had grown deathly afraid that Johnny might leave, just to get back to books. 'Oh, ain't we lucky?'

They were. She knew it. Knew it now, knew it then, knew it every time she woke up, knew it as she shovelled the steaming, stinking piles of cow dung out of the byre, as she was doing now. Lucky Kitty Drinkwater, lucky Johnny Moneymor – even lucky Maldwyn Evans, with his neglected old farmhouse and his much-loved animals.

We're a fambly, good as, Kitty told herself as she shovelled. And presently, washing up in the sink with the delicious smell of bacon frying in the room behind her, she caught a glimpse of her reflection in the window pane and thought that her own mother probably wouldn't know her. Short, richly red-brown hair curled loosely around her head, her eyes were bright, her cheeks glowed pink with health whilst her limbs were rounded and strong, her smile self-confident. The girl whose reflection looked back at her from the window pane was a far cry from the skinny waif who had so often felt the weight of Sary Drinkwater's hand, who had stolen food just to keep alive, who had been afraid for twenty-two hours out of every twenty-four.

I'm not the same person, Kitty thought wonderingly, rubbing herself dry on the rough towel. I've forgotten what it's like to be hungry and scared all the time. Sary's Kitty died the night she lost them trimmings. Johnny's Kitty was born soon after. And I know which I'd rather be, which I'm glad I am!

*

186

A few months later, Art watched the Liver birds getting bigger and bigger as his ship steamed up the Mersey and wondered at his own lack of excitement.

It was over a year since he had sailed down the Mersey on the tide, determined that if he couldn't settle to banking without even the prospect of winning Lilac's love, at least he would have adventure.

But he soon discovered that an assistant purser's life was not for him; there were pretty girls in plenty on the big passenger liner which had employed him, but he thought them affected and insincere. He hated their loud laughs, short skirts, and apparently non-existent morals. Their drawling voices and upper-class accents often defeated him – one cannot keep up a conversation in which one's principal remark is 'What did you say?' – and their humour embarrassed him. But when the female passengers saw that he was young, nice-looking and single there was no stopping their pursuit. He was fair game in a world where women considerably out-numbered men and the bright young things chased him remorselessly.

There were pretty girls on the staff, of course, but an assistant purser was supposed to entertain the passengers, not the staff, which meant he must be extremely polite to the men and let them beat him at deck tennis and cards, and it was soon made plain to him that he was expected to gently flirt with any young woman who wanted to flirt with him. So Art jumped ship in New York and signed on as a deck-hand on a small freighter which chugged up and down the East Coast, transporting anything which needed moving from one place to another.

He stuck it for three months, then signed off at the end of the voyage and worked in a gentle-man's outfitters for a while. He got the job because the proprietor was fascinated by his English accent and thought it lent class to his establishment. But he didn't like the subservience of shop-work and this time he gave notice and signed on as a steward on a liner which was Liverpool bound. He was lucky to get the job; unemployment was biting as deeply in America as it was beginning to bite in Britain and Art thought gloomily that if he was going to starve anywhere, he'd as soon it was Liverpool.

And now here he was, standing at the ship's rail, staring at the city as it gradually grew larger and larger and feeling a great lump in his throat and an unaccustomed blurring in his eyes.

Home! He'd been away for nearly twelve months – he had left in December and it was now November of the following year – and in that time he'd grown up a lot. He didn't see himself going back to the bank, he thought he'd go mad with the boredom of it, but he knew for certain that he wanted to be based in the Pool, even if he was never ashore for very long.

He would go to sea; he knew that now. He'd work his way up, take examinations, slog at it, and eventually he would get his ticket. He didn't fancy a liner, though. He rather thought he'd like a coaster or a trawler rather than a passenger ship. He wanted the sea, hard work, and a degree of forgetfulness. He had noticed that when he was working really hard, slogging as he called it, he didn't think of Lilac from one hour to the next, and that was what he wanted – to reach a point when he simply never thought of her. Then and only then, Art thought, would he be free, able to concentrate on his own life.

I want a home and a family, Art dreamed as his ship steamed slowly and cautiously into her berth. I'm an ordinary bloke with ordinary hopes and desires;

a girl who loves me, a couple of kids, a neat little house like Nellie and Stuart's place in a nice little suburban road like Penny Lane . . . that would make me happy.

Once, he had truly believed that the only thing which would make him happy would be marriage to Lilac, but now, after more than a year of wandering, he knew better. Happiness did not have to depend on only the other person; if you changed your outlook and attitude, turned your life upside-down and lived very intensely, then suddenly you realised that there was more to life than winning the love of one particular person, even if she was someone who had meant a lot to you.

Accept that she will never be yours and look for second best, Art had advised himself grimly at some stage during the past twelve months. And without even realising it, he had taken his own advice. His broken heart, if you could call it that, was on the mend. Returning to Liverpool meant that he could face seeing Lilac with someone else and still go ahead with his own life.

But as the city got closer, so close that he could hear the street-cries of the vendors on the waterfront, he did feel a little pang. If things had been different, if he'd had a girl – *the* girl – waiting for him, standing on the quayside waving to his ship, jumping up and down with excitement because any moment now they would be in each other's arms, how happy he would be!

Give yourself a chance, O'Brien, Art ordered himself as, bag in hand, he went down the gangplank after the ship had docked. You'll find the right girl for you, even if her name isn't Lilac Larkin. And you'll live happily ever after, see if you don't!

'I'm worried about Li, that's the truth, Stu. In this past year she's had more young men than I've had hot dinners and she hasn't settled with any of them. If you ask me, it was always Art, it's just taken her a long time to see it. And now she knows she wants him, he's gone, and that means she can't settle to anyone else.'

'He'll come back, sweetheart,' Stuart said comfortably, pulling the blankets over his shoulders. He was always first in bed because his preparations consisted simply of a quick wash, an incredibly quick shedding of all his clothes and a dive between the sheets. 'Come to bed, leave your hair straight for once.'

'I shan't be long; five minutes,' Nellie said with considerable optimism. She sat down before the dressing-table; Stuart could see her reflection, the troubled expression on her small, much-loved face, her long white cotton nightgown with the frill round the neck which made her look like a choirboy – or a leg of pork. Stuart had teased her about it several times and now he snorted softly, *oink, oink!*, and saw her smile before reaching for her night-cream.

Stuart loved watching his Nell prepare for the night ahead with as much serious attention as though she would fall to pieces if she didn't follow her familiar routine. Smiling to himself, he watched as Nellie did all the daft, lovable things which women apparently thought necessary before succumbing to the lure of the sheets. She tied her smooth shining hair up in curl papers so that the ends would turn under when she undid them in the morning. She had had her hair cut fashionably short a year ago, much to Stuart's sorrow, and now had to curl it, whereas when it had been long she had just fixed it in various pretty, feminine styles

– a knot on top of her head, a bun at the back, a long roll – which had caused her far less trouble.

After she had done her hair she spread some sort of cream stuff all over her face, then wiped it carefully off again with a piece of cotton wool. Then she sluiced her face with clear, cool water and patted it dry. She rubbed cream into her hands and then pressed her cuticles back with an orange stick and filed her nails into smooth curves with an emery board.

In the little adjoining room baby Elizabeth slept. They had both checked that she was asleep, hanging over the cot and exchanging proud glances at the beauty of their sleeping daughter. She had Stuart's dark hair and eyes and Nellie's fair skin and sweet smile, and something else entirely her own, an innocent mischief which made both her parents her adoring slaves.

Now, having finished her preparations, Nellie stood up. She walked towards the bed, then hesitated as she always did.

'Was that the baby? I'll just make sure she's all right.'

'She's fine; fast asleep,' Stuart said to his wife's back. She did this every night as well. He supposed that she would still do it when Elizabeth was a woman, if she was living under their roof.

Nellie pushed the intervening door open with infinite care. Though they both agreed that Elizabeth was an angel, she could scream and yell like the devil incarnate when woken from a sound sleep. Nellie moved out of sight for a second, then returned, smiling.

'Sleeping like a baby,' she whispered, closing the door gently behind her. She hopped neatly into bed beside Stuart, leaned back on her pillows and reached for her book. Usually they both read for a while before turning the light out, but tonight Stuart did not even bother to take his own book off the bedside table; he guessed that Nellie wanted to talk.

Nellie opened her book. She glanced at the page, then put a finger in it to keep her place and turned to him. 'Stuart, there must be some way of getting in touch with Art! I mean, surely he wouldn't have signed on with a foreign ship? And anyway, ships dock sometimes . . . he must be in England occasionally. I wrote to my friend Beryl and she went round to the Corry and talked to Art's sister Etty, but they've none of 'em heard a word from Art since he left the bank. You don't think something awful's happened to him, do you?'

'No, of course not. But according to Lilac, sweetheart, he did have cause to believe she simply wasn't interested. She said Art proposed marriage and she sent him off with a flea in his ear. She admits she was pretty horrid, and to a man deep in love such behaviour is worse than just horrid. If you'd done something like that . . . deep despair takes some getting over, believe me.'

'I know,' Nellie said feelingly. 'When I thought you'd forgotten all about me . . .'

Stuart leaned over and kissed her smooth, faintly scented cheek.

'Silly puss, as if I could! But anyway, Art will get over it and come back here. Give him time.'

'But suppose Lilac goes and marries the wrong man?' Nellie wailed softly. 'I didn't care for that fellow she was going round with last Christmas, and the new one . . . well Polly says she seems to go for the type of men other women avoid, the dangerous ones who just want a good time.'

Stuart sighed. He was extremely fond of Lilac, he hated seeing her becoming hard-faced, chucking young men over on a whim, seeming more interested in their ability to pay for her fun than in any intrinsic worthiness of character.

'All right. We'll go up to Liverpool for a weekend soon,' he said comfortingly. 'You'll only be happy when you can talk to Lilac face to face; I do understand that. Shall we say the end of the month?'

'Oh Stu, you are kind to me,' Nellie said ecstatically. 'I'll feel so much happier if I can talk to our girl meself, instead of writing letters or trying to make sense over the telephone. Can we go Friday and come back Monday, mek a long weekend of it?'

'I'm sure we can manage that,' Stuart said. He took Nellie's book out of her hand and lay it down on the bedside table. 'Now you'll want to thank me properly, so we might as well turn out the lamp.'

Nellie doused the lamp and in the warm darkness turned to him. Stuart felt her soft arms entwine him, her soft lips seeking for his across his cheek. His heart began to beat faster and he untied the neck-string of the demure nightdress with fingers that trembled, and pulled it down over his wife's creamy shoulders.

'Nellie, Nellie, Nellie,' he murmured as she pressed close. 'Oh, what a lucky devil I am!'

Lilac got the letter saying that Nellie and Stuart were coming to the city for a long weekend just before she left for work one morning. She was delighted, excited, even a little apprehensive, for much though she longed to see them she knew she would have to come clean about a number of things which she hadn't fully explained in letters or over the telephone.

For a start, she no longer worked at the bag and sack factory. She had told Nellie about her new job of course, but not how she had come to get it. It had all come about when she had realised that she had lost touch completely with Art, that the O'Brien family neither knew nor cared where he was, that the authorities merely said his whereabouts were not known to them. Then the iron had entered Lilac's soul. She couldn't get Art out of her mind, she couldn't take other fellows seriously, so she decided the thing to do was to fill her life totally, to find as many men-friends as possible, and to wait.

Accordingly she had told Alan that she was not interested in seeing him again and had deliberately set out to meet the type of man who she felt could give her a good time without trying to tie her down to marriage or a permanent relationship. She went to modern dancing classes at the dancing academy on Edge Lane and became very proficient very quickly, for she was a natural dancer. She also made a new friend who was to show her how to escape from the drudgery of the factory into something far more amusing – something which also paid well, as she was soon to discover.

Her new friend, Charlotte Unwin, was in looks at least the exact opposite of Lilac. Her father, she said, was a Spaniard, her mother Irish, and this fiery combination had resulted in Charlotte having luxuriant black curls, olive-tinted skin and a figure as curvaceous and footsteps as light as any Irish fairy.

The two girls took to each other on sight. Perhaps it had something to do with the fact that Charlotte's young husband had disappeared with a chorus girl from a Cochran review at the Empire Theatre on Lime Street. She told Lilac bluntly that men were not to be trusted, but that didn't mean she was averse to netting another one.

'Only next time,' she told her new friend, 'I'll have more sense than to talk about love or forever; it'll be *what's in it for me?* next time.'

It was Charlotte's suggestion that the two of them might go into partnership and rent a room on a popular thoroughfare where they might teach seamen, as well as others, the intricacies of modern dancing.

'They need patience an' a pretty lass to give 'em confidence,' she said. 'Most of the dancing academies teach girls, but we'd specialise in fellers. We'll be Miss Charlotte an' Miss Lilac an' they'll be queuein' up jest to get in at the door.'

'Sailors? Queueing to learn to *dance*?' Lilac said derisively. 'They'll think we're teaching something very different, you mark my words, and I don't intend to have anything to do with *that* sort of thing.'

Charlotte flashed her Mediterranean smile, then rolled her eyes expressively.

'Oh aye, they may come in for the wrong reasons, queen, but they'll stay 'cos they can see the point o' larnin', if it gets 'em into the arms of girls like us.'

'What do you mean by arms?' Lilac said suspiciously. She had only known Charlotte a couple of months.

'I means jest what I say. Arms as in dancin', not whorin', if that's what you was thinkin'. Listen, are you on? Because in my considered opinion, the pair of us could make a tidy living if we rented the right sort of premises and found ourselves enough pupils. Only we'd have to mek it clear from the start that it was regular teachin' for older people, not for kids an' flappers. There's plenty caterin' for them already.'

'I'm on, for a bit at any rate,' Lilac decided. 'If it works . . . well, we'll see.'

It did work. And not only did they soon find themselves with more pupils than they could cope with so that they had to hire other girls to work for them, they also began to meet quite a different type of customer to the ones they had envisaged when Charlotte first got her bright idea.

And oddly enough, the dancing school really helped Lilac, if not to forget Art, at least to keep his loss from the forefront of her mind. And when she discussed it with Charlotte, her friend admitted that with so much to do and with success so close, she hardly ever woke in the night to weep for her absent husband.

As the school flourished, their fame as teachers of modern dance and as girls in whom beauty and character mingled began to spread. Respectable people, particularly older men, came to learn from them and after a few lessons, often asked one or other girl out to a theatre or restaurant.

Charlotte was choosy, Lilac more so, but they began to have an enviable social life, though there were always some people who raised their eyebrows. Then respectability, which had hovered doubtfully, arrived on their doorstep. At Lilac's insistence they opened the dancing school to young ladies as well as men.

'Never mind if they say it's a marriage bureau, so long as they come to our classes and pay our fees,' Lilac said decisively, when Charlotte complained that one particularly pretty girl had stolen a patron from under her nose. 'We're neither of us interested in permanence, not yet, so we shouldn't worry ourselves when the flappers are prepared to take on men who may interest us only briefly.'

'You're right,' Charlotte sighed. 'George Harris was rich, but he had two left feet and bad breath. Miss Nichols is welcome to him.'

The dancing school, successful though it was, did not keep both girls occupied during the day. Charlotte saw to the books, kept the rooms in good order and trained the staff, whilst Lilac took a job as receptionist at a big hotel, the Delamere, situated in a prime position on Tythebarn Street. She found the work congenial and not too hard. She was offered the job by the proprietress after she'd organised a display of modern dance in the Delamere's ballroom, and she accepted with some trepidation. Factory life had made her believe that she could do nothing else, but in fact the job of receptionist suited her very well. She sat behind a flower-decked desk looking immaculate and smiling a welcome, she did the books, learned to use a typewriter . . . and fought off amorous male customers so tactfully and with such success when she was on the late shift that the proprietress, a harsh-featured woman called Mabel Brierson, told her she was worth her weight in gold and would undoubtedly own and run her own hotel, some day.

So Lilac was beginning to have a very good idea of her own worth, and she did not intend to throw herself away on any handsome young sailor or poorly paid clerk. If it had been Art it would have been different; even thinking about him still gave her a warm and breathless glow, but she was beginning to wonder if her old friend would ever show his face in Liverpool again. Certainly he had never visited The Waterfront Academy of Modern Dance, Props Miss Lilac and Miss Charlotte.

But the letter from Nell put her in a spin.

Her sister knew all about the job as receptionist,

knew that Lilac taught dancing in the evenings, but had no idea what a very successful venture the dancing school was, nor how convenient a place for meeting men with money and time on their hands. And if Nellie had known she would not have approved; Lilac knew that five years ago she herself would have been horrified at the mere suggestion of deliberately setting out to meet fellows, but now it was different. A factory girl only met clerks and deck-hands. A receptionist might never click with a customer. But a dancing teacher . . . ah, that was a different kettle of fish altogether. She and Charlotte had made up their minds to marry for money if they could not marry for love, and because of the school at least they had the choice. Men of all shapes and sizes, men from every walk of life, crossed their paths and were closely scrutinized with a view to matrimony.

'Not that I'd dream of marrying whilst there's a chance that Art and I might make up,' Lilac admitted wistfully. 'Besides, I do enjoy life; I'd rather not marry at all than pick the wrong man.'

'I'm not marryin' again yet, either,' Charlotte confirmed. 'We're mekin' money, and having a lot of fun at the same time. But later, when we're gettin' really old – say when we're twenty-six or twenty-eight – then we'll mebbe need a rich feller!'

'By that time it'll be too late,' Lilac said, chuckling. But Charlotte, though she laughed too, said Lilac knew very well what she meant – and Lilac acknowledged it. One day they would get tired of dancing with every Tom, Dick and Harry, tired of having their feet trodden on and their dresses tugged off their shoulders, tired of theatres, cinemas and restaurants, even. Perhaps they'd get tired of waiting for the men in their lives, too, for whatever Charlotte might pretend, Lilac knew very well that her friend was always scanning the crowded room with the same wistful thought that haunted Lilac herself: will he come? Will he be here, tonight?

'My sister and her family are coming to see me tomorrow and staying till Monday, so I shan't be teaching,' Lilac reminded Charlotte on Thursday evening. 'Mrs Brierson's given me time off . . . we'll have fun, the four of us.'

She knew Nellie would ask awkward questions and Stuart would eye her shrewdly and listen to local gossip and perhaps even put two and two together and make four, but she would still have fun because she loved them all so much, the young Gallaghers. Besides, she was hostess and she loved entertaining. She had moved out of Lord Nelson Street and into a flat on Mount Pleasant when she got the hotel job, and as soon as she had read Nellie's letter she made her plans for the weekend. She would sleep on the couch in her living room so that Nellie, Stu and little Elizabeth might have her bedroom. She had planned meals, entertainment, cosy sessions round the fire in the evening whilst baby Elizabeth slumbered in the next room. It was November, the days shortening, and the weather had passed through every possible phase in a couple of weeks. Rain had fallen, and sleet; they had enjoyed a couple of days of brilliant sunshine; fog, always prevalent in a city so close to a river estuary, had blacked them out for three solid days, and even now, after a pleasant enough afternoon, there was a decided nip in the air as soon as darkness fell – a good excuse for a fire, roast chestnuts, and bread toasted on a fork held out to the flames.

Friday arrived at last. Lilac was at the station fifteen minutes early, with a beautiful teddy bear for Elizabeth and a heart full of affection for Nellie and Stuart. They got off the train, tired, pale, even a little confused, with a very large suitcase and the baby clutching Stuart's shoulder and wailing, and found themselves whisked off in a taxi and welcomed to Lilac's shining flat with a meal in the oven keeping warm and a bottle of wine standing in the sink, keeping cool.

'You're living in style, queen,' Nellie said, sounding pleased yet puzzled. 'My goodness . . . wine!'

'I've a good job and a good boss. The wine came from Mrs Brierson, with her compliments,' Lilac explained. 'What does little Elizabeth eat, Nell? I've done a casserole of beef with suet dumplings for us, it's nice and warming on a chilly evening – but I was at a loss what she would like.'

'She's a young lady now she's had her first birthday, and will have a tiny bit of the stew with some bread and butter,' Nellie said. 'Dearest Li, do you mind if I go through and change her into her night-things and clean her up? She's fractious now, and cross, but once she's clean and fed she'll be a different person – and so will I, because there's nothing so tiring as a grizzling child.'

'You carry on. Stu will help me to dish up and lay the table. We can gossip whilst we work,' Lilac said. As soon as Nellie had bustled from the room with the baby in her arms she turned to her brother-in-law. 'Sit down Stu, this minute. When I need your help I'll tell you what to do.'

'That's nice, because I'm extremely tired,' Stuart said, sinking into Lilac's rocking chair. 'What a pleasant room, my dear, and how cosy you've made it. Let me do something soothing, like boiling a small pan of milk with a little sugar in it for Elizabeth's drink, and we'll talk. I don't mind telling you Nell's been in a real state about you. She thinks you've got too many fellers and you change them too often. She doesn't believe you're really happy. In short, chuck, she still has hopes of you and Art.'

Lilac, pulling a pan of potatoes over the heat, looked thoughtful.

'Nellie always did know me better than I knew meself,' she said. 'I've tried and tried to contact Art though, Stu, and there's no way. Nell is right, I do go out with a great many young men, but there's safety in numbers, they say. This way I can wait for Art without being bored and dull. And I sometimes think I'll wait for ever, rather than give even the thought of him up. If *only* he'd left some sort of address with someone, so I could write. But he's bound to turn up here some day – isn't he?'

'I think so. Us Liverpudlians are queer folk, queen. We're attached to this dirty old city by a strong cord and it tugs us back eventually no matter how far we roam. Look at Nell, she's got a nice home – well, you've seen it – and a lot of friends, yet she can't wait to come back here. Any excuse and she's planning a quick visit. I reckon I can keep her down south for another two years and then it's bring her back or see her seriously unhappy. And I wouldn't want that.'

'What about you, Stuart? You were born and bred here, same as Nell and me. How do you feel?'

Stuart had boiled his little pan of sweetened milk. As Lilac watched he poured it into a mug with a spout and began to run it under the cold tap. 'Cooling her majesty's booze; she can't cope with drinks unless they're blood heat,' he explained. 'Me? I'm the same, love. Just the same. I can't wait to get back.'

*

The weekend flew by, of course. Nellie and Stuart proved to be extremely understanding about the dancing school and were very impressed when Lilac took them round on Saturday evening when the classes were in full swing.

'Your partner can Charleston up a storm,' Stuart said admiringly as Charlotte, long beads swinging, headband low on her dark brow, proceeded to make the wild, wiggly dance look both easy and exciting. 'You have some very superior pupils, Lilac love — that's a First Officer off a liner over there, still in uniform!'

'Who pays the band? They must cost you the earth!' Nellie exclaimed, but Lilac was able to reassure her.

'They don't cost a lot because there's so much unemployment in the Pool. They're all unemployed during the day and they make a bit at night by playing for places like this. They're rather good though, don't you think?'

'Awful good,' Nellie said. 'The trumpeter keeps smiling at you, Li. He seems a nice young man.'

'Oh, that's Spudsy Bishop. I was at school with him . . . well, I wasn't actually since he was at St Ant's, but I knew him pretty well. He was in Art's class, in fact.'

'Oh. Does he . . . do you . . . ?'

Lilac laughed.

'No he doesn't and we don't! I've no time, Nell, and precious little inclination to tell you the truth. I'm . . . I'm still waiting for . . . for . . .'

'Good,' Nellie said, nodding her head decisively. 'You're right to do so. He'll come back, I'm sure of it.'

Lilac took the Gallaghers to the hotel of course, and

the staff were charmed by Elizabeth and pronounced Nellie and Stuart a very pleasant young couple. Mrs Brierson insisted on entertaining them to coffee and biscuits in her suite of private rooms and told Nellie that she valued Lilac very highly.

It was what Nellie most wanted to hear. And when Stuart tactfully took Lilac for a walk whilst Nellie saw to the baby, his first remark was a promise that Nellie should not hear what he was about to say.

'That sounds bad,' Lilac said rather apprehensively. Stuart had gone off visiting friends a couple of times, leaving the girls in the flat together. Newspapermen being the way they were, Lilac guessed that Stuart might have enquired about The Waterfront Academy of Modern Dance and its proprietresses, Miss Lilac and Miss Charlotte.

'I wouldn't say it was bad, chuck, but you must be careful. A feller told me that when you started the dancing school it was widely believed you were running quite a different business from what you advertised – get me?'

'Yes. I *told* Charlotte that would happen but she said so long as the fellers came and saw for themselves, it wouldn't matter. And it hasn't mattered, not really. We're very respectable now.'

'Oh aye, now you are, so I won't reproach you – but you wouldn't want Art hearing rumours about you and perhaps believing them, would you?'

'My God . . . you don't think . . . is *that* why . . .'

Stuart laughed and squeezed her arm reassuringly.

'No, I'm sure it isn't. But two young girls running a business have to be whiter than white, chuck. When you start your own hotel, and Mrs Brierson seems to think you will one day, then your reputation must be above reproach. So bear it in mind, eh?'

'I will,' Lilac said fervently. 'And I'm ever so grateful to you for not saying anything to Nell, because she'd be upset and there was nothing like that, I promise you.'

'You don't have to promise me; I know it. Come on, better turn round and go back to the flat or Nellie will wonder what we've been discussing for so long.'

On the Monday, Nellie and Stuart went the rounds saying goodbye, telling everyone it wouldn't be long before they came home, promising to write. Their train left at noon, so Lilac offered to take Elizabeth out for a walk whilst her parents packed and Nellie was delighted to have the child taken care of whilst she and Stuart were busy.

It was a very cold morning. Elizabeth was warmly wrapped up in a bright red coat and hat, with sturdy shoes on her tiny feet when she set off with her aunt. But she couldn't walk far, and since she had greeted Lilac's suggestion of going down to the docks with great enthusiasm, Lilac ended up carrying her most of the way.

Elizabeth loved the shipping. Down to the pierhead the two of them trundled, then along the docks, Elizabeth now walking, now riding triumphantly in her aunt's arms. She still wasn't talking much, though she could mum-mum and dada-dada with the best, but she could wave, and smile, and crow with delight and she did a great deal of it as Lilac pointed out the big ships, the water, the bustling people on deck.

They reached the deep-water berth where a big liner was about to sail and stood watching the preparations for a bit. Elizabeth jumped up and down, sat on her well-padded bottom, allowed Lilac to lift her up onto her shoulders the better to see what all the noise and bustle was about.

Just before the liner steamed out, Stuart joined them. He took the baby from Lilac and the three of them waved enthusiastically to the crowds on deck, most of whom waved good-naturedly back.

'Wasn't that fun, queen?' Stuart said to Elizabeth as they turned away to return to the flat. 'Now let's hope you've been so active that you'll sleep all the way to Balham!'

Art saw them. He had prowled the city, waited outside the bag and sack factory, even visited the house in Lord Nelson Street where Lilac had lodged, and gone round to 39 Penny Lane. He had had no luck, but then he didn't rightly know if he wanted any luck. He wanted to see her yet he dreaded it – rightly, as it turned out.

He had signed on as assistant purser again, but this time on a much smaller liner, one that crossed the Atlantic less with party-going in mind than business trips. He had been working hard ever since the passengers began to come on board and stopped for a moment when the flow slackened, went over to the porthole in his crowded office for a breath of fresh air.

She was there, within thirty feet of him, her beautiful hair tugged loose by the wind and by the baby in her arms, looking up at the ship as she began to steam out of her berth, waving, smiling.

He stood as if turned to stone. He could only stare, whilst all the unacknowledged, subconscious hopes he'd nursed for the past year crumbled to dust.

They were getting smaller, smaller ... Lilac just

a tiny figurine, the babe a dot in her arms ... and then a man approached them. He took the baby, held it comfortably in one arm, put the other gently round Lilac's waist for a moment. Then the three of them waved and waved ...

'Mr O'Brien, if you've nothing better to do, perhaps you could give me a hand with these figures?'

Art turned away from the scene. There were tears in his eyes, tear-tracks down his cheeks. He rubbed at his face fiercely, trying to calm himself, but the purser, who had reminded him of his duty, was looking down at the pages on the desk.

'Sorry, sir,' Art said huskily. 'Saw someone I thought I knew. Pass the stuff over, I'll get on with it now.'

Chapter Nine

The year that Kitty was fourteen, Maldwyn bought her a proper dress. Before, she'd scrimped and saved out of her egg money or any bit of cash she was paid for anything and kept herself in working clothes, but this time Maldwyn said she should have the dress and Johnny, looking at her critically as they washed up after their meal, agreed.

'You've growed out o' everything you've got, Kit,' he said. 'Kecks is fine for workin' in, but you want a decent dress for market days an' that.'

'I can buy a skirt,' Kitty protested. She looked down at herself and noticed, for the first time, how much leg stuck out at the ends of her trousers and how much wrist from the ends of her shirt-sleeves. 'Anyway, I've gorra skirt, come to think. Won't that do?'

'It iss not good enough for what I've got in mind, lass,' Maldwyn said. 'Look, Johnny'll tell ye.'

He limped off, a huge man, shy as a girl and as gentle as one, too.

Kitty turned to Johnny. 'What's 'e mean? What's 'e gorrin mind, Johnny?'

'It's the farm,' Johnny said slowly. 'Maldwyn wants us to 'ave it when 'e's dead an' gone. You an' me, Kit. I said we didn't expect nothin', that we'd no right, but 'e said we'd earned it. Better'n that nephew of 'is, 'e said, cos Elwyn Ap Thomas don't know one end of a pitchfork from t'other. Elwyn's goin' to be a

'countant, Maldwyn says. Mal 'asn't got no time for
'countants.'

'That's true,' Kitty agreed. 'Cor, fancy 'im wantin'
to leave the farm to us, Johnny! But they won't let 'im,
eh?'

'Mal says they will. Says 'e'll tie it up all legal an'
sign things wi' a lawyer. Wants it to 'old water 'gin
any court in the land.'

'Oh. But the dress . . .'

'We'll 'ave to go up to Corwen wi' Mal, an' see the
lawyer,' Johnny said patiently. 'Mal says we've gorra
look real respeckable, else the lawyer will think 'e's
off 'is chump.'

'Oh, I do understand, then,' Kitty said thankfully.
'But there's no 'urry, is there? Mal's got over 'is bad
foot a treat, 'asn't 'e?'

'Yeah, but . . . 'ow old d'you think he is, Kit?
Maldwyn, I means.'

Kitty frowned. To her an adult was an adult, unless
he was bald or had snow-white locks. Maldwyn's
grizzled hair was still more dark than grey and his
weatherbeaten visage looked just like everyone's face
round here.

'Umm . . . thirty?' she volunteered at last, seeing that Johnny honestly wanted to know what she
thought and didn't intend to give her a clue.

Johnny shook his head.

'Nope. Older'n that.'

'Oh. Forty . . . no, say fifty.'

'Older'n that.'

'He ain't never sixty!' Kitty said in an awed voice.
That was a ripe old age, that was, and Maldwyn got
about just as well as she and Johnny would if they
had a bad foot.

'The truth is, queen, 'e's seventy-two. That's what

'e told me an' Mal never lies, it's one of 'is things.'

'Seventy-two!' Kitty whistled. 'No wonder 'e wants to mek 'is will, then!'

'Yeah. So you let 'im buy you the dress, an' we can get it all sorted out.'

'All right. I'd like a dress,' Kitty said thoughtfully. 'But give us the farm . . . they'll never let 'im, Johnny.'

Maldwyn took them to a lawyer in Corwen, but left the two youngsters in the outer office whilst he and Mr Brindley Travers talked. There were a few magazines on a table in the outer office so Johnny and Kitty amused themselves by reading, but presently Maldwyn came out again and gestured to them to follow him down the stairs and back into the street.

'English, he is,' he said in a low voice, jerking a thumb towards the door from which they had just emerged. 'Not a nice person, I'm thinking. We'll catch a bus to Wrexham.'

'Where's Wrexham?' Johnny asked as they clattered along the pavement, all three of them in their best boots. 'What did 'e say, Mal?'

'Seemed to think I wass running mad to leave the farm away from family, though as I said, families stick together in times of trial and hardship, they don't go their own ways like that Elwyn has. So I thought, get going Maldwyn or this feller will 'ave the pants off you, and not a word of Welsh to 'is name either! Wouldn't trust 'im with a bundle of hay, let alone my farm. We're lucky though, there's a bus in ten minutes to take us to town.'

'So why Wrexham?' Kitty said as they reached the omnibus stop. 'Do you know anyone there?'

'I do. Man wi' an office on Charles Street, not far

from the hotel . . . the Wynnstay Arms. Feller named Hywel Hughes. A friend, like. Trust him wi' me life, I would.'

'Oh, then that's all right,' Johnny said cheerfully as the vehicle they wanted came trundling up the street towards them. 'Wouldn't like to t'ink I'd put on me best kecks for some English bugger what 'ud cheat 'is own gran'mother!'

Maldwyn chuckled and pushed Kitty ahead of him on to the omnibus step.

'You'll like Hywel,' he assured them. 'Trust 'im wi' me life I would.'

Kitty was collecting eggs. She knew most of the places the hens laid, and in summer, when the hens laid more eggs than they could use, she took them to Corwen Market and sold them to the townsfolk along with butter, cream and a few vegetables or a couple of past-lay hens. Today being market day, she would go into town in the trap with the brown pony, Tilly, between the shafts. Once, Maldwyn or Johnny had always accompanied her when she went to sell, but not any more. She had grown tall on the good farm food and though she was slim she was also tough and capable. She could put up her small stall herself, and sell her goods, and if anyone tried to molest her or take her money it would be the worse for them. Patch always went with her and Patch could give a troublemaker a nasty nip on the ankles if nothing worse.

Besides, Kitty thought, laying the big brown eggs tenderly in her basket, it wasn't as if there ever was trouble at Corwen. Most of the farmers and their wives knew her and although they still tended to speak in Welsh amongst themselves they often included her in their conversations, especially now that she was beginning to be fluent in Welsh. Indeed, often she spoke the language instinctively; Maldwyn spoke Welsh as his first language and she had picked it up almost without noticing, suddenly realising that she understood and could answer in the same tongue.

From the byre, she could hear Johnny whistling. They had milked the cows earlier and Johnny was mucking out whilst she collected the eggs. Maldwyn would be getting breakfast – they took it in turns – and as soon as they'd eaten she would go out to the field, bring the pony in and harness her up to the trap. Maldwyn and Johnny would do all the work about the farm today, including her share, whilst she sold their eggs, chickens, butter and vegetables. Last night she and Johnny had collected the string beans. They had had a good summer and the beans hung thick and heavy, far more than they could eat or salt down. Maldwyn had pulled a basketful of carrots for her, too, and had washed them under the pump. Carrots sold better all bright and clean, though they didn't keep so long – but townsfolk didn't seem to care about things like that.

The little black hen with the torn comb usually laid right at the end of the orchard, so Kitty went that way, pushing through the long, dew-wet grass and singing to herself. September was a good month, and October wasn't bad either – she would have a great many apples to pick and bottle, and store away in the apple loft. At the bottom of the orchard there was a thick old hawthorn hedge, less to keep stock out than to protect the apple trees from the winds of winter, and it was here that the little hen scraped herself a scrappy, twiggy nest and laid her clutches of eggs.

Kitty leaned into the hedge and felt about. Her fingers closed round the eggs ... two, three, four ... and she backed out again, bringing three eggs with her. She would leave one for the little hen, so that she laid there again rather than wandering off and forcing Kitty to wander after her.

It was a bright morning; Kitty crossed the orchard, stopping by a particularly fine bush apple. She tested the fruit, but they still weren't ripe. Nevertheless she picked one and bit; sharp juice flooded her mouth and the crispness of the green-tinted flesh was good. She ate the apple, flung the core into the long grass and then went back to the house. She went into the kitchen and carried the basket carefully over to the low stone sink. Most of the eggs were clean and smooth, but one had chicken-dung all over it. Maldwyn, easing fried eggs out of the pan, grinned at her as she wiped the dirty egg clean.

'Ever made bramble jelly?' he asked. 'I thought we'd go after blackberries tomorrow, then you can sell bramble jelly when we need all the eggs the 'ens lay.'

'I made blackberry and apple last year, but it didn't go too well,' Kitty said, putting the cleaned egg back in the basket with its fellows. 'Do they prefer jelly, then?'

'Yess indeed; no pips, see? If you've false teeth a reg'lar nuisance are berry pips. We could tek our tea with us, go over the 'ills a ways.'

Kitty, agreeing, smiled to herself. Seventy-three Maldwyn might now be, but he was a child in some things. He adored picnics, always insisted on food being carried out to the hayfields in early summer, and later to the harvest fields. And he still didn't seem more than forty or forty-five to her as he limped about the farm, doing his work.

Thinking about his age made her remember the great will-making which had taken place in the market town of Wrexham about a year ago. Maldwyn had been right, they had all taken a liking to Hywel Hughes, a tiny fat gnome of a man, cherry-cheeked and cheerful, who had drawn up the will and had it witnessed by two passers-by. One witness was a soldier, home on leave from the army, the other a bright-faced lad from one of the hill farms at the back of the town. Maldwyn had insisted that strangers should be witnesses because he didn't want his nephew being told before time about the will.

'We don't want no trouble,' he had said gruffly. 'Try and persuade me to change my mind, Elwyn would . . . greedy for money, see? No love of the land, no fondness for me, but greedy. Once the deed's done, though, and I'm gone . . .'

'We'll 'ave trouble, I'll stake me 'at on it,' Kitty had said privately to Johnny later that same day. 'That old Elwyn, 'e won't lerrit rest, 'e'll come naggin' at us.'

Johnny shrugged.

'Don't matter,' he said laconically. 'A will's a will, see? A legal docyment what you can't overturn, that's a will.'

But right now the pony must be put in the trap, the trap must be loaded, and she must be off. Kitty loved market days, and was delighted when Johnny brought the pony and trap into the yard, all tacked up and ready to go. Johnny was grand, she thought affectionately. He did everything he could to make her life easier. At just seventeen he was tall and gangly, stronger than he looked but still with the boyish grin and the twinkle which had taken her fancy so strongly when they had first met.

'Ready, Kit? Put them eggs aboard, an' the beans, an' you're ready for the off. 'Ave you 'ad your breakfast yet?'

'Not yet. I'll gerrit down me quick, though.'

They ate breakfast, enjoying every mouthful. The tea was a bit weak; Maldwyn said they were almost out of tea and Kitty must be sure to buy some before she left Corwen. Just as she was about to swing herself up into the driving seat of the trap he pressed some money into her hand.

'Buy yourself a bite o' dinner,' he whispered. 'Don't go 'ungry till you gets 'ome, Kitty lass.'

Kitty took the money and gave him a hug.

'You're a prince, Mal,' she said. 'Oh, we does love you, Johnny an' me! I won't knit you another muffler – can't say fairer than that, eh?'

Maldwyn laughed and rumpled her hair. That first winter he had uncomplainingly worn the uneven, holey muffler which Kitty had painfully knitted for him, only admitting how useless it was when she had spent her egg money on a beautifully thick one, on sale at a local clothing emporium. Since then, mufflers had been a joke between them.

'You can make me some bramble jelly, instead,' he called as she swung herself into the driving seat. 'Awful fond o' bramble jelly I am!'

Soon, Kitty and the little brown pony were jogging along the road, heading for the town. She could see over most of the hedges from her lofty perch and was struck, as so often before, by the beauty of her surroundings. To her left the high hills were ablaze with the rich purple of heather and the richer gold of the gorse. The trees were still in full and glorious leaf and when the road crossed a small stone bridge the stream beneath it reflected the innocent blue of a cloudless sky. It was hard to look back down the years – gawd, it was fully three years since she had run away from Paradise Court – and remember her life in those far-off days, the grim, grey hopelessness of it. It was almost impossible to realise that only fifty or sixty miles away – she was still vague over distances – people lived in conditions which she now considered a hell on earth, not even loving one another or taking care of the children of their bodies, but resenting them, beating them, sometimes, she knew, killing them. She often wondered what her mother had made of her sudden flight, whether anyone had searched for her, but had concluded that it scarcely mattered. If her mother had informed the police, the search had never extended to Corwen, or indeed to North Wales. After all, she had never pretended to be anyone other than Kitty Drinkwater and the name had never raised an eyebrow down here.

The road curved round to the left and Tilly followed it, her hoofbeats muffled by the soft road-dust. Presently, however, they met the cobbles of the town and Tilly slowed her brisk trot to a walk. The little grey town was beginning to fill up already, some stalls were set up, others in the process of erection. Kitty made her way to the market yard and tied Tilly to a tethering post. She watered her with a handy bucket, fed her a couple of apples and then began to carry her goods to her table, next to Mrs Dewi Jones's fancier stall.

Customers wandered along, poking, measuring. They exchanged jokes, gossiped, tasted butter or a piece of broken biscuit. Kitty sold a dozen eggs to a woman in an old-fashioned black cloak who asked kindly after Maldwyn and said she'd call one of these fine days and had Kitty seen the travelling fishmonger this morning?

The day jogged on its familiar course. Kitty bargained briskly, laughed a lot, swapped a bag of her string beans for a pot of heather honey. The sun rose in the sky and wasps buzzed round Mrs Dewi and had to be repulsed. They were after Mrs Dewi's plums, her big early Victorias, so Kitty swatted wasps with a folded newspaper and bought some of the plums as a treat for Maldwyn – he only grew the small purple ones – and planned plum jam, or perhaps a plum pie.

The minister came up to her stall and congratulated her on her butter. 'Best in Corwen,' he joked. 'Well, not bad for a stranger, eh, Mrs Ellis-Wynn?'

'Oh, I wouldn't call her a stranger, Reverend,' Mrs Ellis-Wynn said. 'Speaks the Welsh like a native she do.'

And Kitty smiled and sold the last of her eggs and was totally, blissfully happy.

It was growing dusk when Kitty reined up in front of the farmhouse again. Lights twinkled warmly from the kitchen. She could hear the murmur of voices, see movement through the thin checked curtains. She climbed down a trifle wearily, the heavy bag with the money in it clutched in one hand. They would be very pleased, Mal and Johnny, she had done better than ever before, sold out! She knew she should get Tilly out of the trap and rub her down before she did anything else, but she always let the men know she was home. No sense in not doing that; it meant Johnny would come out and help her and Maldwyn would begin to dish up. She had eaten a beef and mustard sandwich and drunk a pint of buttermilk earlier, but that had been hours ago and right now she was starving hungry again.

She looped Tilly's harness round the tethering post and pushed open the back door.

Johnny was sitting by the fireplace. He looked up, startled, when she entered the room. He was white as a sheet and looked ill.

'Johnny? What's wrong? What's happened?'

She knew something was wrong, the whole room reeked of it.

'Oh, Kit . . . come and sit down.'

Johnny was on his feet, coming across to her, concern on his face, his eyes red and swollen. Kitty stepped back.

'Maldwyn? Where's Mal? Why isn't he here?'

But she knew. Knew as soon as she saw Johnny's red eyes and the pallor of him, the stricken expression on his face.

'Oh Kitty, love, Mal's gone. It were a stroke, the doctor said. Not long after you left, queen. Mal's dead.'

After that, everything happened in a sort of fog. The minister came and he, the doctor and Johnny arranged the funeral. The work went on. Patch slunk round the house close on Kitty's heels; they heard her whining in her kennel after they'd gone to bed, so Kitty went down and fetched Patch up to her room. She and the dog curled up on the bed and comforted one another in their loss.

Neighbours came. Maldwyn had been well liked, loved even, for his generosity, his strength which he would lend to any in need, his strong, abiding faith. Everyone offered help to the children but Johnny and

Kitty knew that what they needed was hard work, to get them over this dreadful, sad time.

'I know 'e was old,' Kitty said to Johnny after the funeral and the funeral tea were over. 'I know 'e was jest an ordinary bloke, in a way. But we did love 'im, didn't we, Johnny?'

' 'Course we did; an' 'e loved us,' Johnny said gruffly. 'Mal loved everyone, wanted the best for everyone. Now 'e's gone we gorra do the best we can for ourselves an' the farm.'

There was no word from the relatives, but Johnny got the will out anyway. He and Kitty read it anxiously and agreed that it was clear as a bell; they had the farm.

Then a week after the funeral they had visitors. Kitty and Johnny were sitting by the fire, having eaten a quick meal. They were both very tired, for even with his lameness to contend with, Maldwyn had always done his share and more of the farm and house work.

Kitty got up and went over to the door as soon as the knock sounded. She thought it was a neighbour, popping in to see how they were getting on, but it was not. It was Elwyn Ap Thomas, his wife and his lawyer, Mr Brindley Travers.

They did not wait to be asked in but entered as of right and seated themselves by the fire even whilst Kitty, thoroughly discomposed, was stammering out an invitation to them to sit down.

'Mr Maldwyn Evans came to me to make a will,' Mr Travers said, very dry and precise and cutting across Kitty's words without compunction. 'But he made no will because I persuaded him that it was not in his family's best interests. Since, therefore, Mr Evans died intestate, or without making a will,' he added the last bit with a malevolent glance at the two young people, staring at him, 'the estate and all his possessions go to his next of kin, Mr Elwyn Iawn Ap Thomas, my client. And this means that you young people are guilty of trespass.'

'There is a will,' Johnny said quietly. 'Mr Evans didn't like your attitude, Mr Travers; he didn't trust you, either. So we went to Wrexham, where Mr Evans made his will at the office of another lawyer, a Mr Hywel Hughes, where it was duly signed and witnessed. I have the will here if you would like to see it.'

Kitty had never heard Johnny talk without his Liverpool twang before. She stared at him, astonished, as he turned away and began to fumble in the dresser drawer. Fancy Johnny talking like a toff!

Johnny found the will and held it out to Mr Travers. The lawyer snatched it, read it, handed it to his client, who read it also. Then Elwyn Ap Thomas made as if to hand it to Johnny – and instead, with an exclamation of impatience, threw the document straight into the heart of the red-hot stove.

'A tissue of lies; a forgery,' he said shrilly. 'The fire's the best place for it! Now I repeat what my legal adviser has told you; you are trespassing. We will give you one hour to get out of this house and renounce all claims to it. If you refuse to go, Mr Travers and I intend to call the police.'

His words went unheeded, for the moment at any rate. Before Kitty realised what he intended, Johnny had dived at the fire, shoving his arm into the red-hot heart of it. As he did so he gave a cry of sheer agony . . . and even as Kitty dived on him to drag him away, Elwyn ran over to him and actually tried to wedge his skinny bottom against the boy so that Johnny was forced deeper into the fire.

'Let him burn if that's what he wants!' he shouted. 'He's a liar and a thief – liars and thieves should burn!'

But Patch soon put paid to that. She snarled once and flew for Elwyn. As Kitty dragged Johnny, screaming, away from the fire, Elwyn began to scream in his turn – Patch was attached to his leg. Kitty saw the white teeth begin to redden round the edges and felt only an enormous satisfaction, a dreadful, deep hatred.

Mrs Ap Thomas was crying, stammering something, the lawyer was contenting himself with threats. Kitty got Johnny to the sink and began to pump cold water over his arm: she had heard Maldwyn say it was how he had treated his burns when he'd fallen back and sat, for a moment, on top of the stove.

'Shoved my bum into a bucket of cold water I did,' he had told her. 'Maybe not what a doctor would do, but it worked a treat, lass! Better I did feel in no time, no time at all.'

But Johnny's burns were bad, really bad. Kitty took a look and shuddered. She wouldn't let him take his arm out from under the constant stream, then suddenly he was pulled away from her. Elwyn, his face contorted, was dragging at the boy's shoulder.

'Out I said and out I meant!' he shouted. 'Out of my house and off of my farm or I'll have the police on you!'

Patch was whimpering. Kitty looked and saw that the dog was holding up a crushed paw; blood dripped slowly from it. Kitty looked round for a weapon and found the big iron frying pan. She pounced on it and backed towards the door, swinging the pan in front of her. Johnny, half-fainting, lay slumped against the sink. Patch, whimpering still, limped painfully over to her on three legs, showing her teeth at Elwyn as she passed him. He must have stamped on the dog's paw, Kitty thought, wincingly. But there wasn't much one girl could do against two determined men and a woman who was prepared to allow them to behave the way they had. She could only do her best to get them all out of here without further injury.

'Get back!' she hissed at the two men, swinging the pan. 'I'll send the pair of yez to kingdom come if you try one more dirty trick! We're goin' for now, but we'll be back . . . because this is *our* place, not yours, willed to us all legal. And we won't forget what you done tonight!'

She backed up to the door, opened it, felt the cool night air surge into the room. She dropped the pan, took Johnny's weight on her shoulder, felt Patch pressing close to her legs . . . and they were in the yard, the door of the farm slammed behind them, alone in the dark with a drizzling rain falling and puddles at their feet.

She thought of the haystack at once, of course, and the byre, the apple loft. But she was afraid. If she lay down, if she let Johnny and Patch lie down, God knew what the Thomases might do. Fire the barn or the stack? It seemed highly probable in view of what Elwyn had already done. She could hear from Johnny's sobbing breath that he was scarcely conscious of what was happening. His pain had taken over; all he could think of were the deep burns on his right arm.

'Johnny, love, you've got to reach the stable,' Kitty said urgently in his ear. 'Come with me . . . one foot at a time.'

It took ages, hours it seemed, but she got him to Tilly's stable and slumped him across the pony's back. She could do nothing about Patch's paw right now, but the dog would follow. If they could just get as far as the Jones's farm . . .

It was two miles. Two long miles. Johnny moaned all the way, she spoke to him but he could not answer, he was in some world where pain and darkness held sway. Patch whimpered and fell back, Kitty and Tilly waited, and the dog caught up.

But they made it. They reached the farm. Kitty knocked and the dogs all barked but no one came to the door. It was probably well past midnight, Kitty supposed, so you could scarcely blame them. And anyway, all they wanted was to be kept safe from the Ap Thomases for the time being. A stable would do. A pigsty even.

Kitty got Tilly into a stable and slid Johnny off into the hay. Then she lay down beside him. He was shivering uncontrollably and still moaning, choking on sobs. She put her arms round him and Patch, still whimpering, curled up close. It must have been an hour before Kitty slept, and her sleep was shallow and deeply troubled. And she, who had been so brave and resourceful awake, wept in her dreams.

Morning brought Eifion, the son of the house. He came into the barn, whistling, and stopped short.

'Duw, what the 'ell . . . ?'

'If your Da heard you, you'd cop it,' Kitty said, struggling into wakefulness. 'Eifion, bach, we're in trouble. Patch 'as got a crushed paw and Johnny's burned real bad. Tek a look.'

He looked, shuddered.

'How did 'e do that?' he whispered. 'Burnt near to the bone 'e is. Why aren't you at the farm? Was it robbers?'

Kitty told him. She told him everything. About the will which Elwyn had burned, about the lawyer lying to them, about Elwyn trying to push Johnny deeper into the fire, and deliberately crushing Patch's paw with his heavy shoes.

'Here, better see Mam,' Eifion said, white-faced. 'What wickedness indeed . . . I know nothing about the farm, but what wickedness to burn a will and try to burn your Johnny.'

'Could you fetch somethin' to carry Johnny on?' Kitty said. 'He's awful badly, I doubt 'e could walk.'

But before Eifion could do anything Johnny woke, groaned, pulled a face and got to his knees, then lurched to his feet.

'Gi's an 'and, there's a good feller,' he panted. 'Gawd, me arm's fair killin' me; what 'appened? What did them people want?'

'Never mind that,' Kitty said, shaking her head at Eifion, who had opened his mouth to remind Johnny of the previous night. 'Can you get to the kitchen? Eifion's mam will see to you.'

They got Johnny indoors. Mrs Jones was horrified over his arm, ran for a soothing lotion, for bandages to keep the air off. But Kitty, mindful of Maldwyn's home-remedy, said that she rather thought Johnny would be better to keep his arm as cold as possible because that was what Mal had advised for burns.

'Oh? Yes, I remember Maldwyn saying . . . and deep though they are, they've not yet blistered,' Mrs Jones said. 'Run water, Eifion!'

Eifion ran water and Johnny immersed his arm in

it. He sighed with relief. 'It feels easier,' he declared. 'What's Patch done to 'er foot?'

Mrs Jones looked at the dog's paw, then settled Johnny in a comfortable chair with the basin of water on a table beside him and knelt to Patch.

'Nasty, but it'll mend,' she said at last. 'Fetch me some disinfectant, Eifion, and then fetch your da; milking he is, but he'll come when you tell him there's trouble.'

When the story had been told in gory detail to Mr Jones he looked worried and upset.

'That such wickedness can happen – such evil,' he said. 'It sickens me to my stomach. But what to do? The will's gone, you say? Quite burned up?'

'I tried to get it out,' Johnny said defensively. His face went sickly greenish at the memory of that dreadful moment. 'But the fire was blazin' in the range, I didn't 'ave a chanst.'

'And who else knows about this will?'

'Mr Hywel Hughes, of Charles Street, Wrexham,' Johnny said promptly. 'He drew it up.'

The Joneses looked at one another. Mrs Jones was the first to speak.

'Dewi, was that the Hywel Hughes . . .'

'Aye, that'll be the one. I don't think you should be too hopeful of help from that quarter, little ones. Who witnessed the will? Did Maldwyn not show it to anyone else?'

'Two men witnessed it. A soldier and a farmer's lad. The lad's name was Jones, though I can't recall his first name, but I remember the soldier's name because he was a scouser, like us. John James O'Hare, that was 'is name.'

'Grand. Address?'

' 'E never give it,' Johnny said. 'You don't, not on

a will. So far as 'e was concerned, 'e was jest a bloke in the street earnin' hisself a bob. Mr 'Ughes gave 'im a bob to be a witness,' he added.

'Please, why can't we go to Mr Hughes?' Kitty said, whilst the Joneses wrestled with the problem of tracing a boy named Jones and a man from Liverpool. 'Mr 'Ughes was ever so nice to us, weren't 'e, Johnny?'

'Aye; but he was old, wasn't he? Older than Mal?'

'Yes, he was a bit older. Two classes 'igher in the school, Mal told us. But why . . . ?'

'His obituary was in the paper, see?' Mr Jones said heavily. 'Well known in these parts was Hywel Hughes and well-liked, too. Not like that Travers fellow.'

'His obi . . . 'is what?'

'The feller's died, our Kitty,' Johnny said, his voice flat. 'Ain't there a law against burnin' a will though, Mr Jones? Kitty an' me 'ud swear to it, wouldn't we, Kit?'

'Ye-es, but they could say, with a certain amount of truth, that since you were beneficiaries, or claiming to be under the will which was burnt, then your testimony was scarcely without prejudice,' Mr Jones said, sounding like a lawyer himself. 'Got to find them witnesses you have, or you're going to have a job to prove your claim.'

'Didn't you ever see the will, Dewi?' Mrs Jones said suddenly. 'Maldwyn was a good friend – did he never show you the will?'

Mr Jones shook his head.

'No, and perjure myself I cannot, nor would Maldwyn expect me to do so,' he said. 'He was straight, Maldwyn, straight as a die.'

'And you didn't see hide nor hair of it?' his wife said persuasively. 'You never heard it mentioned?'

'Oh aye, it was mentioned, several times. Maldwyn told me he intended to leave the farm to the boy . . . and to Kitty, of course . . . and I applauded the idea since the young people had worked hard for him. But not a line in writing did I see.'

'Oh well; perhaps you will find the witnesses,' Mrs Jones said, looking hard at the two of them. 'The law's a strange thing – that a lawyer can perjure himself without a second thought but a farmer cannot . . . and if that Elwyn Ap Thomas comes here to live, he'll regret it if it's the last thing I do.'

'He'll sell,' Johnny said sombrely. 'That was what Maldwyn allus said – that 'is nephew cared for nowt but money.'

'It'll take a while to prove, wi' no will to back him up,' Mrs Jones said thoughtfully. 'There's a cousin in Australia and another nephew in Canada – swear to it I will. That'll give you time to find those witnesses, the pair of you.'

'And in the meantime, you've a home here,' Mr Jones said decisively. 'That arm must mend, Johnny bach, before you go searching for anyone. And when you do go, we'll keep Patch safe against your return. They won't want her but she's a grand worker with the flock, grand. Now let's have some breakfast, Bronwen my dear, and later I'll drive into Corwen, have a word with a legal friend or two, see how you stand.'

'We'll never forget what you done for us,' Kitty said, her eyes bright, suddenly, with the tears which she had never shed when she was struggling to bring them through safe. 'Even if we ne'er 'ave the farm, we won't forget, will we, Johnny?'

And Johnny, leaning back in his chair, his eyes dark-rimmed with pain and fatigue, agreed they never would.

Johnny and Kitty stayed with the Jones family for a week. At the end of that time Johnny took Kitty aside to the barn for a serious talk.

'We can't stay, Kit, no marrer 'ow nice they is to us,' he said bluntly, as soon as he had made certain they were alone. 'We're wastin' time, chuck. We gorra find them witnesses.'

'Yes, I suppose . . . only isn't Mr Jones's friend doin' 'is best for us? Mr Jones said 'is friend would go to Wrexham, try to see if 'e could tek a look at that Mr 'Ughes's papers an' that, see if there were a record, like. Shouldn't we wait for 'im to say what 'appened?'

But Johnny was of the opinion that time spent waiting was time lost.

'The sooner we git after them fellers the likelier we are to find 'em,' he urged. 'Let's start to tramp tomorrer.'

Kitty felt they were being too hasty, but on the other hand, she felt guilty at eating the Jones's food and sleeping in their truckle beds, especially if they were never going to gain their inheritance and so would be unable to pay the family back for all their kindness.

And Mrs Jones agreed with them that they should be doing something.

'I remember reading somewhere that possession was nine-tenths of the law, and them Thomases will be snugging down an' taking over more with every day that passes,' she said worriedly. 'What's more, if they sells it whilst you're doing your finding out, it 'ud be rare difficult to get the farm back I shouldn't wonder. As for Patch, you may leave her here and she'll be well looked after, I'll treat her like my own. Then you must come back, see, to pick up the dog and decide what to do next.'

This made sense to Johnny, and even Kitty could see the logic of it. What worried her, though, was that she could see Johnny was anxious to be off, not necessarily because of the farm, but because he didn't really think they would ever get their inheritance, and wanted to return to the tramping life while his arm mended at least.

'We will try though, won't we, Johnny?' she asked anxiously as the two of them left the Jones's on a crisp, bright morning, with blackberries all over the hedges and button mushrooms spangling the pastures. 'We won't just give up an' let them 'ave it all?'

'Course we's goin' to try. Only first we gorra pick up our gelt,' Johnny reminded her. 'I took the money Mrs Jones lent 'cos I don't want *no-one* to know we're not penniless, see? If them Thomases ever found out . . .'

'Do you know, I'd forgot the wages?' Kitty said, considerably heartened at the recollection of Johnny's secret hoard. 'That'll keep us in grub for a week or three, eh, Johnny?'

'Oh aye, that'll see us awright. So we'll 'ide up in the old shepherd's 'ut till dusk, then go down and get our gelt, then be on our way.'

'Where'll we go first?' Kitty enquired.

'We're goin' straight to Wrexham to see if we can find that lad, though I admit without 'is name it's a faint 'ope,' Johnny told her. 'And after that it's back 'ome, queen, because wi' a name like John James O'Hare that sailor should be easier to find. My, but ain't it good to 'ave a purpose again?'

And Kitty, striding out step for step with him

228

through the bright, cold morning, with a thick coat on her back and food in a bag slung over her shoulder, had to admit that it was better to be trying to claim their rights than just sitting at the Jones's farm, feeling thoroughly miserable.

The day spent in the shepherd's hut proved rather more interesting than they might have wished, and that was because, not an hour after they had settled in, they heard someone approaching up the hillside, pushing stealthily through the thickness of dead bracken, making for the hut.

'Git under the 'ay,' Johnny hissed at once. 'It can't be them Thomases, but jest for sure . . .'

They hid under the hay, scarcely daring to breathe. As they lay there, they heard soft little movements outside and then someone – or something – pressed a nose to the crack of the door and inhaled deeply. Then, even as Kitty began to scramble out of concealment, there was a short, sharp bark. A let-me-in bark.

'Oh Patch, whatever are you doing here?' Kitty said, hurling the door open and dragging the dog inside. 'Oh dear, what will the Joneses think?'

'They'll guess,' Johnny said. 'Wonder if she'd go back if we told 'er to?'

'No she wouldn't,' Kitty said stoutly, both arms round the dog's neck. 'She's comin' with us, Johnny. She'll be no trouble, honest to God!'

'Well, it might be best,' Johnny said vaguely. 'I just 'ope no one saw 'er.'

'Nor 'eeded that bark,' Kitty said rather apprehensively. 'I'll tek a look outside I think.'

But when she opened the door and peered down

the hillside, there was no sign of life from the farm. In fact she spent most of the day spying on the Ap Thomases, and very boring it proved. Not until noon did they put in an appearance, and then it was Mrs Thomas, curl papers in her hair and slippers on her feet, slopping out to the yard and across to the byre.

'They 'aven't got the cows in; don't they know cows 'ave to be milked?' Kitty said angrily. 'What's 'appening to 'em? They won't 'ave no stock left.'

'They sold the cattle day after we left; I never said nothin' because there weren't nowt we could do,' Johnny said. 'Best that way, at least the beasts won't be sufferin' from their iggerance.'

'True. Then why did the ole woman go to the byre?'

'Daft Penrhos is workin' for 'em,' Johnny muttered. 'They kep' one cow so Eifion told me.'

'Oh. But Penrhos really is daft; 'ow can 'e work for anyone?'

'Dunno. Forget it. 'Sides, they coul'n't git anyone else to go there. Folk think they're 'orrible, even them what sez blood's thicker'n water.'

'Oh.' Kitty withdrew from her spyhole for a moment. 'I wish the sun 'ud go down.'

'It will. 'Ave a sleep, chuck, or you'll not want to walk tonight.'

Kitty thought she would never sleep, but she did; boredom drove her to it. And when she awoke it was because Johnny was gently shaking her shoulder.

'Wake up, queen,' he said, very low. 'You'll 'ave to watch for me. Keep Patch quiet, though.'

Together, the three of them stole down the hillside. The stars were out and a thin curl of silver moon lit the night. The kitchen window was the only one illuminated at the farmhouse and the smoke from the chimney went up straight as a die. Johnny touched Kitty's arm and indicated it.

'No wind. Good.'

He led them round the farm and past the old orchard to a piece of pasture where Tilly sometimes grazed. It was pitted and pocked with rabbit holes and as soon as they reached it, Johnny began to peer at them and to count under his breath.

'One, two, three, four, five . . . turn right. One, two, three . . . turn left. One two three four . . .'

He wove around, finally coming to a halt beside one particular burrow.

'Right. Don't watch me, queen, watch the 'ouse.'

Kitty turned her back on him and stared at the lighted window, but before she had grown bored with the view or tempted to peep there was a light touch on her elbow.

'Gorrit! I've took the lot, no point leavin' none. Come on, let's 'ead for Wrexham!'

Chapter Ten

Gibraltar isn't a very big place, and it is said, by Gibraltarians, that if you stand in Casemates Square at the bottom of Main Street, everyone who is anyone will pass by you in the fullness of time. Art, wandering along with his hand solicitously cupping the elbow of a pretty young lady, was about to test the truth of that saying.

'Hey, Art! Arthur O'Brien, don't you dare walk by me and never a word!'

Art stopped so suddenly that his companion gave a squeak.

'Oh, Art, 'ow rough you are, you jerked at my arm! Who calls to you? Ah, a young man – do you know 'eem?'

'Well, well, well!' The young man, short and broad with curly hair and dark eyes, seized Art's hand and pumped it up and down. 'I never thought to see you here . . . how are you, old feller?'

'Tippy Huggett! What on earth are you doing in Gib?'

Tippy laughed, still holding Art's hand as though loth to let him go.

'Just visitin', same as you, I daresay. I signed on as a deckhand on a cruise ship – the *Mersey Wanderer*; lovely vessel. She's lying offshore even as we speak, so I come over to buy me mam some pretty china. It's said to be cheap here. Art, where in 'eaven's name 'ave you been these past years? Why, only the

232

other week I was ashore in the Pool and I met young Lilac whatsername . . . she were askin' after you.' He seemed suddenly to become aware of Art's companion and his face crimsoned hotly. 'On'y a friend, like,' he said hastily. 'Jest interested, that's all.'

The girl smiled at him, her teeth a flash of white in her dark face. Art turned to her and said something in a foreign tongue. The girl nodded, gave Tippy one last curious glance out of a pair of magnificent dark eyes, then turned and disappeared into the crowd.

'Who were that?' Tippy asked curiously. 'She was very pretty, mind. A friend o' yourn?'

'Local girl; mother's my landlady,' Art said almost absent-mindedly. The burning question on his mind had nothing to do with Hortensia. 'I sail from the port of Gibraltar now, when I'm not working ashore, that is. I haven't been back to the Pool for, oh, ages. What were you sayin' about Lilac? I know she's married, but . . .'

Tippy stared, then frowned.

'She ain't! Well, if she is, it's a well-kept secret. She's Miss Lilac you know, of The Waterfront Academy of Modern Dance on Mount Pleasant; t'other one's Miss Charlotte. They've got a great little business I'm tellin' you, great.'

'But I saw her! Leastways I saw her wi' a babe in her arms, bouncing it up and down and making it wave to the ships. So I thought . . . naturally I thought . . .'

'Oh, the baby! That'ud be her niece, Nellie's lass,' Tippy said knowledgeably. 'She dotes on little Elizabeth they say. But your Lilac's doing well for herself and just about everyone knows her. She's the receptionist at the Delamere Hotel – you know, the big, smart hotel on Tythebarn – and she has that dancing school.'

'And she isn't married? You're sure, Tippy old pal?'

'Certain, sure,' Tippy said stoutly. 'She reckons you are, though. Says that must be why you haven't come back. She keeps her eyes open, asks all over. And since a good few of her pupils at the school are seamen she'd probably hear if you did come back.'

'Dancing! Here's me thinking her a prim little house-wife darning socks and making meat pies, while really she's working in a posh hotel half the time and teaching dancing the other half.' Art grinned from ear to ear. 'Well I'm damned! And definitely not married, you say? Engaged, though? I guess she's engaged?'

'Nope. Told me last time I asked that there was safety in numbers and besides, she was waitin' for someone.' He grinned at Art. 'I didn't ask who that might be, old friend, because I thought I knew. And judging from the look on your face, I weren't so far wrong.'

'But we – we had a real bust-up,' Art protested. 'Called each other every name we could give tongue to. And after that I tried to find her and couldn't. Not immediately, of course, while I were still mad, but later when I'd cooled off a bit.'

'No, well, she left the bag and sack factory, see. *And* the place in Lord Nelson Street. I suppose you looked at one or t'other? And she said she did try to find you, haunted Exchange Flags, went over the Mersey to Hamilton Square and asked the clerks in the bank if they could 'elp . . .'

'And I'd gone, o' course,' Art said with a groan. 'I tried the factory and Lord Nelson Street, but I felt an almighty fool so I didn't ask, not for ages. I kept well out of sight and just hoped to walk into her, be accident-on-purpose, if you get my meaning.'

'Well I'll let you into a secret; I heard Lilac even

went back to the Court; yes, she bearded your family in their den, and your mam never liked her you know, then she tried the shipping register and spent all her spare time at the docks, even asked your old friends what 'ad become of you. Only we didn't know either, see, so we couldn't help. But *now* . . .'

'Tippy, tell her . . . oh Gawd, if only I could just up and go, but I've got a responsible job here, I'm with a small concern, I couldn't just let them down. Look, will you take her a letter? No, go round and see her, tell her I'm coming home as fast as I can . . . here, don't you go off, I've got a room up Bell Lane, over a confectioner's shop. Come up there with me, we'll have a bevvy together and a meal and you can write her address down so I can drop her a line. Tippy, you were always a good pal – you've done more for me than you know! She *isn't* married, she don't have a kid . . . and she's waiting for . . . for someone. I can't believe it, you know, I keep thinking in a moment I'll wake up and it'll have been another dream.'

'Well, it ain't no dream and neither am I,' Tippy assured his old friend. 'Look, I don't know your Lilac's address because I'm not in the habit of visiting ladies' flats . . . well, not other feller's ladies, anyway . . . but if you send the letter to Miss Larkin, care of the Delamere Hotel on Tythebarn Street, that'll find her.'

'Wonderful,' Art said. 'I'll never forget this Tippy, never! For as long as I live you'll be me bezzie!'

'I thought I were your bezzie anyway,' Tippy said. 'Even when you didn't write, didn't get in touch, I still reckoned you were me best pal and kinda hoped I were yours.'

'I've been a fool,' Art muttered. He turned left off Main Street and drew Tippy up a steep and narrow alleyway between tall, thin buildings with balconies above their heads. About fifty yards or so up the alley he stopped outside a heavy mahogany door. He unlocked the door with a large iron key and it swung inwards, revealing a tiny square lobby and a flight of stairs.

'Here we are; follow me but go careful, the stairs are steep and pretty dark.'

The two young men climbed the stairs and stopped again on a narrow landing. Art put another key into another lock and flung that door open too.

'My place,' he said. 'It's small, but it does me well enough.'

Tippy looked around. He saw a pleasant room with a double bed on one side and a screen folded back beside it. A long, narrow window was curtained in a good deal of white lace but since it was open, the curtaining was blowing out more or less straight so that Tippy could see the houses opposite, no more than six or eight feet away. There was a square of carpet on the floor, a kitchen section with a gas ring, a low sink and a wooden draining board, and the rest of the room held books, flowers, pictures and ornaments, a small desk, a dining-table and chairs.

'Neat, eh?' Art said with obvious pride. 'Hortensia is a good homemaker and she's proud of the way she keeps my room. Always fussing around she is, getting me bits and pieces.'

'Hortensia?'

'The girl I was with. Hortensia Valilodad.'

'Art! So Lilac was right, you are married!'

Art looked offended.

'I am not! I suppose I could call her my landlady, since her parents own the whole block, but in fact she's just a friend. She's taken me under her wing, cooks for me, cleans for me . . .'

'Sleeps with you?' Tippy said bluntly.

Art looked self-conscious.

'I've been that lonely, Tip, and unhappy, too, thinking that Lilac had gone and married some feller . . . and it's not as if we live together or anything like that, it's just that occasionally . . . and she needs pretty things which I'm happy to give her – I earn good money: if I can bring her a bit of happiness . . .'

'I guess I don't want to know,' Tippy said hollowly. 'But Art, if you're going to write to Lilac, go home to the Pool . . .'

'It won't happen again,' Art assured him. 'I told Hortensia a little bit about Lilac, so when I tell her I'm going home, that Lilac isn't married after all, she'll understand. She's a sweet girl, not like some. All she'll want will be my happiness, I assure you. Now what do you want to drink? The ale's quite good and I bought a loaf and some cheese this morning . . .'

After Tippy had gone, Art lay on his bed gazing at the ceiling and thinking about Lilac. What a fool he'd been to jump to conclusions, not to check that she really was married, had a child. And how could he have forgotten that Nellie had been expecting a baby . . . of course she lived in London, but he should have guessed that she would come back to see her beloved adopted sister. And the man who had put a casual arm round Lilac's waist – now that he thought about it seriously, he realised it had been a brotherly rather than an amorous gesture. It had been Stuart, of course – what a complete and utter duffer he had been! But Tippy had removed his obstinate, self-imposed blindness and now at last he could see!

*

'Pig and son of a pig! Take that . . . and that!'

Crash! went the blue pottery vase on the wall beside Art's head, scattering water and spikes of Spanish lilies as it flew through the air. Hortensia, her dark eyes flashing magnificently, her bosom heaving, reached blindly for the next object, and a silver fruit bowl, complete with its usual complement of oranges, grapes and bananas, took wing. Art ducked and winced as it met the window-pane squarely and crashed through it, then winced again as a startled roar announced that the fruit bowl had scored a direct hit on an innocent passer-by.

'Hortensia, listen to me! I never promised . . .'

'You . . . are . . . a . . . dog!'

The ivory paper knife in the shape of a crocodile was lighter than the fruit bowl. In the interests of not utterly thwarting the thrower, Art did not duck and gasped as the paper knife caught him across the Adam's apple.

'Ouch! Hortensia, if only you'll listen for a moment . . .'

'Deceiver! You took my innocence . . . in my mother's house . . . English swine, liar, thrice-cursed!'

She was running out of throwables, Art saw thankfully. Unless she started on the saucepans and the cooking utensils of course.

'Darling Hortensia, we had an agreement . . .'

'Pig! I say you are a pig and a liar! An agreement . . . poh-poh! I spit on our agreement!' she spat. 'You told me you loved me, you said one day . . .'

She started on the saucepans. Art, who had bought them and had chosen cast-iron knowing it to be the heaviest and longest-lasting of materials, began to duck in earnest.

Lilac had had a really awful day. The hotel had been fully booked but she had been approached by a regular customer who wanted a bed for a couple of nights. She had juggled and moved people around and at last managed to persuade two ladies that they would be better off sharing a room rather than paying twice as much for a room each. The regular customer was grateful, but the chef, a man of great talent but uncertain temperament, was not.

'I have no spare salmon; it is all very well, Miss Larkin, to say that one can always fit someone else into the dining room, but food can only be stretched so far. First it was thirty-eight, then forty, then forty-four. But forty-five people, if they all mean to have the salmon, will all go a little hungry and will blame me – me, who does the marketing, prepares the food, plans the menus . . .'

'I'm sorry, Monsieur Arrat,' Lilac said sincerely. 'Can you not serve one person with melon in place of smoked salmon?'

'I have no melon,' Monsieur Arrat said sulkily. 'There was none in the market this morning, it will have to be tinned grapefruit, and no guest would choose tinned grapefruit when he could have my smoked salmon nestling in a bed of scrambled egg. Since it is all your fault you had best go and purchase some more salmon before all the shops shut.'

So Lilac, who should have been heading homeward, had to make her way to Byrom Street, to a fishmonger highly regarded by Monsieur Arrat. She bought smoked salmon, added half a dozen fresh eggs so that she might make herself an omelette when she

239

finally reached home, and set off for the hotel once more.

She arrived to more chaos. The chef was satisfied with the extra salmon but the housekeeper had counted the sheets back from the laundry and found two missing. She had sent a kitchen maid round to Chung's Chinese laundry on Smithdown Road because her chambermaids, who should rightly have gone, finished work at four. So Lilac's first task was to face Monsieur Arrat once again when he discovered that his favourite peeler of potatoes, who should have been hard at work on the next day's supply, was missing from the scullery.

By the time she had sorted everyone out, forced the housekeeper, a bad-tempered old woman who should have been retired years ago, to apologise to the chef, gone into the kitchen herself and arranged the wafer-thin slices of smoked salmon in curls, ready for the creamy scrambled egg, she was almost as inclined to scream as the chef had been. And far from going home and throwing herself on to her bed to rest, she was due down at the Academy in ... gracious, in an *hour*, to take her turn at teaching the latest craze to cross the Atlantic, the Black Bottom.

So when Mrs Brierson called to her as she was crossing the front hall she very nearly pretended to be deaf and continued on her way.

Nearly, but not quite. After all, it was scarcely her employer's fault if things had not gone right. Lilac smiled and turned towards the desk.

'Yes, Mrs Brierson?'

'A letter for you, Miss Larkin. It came care of the hotel, but I think it's personal. Here you are.'

An ordinary brown envelope with handwriting on it. Lilac took it, glanced at it as she went to pop it into her handbag – and froze. She stared down at the well-remembered writing like a bird stares at a snake. It was Art – Art writing to her, after all this time! It had been years, without a word, and now a letter – what could it mean? Good news ... or bad? Suppose he was writing to her to tell her he was married, with children? If so, she would rather not open the envelope, would sooner stay in ignorance for the rest of her life ...

No. That wasn't true; not knowing had been the worst part. Very soon she would know and either way, she guessed it would be a relief.

'Miss Larkin? My dear, you've gone quite white! Does the letter contain bad news, perhaps?'

'Bad news? No, indeed. It's a letter from an old friend, a friend I've waited to hear from for these past two years. It's good just to see his writing again to tell you the truth, though I was ... am ... surprised that he's got in touch after so long.'

Lilac continued with the movement of pushing the envelope down into her handbag. She smiled up at Mrs Brierson and her employer, clearly relieved by her words, smiled back.

'Well, that's good news, as you say. Good night, Miss Larkin.'

'Good night, Mrs Brierson,' Lilac said, her voice lifting. She hurried out of the hotel and, in the road outside, looked at her handbag longingly. Should she stop and open it now? But the March evening was chilly and besides, she wanted her own room, her own company, when she opened the precious envelope and read the letter she had waited so long to receive. She hurried on her way, suddenly realising that she'd not so much as looked at the stamp or the postmark, all she'd done was stare at the handwriting.

He might be anywhere – he might be in this very city!

But by the time she reached her flat common sense had reasserted itself. If he was in Liverpool he would scarcely have written, he would have called round. No, he must be away somewhere . . . but she would know soon enough.

She reached the hallway, climbed the stairs, unlocked her door. She loved her little flat, took a great deal of pride in it, but this evening her eye flicked heedlessly across the potted fern by the front door, the arrangement of daffodils and narcissus in the tall white vase, the pictures in their gilded frames, the soft, Welsh wool rugs. All she wanted was to get the lamp lit so that she might settle down in her chair and read her letter.

She lit the lamp, threw off her coat, plumped down on the scarlet velvet cushion laid negligently on the seat of her chair. She took out the letter, slit the envelope with a trembling finger, and drew out the two lined sheets of paper. For a moment she simply checked that she had not made a mistake, that it really was from Art. She found that she remembered in greatest detail everything about his writing, how he dotted each *i* and crossed each *t*. Yes, she knew it was he, without reading a word. She sighed deeply, happily. Then began to read.

Dear Lilac,

I'm sorry; there, I said it first! I made a God-awful fool of myself that day in Miss Young's Dining Rooms and I've been sorry ever since. It was loving you too much you see, queen – when you love someone like that everything they say is terribly important, terribly serious. So all I could think was that I'd muffed it and lost you for ever. And Lilac, love, if I had really lost you for ever then I didn't want to go on living, didn't care if I lived or died.

I ran away after that. I told myself I was going to be independent of you, make a life for myself without you, but really all I was doing was running away, and there's nothing to be proud of in that. I did come back though. After a twelve-month. I searched all over but you'd good as vanished, or so it seemed. I know now that you'd changed your job and moved away from Lord Nelson Street, but at the time I thought you'd probably met someone else and married them. Daft, eh? And then, when I'd given up and signed on for another voyage, I actually saw you. Down on the dock, with a baby in your arms and a fellow beside you.

I know now that it was Nellie's baby and Nellie's fellow, too, but at the time the bottom fell out of my world. I reached Gibraltar and saw a job advertised, for someone to do the paperwork and accounts for a small shipping line. Sometimes I'd be on board their cruisers – they have two passenger ships – and at others I'd be in Gib, doing the paperwork etc.

I took the job, got myself a flat, began to try to forget. Only I couldn't, not quite. And then I met Tippy Huggett and he told me you weren't married, nor engaged. He said he thought there was a chance for me . . . I was over the moon, queen, over the moon! If I could have I'd have handed in my notice right away and hopped on the first Liverpool-bound vessel I saw, but I've got a deal of responsibility here and I couldn't do it to them, they're decent folk, they depend on me.

Besides, queen, I don't know how you feel! Could you drop me a line, let me know whether there's any

hope? I'll give you my address at work, since I've
recently changed my lodgings. And if there is a chance
of us getting together again . . . well, I'd move heaven
and earth for you, my darling girl.
　With love from
　Art

Lilac read the letter through three times, very slowly. The first two times her hands were trembling so
much that the paper fluttered like a leaf in the wind,
but by the third read she had got a hold of herself
and she simply let the flooding, overwhelming joy
take charge. She hugged herself, she kissed the
letter, she thanked God, Tippy Huggett, Art, even
the ship which had brought the letter, the postman
who had delivered it. Then she jumped up and went
over to the kettle standing on the ring and lit the gas
beneath it. She felt absolutely certain that at long last
things were starting to go right. She clutched the letter, her magic talisman, her good fortune, and kissed
it again, noticing that she had, at some stage, shed
tears all over it, which was not the sort of thing she
usually did, being a sensible and down-to-earth young
woman.

But I'm not sensible or down-to-earth, not where
Art's concerned, she told herself giddily. I'm in love,
I'm in love, I'm in love!

Presently the kettle boiled and she made herself
a cup of tea and read the letter again. And again.

Then she sat down and wrote a reply.

Kitty and Johnny stayed in the Wrexham area for
a while, then left, their search a failure.

'Askin' for a feller called Jones is like askin' for a

fish in the sea,' Johnny said disconsolately. 'Everyone's called Jones, jest about. And everyone shops in Wrexham on Beast-market day, every blamed one. We aren't agoin' to find 'im, so we'd best search for t'other un.'

'Yes, awright,' Kitty agreed, not without some reluctance. She no longer feared her parents – she doubted if they would recognise her if they met in the street, nor she them – but she was afraid of the city. Even when she was full-grown with a job and money in her pocket she thought she would never forget the miserable conditions at her home in the Court, nor the hunger which had gnawed at her morning and night, a hunger deliberately fostered, she had come to believe, by her mother. And not only did she remember the hunger, she would never forget the complete lack of love, the hatred even, which her parents had shown towards her.

But then she remembered the other Liverpool, the one of her summer wanderings, when the city had taken her to its warm and generous heart. Liverpool had sheltered her beneath its posh doorsteps, fed her from its rubbish bins and its vegetable gardens, shown her its parks and gardens, its beauty at dawn and sunset, its miles of glorious waterfront. And it was not just the city, it was the people, many of whom had been kind to her. Best and first was Mrs O'Rourke of course; Mrs O'Rourke had quite simply given her a reason for living. Then there was the girl from Penny Lane, the stop-me-and-buy-one boy, the people who gave her pennies for carrying their parcels or food because they saw she was hungry. There were others; a scuffer, telling her off for loitering in the park because a rich old woman had complained, and slipping her tuppence when no one was looking;

245

coming back next day with a pair of clogs and a grey woollen cardigan. She'd lost the clogs to a bigger child and popped the cardigan one day when food was scarce, but they'd been given from kindness and she had appreciated it.

And Johnny. When he was scarcely more than a kid himself he'd taken her under his wing, cleaned her up, chopped off her verminous hair, destroyed her filthy rags and given her some self-pride. And he was a Liverpudlian, just like her.

Yet still, when Johnny announced that they would go home now, cross the Mersey, she felt a stab of fear, of very real reluctance. She put a hand on Patch's collar, gaining comfort from the dog's closeness; Patch would not desert her, no matter what. Suppose her mam had set the scuffers on her? Suppose her dad was home and recognised her, beat her up? But it was pretty unlikely; only a ninny would worry about things like that and she was no ninny, she was Johnny's chosen companion, she had all but been the owner of half a farm – and might be again if they could track John James O'Hare down!

'So will we hoof it, or travel like lords?' Kitty asked Johnny as they came out from the barn where they had spent the night. 'Weather ain't up to much.'

Johnny looked up at the sky and sniffed suspiciously. The wind was getting up and the clouds overhead were moving fast. Even as he looked, a faint, misty rain began to fall.

'Hmm . . . what'll it cost on a train, eh?'

They enquired and Johnny shook his head, half sadly but half gladly too, Kitty was sure.

'Nah, we aren't partin' wi' that much gelt! 'Sides, they wouldn't be too keen on lettin' Patch ride, I daresay. We'll do it on foot in a couple o' days.'

'Right. I like to hoof it,' Kitty said loyally. 'And we ain't in that much of an 'urry, eh, Johnny?'

'We'll tek it easy,' Johnny promised, and indeed they both enjoyed the walk.

It was evening on the third day when they reached Birkenhead. They caught a ferry, Patch squeezing between the two of them as unobtrusively as possible, and stood silently at the rail watching the port gradually approach, then disembarked with the other passengers.

'We aren't sleepin' rough in the streets, we'll go to a lodgin' house,' Johnny said authoritatively as they began to move uphill. 'There's doss 'ouses for sailors along the waterfront, we'll go there.'

'I can't, not a doss 'ouse for sailors,' Kitty reminded him. 'Don't be silly, Johnny.'

'Sorry, I forgot. But there's places where we can both go . . . I'll get us a bed, don't worry, queen.'

They found a cheap lodging after several unsuccessful efforts. At the first place the bedding was filthy and stank of stale sweat and urine. Kitty, with wrinkled nose, told Johnny it wouldn't do and the pair of them turned away, followed by screeches from the offended landlord. At the second place they were told they would have to share a bed and tie the dog up outside and though they agreed to do so, when they went into the room every bed was already occupied by at least one person.

'Tell one of 'em to shove up,' the landlord hissed. 'Den slip in beside 'um.'

They were luckier on the third attempt. They were each given a bed-roll of reasonably clean materials – a thin straw mattress, a lumpy pillow and a blanket – and shown into a large room where a number of people already lay sleeping on the floor. Patch, it was agreed, might sleep on the floor by their bed.

'I didn't want to share,' Johnny muttered. 'Not with some of our wages still left, but us'll 'ave to mek do tonight. I'm wore out.'

So the two of them put their mattresses one atop the other, wrapped themselves in their blankets and cuddled up like puppies. And very soon Patch sneaked onto the mattress with them, adding her warmth to theirs. Kitty thought she would never manage to sleep but it had been a long, hard walk through some pretty rough weather. They both slept within ten minutes of their heads touching their pillows.

Next day Johnny decreed they should split up.

'I'll do the docks, you an' Patch do the streets at the back o' the docks,' he said. 'Don't forget – John James O'Hare. Tell anyone what asks there's a reward, that'll fetch 'im out if 'e's around.'

'I'll try the boozers an' the schools,' Kitty volunteered. 'An' the snooker 'alls an' the workin' mens clubs.'

Johnny stared at her.

'Kit, I knew you was a bright kid, but you's bloody brilliant!' he said. 'You'll strike gold afore me I've no doubt . . . where'll we meet?'

'Inside the Shamrock Café on Preesons Row, if they'll let Patch inside,' Kitty said promptly. 'If not, outside.'

When she had lived in the city she had often hung round the Shamrock, wooed by the rich and delicious smells which came from it and also by the friendly way satisfied customers, seeing her wistful face as they came out again, would chuck her a penny or even save her something to eat – a crusty bread roll spread with butter, or a little cake with currants in.

'Preesons . . . oh, yeah, I know it; just off Derby Square, ain't it?'

'That's it; opposite the Victoria Memorial. What time?'

'Oh, say six o'clock. We don't want to go on after dark. If I'm not there on time it could mean I found 'im, though, so 'ang about a bit.'

'What if you're hot on his trail though, Johnny? Or what if I am, come to that? Where'll we meet then?'

'Back at the lodging 'ouse, I reckon. Here, I'll gi' you some cash so's you can git yourself a meal or a bed. But I reckon we'll meet at four.' He raised a hand, turned to go, then turned back. 'You sure you'll be all right, Kit? Sure you wouldn't rather we stuck together?'

Kitty would much rather have stayed with Johnny but she saw his point; Liverpool was a big city and John James O'Hare just one rather insignificant young man. To find him could take weeks, but if they split up and searched separately it could halve their labours.

'Nah, it's awright, this way's surer. An' I've got Patch; she wouldn't let no one 'arm me. See you at six, then.'

At six o'clock prompt, Kitty was walking up Preesons Row. She had met one O'Hare, though he turned out to be Tom and not John, but meeting him had been a lucky chance which cheered her up considerably and made her think that maybe their search would be crowned with success after all.

'An' aren't I sorry I'm de wrong feller, an' you

249

wit' Irish eyes an' de sweetest smile?' Tom O'Hare said genially, when Kitty had explained her quest. 'But haven't I a brudder, Jamie O'Hare, and a cousin wit' de very name you mentioned? Cousin John's a seaman, too, he may be in port now for all I know. I'll mek some enquiries for yez, sweet'eart . . . tell me where to find you again!'

'Me and my brother are meeting at the Shamrock Café in Preesons Row at six this evening,' Kitty said, making a lightning decision. 'If you've any news, we'd be real grateful if you'd join us there then.'

'Well, unless I get a ship soon me time's me own,' Tom O'Hare said, and suddenly his face looked sad for a moment. 'I'll be glad to do what I can to 'elp, chuck.'

So despite having called in at a dozen pubs and engaged a great many people in what turned out to be fruitless conversations, Kitty was still feeling rather pleased with herself as she reached the Shamrock. She glanced round but there was no sign of Johnny, so she went inside, Patch as close as a shadow, her soft nose touching Kitty's calf.

It was as lovely as she had always imagined it to be. With Johnny's money in her pocket and her nice clean clothes on her back, with her hair neatly bobbed and her body well-nourished, Kitty allowed the waitress to take her to a window table, sure that no one would ever recognise in her the little waif of years ago. She explained to the waitress that Patch was well behaved and would lie quiet, and said she was waiting for a friend. However, as the time began to pass she decided she might as well eat – after all, Johnny might easily have had some luck and be talking to their quarry this very minute. She ordered brown Windsor soup, scrag-end stew and two veg, followed by strawberry blancmange, and she bought a cornish pastie for Patch, who ate very daintily, without crumbs. The meal cost tenpence, and was accompanied by a round of bread and butter and a cup of tea. We should come here every day, Kitty thought enthusiastically, drinking her soup the way Maldwyn had advised, from the side of the spoon and without any slurping, either. We won't get better value than this anywhere, and all three of us have got to eat!

She knew she was eating quickly and tried to slow down, but even so the meal was finished before Johnny had put in an appearance. There was a clock on the wall saying ten minutes to seven; Johnny wouldn't expect her to wait any longer, she would have to leave. But they'd meet up at the lodging house, later. Kitty put her face close to the window and peered out. There was someone out there ... she hadn't misunderstood Johnny's directions, had she? He had said meet inside and not out?

She half-rose from her seat, then sank back again. It was a child outside, not an adult, hovering as she, Kitty used to hover, sniffing the lovely smells of hot cooked food, thin as a stick and clad in a raggedy little dress which barely covered her bony bottom.

That might have been me, Kitty thought, awed. Poor kid ... she looked round her. She had eaten her entire meal, but that could be remedied. She beckoned the waitress over.

'Excuse me ... could I have a – a bacon sangwidge to tek out wi' me? And one of them curranty cakes?'

'That's another fourpence,' the waitress said. 'Shan't be a tick, miss.'

She disappeared and came back moments later with a thick, steaming bacon sandwich and a currant cake. She put them into separate brown paper bags and handed them to her customer.

'There y'are, miss. I 'opes as 'ow you enjoy 'em.'

'Thanks. Goodnight.' Kitty struggled into her coat, touched Patch to rouse the dog, and then, with some reluctance, left the warmth and brightness of the small café for the chilly darkness outside.

For a moment she thought the child had gone, then she saw her again. She was coming across the road like a moth to a flame, and as she passed close by, Kitty spoke.

' 'Ere, I couldn't eat all that lot – like to finish it up for me?'

The child turned towards her and in the glow from the gas lamp overhead, Kitty saw her face.

A thin face which had once been round and rosy, with the blonde hair once tied back with white ribbon straggling unkempt and verminous down to her shoulders.

Recognition was instant and two-fold.

'My Gawd . . . Bet!'

'Well, if it ain't our Kitty! Oh Kit, where've you been? You do look grand . . . is that f'me? Oh, I's so 'ungry . . .'

Betty Drinkwater, for it was undoubtedly Kitty's little sister, almost snatched the proffered sandwich. She crammed it into her mouth, the grease running down her chin, and swallowed it in huge, wolfish bites. Kitty bent over the better to see the child. Tears rose, unbidden, to her eyes and trickled down her cheeks.

'Betty?' she whispered. 'What is it? What's 'appened? Our Mam allus fed you littl'uns proper, it was on'y me what went so short I could've ate road-dirt. Where's the twins? An' the others?'

'Arny were run down by a tram and died in the 'ospickle,' Betty said thickly, through the sandwich. 'Bob ran off a long whiles back. Our Da went off about then ... three year ago, it'ud be. Mam said 'e might of been killed, but someone told Bob 'e'd gorra lass into trouble out Crosby way. And Mam's real ill, awful ill. I's scared she'll die an' leave me to fend for the kids. I does me best, Kit, but I's allus hungry, allus cold.'

'I remember,' Kitty said feelingly. 'Oh Betty, whatever can I do? Mam hated me, you know, if she sees me face she'll probably snuff it anyroad, from shock and 'orror – I suppose she thought I was dead, eh?'

'Never said,' Betty mumbled. She was finishing off the sandwich, holding on to it so fiercely that her fingers were almost meeting through the bread. 'Good riddance, she said, and suffin' about serpent's teeth.'

'There you are, then, she ain't goin' to welcome me back, exactly.'

'No ... I mean yes, she would!' Betty exclaimed. She looked up at Kitty, tears trembling on her lashes. 'Oh Kit ... please come back, please! I's on'y ten, I dunno which way to turn, honest to God! I jest know they'll all die an' it'll be my fault an' I'll 'a been a bad sister to 'em.'

'Well, I was supposed to be meeting a friend,' Kitty said doubtfully. 'Look, 'ang on a minute, I'll leave a message wi' the waitress just in case 'e turns up. But I'll see 'im later, explain.'

Kitty went back into the Shamrock, asked the waitress to tell Johnny, should he turn up, that she had had to leave but would be at their lodging house before ten that night, and went outside once more.

She took Betty's hand and perhaps it was that which decided her. She had taken the child's hand

253

many times in the past and had always liked the feel of the plump little girl's cushiony palm against hers. But now Betty's hand was just like a claw, whereas Kitty's own hand had flesh on it, and muscles in the wrist.

'You really will come 'ome? You an' the dawg? Jest for a minute, to see our Mam?' Betty said tremulously. 'Oh, Kit, you're real good; I allus knewed you was the best of us. Arny an' Bob were 'orrible to you and when you went they was 'orrible to the rest of us. Arny was wuss'n Bob, even.'

'Shouldn't speak ill o' the dead,' Kitty reminded her sister gently as they made their way across Derby Square and dived down Castle Street. 'Still, you've 'ad a bad time, chuck, I can tell.'

'It weren't too bad till our Da went,' Betty admitted. 'There was food, when 'is 'lotment come, and Mam went on wi' 'er sewin'. But fust our Da went an' then Mam were took bad . . . there won't be nothin' for 'em tonight . . . ' the child stopped dead in her tracks, her expression stricken. 'Oh, Kit, an' I ate that sangwidge!'

'I'll buy a loaf an' some cheese, when we reach the Scottie,' Kitty said hastily, seeing that more tears were about to fall. 'Don't worry, we'll feed the kids tonight.'

Far from cheering Betty up, however, this seemed to bring on a fresh attack of misery.

'You was often 'ungry, Kit, an' I knew you was, an' I never give *you* owt 'cos I were afraid of our Mam,' Betty wailed. 'Mam said you was such a wicked kid, see, an' you was older'n me an' I didn't know, then, 'ow it 'urt to 'ave an empty belly.'

'Well, we both know now,' Kitty said ruefully, feeling that tears were not too far from her own eyes. 'An' we'll do our best to see it don't 'appen again. Come on, queen, step out or we shan't get back to the Parry afore the shops close.'

She meant it as a joke since the shops would not close until nigh on midnight, but Betty took her seriously and scuttled along clutching her sister's hand, scarcely bothering to talk any more.

And presently they reached the Scottie and Kitty pulled Betty into George Lunt's for a large loaf, and a little further up the road into Costigan's grocer's shop for the cheese. But knowing that the money Johnny had given her would have to last, she bargained in Lunt's for a yesterday's loaf and told Mr Costigan that she would take cheese-ends if he'd any going cheap.

'An' I'll tek a couple o' tins o' conny-onny,' she added grandly, 'an' a twist o' tea.' She remembered that her mother often drank tea when she had run out of more alcoholic beverages and besides, milk was good for the kids. It seemed strange to acknowledge that her mother would not have milk in the house because she'd become used to a constant supply on the farm. But the milkman only came round Paradise Court in the mornings and Sary had never patronised him; she used the sweet, thickened condensed milk in her tea and in anything else which needed the addition of milk.

Without being asked, the man in Lunt's had given them a paper carrier bag, so the cheese and milk were piled on top of the loaf and Betty hung onto Kitty with one hand as though she feared to let her go. With her other hand she was busy eating the currant bun the baker had popped in on top of the loaf.

It was strange, turning off Scotland Road into Burlington Street after so long. They passed the fishmonger whose boy had been the start of all

Kitty's adventures – Kitty thanked him from her heart as she went – and then crossed over Titchfield Street, passed a couple of court entrances and there was Paradise Court itself, looking to Kitty's eyes more like purgatory than paradise at that moment.

They went into the Court itself. It was very much smaller than Kitty remembered, and unbelievably shabby. The flags were layered in filth, the one gas-light sputtered fitfully, showing leaning doors, cracked window panes, a broken chair and an abandoned mattress with the stuffing leaking out. As though Kitty's horror was palpable, Patch pressed harder against her leg and gave a small whine. Kitty automatically fondled the dog's smooth head, then stared around her once more.

'Gawd,' she said in an awed whisper. 'Gawd, it's wuss'n I remembered, an' that's sayin' suffin'!'

'Yeah, the welfare lady said it were run-down,' Betty murmured. 'There's almost no one 'ere in work, though, our Kit. It ain't just our Da an' Mam, there's others an' all.'

'What about the Hallorans? An' the Percivals?'

'They left. Moved, I means. It's bad 'ere now, our Kitty. It's the Fletchers what done it.'

'Done what?'

'Oh, brung it low. They're allus in trouble an' they're a big fambly. Mam, Da, a couple o' aunts, an uncle, three big gels, a dozen kids . . . Mam says the gels 'ave sailors in.'

'Oh,' Kitty said, following Betty's example and keeping her voice low. 'It's quiet now, though.'

'Oh ah; they'll be at the boozer,' Betty explained. 'Better come in, our Kitty; that's our Eth cryin'. Poor bitch, she's 'ungry. Ruthie don't holler much; younger, see. Used to it, I dessay.'

Betty stumped up the step and pushed open the creaking door.

'Mind the Drop,' she said. 'They're in the front.'

They were. Two small girls, all thin and ragged, though neither quite as thin as Betty. Eldest always gets it hardest, Kitty thought, then moved forward, doing her best to smile. The lamp was lit but it was sending out some pretty fierce fumes; she wondered if the children could see who she was or could recognise her if they did. Four years is a long time when you're only eight or nine.

Betty took hold of her hand and led her forward; Kitty could feel Betty's pride in her, as though by producing their big sister she had done everyone a big favour.

'Here's Kitty come 'ome,' she said softly. 'Eth, stop snivellin', she's brung food, an' a dawg! Did you 'ear that, Ruthie – we got grub!'

Two ragged heads swung towards her; two pairs of dull eyes brightened. Kitty produced the loaf, the tins, the cheese. The smallest girl, a child no more than two years old, held out her hands, cupped, in a gesture of begging so painfully eloquent that Kitty had to swallow a lump in her throat.

'Bread an' milk,' she said to Betty. 'I'll open the tin, you crumble some bread into – into somethin'. I don't remember Ruthie, she must've been born after I left.'

'I 'member you, Kitty,' Eth said.

She must be nine, it stood to reason she was nine, but you could have thought her five or six. And there had been others, there was Phyllis, and Mo . . .

'Where's Phyllis and Mo?'

'The Welfare took 'em, just after you left; never

seed 'em since,' Betty said briefly. 'Mam said they'd be better off.'

'I remember when you was 'ome, Kitty,' Eth said suddenly. 'Mam were allus . . .'

Her voice died away. She looked avidly at the chunk of loaf which Betty was crumbling into three empty bully-beef tins.

'Can someone fetch water?' Kitty said.

Eth got to her feet. Her nose was running and she staggered as she tried to walk. Quickly, Kitty caught hold of her and sat her down again, on the bundle of old newspapers and rags which dominated the room.

'S'awright, queen, I'll go meself. You'll feel better presently, when you've ate.'

She went out to the yard, the kettle in one hand, and filled it at the communal tap. Returning to the front room, she looked hopefully at the grate. No wood, no coal, nothing but long-dead ashes. And it was a chilly evening.

'No fire? Oh well, I daresay it'll go down just as well cold,' she said cheerfully, hacking a hole in the can with a rusty tin opener and mixing the milk with water until it was of a pouring consistency. She made the bread and milk and handed the children the tins. They ate with their fingers, lacking spoons, and with feverish haste. Then they looked at her; they said nothing, just looked.

'Bite o' bread an' cheese?' Kitty said. 'Ain't much else, but I'll go round next door presently, get 'em to boil us a kettle. Then we can 'ave a drink o' tea.'

'Oh Gawd, I forgot! Mam . . . come up an' see Mam, there's a dear, Kitty,' Betty coaxed. 'She's poorly . . . you might know wha's wrong.'

'I shan't, an' the sight of me is bound to mek 'er worse,' Kitty said uneasily. 'Oh, awright then, I'll jest tek a look.' She turned to Patch, sitting gnawing on an ancient bone she must have found somewhere. 'Stay 'ere, there's a good gel.'

Betty lit a stub of candle and they left the two little girls single-mindedly chewing bread and cheese in total silence and climbed the rickety stairs. At the head of them was a tiny landing, with the children's slope-roofed room to their left and the main bedroom to their right. Kitty peeped through the doorway, not venturing to enter, expecting either a storm of abuse or possibly even a missile. But there was nothing. Not even movement.

Encouraged, she ventured further.

Sary Drinkwater lay on her back on the old brass bedstead. She had a pile of rags over her and her hair hung over her face in a wild tangle. She heard the two girls in the doorway and slowly her big, untidy head swung towards them.

Her face was frightful. Her eyes were bloodshot and screwed up against the fitful candlelight, her skin was blotched and purplish, her toothless mouth hung open; saliva ran down her chin and puddled the rags beneath her head.

'Mam, 'ow d'yer feel? We brung food, an' there'll be a cuppa presently.'

'I could do wi' a cup.' Sary's voice was slurred and her eyes seemed scarcely to move, but she had taken in something at least, as her next remark proved. 'Who's your pal?'

Kitty put out a warning hand but it was too late; Betty was in full flood.

'Why, Mam, it's our Kitty, come 'ome to look after us till you're well agin! Doncher reckernise 'er?'

Sary peered, then half-closed her eyes.

'Kitty?' she said in a wondering voice. 'Not Kitty Drinkwater?'

'That's right, Mam,' Kitty said, preparing for flight. 'I jest popped in to . . .'

'Kitty! Me eldest . . . me best . . . Gawd, I thought you'd gone for good, thought you was dead . . . an' you've come 'ome! Oh Kitty, love, things 'ave been that bad for us sinst you left, things 'ave gone cruel 'ard. Oh praise be, she's come 'ome!'

Kitty said gruffly that she had indeed and backed carefully out of the room. Downstairs again she wondered, as she worked on the food, what she was to do. Betty had convinced her that the family were in dire straits, but the interview with her mother suggested to her that things were worse than even Betty knew. Sary Drinkwater was not ill; she was mad. And madwomen, Kitty suspected, didn't get better. Did this mean that she would have to stay here in this vile and abominable place, rear her three sisters and feed them all by her own efforts *and* see to the great, creaking hulk of a madwoman in the bed upstairs?

I'd sooner die, Kitty thought desperately. I can't do it, I'd much sooner die.

But she knew – none better – that death didn't come for the asking, and that duty, that horrible word, had a way of forcing itself upon you. Could she leave Betty, Eth, and little Ruthie to starve? Could she leave them, even, to the mercy of the madwoman upstairs? I had Mrs O'Rourke for a bit, and I managed somehow, she told herself. They've got nothing, and they won't manage, they aren't strong enough.

But others as strong as she and with more reason to stay had just run off. First Da, then Bob. Why should she stay, when they'd deliberately driven her out all those years ago? Why couldn't she give them the rest of her money, spend one night with them and then cut and run, back to Johnny, and the hope of the farm, the promise of the open road and good company?

I'll see what Johnny says, she told herself much later that night, when she and Patch sneaked out of the house and set off across the city in the direction of their lodging house. He'll advise me, tell me what to do for the best.

But Johnny wasn't at the lodging house.

'Seen neither 'ide nor 'air of 'im,' the landlord said. 'Still, you an' the dawg's welcome if you've got the dosh.'

'Not tonight,' Kitty said. She felt numb with fear. What she most dreaded had happened, she had lost touch with Johnny! Then she remembered that they could both read and write. 'Look, can I leave a note for me brother? You'll give it to 'im when 'e does come?'

'Aye, I'll give it 'im,' the man agreed. 'Want a bit o' paper?'

He found Kitty a crumpled sheet and a stub of pencil and Kitty, after much thought, just told Johnny that she'd gone back home to help out and could be found at 8 Paradise Court.

' 'E'll come for us,' she told Patch as they walked back across the city. 'Johnny'll not leave us 'ere.'

She returned to the lodging house after a couple of days. The landlord said no one had been, no one had asked for her. Kitty could only think that Johnny must have found their witness and taken him back to Wrexham or the farm. After she'd gone, the landlord chucked her note on the fire. No use keeping it since he'd forgotten all about it when the lad had come looking. Best put the whole thing out of his mind. Cheeky mare, using him as a bloody notice-board!

After three days, she decided Kitty would have to leave the family to fend for themselves and actually go in search of Johnny. It was clear that their plan had failed in some way and she could not contemplate staying here in this dreadful house. That's what I'll do, tomorrow, she vowed to herself late that night, as she and Patch joined the little girls in the pile of rags and old newspaper which was their bed. Tomorrow I'll give 'em what's left of Johnny's money and split. There's so little I can do anyway ... I'm only one, they need an army of helpers to get them right. Well, I'd better get a doctor to the old woman 'fore I go or she'll pop her clogs and the kids'll get sent to the workhouse or worse – what's worse, come to think? And I'll clean the place up or they'll die of filth and vermin ... I saw a rat in the back kitchen, scuttling across the floor bold as brass, good thing we finished up the bread and cheese!

So she promised herself an escape in the forefront of her mind, but in the back of her mind, where truth lies waiting, she knew she could never do it, never desert them. And when sleep claimed her she wept in her slumber and her sobs woke little Ruthie, who burrowed through the rags and curled up against Kitty's chest and seemed to comfort her a little, for the weeping gradually slowed and stopped.

But Kitty's dreams were dreadful.

Chapter Eleven

Lilac had always been a hard worker, even-tempered and patient, but once she had written to Art telling she was every bit as sorry as he – sorrier – and received a reply which could only be described as lyrical, she was so cheerful, so happy, that even Charlotte remarked on it.

'And not only are you grinnin' from ear to ear day and night,' Charlotte said accusingly one morning, 'but you're singin' and laughin' and gettin' through a huge amount of work . . . it ain't natural, our Li!'

'What's unnatural about happiness?' Lilac said, on her hands and knees polishing the dance floor. 'Anyway, you should be grateful; Mrs Higgins never got a shine like this on it – you can see your face, just like in a mirror!'

'That's what I mean . . . who wants to see their face in a dance-floor? A quick mop-over would have done very well.'

'It needs polishing,' Lilac said, rubbing away. 'To tell you the truth, Charlotte, I've got so much extra energy that I hardly need to sleep at night! I know Art and I won't be able to get together at once, because he's got to arrange for someone to take his place for a couple of weeks . . . that's what we've decided, incidentally, that he'll come here for a fortnight whilst we do our arranging and get ourselves wed, then we'll go back to Gibraltar for a bit, just until Art can arrange something over here. And we're going to have a little honeymoon in New Brighton, because when we were kids Art was always saying that one day we'd go there, and the day we fought and he went off we'd planned to spend the afternoon there. So a honeymoon there will be a long-delayed treat . . . oh, I'm looking forward to that little honeymoon just as much as if it were Venice or Rome we were visiting! After that we'll go back to Gib and he'll start trying for jobs over here.'

'How can you get a good job in Liverpool from Gibraltar?' Charlotte said doubtfully. 'It's hard enough when you're actually livin' here!'

Whilst her friend polished the floor she was rubbing up the window panes, plumping the cushions on the small chairs and dusting the skirting boards.

'Yes, I know, but Art's awful good at mathematics, a real genius. And he's had all that experience now in running a small shipping line, so he hopes perhaps one of the big shipyards – Cammel Lairds or somewhere – will take him on.'

'Yes, I suppose that's possible,' Charlotte admitted. 'But things are pretty bad right now, they say even people in quite good positions are losing their jobs. And you're doing so well, queen – the hotel can't manage without you, the dancing academy needs you – why quit when you're on top?'

'I've already told you; because Art is also doing well, and making good money. And though I really enjoy reception work and I love the dancing school, for Art I'd – well, I'd give it all up.'

'So that's being in love, is it?' Charlotte mused. She stood on one of the spindly chairs and reached up to dust the upper sash. 'And all these months I've been wishing it would happen to me – I must have been mad!'

Lilac giggled.

'I've decided I don't know the first thing about love,' she said frankly. She knelt up the better to consider the matter. 'First I thought it had to be exciting, then I thought it had to be dangerous. Then I decided what I really wanted was security, and love would have to be accompanied by loads of money . . . and then I lost Art and I knew what I wanted. I wanted him, Charlotte, at any price, under any circumstances, I wanted him until I ached with it, until it was all I could think about. So now we've mended our quarrel and are planning a life together, I can't help but be happy. But I don't know whether it's love, or whether it's something quite different, I just know that without Art there isn't much point to my life. Is that love? You tell me!'

'I guess it is,' Charlotte said rather wistfully. 'It's so long since I was in love that I find it quite difficult to remember. I wonder, do fellers feel the same?'

'Art does,' Lilac said contentedly. 'He's just like me; his letters are one long grin . . . if you understand me.'

'I do,' Charlotte sighed. 'Oh, Li, you are so lucky!'

Over in Gibraltar, in his temporary room in Irish Town, Art went through the days in a similar daze of happiness to that which Lilac was enjoying. He had found the perfect flat for a young married couple; it was on Town Range and it overlooked Trafalgar Cemetery in which lay the men who had died at the Battle of Trafalgar many years before. It was a pretty cemetery, with big old trees, beautifully kept gravestones, and it was cool and peaceful even in the warmest weather. Because the new flat was right at the top of an old house it was quite private, which would be better, Art considered, for a newly married couple, and it had recently been modernised. It was near the shops so marketing would not be a problem, but near the harbour, too, and Lilac would be able to catch a bus to Rosia Bay whenever she wanted to spend an afternoon on the beach.

But we probably won't stay here long, Art told himself as he arranged for a year's rental on the flat. We'll be wanting to get back to Liverpool ... I mustn't forget Lilac's dancing school; she and her friend Charlotte have built it up from nothing, it would be a sad shame to let it go. And anyway, once our children are in school she might be glad of a little hobby.

Children! The thought of having a family, living in a neat little house like the one Nellie and Stuart had shared in Penny Lane, was a dream of which Art thought he would never tire. He could just imagine it all, the neat red-brick house with a little garage at the side for his motor car (when he could afford one) and four good bedrooms upstairs, one for the girls, one for the boys, one for he and Lilac and the last one a spare room, for guests. Then downstairs the big, modern kitchen with a gas cooker and an Aga to heat the water. A proper front room, all carpet and cushion covers, a back garden for the veggies and a front one for flowers. Oh aye, he'd got it all planned out, all right.

He didn't want a big family, even though the Catholic faith frowned on birth control. Art had attended Mass on a Sunday and gone to Sunday School, listened to the Father and done his best to be a good person in his own quiet way, but where Lilac was concerned everything else went by the board. He had quite made up his mind that he would be the

266

best husband ever, so there was no point in having kids like doorsteps and ruining Lilac's health and figure. Too many kids keep you poor, Art thought, and I don't want my kids to have what I had – more kicks than kisses – nor to find them turned over to an orphan asylum like Lilac was, if the worst happens and one of us dies. Didn't the good God give me self-control, as well as this great love of Lilac burning in me breast? Well, I reckon we'll have two boys and two girls and then shut up shop. There's something nice and satisfying in a family of six . . . a bit of a squeeze in me new car, perhaps, but we'll fit in somehow when we go off to New Brighton for the day, or across the river and into the blue hills of Wales.

He talked to his employer about a fortnight's holiday; Mr Bassano was willing. His small company was flourishing, he liked Art, appreciated the additional time the younger man put in without ever expecting more money or any sort of perks. What was more, Art was straight, told his employer everything and made sure that Mr Bassano was not cheated.

'Take a fortnight . . . take longer if you need it, Mr O'Brien,' Mr Bassano said generously. 'When you bring your young lady-wife back with you we'll have a grand party to celebrate your wedding . . . but you will come back? I don't know how we managed before you came.'

Art assured his employer that he would most certainly return and began preparations for departure. He moved out of Irish Town into the flat in Town Range and spent happy evenings choosing furniture, pictures and ornaments. Hortensia's farewell fling meant that he had had very few breakables left when he moved out, but he enjoyed buying new ones, anticipating, with each purchase, Lilac's pleasure in the pretty or practical, mundane or unusual.

He was wandering back up through the town one evening, having had a drink with some friends, when he heard his name called. He had been about to cross Convent Place but had paused to watch the guard change in front of the Governor's Residence, and on hearing his name he turned and saw Mr Bassano, waving vigorously. Art stopped and waited for the older man to catch him up.

'Mr O'Brien, I'm glad I caught you,' Mr Bassano panted. 'My old friend Albert Edwards has come to me . . . his purser aboard the *Queen of the Straits* has been taken ill; he's done some juggling around and now tells me that he has a berth for a temporary purser aboard the *Queen* . . . she's a sizeable cruise ship and she sails tonight for Liverpool, she'll be berthed there for two or three days . . . would it help you to clear up your arrangements if I released you for the duration of this voyage? Albert would be grateful, and I daresay we might manage without you for the period in question.'

Art could scarcely believe his ears; a chance to get back to Lilac now, to talk over their plans in person . . . to hold her in his arms for the very first time!

'Me? Go back to the Pool for a couple of days? Oh, Mr Bassano, it would be – I can't tell you—'

'Good. You sail in three hours. Can you be ready?'

'I'll be there in fifteen minutes,' Art gasped. No time to telegraph or telephone . . . but what does it matter? 'This will make things so much easier . . . thank you, Mr Bassano!'

And Art was as good as his word; he was aboard the *Queen of the Straits* in less than an hour and working in the purser's cabin ten minutes later. And that night, when he eventually got to bed, having got his books up to date and his passenger lists sorted, he was too excited to sleep.

Liverpool! He was going home for the first time for ages. Unexpectedly, without a fanfare, no one waiting at the docks for him – and it was the best thing which had happened to him since he was a nipper and had first set eyes on little Lilac Larkin in her pink silk dress!

They docked at eleven in the morning. The waterfront was busy but not unusually so. Art had stood at the rail as they approached the port, devouring it with his eyes. Never before had the Liver birds seemed more welcoming, never before had the city shone so white and gold in the sunshine, the sky such a perfect arc of blue above! He knew he would not be met but to his surprise, on stepping ashore he was greeted.

'Well, if it ain't Art O'Brien!' A hand seized his shoulder and spun him round, another hand seized his. 'How do, whack! Don't say you've forgot your old friend Matt?'

Art gaped.

'Well, blow me down, if it isn't Nellie's little brother! I've not seen you since you went to sea . . . oh, it must be half a dozen years back.'

Matthew McDowell grinned, still holding Art's hand.

'There weren't nothin' much to go back to the Court for, not once Aunt Ada died and Nellie moved out. I say, that's a lovely feller Nellie's got herself, ain't it? I bin dockin' in London these past few years, and it's been grand to 'ave our Nell an' 'er Stuart to visit, a family on the spot, like. But didn't I 'ear you was in a bank or an office or some such t'ing?'

'I was, but I left. I'm at sea on and off . . . look, do you remember Lilac?'

'What, the kid our Nell took on? Little Lilac Larkin?' Matt's grin widened. 'I 'member her chuckin' a pile o' spare ribs at your 'ead and kickin' an' swearin' . . . eh, grand little kid!'

'Well, I'm going to see her later, but I'd like a bevvy an' a cheese barm first. Come with me? We could go to the Sparling Hotel, it's only just across the road. Have a chat about old times.'

'Well, I dunno . . .' Matt said slowly. 'On t'other 'and, I'd like to see young Lilac again.'

This was not at all what Art had bargained for but his doubts must have shown in his face, for Matt thumped him on the shoulder with a friendly fist, accompanying the gesture with a guffaw.

'S'awright, la', I were 'avin' you on! You was always sweet on our Lilac from the time you was little, I do 'member that much! Right, let's go to the Sparly, 'ave ourselves a bevvy or two. You stayin'at the Corry, then?'

Art shook his head.

'Nope. I send money . . . but I'm only here for a couple of days, I'd sooner book into a lodging house near where Lilac works, so we can have some time together. We're getting married in a few months.'

'Tyin' the knot, eh?' Matthew whistled. 'Well, good for you, young feller! Lilac were in the bag and sack factory, but our Nellie said something about betterin' herself, hotel work, was it?'

'Oh aye, it were hotel work, and she's done well for herself,' Art said proudly. 'She's the receptionist at the Delamere Hotel on Tythebarn Street, and she's got a—'

'Dancin' school on Mount Pleasant,' Matthew finished for him. 'That's right, our Nell said to pop in there some time, get meself a few lessons in all the latest steps. Well, since it's all in the family, Art old feller, why don't you book in at the Delamere? She'd gi' you special terms, no doubt.'

Art stared, eyes rounding.

'Well, I never would have thought of that! Yes, why not? I'd like to see the look on her little face when I walk in, bold as brass, and ask for the best room in the house!'

'You won't git more'n two words out afore she's hangin' round your neck,' Matt said shrewdly. 'Tell you what, let's 'ave a bob on it, eh? Ten to one she'll be givin' you an 'ug afore you've opened your mouth.'

'You'd probably win,' Art said ruefully as they turned into the Sparling Hotel. 'Look, I'll buy the grub and the bevvies now an' if she gives me time to ask for the best room in the hotel, you can pay me back.'

Art and Matt enjoyed their meeting, their meal – which turned into something a good deal more convivial than a barm and a bevvy – and above all, reminiscing about old times. Art had not kept in touch with the inhabitants of the Court because working in a bank and then leaving the city had isolated him, but Matt knew everyone and everything and was only too happy to pass on all the news.

'I got relatives all over,' he said proudly, as the two of them sat at a window table, sipping their ale and waiting for their food to arrive. 'There's me brother Charlie down south, me cousin Lou in New York and me other cousin, Jessie, in France . . . she

271

married again, you know, a Frog of all t'ings . . . and then me mates are mostly at sea . . . odd, ain't it, that I still get this yearnin' for 'ome, and that 'ome is still the Pool?'

'We all suffer from it,' Art said wisely. 'I've got a good job in Gibraltar, ashore mostly, an' I'll be taking Lilac back wi' me when we're married, but we shan't stay abroad. It'll be Liverpool again for us, just as soon as I can get a decent job back here. Mind, we'll do awright in Gibraltar; it's a good place to be.'

'Oh aye; 'alf the navy an' most of the garrison would agree wi' you there,' Matt said. 'Here comes our grub – eh, you can't beat the Pool for good grub!'

Lilac came on desk duty at lunchtime, having spent the morning sorting out the books, the rooms and the staff. The chef wanted to change the menu; an artist of his calibre, it appeared, could not be content to cook the same food week after week after week. He desired to make a raspberry mousse encased in puff pastry and served with fresh cream for dessert.

'In October?' Lilac said despairingly. 'Why not make it an – an apple mousse? Or a lemon one? At least I could send someone round to the shops for lemons without being laughed at.'

'You meestake,' Monsieur Arrat said, wagging a finger the size and shade of a pork sausage under her nose. 'Or per'aps I should say you underestimate ze wonders of ze rrrrailway.' He always became very French when thwarted. 'Scottish raspberries, Mees Larkin, Scottish raspberries!'

'Oh? Are they in season now? I'm sorry, I didn't know,' Lilac said humbly. It paid to be humble when dealing with an aristocrat of the pastry board, like Monsieur Arrat.

He nodded earnestly, beaming at her and patting the air with one hand as though an invisible child stood before him.

'Zey are in season. And I wish also for ze best beef, in strips . . . 'ow ees eet called . . . ?'

Having sorted out the menus for the week to the chef's satisfaction, Lilac then accompanied a new chambermaid round a bedroom, showing her how a bed was made, how a well-handled feather duster could remove cobwebs from lampshades, picture rails and long net curtains, all without knocking anything askew, and how a little vinegar applied to a mirror and then buffed vigorously with a soft duster could bring an immaculate, smear-free shine.

After that it was cashing up and telephone bookings, after that it was seeing the sewing woman about sides-to-middling some well-worn best sheets so that they could be used for the staff bedrooms in the attics, and after that Lilac had a light lunch on one end of the kitchen table whilst the staff flew around getting ready to serve twenty-eight guests with something a little more elaborate than Lilac's cold beef and pickle sandwiches, and coffee.

She had just finished her ice-cream when Mrs Brierson came into the kitchen, fanning herself with the reservation book.

'Well, if Mr Robeson tries to book in again, Miss Larkin, I hope you'll send him packing . . . or rather, assure him we're fully booked,' she said with a rueful smile, sinking into the chair opposite Lilac's. 'Not only does he complain about everything, but he insists on doing so at the top of his voice in the most public place he can find. And now Miss Jenkins in Room

8 tells me that he made a very strange remark to her when he met her on the landing in her dressing-gown! Have you nearly finished your luncheon, my dear? I've left Miss Skidmore on the desk, but she isn't really qualified . . . I felt I must have a break and a cup of coffee or I'd expire.'

Lilac got to her feet.

'I had almost finished,' she said. 'If I may, I'll take my coffee up with me. I'd love to know what Mr Robeson said to Miss Jenkins though I don't suppose we'll ever find out. Thanks for a very nice luncheon, Monsieur Arrat,' she added diplomatically.

The chef, about to serve home-made bread rolls with cream of asparagus soup, nodded distractedly, and Lilac took the reservations book and left the room, climbing quickly up the stairs to the reception hall. She sat behind the desk and drew the account book towards her; best check who had already paid their bills and who still needed reminding.

Her head was bent over the book when the swing-door from the lobby was pushed open. She saw, out of the corner of her eye, a tall figure enter, and so instead of studying the figures she pushed the accounts to one side and drew out the reservations book. She ran her finger down the page . . . it appeared they had only three new guests so far today, and as Miss Jenkins and Mr Robeson had both left and the Elgin family had paid and gone soon after breakfast there were still a fair number of the better rooms available.

The man approached across the well-polished wood-block floor. Lilac kept her finger on the new line but looked up at him, beginning the bright, pleasantly professional smile with which she greeted would-be guests.

'Good aftern . . . Oh! Oh, oh, oh!'

She was out from behind the desk and throwing herself into Art's arms before he could even open his mouth. She clung like a burr, like ivy to a wall, like a lass to her lover, whilst Art held her gently, then tighter, then tighter still, and kissed the top of her red-gold head and then lifted her off her feet to claim her mouth.

Lilac pressed unbelievingly against him. The warmth of him, the strength, the wonderful familiarity of him – yet they had never cuddled properly before, just the odd snatched kiss, her scolding, him apologising, and the feel of his hand, big and warm, round hers, their sides touching as they walked along the pavement, argued, fought ... made up. She sighed, a great sigh fetched up from her boots, and relaxed, letting happiness, incredulity, stunned belief in the miracle, all wash over her in turn.

He was here! She knew that this must be a dream because really he was hundreds of miles away, on that little rock sticking out into the Atlantic Ocean which was Gibraltar, but yet he was here, in her arms. They were going to get married, he was coming back in a couple of months and they would marry and ... oh dear God, the feel of him, the safeness, the security of his touch!

Art broke the embrace first. He held her away from him, his grey-green eyes scanning her face as though he could never see enough of it, his toffee-coloured hair crisply short as she remembered it, his teeth white against the tan she had never before seen on his normally city-pale face. But it was the face she wanted to see, and the fact that she suddenly saw that he was not only her beloved Art, but also an extremely handsome young man, did not matter. It was a bonus, but one that was simply not necessary. I would love him, she thought with deep contentment, if he was ugly as a pan of worms; when he's old and bent and grey I'll love him still. What a curious thing love is, when just his touch can start a long, slow burn of desire for him within me, yet I don't want to go to bed with him particularly, I just want to be with him!

'Well, sweetheart – surprised?'

'Oh, darling Art – *so* surprised! You said not for another eight or ten weeks, my hair's a mess . . .' she touched the smooth, red-gold mass of it, bunched up on her head in a velvet band, falling on either side of her face in tiny, wispy kiss-curls. 'And I'm wearing the most miserable old dress and ugly old flat shoes.'

'You look wonderful. You'd look wonderful in rags, in—'

'Miss Larkin! Whatever would your fiancé say?'

Mrs Brierson's voice cut across his words, and despite the laugh in her voice they jumped apart guiltily. Lilac's cheeks felt suddenly hot and she saw Art's eyes shift uncomfortably. She turned towards her employer, standing behind the reception desk.

'Mrs Brierson, I'm sorry, I took one look at Art – Mr O'Brien – and everything just went straight out of my head! He isn't supposed to be here for at least a month . . . I still don't know what's happened . . . it's just so wonderful to see him! Oh Art, I'm on duty for another five hours . . .'

Art turned to Mrs Brierson and sketched a tug at a non-existent cap.

'How do you do, Ma'am? You'll be the Mrs Brierson I've heard so much about,' he said gravely, extending a broad, tanned hand. 'I was about to book meself a room in the hotel when this young person rushed round the desk and grabbed ahold of me. Your staff

276

can be very welcoming to a man fresh from a long sea voyage, I must say!'

Mrs Brierson laughed and blushed and shook Art's hand.

'How d'you do, Mr O'Brien,' she said, twinkling up at him. Lilac saw proudly that his looks and charm had quite won her employer's heart. 'I'm sure you really are Mr O'Brien, for Miss Larkin is a most restrained young person as a general rule.' She turned to Lilac. 'In the circumstances, Miss Larkin, perhaps you would like to take the rest of the afternoon off? I'll book Mr O'Brien into Room 6, with the compliments of the management.'

'I can pay me whack,' Art protested. 'I was going to do so, it never crossed me mind . . .'

'My dear young man, Miss Larkin is as good as an extra right hand in this hotel; when you and she come back to Liverpool, if she is still interested in this sort of work, I intend to ask her to take her job back, and how I'll manage for the year or so you'll be in Gibraltar I don't know,' Mrs Brierson said frankly. 'That is why I've been talking to business friends about getting you employment over here . . . but having met you, I'm sure you'll find yourself work very quickly – and good work, too.'

'Oh, Mrs Brierson,' Lilac sighed, still clutching Art's arm as though reluctant to let him go, and beaming at her employer with starry eyes. 'We'll come back as soon as we can, won't we, Art? And nothing would make me happier than to work here again . . . I so love the work, the staff . . . you've been so good to me, made me so welcome, taught me so much . . .'

'Good, that's settled then. Now if Mr O'Brien would just sign the register, I'll show him to his room whilst you get your things together, Miss Larkin. Then if you could bring Miss Skidmore in from the office and tell her to stay on reception until she's relieved we shall be organised. And we'll see you in the morning.'

'Miss Larkin, you're a very fortunate girl; that is the nicest young man I've had under my roof for a long while. And to think you sent him packing years ago – and you could have been happily married all this while!'

'I didn't appreciate him until he went,' Lilac said happily. She had come into the hotel next day to find all the staff singing Art's praises. He was sensible, helpful, he made the girls laugh, and had sent a message to the chef to say that dinner last night had been the best meal he'd eaten for many years. And now to have Mrs Brierson, a woman she respected deeply, telling her all over again how lucky she was to be engaged to Art, put the seal on her pleasure.

'What's more, you're having the day off,' Mrs Brierson said now as Lilac went to slip out of her jacket. 'You've got a great deal of arranging and planning to do; Mr O'Brien explained. He says it will be an early December wedding – such a festive time of year, my dear – so we're doing the reception here, a really first-class buffet, the chef told him what would be seasonal then. And Mr O'Brien wants you to get your dress at Blacklers, I told him they do the most beautiful wedding gowns . . . I've already discussed menus, the guest-list, bridal attendants . . .'

'Is there anything left for me to do?' Lilac said, standing behind the reception desk and looking round her rather dazedly. 'Flowers? My bouquet? Who are my bridesmaids?'

'Well, Mr O'Brien knew you wouldn't want too

much fuss since it's got to be a Register Office wedding, so he thought your niece Elizabeth should hand you a lucky horseshoe, and his sister Etty and your friend Charlotte might be your attendants.'

'Lovely, just who I'd choose,' Lilac said. 'Did Art ... Mr O'Brien I mean ... tell you what he gave me, yesterday afternoon?'

'No, dear,' Mrs Brierson said vaguely. She appeared to be making more lists and was running her eye absently down the latest one as she talked. 'What was that, then?'

Lilac held out her left hand, waggling the third finger slightly.

'Look!'

'Oh, the prettiest ring!' Mrs Brierson exclaimed, taking Lilac's slim fingers in hers. 'I declare, that *is* a lovely ring. What is the stone?'

'It's an amethyst surrounded by diamond chips,' Lilac said proudly. 'Art said it was the nearest he could get to Lilac – isn't it pretty? I love it so much! And it fits, so he even got the size right.'

'And have your bought the wedding ring?'

'We're getting that today,' Lilac said. 'I telephoned my sister Nellie to tell her the date and talk about the arrangements – we've booked a wedding car and the Register Office for eleven o'clock – and she and Stuart will definitely bring little Elizabeth up the day before, so we can all be calm and relaxed on the day itself.'

'Wonderful,' Mrs Brierson said. 'You'll make the prettiest bride, Miss Larkin – we at the Delamere will all be very proud of you!'

The day Art sailed he looked down at the dock

and remembered his homecoming a couple of days earlier. Then, not a face turned in his direction, not a hand waved. Now he could see Lilac and Charlotte clutching each other, waving, Lilac blowing kisses. Near them stood Mrs Brierson, also waving and daringly blowing kisses whilst in the background Monsieur Arrat, Miss Skidmore, some of the chambermaids and the girls from the kitchen clustered, waving hankies and tea-towels and shouting to him that it wouldn't be long before they saw him again.

They had taken him to their hearts because of Lilac, of course. She was such a marvellous girl, no one could resist her. But he was not just a passenger on the ship, he was still the purser, so after waving until Lilac was just a tiny dot amongst all the other dots, he went below and began on the pile of paperwork which sailing always brings in its wake.

He wished he could have had long enough to take her to New Brighton, though. They had almost got there so often, it would have been nice to have arrived home and whisked her across the Mersey on the ferry to the seaside place which had been their childhood Mecca. Odd how the place haunted them – always there, always beckoning, but they somehow hadn't managed to make it. Well, never mind, they would honeymoon there, it had been agreed between them.

He was just finishing his paperwork when there was a slight commotion outside the cabin door and a woman entered, holding a young girl by the hand. She was a pretty, dark-haired woman in her fifties, Art guessed, and the child must be about eight or nine. She held a skipping rope negligently but Art got the impression that for two pins she would have started skipping, there and then, in his neat and tidy office. Young rip, he thought, and then looked properly at the child. Immediately he was struck by the little girl's extraordinary likeness to the young Lilac – she had the same gleaming, reddish-gold hair, the wide blue eyes, the trick of looking down at the ground and then up again through her thick, light lashes. And somehow the same jaunty, devil-may-care attitude, too, though Lilac had been a penniless orphan and this was a little lady with a family rich enough to send her to Gibraltar aboard a cruise ship.

'Ah, purser; my name is Nicholson, Mrs Edward Nicholson. My grand-daughter and I are travelling with you to Gibraltar, where Lucy's father is stationed with the Royal Navy. Lucy's going to stay with him for a few weeks, but unfortunately we have been allocated an inside cabin and I was wondering, since the ship isn't fully booked, whether I might pay the extra and move to an outside one? The truth is, Lucy needs fresh air. She suffers from asthma and finds the cabin stuffy, which has already led to one attack.'

'I'm sure something can be arranged, Mrs Nicholson,' Art said, getting out the big passenger-list. 'Let me see ... ah yes, I've found you: Mrs Edward Nicholson and companion, travelling from Liverpool to Gibraltar. You're on 'B' deck, in cabin three, right?'

'That's right.'

'Well, we've an outside cabin free on 'A' deck. Yes, it would probably suit you and your granddaughter quite well. I'll just lock up here and then I'll take you up to it myself.'

'That's most kind,' Mrs Nicholson said gratefully. 'Although Lucy sits up to dinner with everyone else, she goes to bed straight afterwards and since I like to sit with her for a little while before she sleeps, an

281

outside cabin would be more pleasant for me, too.'

On the way to the cabin Art mentioned, casually, that Lucy bore a remarkable resemblance to his fiancée, a Liverpool girl named Lilac Larkin. Mrs Nicholson raised her brows.

'Indeed? Well, Lucy takes after her father, not her mother . . . my daughter Alicia was as dark as I am myself. I don't know Frank Dobson very well, in fact this will be only the second time I've met him, so for all I know your fiancée and he might be closely related.' She paused to glance at the child, now running ahead with her skipping rope, occasionally skipping as calmly and efficiently as though she were still on dry land and not the heaving deck of the *Queen of the Straits*. 'To tell you the truth, Mr O'Brien, there was a family disagreement.' Mrs Nicholson lowered her voice. 'My daughter married to disoblige us, as the saying goes. She had been engaged to a suitable young man . . . he was heartbroken when she eloped . . . but I daresay he's happy now, with his new wife and little family. And much though I miss my dearest Alicia – it must be nine years since she died – Lucy is a great comfort to me. She is the sweetest, most thoughtful girl.'

'And is she going to live with her father?' Art asked as he waved Mrs Nicholson ahead of him down the companionway. The child was already at the bottom of the stair, skipping in earnest now, the rope banging with smooth regularity against the well-polished floor. 'Is he settled in Gibraltar, for a time?'

'That is the intention,' Mrs Nicholson said cautiously. 'I've been a widow for fifteen years and am about to re-marry. We thought it best if Lucy went to her father for a while, so that Mr Addison and I might settle into our new home. But I couldn't give

Lucy up for ever,' she added quickly. 'We have resolved, Captain Dobson and I, to share her so far as is possible.'

'That sounds sensible,' Art said, throwing open a cabin door. 'Miss Lucy, you've gone too far – come back and examine your new cabin with your grandmother.'

Lucy ran back, beaming.

'Oh, a *window*,' she exclaimed joyfully. 'Oh, isn't this nice, Gran? We'll be able to see the sea and the gulls and have a breeze when it gets hot. Thank you, Mr O'Brien.'

'It will do very well,' Mrs Nicholson said, having taken a good look round. 'Could you arrange for one of the deck hands to bring my traps along here? I'd like to settle Lucy in by bedtime.'

During the days that followed, Art saw quite a lot of Lucy Dobson. She was a lively and intelligent child and it was soon obvious that whilst her grandmother adored her, she was no longer of an age to play games for hours at a time with her little tomboy of a granddaughter. Art, however, was glad of someone to amuse and came out of his office daily to play deck quoits, to teach Lucy new skipping games, to play cards in the evenings and to advise on a fancy dress when the weekly fancy dress ball loomed.

He was on his way to meet Lucy when the storm blew up.

It came from nowhere, the way storms at sea so often do. One minute it was calm enough beneath a lowering sky, with leaden clouds chasing one another across the horizon. The next moment a low rumble of thunder was followed by another and another, by lightning flashes, forking from the highest heavens deep into the sullen, surging sea. Then the rain came, great shining rods of it, bouncing off the suddenly boiling surface, hitting the deck so hard that the spray leapt head-high, forming puddles and lakes on the tennis court, running in rivers around the hatches on the foredeck.

Art watched from a convenient shelter and wondered just where Lucy had got to. She was an adventurous kid, she'd already been extracted from the engine room with a ruined cotton dress, and dissuaded forcibly from trying to climb the funnel. She loved the kitchens and pottered round there, helping with anything that she was big enough to do, hindering quite often, though always without any evil intent. If we'd been a sailing ship she'd have been balancing on the yard, darting in and out of the lightning strikes, Art thought rather balefully, for he had grown extremely fond of Lucy and rather resented her grandmother's casual acceptance of her charge's various adventures.

Art had arranged to meet Lucy on deck for a game of boule, a diversion which was proving popular amongst the younger element on board, but clearly she had realised that there would be no deck games until the storm abated and so had remained below. He was about to leave his look-out when he saw, dancing along the deck with her skipping rope dangling behind her, Lucy's small figure. She looked even smaller than usual with her clothing and hair drenched through, but she grinned at the sight of him and waved the wooden handle of her rope.

Art dived out of hiding and was soaked before he'd gone more than three yards. He gestured furiously to Lucy – the ship was heaving and tossing, it wasn't safe on deck, he realised, even if you didn't count the lightning and thunder.

'What?' Lucy shrieked across the short distance which separated them. 'What do you want? It's *lovely* out here – Gran wouldn't book us tickets on a big ship with a swimming pool because I can't swim yet and she said she'd never have an easy moment, but this is almost as good—'

Behind her, Art saw the wave coming. A great green monster, as high as the ship's rail, it raced towards them faster than an express train and every bit as dangerous. He waved his arms, shouted, began to run . . . and saw the wave hit the ship, curl above the rail, and come crashing down on the deck, several tons of green water, sharp with salt and weed, pebbles and sand.

He saw Lucy taken. That was it, she was taken, just as though the wave had curled a great green hand round her skinny little person and scooped her over the side and into the ocean. Art grabbed a lifebelt, heaved at the warning bell with all his strength, heard it begin its clangour . . . and scrambled over the rail. For a moment he stood poised – he heard voices behind him and roared a brief explanation, 'Kid overboard!', as loudly as he could against the elements. Then he saw in the water below him, just for an instant, a frightened white face, a swirl of red-gold hair – and he dived.

He reached her. Somehow, he didn't quite know how, he got hold of her, floated on to his back, forced her into the lifebelt, got her up on his chest and began to turn back towards the ship. The sea was running high still, and now that he'd got Lucy in a firm grip he was hanging on to her and the lifebelt, concentrating on keeping afloat, hoping to be seen because if they weren't there could be only one end to Lucy's latest escapade.

They were seen; a rope came snaking over the side, more lifebelts were thrown, they were lowering a boat. Lucy had been shuddering with cold, he thought her unconscious, but suddenly she turned her head and grinned weakly at him, looking so like the small Lilac that he could only grin back, knowing he should be angry with her but wanting only to see her safe, up on deck with her grandmother crying and cuddling her, regretting, at last, her lackadaisical stewardship of this most precious cargo.

He got her into the boat; the two men on board hauled her over the side and dropped her on to the bottom-boards, then turned to Art. But the boat had drifted too near the hull and they had to leave him to tread water for a moment whilst they worked desperately at the oars to avoid being crushed against the echoing steel plates. And Art, whilst they struggled, found himself fighting a force which was stronger than the arms of the men in the boat, stronger than Art himself; he was being drawn back and down by the currents which swirled around the ship's hull.

For a moment longer he fought it, not realising why he was gradually moving away from the boat, despite his attempts to get aboard. He saw Lucy, on her knees, holding out her small hands to him, her expression desperate. He even heard her voice, clearly, above the storm.

'Mr O'Brien . . . Art! Come to Lucy, swim to Lucy!'

Then the sea sucked him down. He fought it maniacally, struggled to rise to the surface as his lungs began to burn with the effort of holding his breath. Then he was dragged deeper, deeper yet, the sea no longer gleaming green around him but black, black.

He realised what was happening to him, knew that he was powerless to prevent it for one brief second before he spiralled down into the lightless deeps beneath, his breath gone, water in his lungs, his body squeezed by the pressures of the depths into the likeness of a rag doll.

His last thought was that he would never take Lilac to New Brighton now.

Chapter Twelve

It was all over the national dailies that he was a hero, that he had died saving a child. Nellie read it idly, standing in the kitchen with a cup of coffee in one hand, waiting for the wash-boiler to reach heat. No sooner had the dreadful news sunk in, however, than she was out of the room and on the telephone to Stuart at his office.

'Stu . . . have you seen today's *Times*?'

'No, not yet,' Stuart said. He worked in a newspaper office, so presumably, Nellie thought, he had enough to do writing for his own paper without reading other people's. 'Why? Is there something we should pick up?'

'No . . . Stuart, c-can you come home? It's Art O'Brien, Lilac's fiancé. Of course there might be two of them, but he was acting purser on the *Queen of the Straits*, I'm sure that's what Lilac said. He – he's been drowned, Stu, saving a little girl's life.'

'Drowned. Art? Oh, dear God, and he and Lilac . . .'

Stuart's voice, which had been indulgent, absent-minded, only interested, she could tell, because he thought there might be a story in it, sharpened into dismay. He had been fond of Art, Nellie knew, but he loved Lilac, as she did.

'That's right; he came home to plan their wedding. Oh Stu, this will kill her – I must go to her! Can you come home right away?'

'I'll leave at once.'

A different tone yet again, crisp, stern. Nellie could picture him hurling himself down all those marble stairs, through the revolving doors and out across the pavement to the nearest tram stop.

Nellie had been using the telephone in the hallway, sitting on a low chair, so now she stood up, replaced the receiver on its stand, picked up *The Times* and walked into the kitchen. Elizabeth was sitting up at the kitchen table, doing a wooden jigsaw. She had a summer cold and every now and then blew her small nose noisily into the hanky attached to her wrist by a length of wool. She looked up as Nellie entered.

'What's 'a matter, Mam?' she said thickly. 'Your eyes is red.'

'Mam's sad,' Nellie said. 'Someone we love is ... is not well. I've rung your Da at the office and he's coming home. We're going to have to go to Liverpool, queen.'

'Liverpool?' The child's eyes brightened though the lids were heavy still. 'To Auntie Li?'

'That's right, sweetheart. We're going to see Auntie Li.'

Elizabeth promptly got down from the table and set off across the kitchen.

'Wait, Miss Impatience; where are you going?'

'To pack me things,' Elizabeth said. 'I'm going to be Auntie Li's flower-girl, in a bootiful pink dress! Can I take dolly Gwen and Red Ted?'

'Oh my God,' Nellie said. The room dipped and swayed; she clutched the sink for support. 'Oh, my God! Oh my baby, my poor baby!'

She sank into a chair and put her face in her hands, then began to cry; for Lilac, for little Elizabeth, for all the pain that this cruel death would engender. Art was beyond tears, beyond pain, yet she cried bitterly, helplessly, for him. He had been so young, so full of hopes and dreams, and they had all been lost in one moment of gallantry, one foolhardy, wonderful moment in which he had saved a life and lost his own.

Nellie was still sitting in the kitchen when Stuart's key grated in the lock. He burst into the house, ran down the hall and, as she got stumblingly to her feet, he snatched her into his arms.

'Oh my love, my poor darling,' he murmured against her hair. 'Get some things together, we'll go by train, we can be with her before dusk.'

'Stuart, you're the best,' Nellie said huskily. 'Look, read the report whilst I pack. I'm sorry I didn't do it earlier, it was the shock, I suppose. All I could think of was the wedding, and . . . oh, Stu, my poor baby!'

She burst into tears again and headed for the stairs. Stuart started to follow her, then turned back and began methodically to tidy the kitchen, pulling the kettle over the heat and setting the teapot ready. Above his head, he could hear Elizabeth prattling away to herself in her small room. Some people might have assumed that when Nellie spoke of her poor baby she meant little Elizabeth, robbed of her chance to be a flower-girl at her aunt's wedding. But Stuart knew his wife better than that. It was Lilac, a young woman in her twenties, for whom she wept, because Lilac, in every sense but one, was indeed her baby.

Lilac sat behind the reception desk. Her face was perfectly white, but her smile, though a little stiff, sprang into being every time a guest came through the front door and approached her. She was calm and collected, because she did not believe the newspaper reports; how could she? She and Art O'Brien were going to be married, she wore his ring, had bought her gown, had planned her trousseau and her honeymoon, had even reserved the best bedroom at the largest hotel in New Brighton.

Staff came and went; Mrs Brierson was as pale as Lilac, but she wept; Lilac did not weep. Why should she, when she knew the whole report to be some horrible mistake, when she expected that any minute Art would come bustling in through the door, to seize her in his arms, kiss her with little kisses, tell her what a sensible lass she was not to be taken in by a sensationalized story?

Presently Monsieur Arrat came up from the kitchen. He looked different; she tried not to stare because it was rude, but his eyes were red, his nose positively glowed and his lower lip trembled. He told her there was a light supper set out for her downstairs and said she should go down to the kitchen now, she'd been on duty long enough.

She stood up and nearly fell. She wondered just how long she had been on duty – she didn't usually get so stiff that her legs failed her. But she walked across the hall behind Monsieur Arrat, pushed open the green baize door and began to go down the stairs. She was halfway down the flight when the blackness came up to meet her, like icy water creeping slowly up her body, devouring her. A terrifying numbness accompanied the blackness, an all-devouring chill which swept over her. She tried to clutch at the bannister rail to save herself, tried to call out ... then fell, swooping headfirst into the ice-cold dark.

Monsieur Arrat caught her before she hit the ground. He had been standing a few paces ahead of her and he simply held out his arms and swept her against his chest. All day he had been lamenting, crying, declaring that he could not work when such a terrible sadness had afflicted one for whom he had so much respect, but now that they needed common sense and practicality more than anything, he shed his affectations and became a tower of strength.

'I'll take her to one of the empty rooms,' he said, in almost accentless English. 'Poor child, she's coming to terms with the unbearable; that takes some doing. Someone must stay with her and when she comes round I will bring her supper up on a tray. With a whisky and hot water, I think.'

'I'll sit with her,' Mrs Brierson said. 'Sadie, go round and fetch Miss Charlotte; tell her what's happened – I'm sure she doesn't know or she'd have been round before now – and Phyllis, make me a couple of hot water bottles for her bed.'

The girls scuttled off to do her bidding and Mrs Brierson saw Lilac tucked up in bed and beginning, drowsily, to come round. She held Lilac's cold hand, murmured soothingly to her and presently despatched a maid to tell Monsieur Arrat that they would have the supper tray in ten minutes, please. Then she settled down to wait for Lilac to acknowledge her whereabouts.

Lilac opened her eyes. Outside the window she could see the sky, deep blue with dusk, but someone had lit the gas and a faint golden glow suffused the room in which she lay. She moved restlessly and realised someone was holding her hand. Her heart bounded joyfully in her breast – she had known Art was coming to her, he was here, he was holding her hand, sitting by the bed. . .

292

She clutched the fingers in hers and it was Mrs Brierson bending over her, saying something about a supper tray. Behind Mrs Brierson, Charlotte hovered, pale, red-eyed. Lilac shook her head at the mention of a supper tray, thoroughly disorientated, unable to remember with any clarity what had happened to her or where she was. After all, if she was still at the Delamere, what was Charlotte doing? Charlotte belonged to another life, her dancing academy life, she would not be at the Delamere! After a moment or two, however, Lilac sat up on one elbow and looked around her. She saw she was in bed, in the hotel, with hot bottles behind her knees and at her feet, with her employer sitting beside her holding her hand, whilst a great, echoing emptiness filled her aching head.

She looked helplessly across at Charlotte, wanting to ask her what had happened, why she felt so ill, but the words would not come. Slowly, she slid down the bed again. She turned her head away from Mrs Bierson and Charlotte and closed her eyes, but she was powerless to prevent the tears from squeezing out under her lids and trickling, slow and cold, down her cheeks.

'Lilac, my dearest child, my own dear girl, what a tragic, wicked waste, your dear boy gone and you far away, unable to do anything about it. Come to Nellie, dearest, tell Nellie!'

Warm arms enclosed her, a warm cheek was pressed to hers. The cheek was wet with tears, the hands clutching hers were trembling. She could feel Nellie's passionate sorrow, the love which enfolded her as Nellie hugged her tight.

'Oh, Nell, it isn't true, say it isn't true,' Lilac begged. Her voice was odd, harsh and croaking. 'He can't be drowned, not my Art, not my dear old Art.'

'You know it's true, love,' Nellie whispered. 'He's a hero, he saved a kiddy's life . . . but that don't help, not when he's gone.'

'Oh, but it's a mistake, it must be! We're going to be married, we're going to New Brighton for our honeymoon, we'd planned it in our letters, he came all the way from Gibraltar for two days just to talk about it! He can't, he can't be drowned.'

'He's dead, queen,' Nellie said gently. 'But you're alive, and you've got to go on living. Come on, sit up and have some of this nice supper what chef prepared.'

'He's dead? My Art really is dead?'

'That's right, queen. Look, a cup of thick soup, some bread – chef's homemade – and a glass of whisky to help you to warm up, all set out so lovingly . . . they're that fond of you, Li, that. . .'

'You're telling me that the newspapers got it right? That it was my Art who dived off the ship and saved the little girl and then got sucked under by the currents round the hull? My Art who drowned?'

'That's right, Lilac love. I've never lied to you, have I? And I'm not lying now. Art's gone and you've got to come to terms with it.'

Lilac nodded slowly and lay back against her pillows. The ache in her breast wouldn't go away, she supposed it never would, nor the hollowness in her mind. Could a person live with such pain, such loss? She asked Nellie whether it was possible and Nellie looked at her with such understanding, such loving sympathy in her big, expressive eyes!

'A person can try, queen,' she said quietly. 'A person has to try.'

If it hadn't been for her iron determination to get her family straightened out, Kitty didn't think she would have survived that first month. Patch helped, just by her constancy and affection – just by being there, when Kitty knew very well that the dog was pining for the countryside – but it was a terrible four weeks for Kitty, after three years of clean air and comfort on the farm. Poor Patch, too, was a country dog, terrified of city ways, city traffic, city people. But dogs are resilient and when they love they put their hearts and souls into it. Patch had loved Kitty from the moment the girl had let her off her chain and fed and watered her when Maldwyn was unable to do so. She had stuck closer to Kitty than a burr, always at her heels, only going off with Johnny or Maldwyn when they needed her to round up stock or bring cows or sheep in off the mountains.

Now, living in a city slum with food scarce and kicks ten a penny, she still stuck to Kitty. She grew gaunt and nervous, though Kitty did her best to see the dog was as well fed as circumstances allowed, but Patch never wavered in her affection and concern for her young mistress. And Kitty, no matter how tired she was, no matter how much she longed for a sit-down, took Patch down to the waterfront or up to the park night and morning and threw a stick for her so that the dog got plenty of exercise to keep her muscles in trim. What was more, Kitty begged bones from the butcher, scraps, rag-ends of meat or fish, and saw, somehow, that Patch was always more or less adequately fed.

295

The family fared equally well; that was to say they were mainly fed. Betty was a big help, carting the two younger ones around with her, using an old pram to carry shopping home and thus earn pennies. But once Sary's initial joy over Kitty's return cooled a little, Kitty often saw her mother staring at her with a horrible sort of calculation in the mean, bloodshot eyes. And the doctor had proved adamant. He would not come to the Court unless he was paid in advance.

So after a month of trying to improve her mother's physical condition, Kitty somehow lugged her parent, by tram and on foot, up to the centre on Brougham Terrace where free medical treatment was handed out, if you didn't mind the waits, the queues, and being treated by many of the medical staff as though you were nothing better than ignorant and unimaginative cattle who were lucky to be examined and should not expect to also be addressed.

They saw a young doctor, a man who examined Sary Drinkwater thoroughly, but with a sort of sneering distaste which annoyed Kitty very much. At the end of his examination he sent Sary off in the care of a nurse who would weigh and measure her and turned to Kitty.

'You the daughter?'

'Yes,' Kitty said equally baldly.

'Hmm. She drinks to excess, of course.'

'Yes.'

'Eats all the wrong food, too . . . fried potatoes? Bread and jam? That sort of thing?'

'When she eats at all,' Kitty said. 'What's 'er food got to do wi' anything?'

'My dear girl, it has everything to do with her state of health! She's overweight, flabby, I daresay she seldom walks . . .'

'She don't 'ave the strength,' Kitty said bitterly. She was disliking this young man more with every moment that passed. 'What I want to know is, what do I do about it?'

'Do? Why, stop her drinking and start her eating properly. She needs milk, meat, fresh fruit and vegetables of course . . . hey! Where are you going?'

'I'm goin' to find if there's a doctor in this place what can talk sense,' Kitty said furiously, turning to glare at him. 'Me Dad left 'ome three year ago an' we don't get 'is 'llowance no more; me brother flew the coop soon after. There's me an' three little sisters, I ain't gorra proper job, I picks up what I can . . . 'ow the 'ell d'you expect me to find food like that for me Mam?'

The doctor looked a little abashed, then rallied.

'I can only advise,' he said pompously. 'She's got where she is today through her own faults, you can't expect me . . .'

But he was speaking to a closed door. Kitty had slammed out.

Getting Sary to see another doctor was hard, but Kitty did not intend her time to be wasted. She bullied her mother into joining another queue and said grimly that unless Sary behaved she would find herself minus an elder daughter by morning. Sary gave her an evil look but consented to join the queue and presently they were ushered into another small, bleak consulting room. To Kitty's relief the second doctor was older, and, if wearier, very much more practical.

'She's had some sort of debilitating fever which has affected her mind, I fear,' he said to Kitty, smiling down very kindly at her. 'She isn't mad, as you feared, but she has lost touch with reality a little. If you can keep her away from alcohol and see that she drinks fresh milk and has something like cabbage or carrots most days, I am fairly confident she will recover. I'll have a tonic mixed up in the pharmacy, but fresh air, exercise and the best food you can manage will do her more good than any medicine I can provide. Now, my dear, what are your circumstances?'

Kitty explained.

The doctor nodded and frowned.

'I really think your smaller sisters should go to the Father Berry Catholic Children's Home on Shaw Street. They will be well-treated, well-fed, and that will enable you to see to your mother as best you can.'

'But they ain't orphans,' Kitty protested. 'They've gorra mam an' a dad; and me, acourse.'

'They have no one to support them,' the doctor explained. 'Your mother is ill and likely to be so for several weeks yet, your father has gone, and you're . . . what, fourteen?'

'Fifteen,' Kitty said. Being a practical young woman she could see the truth in his words. 'Right. 'Ow do I gerrem into this place?'

So the deed was done, with the doctor's help. Ruthie might not have understood what was happening to her but Eth did, and the look of relief on her small face when she was taken into the home and warmly welcomed, when she watched as Ruthie was picked up and cuddled by a fat nursery-maid and was shown the clean, warm clothing she would wear, went a long way to convincing Kitty that she had done the right thing. What was more the little girls were reunited with Kitty's other sisters, Phyllis and Mo, who had been at the Home for over a year and were very happy there.

Kitty told the girls that this was not a permanent thing, that they would only be cared for until

Sary Drinkwater was able to take them back. But in her heart she could not see Sary ever again being sufficiently responsible to take care of her children. Even when Sary's health improved she was clearly not a happy woman and the future seemed to hold no charms for her.

'Me dad leavin' must of cut 'er up more'n I'd ha' guessed,' Kitty remarked to Betty on a day when their mother refused to leave her bed. 'Poor Mam, she really must of liked the old soak.'

'Well, I didn't,' Betty said. 'Mam was always me favourite. She were awright when she were well, was me Mam.'

Despite missing the two younger girls, coping was easier once it was just Kitty, Betty and their mother, with Patch as moral support. Easier in one way, that was. Sary, who never seemed to take the slightest notice of her children, was told that the younger ones had been taken to someone who would feed and clothe them whilst she was too ill to do so, and accepted the explanation without more ado. Betty wept for a couple of nights and gave Kitty long, pained stares . . . she was presumably thinking that she had done her best to keep the family together yet this big sister had handed the little ones over without a murmur . . . but Kitty herself really missed Eth and Ruthie and felt guilty into the bargain, until she had visited them a couple of times after they had settled in.

The orphanage was a plain place, and practical, but the children were fed and neatly clothed, well taught, and if not loved, at least cared for in a responsible manner. Eth was soon seen to be in her element as the staff took her in hand, and Ruthie had been happy from the start, not only enjoying the food and the clothes, but revelling in the constant attention. Kitty, horribly aware of her own shortcomings as a provider, was glad to see the little girls growing sturdier with each visit, and soon stopped blaming herself for letting them go. The alternative was too horrible to contemplate, for even after a month her mother seemed little improved and the work Kitty managed to get scarcely fed the three of them. It would never have stretched to five.

'What did you do when you wasn't 'ere, Kit?' Betty asked, one chilly evening as the two of them and Patch snuggled down in the pile of rags. 'Was you very un'appy all alone?'

'I weren't alone, chuck, I were with a pal,' Kitty said slowly, a hand buried in the thick ruff of fur round Patch's neck. 'We was in the country, me an' me pal, on a farm. I 'spec' we'll go back, one day.'

'A farm? Wha's a farm?'

'Oh Betty, you know very well! Pigs an' cows an' that. Medders, fields . . . honest to God, kiddo, you must ha' seen about farms in books!'

'Oh, books,' Betty said. 'I can't read good.'

'I'll teach you if you like,' Kitty said. 'You goes to school, though.'

'Oh, aye, but only when I 'as to. I'll be 'appy when I can stay 'ome wi' you an' our Mam.'

Kitty did not reply. She knew very well that Betty sagged off school as often as she could but she simply could not take on the task of forcing the younger girl to attend classes. Besides, when school was in it was easier for Betty to get the odd job – fetching shopping for the old or the idle, wheeling the pram down to the docks for broken boxes which she could sell for firewood, lugging coal or potatoes home from the market – whereas in holiday time every kid was out there trying for work.

'Kit?'

'Yes, chuck?'

'Tell me about your farm.'

'Well, it's at the foot o' the Berwyn range – them's mountains. They're real lovely, are mountains. Blue an' misty sometimes, clear an' 'ard agin the sky others, spread wi' all sorts o' greens in the spring an' purples an' pinks in 'igh summer when the 'eather's out.'

'Mmm, sounds real lovely. Is that where you got your Patch from?'

'That's right. One mornin' me and me pal 'ad been sleepin' warm in an 'aystack . . .'

She told Betty about their arrival at the farm, Maldwyn's injury, his kindness to them. And when the child slept she went on thinking about the farm – and about Johnny Moneymor.

What had happened to him – more important, what did he think had happened to her? Had he found the witness to the will, taken him back to Wrexham, fetched a lawyer to confront the thieving Ap Thomases with their lies and treachery? Had he searched for her, Kitty? Somehow, she was sure he had, but it was too late. No one could search for ever and if he was still prosecuting his claim then he would have to be in Wales, and if he had been successful and had won, then he would have to be on the farm, taking care of things, protecting his property. Their property.

Because of course Johnny knows that I know where the farm is, whereas all he knows about me is that I used to live in Paradise Court but swore I'd never return there. He didn't get the note, that's for sure. So he might hunt for me up and down the Scottie, but likelier he'd go to Penny Lane because he knew

I had a friend there, or he'd hunt through the docks and the area he told me to search. The one place he wouldn't look is the Parry, so I'm safe enough here.

But that was silly, because she wanted her pal more than almost anything, certainly more than she wanted this collapsing house or her mean-eyed mother. But she couldn't just leave them to manage without her, not when she knew very well that they wouldn't. See them right first, she told herself meaninglessly, because seeing them right was an impossible task. See them right first, and then go your own way.

But thinking about the farm, and Johnny, was an escape from the bitter poverty, the ugly dilemma, in which she found herself. The apparent friendliness which Sary had shown at first had soon dissipated; her mother would have used violence against her, save that Kitty was clearly the stronger and fitter of the two. I'm more of a gaoler than a daughter, Kitty thought bitterly, for she hid her money away from Sary, never allowed her a penny to herself. If she did, she knew very well it would all be splashed out on drink, and that she dared not allow. And not only did she keep Sary short of cash, she also kept her either in the house or accompanied her outside it. Her mother would steal to get alcohol, and on the only occasion she had managed to get herself as far as the Black Dog unaccompanied she had also got herself very drunk indeed. Kitty guessed she had begged drinks, and supped the dregs in glasses, and because she hadn't drunk for so long, Sary had speedily become incapable. It had taken the combined strength of Kitty and her younger sister to drag the screaming, cursing hulk which was Sary Drinkwater out of the gutter and back to the house in Paradise Court.

'Nex' time we'll leave you lie,' Kitty had hissed breathlessly as they dropped Sary unceremoniously on the bottom stair. 'I'm warnin' you, Mam, there 'adn't berrer be a nex' time!'

But it was no life for any of them, Kitty thought now, as the dog's warmth mingled with that of the two girls and made the bed almost comfortable. And what'll we do when the weather worsens? Even now she was always tired, always hungry, always worried. September and October had been relatively mild, but now it was November, and when it grew really cold she doubted her ability to keep them warm and fed. Sary was clearly far from well and cordially hated her gaoler-daughter, even though everything Kitty did was for her ultimate good. But you can't teach an old dog new tricks, Kitty thought, stroking Patch's silky ears. Her mother had always been a violent woman, a heavy drinker. Nothing would change that now, except for old age and infirmity, and Sary was only thirty-eight, though she looked and acted sixty.

But it was no good thinking like that or she'd never sleep. Kitty curled up with an arm round Patch's neck and directed her thoughts back to the farm. Wouldn't it be marvellous to wake up in her own little room, with the mountain range glowing with sunrise outside her window and the heather's purple deepening to brown? Downstairs a big log fire, outside the clean, fresh mountain air, the winter-pale grass, the trees with their bare branches dusted with frost.

Some kids are so lucky, she thought drowsily, her mind eased and gentled by her recollections. Some kids have all that from birth, it's as natural to them as city streets and hunger are to kids like Betty, to women like me Mam. Why, if things had been different . . . .

She sat bolt upright, ignoring the cold air which her sudden movement had brought swirling into their nest. If things had been different . . . well, why should they not be? Why should she, her mother and her sister, to say nothing of Patch, not set out on the road, as she and Johnny Moneymor had done? God knows they could not be worse off than they were at present, and at least if they were in the country they would have fresh air to breathe, fresh water to drink, and the clean fields and meadows to walk in. Patch would be better – she worried more about the dog than about the rest of the family since she had brought Patch to this dreadful pass – Sary and Betty would be better and she, Kitty Drinkwater, would probably be able to earn them a living of sorts.

Even if the Thomases are still at the farm, I can earn my living in the country, Kitty thought. I can milk a cow, clean a byre, drive a pony and trap, sell at a market . . . her skills, which were non-existent in a city, suddenly began to mount up to something worthwhile when you thought about the country. Why, I could keep house for a bachelor farmer, she thought excitedly, remembering how Maldwyn had painstakingly taught her to cook, to make and to mend, to clean and polish. Oh yes, of course, why hadn't she thought of it before? It was in the country that their future lay, Mam's and Betty's as well as hers and Patch's. She would talk to them about it the very next day!

'Go off, 'oofin' it? Wi' winter comin' on? You're mad!'

Sary Drinkwater heaved a huge shoulder up in the air and burrowed further down under her filthy bedcovers. The gesture said louder than words that she did not intend to budge from her bed unless she was forced. Kitty gritted her teeth and caught hold of the dirty blanket. She tried not to notice the tiny movements of bugs in the matted wool; they'd die off when the weather worsened, she told herself – so long as we don't follow suit, she added, with grim humour. She heaved and the blanket slid half off the bed.

'Get *up*, Mam,' she said sharply. 'The doc told you fresh air an' exercise. We're goin' for a walk to the country, me and Bet, an' you're coming' with us.'

'No – I – ain't!' Each word was accompanied by a heave on the blanket and Sary was still a strong woman. 'You goes, the pair of yez, an' good riddance I say!'

'We will go,' Kitty threatened. She turned and stormed out of the room, with Betty and Patch close on her heels. At the bottom of the stairs she turned to her sister. 'What'll we do, Bet? I can get work in the country, I've got friends there, but there ain't much I can do in the city! Shall us go, you an' me?'

Betty heaved a sigh and shook her head.

'She'll die if we leave 'er,' she pointed out. 'She'll be up the boozer a-beggin' bevvies – or stealin' 'em – afore you can say scuffers. We'll 'ave to sit it out till she's gorrer full senses back.'

Kitty sighed and nodded, biting back a sharp retort that their mother would be a fool even if she had her full senses, as Betty called them, returned to her tomorrow. But she did try to make her point.

'Mam lives for the booze now, flower,' she said gently. 'I dunno as 'ow I can stay for ever, an' with Mam that's what it'ud be.'

'I know; but Mam was good to us when she were 'erself,' Betty said. 'Not to you, Kit, you've gorra right to go, I know it, but she were awright to the rest of us.'

'You wouldn't go to the children's home, like the others, I suppose?' Kitty said without much hope. 'They'd feed you there, an' that.'

'If I did that Mam wouldn't even try to git better,' Betty observed shrewdly. 'She'd sink like a stone, I tells you.'

'Yeah; you're right. Well, we'll go on tryin' for a bit, then,' Kitty said wearily. 'See 'er through the winter. Best tek the pram down to the docks, see if you can find some broken boxes to sell. I'll bide 'ere wi' Mam and try to think it through.'

She was still thinking, without getting anywhere at all, when there was a tentative knock on the door.

Johnny! Kitty thought; he's found me! And she flew across the room and hurled open the front door.

'Oh, Johnny, I's . . .'

It wasn't Johnny. It was a buxom, smiling girl a few years older than Kitty herself. Kitty recognised her as one of the Fletchers who now lived in what had once been Mrs O'Rourke's neat house. She smiled rather diffidently; the three big daughters, and this was one of them, were always friendly and cheerful, and though the males of the family did roar out songs and a few curses when they came back from the boozer, though the females seemed to have rather a rapid turnover of gentlemen friends, Kitty thought the Fletchers were a cheery crowd. At least they were a change from the rest of the inhabitants of Paradise Court, who tended to keep themselves to themselves and clearly considered, despite Betty's strictures, that it was the Drinkwaters who had brought the Court low rather than the arrival of others.

''Ello, chuck,' the girl said. She had thick yellow curls, bright blue eyes and a wide, friendly grin. Her front teeth had a little gap between them which somehow made her look younger than she probably was, more Kitty's age. Kitty could tell that the yellow curls came out of a peroxide bottle and that her pink cheeks also owed something to artifice, but she admired the older girl nevertheless. 'I t'ought it were time we interdooced ourselves, seein' as we're neighbours, like. I'm Marigold Fletcher, an' you'll be. . . ?'

'I'm Kitty Drinkwater,' Kitty said. She held out her hand. 'How d'you do?'

That was what they said in books, but Marigold looked taken aback for a moment, then seized Kitty's hand in a warm and friendly grip.

'Ow do, Kitty,' she said heartily. 'I come to ask 'ow's your mam?'

'Poorly, thanks,' Kitty said gloomily. 'I were tryin' to get 'er to come for a walk . . . jest a bit of a way at first, the doc say she oughter 'ave exercise an' fresh air . . . but she won't budge from 'er pit.'

'Eh, dat's a shame. I brung 'er a rice pudden', still 'ot. Think she could swally a mouthful?'

'She could, I'm sure,' Kitty said, holding out her hands for the pudding basin the girl had been holding behind her back. 'Ooh, you are good, you are kind . . . it's been queerin' me 'ow the 'ell I were to get 'er a meal today . . . gelt's runnin' low to tell the truth.'

'Yeah . . . well, I wondered if you'd like to do a bit o' work for me,' Marigold said. She dimpled beguilingly at Kitty. 'I been an' got meself a room on Grayson Street – for me business, like – but the fellers don't know where to find me. If they come 'ere, our Daisy an' our Vi'let will oblige, but the fellers from the dock won't bother to search me out, see? An' someone told me you wrote lovely, so I bought a pad an' a pencil an' I thought you could write me some lickle notes, like? I'd pay, acourse,' she added hastily.

'Be glad to,' Kitty said joyfully. A job where she could stay and keep an eye on her mother would be ideal. 'Gi's the paper, I'll do some right away.'

'Good. An' will you deliver 'em for me? Down at the docks where the big ships come in? I'm fed up wi' walkin' up and down meself, so I'll pay you two bob a day so long as you write out twenty or thirty and deliver the same number. What say?'

'Well, aye, but who do I deliver 'em to?' Kitty said, rather mystified. 'I wouldn't know your friends from Adam, would I, eh?'

Marigold giggled and the pink in her cheeks deepened.

'Well, I'd like to say officers only, but I reckon I might do meself in the eye that way, eh? So 'ow about any feller off of a ship what's just docked?'

'Ah, I see,' Kitty said. Now she understood – Marigold wanted sailors to pay her for . . . well, whatever it was that sailors paid bad girls for . . . but she didn't want to walk the streets herself, not now she'd risen to the heights of renting her own room. 'But Marigold, suppose the fellers thought it were me what was toutin' for business? What then, eh?'

'Just given 'em some lip an' keep the dog by you,' Marigold advised after some thought. 'You'd be awright, the fellers like . . . well, they like a woman wi' some flesh on 'er bones, you're a kid, really.'

'It's worth more'n a couple o' bob a day, though,' Kitty said pensively. 'I'd 'ave to get someone to sit wi' me mam, else she'd start knockin' back the gin before you could say mother's ruin. If I 'and them papers to twenty fellers . . . .'

'Oh ah, I see what you mean, but I won't git

twenty customers from twenty papers,' Marigold said quickly. 'Oh, you 'ave to put yourself in the way of a dozen, mebbe more, blokes to get one or two customers.'

'I daresay. But once they knows where you are you won't need me, so I gorra mek the money whiles I can,' Kitty pointed out righteously. 'Five bob a day an' you're on.'

'Five bob! Gawd, you'll 'ave me flat on me back in the gutter at that rate,' Marigold protested, though still so good-naturedly that Kitty guessed she was willing to pay more. 'Say four an' a tanner?'

'Five bob,' Kitty said placidly, sensing her advantage. 'Can't give up me time for less.'

'Right. Five bob, then. Start tomorrer?'

'Start now; gi's the papers,' Kitty said with her usual practicality. 'I'll keep on till you've got enough steadies, then I'll 'ave to find summat else. Where's the copy?'

'Ain't got one,' Marigold admitted. 'I thought you'd do it better'n me. Just say that it's Marigold, now available at Number 20 Grayson Street. Prices reasonable.'

'Hadn't you better say you're teachin' French or something?' Kitty said, starting to write the message on the first sheet of thin paper of the pad Marigold had thrust into her hand. 'Ain't this agin the law?'

'Well, goin' wi' a feller's agin the law, but you can write teachin' French so long as they don't b'lieve you,' Marigold said generously. 'I don't want no fellers wi' brains in their 'eads a-bangin' on me door.' She giggled. 'If you see what I mean,' she finished.

'Look, I can't do a good job standin' 'ere,' Kitty said presently. Trying to write with a stub of pencil on the thin paper, with the pad balanced on her rather inadequate knee, just wasn't possible. 'You go orf, Marigold, an' I'll bring 'em round later. When does you move into Grayson Street?'

'Move, whaddyer mean?'

'Well, when do you start to live there?'

'Live there? I ain't goin' to live there, chuck, I'm just a-goin' to carry on me business there,' Marigold explained. 'So I'll be at number twelve if you want me.'

'Oh! Right,' Kitty said. She waited until Marigold had gone into her own house, then closed the door thoughtfully. She now had a well-paid job for a short while; she must make the most of it and decide what to do when it finished because she was icily determined not to simply give in and stay at the Court with Sary and Betty.

'I'll do me best by 'em both,' she told Patch as the dog sat at her feet, watching her pencil copy out page after page of Marigold's message. 'But I won't give up me life to 'em, it ain't fair and I won't do it.'

Patch sighed and laid her head gently on Kitty's knee; Kitty smoothed the silky fur and sighed too.

'It ain't fair on you either, Patchie,' she murmured. 'But we'll be all right; there's gorra be a way out, there's jest gorra be!'

The job was all right, though tiring and slightly risky. It turned out that she often had to conduct the customers to Grayson Street, since sailors in need of a woman in a strange port aren't prepared to buy street maps. They would sooner pick up some floosie actually on the spot, even if she didn't have much more to offer than a cheap five-minute gallop and a wall to lean against.

However, Patch lessened the risk considerably. Some men she liked, in which case she trotted quietly at Kitty's heels through the darkening streets, never needing more than a word now and then. But some men she disliked, and Kitty soon grew to realise that Patch was a far better judge of character than she was herself. A smart young man with well-brushed clothing and hair Brylcreemed flat to his scalp might be the very one to take a grab at Kitty, thinking to save his money and get what he wanted by stealing it – Kitty was still not at all sure what went on between Marigold and her customers, but she did know it wasn't for her – but Patch soon put a stop to any such thoughts, let alone actions. She would get between Kitty and the man and her hackles would rise up all along her back until she looked the way Kitty imagined an angry wolf would look. And she kept up the most ominous grumbling growl all the time, too, only ceasing when they reached number 20. The only man to decide she couldn't hurt him had been badly bitten, far too badly to want to continue to defy the growling, stiff-legged Patch, so Kitty thought that her personal safety was assured whilst she and the dog were together.

The money she earned from Marigold was good and Mrs Fletcher, a woman as good-natured and easy-going as her daughters, had agreed to keep an eye on Sary whilst Betty and Kitty were out, so things began to improve a little for the Drinkwaters. Food was more plentiful, Sary's health began to improve, Betty positively blossomed.

Spring came and Kitty saved her money and bought herself a cotton skirt and jacket and her mother a lightweight shawl. Betty had a new dress and Kitty got a neighbour to mend the door of number 8 and spray the walls and floor with disinfectant. Sary cooked for them sometimes and Betty attended school now and then.

'I can see the day when I can leave 'em to their own devices ain't that far off,' Kitty told Patch, as the two of them paraded up and down the waterfront with their papers. Kitty, having been eyed askance by both senior officers and policemen on several occasions, had taken what Marigold thought was a really brilliant step. She had gone to the Shamrock Café, where she was still a customer from time to time, and asked them if they would like advertising leaflets drawn up and handed out down at the docks, since she was already performing this service for a young gentleman who gave lessons on the ukelele. The proprietress, who had noticed Kitty as a decent young girl who though plainly dressed always paid her bill promptly, agreed, so now Kitty was paid twice over for her services and if questioned by authority, could always show the Shamrock's menu, innocently printed on pretty pink paper.

She had begun to make good money from her two jobs, and was saving up so she could leave Bet and Sary with some money. She was planning this one day when she went to eat her carry-out, sitting on a bollard by Wapping Dock, and discovered that she wasn't hungry.

This was a rarity. Kitty stared at the bacon sandwich and the apple and then at Patch, who was watching her hopefully.

'You're welcome to it, old gel,' Kitty said, breaking the sandwich into pieces and feeding them to the dog. 'Now as I come to notice, me throat's awful painful, it don't feel a bit like swallerin' food. I could do wi' a drink though.'

She got herself water from a dock-tap, then resumed

her slow saunter alongside the shipping, but as the day progressed, so did her feeling that all was not well with her. The sore throat was bad enough but presently she became aware that while other people were buttoning their coats against the wind, she felt so hot that she had removed her own jacket and tied it round her waist by its arms. That wasn't natural, not even on a mild March day – I reckon you're gettin' a cold, Kitty Drinkwater, she told herself accusingly. Well, you can't afford to be ill, not wi' Mam comin' on well an' Marigold doin' so nicely. She'll get someone else to find fellers for 'er, and then where will us be?

She got herself home and into the pile of rags; her mother had proper bedding now, decent stuff, but she and Betty were saving their money. Kitty was still hoping she would be on the road before too long so spending money on bedding would be a waste.

Next morning she didn't know how to get up; her throat was raw, it hurt her to breathe, and her eyes felt as though someone had cooked them overnight for a joke. She staggered downstairs, saw Betty off to carry parcels from Paddy's Market to the buyer's homes, made her mother tea and porridge, watched her eat it and somehow got herself over to the Fletcher's.

'You look flushed, dearie,' Mrs Fletcher said. 'Ow's your mam?'

'Think I gorra cold comin', but me mam's grand,' Kitty said with satisfaction. 'She's beginnin' to look more like herself. Still . . . keep an eye on 'er, Mrs F.'

'Be in there as soon's I've 'ad me breakfuss,' Mrs Fletcher promised. 'See you later, Kit.'

Kitty went to Marigold's room first, as she always did. Marigold answered the door in a rather dirty dressing-gown with her beautiful golden curls done up in papers and her face as red as a beetroot. 'Don't bring no one back today, chuck,' she said hoarsely. 'I ain't quite meself; I feels rare bad.'

'Me too,' Kitty said ruefully. 'Reckon we've both got 'ead-colds.'

She decided to go round to the Shamrock for some more menus but she never reached it. She began to feel odder and odder; the sky kept dipping and dancing above her head, the tall buildings shrank one minute and grew like grass the next. She sat on the kerb and put her head on Patch's shoulder and had a little weep because she felt so poorly, then she tried to get up and move along. Someone was telling her to move along, she could hear a voice but she could see nothing, only a sort of patchy red and black.

Presently the patchiness turned black altogether and she slumped forward into the road, unconscious.

Frantically, Patch grabbed her by the sleeve and tried to drag her back to safety, then she barked and barked and barked. Someone came along, saw Patch and the girl in the gutter, leaned down and stroked the dog. Patch sniffed cautiously. This was a good girl, a nice girl, a girl she could trust with her beloved Kitty. Patch wagged her tail and sat down, handing over responsibility. And the nice, good girl took one look at the hot and feverish little face, pulled Kitty clear of the roadway, then telephoned the nearest hospital.

'A young girl's collapsed on Preesons Row, just outside the Shamrock Café, opposite the Victoria Memorial,' she said crisply. 'Please send an ambulance at once; I'll wait with her.'

And very soon the ambulance came clattering round the corner and the young lady got into the vehicle, then jumped out again. 'Can you not take the dog? It's our only hope of identifying her,' she said to the ambulance men. 'If not, I'd better stay with it and make my way to the ward on foot.'

'We'll tek the bloody dog,' the driver said as the other men stared at one another. 'Why not? It won't be aboard for more'n a few minutes.'

So the ambulance rattled off to the Isolation Hospital, because the ambulance men knew scarlet fever when they saw it, and Lilac Larkin sat by the swaying bed and stroked Kitty Drinkwater's hot, dry little hand and held onto the dog's collar so it wouldn't be flung about by the motion of the ambulance and wondered just what she had let herself in for this time.

'You shouldn't oughter 'old 'er 'and, Miss,' the ambulance man said presently. 'Scarlet fever's infectious; a killer, if you don't mind me sayin' so, Miss.'

'I'm not worried,' Lilac said, and the ambulance man assumed that she had had the disease and did not fear a recurrence. It did not occur to him that such a pretty, well-dressed young lady simply might not care if she lived or died.

Chapter Thirteen

They tried really hard, at the isolation hospital, to find out who Kitty was so that they could get in touch with her relatives, but Kitty put them completely on the wrong track by telling them, when she was at her worst, that her name was Kitty Drinkwater and she and Patch came from a farm a few miles from Corwen.

'Can you give us the name of the farm, or the village, even?' the ward sister said persuasively. 'We need to get in touch with your people, dear, so that we can try to prevent the disease from spreading through your family. And it would help us if we knew how you'd contracted the illness.'

She was rather taken-aback when Kitty announced that she'd doubtless got it from a sailor. And then Lilac, without meaning to, cast fresh confusion on Kitty's story.

'She may have come from a farm in Wales once, but now she hands out leaflets for the Shamrock Café,' Lilac explained, laughing at the nurse's bemused expression, and showed the older woman a menu which she had found in the pocket of Kitty's light jacket. Perhaps fortunately Lilac knew nothing about the other leaflets, the ones advertising the services of Marigold, and Kitty, even in the darkest days of her fever, said nothing to give anyone a clue.

Patch was not allowed in the hospital, though.

Not even Lilac's most persuasive arguments could work that particular magic. 'She'll respond to her dog,' Lilac said hopefully. The ward sister sniffed. 'She'll come round and speak to it, the way mothers do for their babies,' Lilac stated. The ward sister sniffed louder.

So Patch lived in Lilac's room when she was in it, and behind the reception desk at the Delamere when she wasn't, and fretted for her little mistress, though she was sufficiently sagacious to know, somewhere in her mind, that Kitty was being taken care of. She knew partly because she was an intelligent animal and partly because, when Lilac returned from hospital visiting, she often used Kitty's name over and over, whilst looking deeply into Patch's worried eyes. So Patch was satisfied that, if she stuck close to Lilac, she would end up reunited with Kitty.

Lilac spent all her spare time at the hospital. Not actually on the ward because that was not allowed, the disease being extremely infectious, but on the other side of a broad pane of glass, through which she could see and even speak to, the small patient. From the moment she had seen Kitty lying in the road a chord had been struck somewhere within her – a sense of fellowship, perhaps, or a vague recollection? She had looked at the small, hot face, the abundant red-brown hair, and felt that she had seen Kitty before. What was more, Kitty needed her – needed her as badly as, several months ago now, that other little girl, Lucy, had needed Art O'Brien. Art had risked his life for a child and lost; she was scarcely risking her life, but at least she was doing something for the kid, doing her best, in fact. And since no one else had come forward, her best would have to do.

So whenever she wasn't working, Lilac sat and talked to Kitty through the pane of glass until one day, one wonderful day, Kitty's heavy lids lifted and the fever-bright eyes stared straight into Lilac's. Lilac saw Kitty's lips move, but could not make out, through the glass, what the other girl was saying. She ran for the nurse, who went into the room, but came back shaking her head and saying that the child was talking gibberish.

'She said something about the girl from Penny Lane . . . you don't come from Penny Lane, do you, Miss?'

'No-oo. But I did, once, or rather my sister did,' Lilac said thoughtfully. 'Now I wonder . . . I thought I knew her, there's something just at the back of my mind where I can't reach it . . .'

'Never mind, at least she's spoken,' the nurse said. 'Likely she'll pull through after all.'

And that was Lilac's first intimation that the staff had previously thought Kitty a lost cause.

It was wonderful to come round to white sheets, cleanliness, sweet air and no responsibility, but to glance sideways and see the face she had so longed to see within feet of her – that really did make Kitty wonder if she had died and gone to heaven! But presently a nurse came in with some foul medicine which she tipped ruthlessly down Kitty's protesting throat and Kitty realised she had been ill, was still ill, and must have imagined that face, for when she looked sideways at the pane of glass it was empty; only the reflection of the nurse with the medicine, the bed and Kitty herself rewarded her glance.

'What's your name, love?'

'Kitty Drinkwater.'

'Where d'you come from? We know about the farm, chuck, but not the exact address.'

Kitty felt a spasm of fear; she should not say, she might get Johnny into trouble if folk thought she was laying some sort of claim on the place. She frowned; her head still ached horribly and the skin had peeled off her forehead and cheeks, leaving them sore and dry-feeling.

'I . . . don't live there any more.'

'Where d'you live, then?'

'Off the Burley; number 8 Paradise Court.'

'Do you mean off Burlington Street?'

'Yes, that's right,' Kitty said, already slipping back into the feverish world of sleep she had so briefly emerged from. 'Wi' me sister Bet.'

'Right,' the ward sister said. 'I'll get a health visitor round there later in the day. We'll soon get it sorted out.'

'Well, you're gettin' better,' someone said the next day. It was one of the nurses, sounding cheerful but a bit surprised, as well. 'Be on your feet in a week or two. Then you'll be allowed to see your friend.'

'Friend?'

'Aye. The pretty one what comes and sits behind the glass; don't say you've not noticed 'er!'

So the face was not a dream, then. Someone was there, someone pretty. Could it be Marigold? Or Betty? But deep inside herself she didn't believe it was either of them. It was – it had to be – the girl from Penny Lane.

Nellie had heard, by letter, all about the little girl with scarlet fever and it had worried her deeply. It

319

was all very well for Lilac to say she thought she remembered the child, that Kitty was so alone, that she was only allowed to sit behind a sheet of glass until the danger of infection had passed, it sounded reasonable enough put like that. But Nellie was afraid that Lilac had simply lost her will to live and was looking for a way out. Lilac had never had scarlet fever as a child so she could easily contract it now, and despite the marvels of modern medicine scarlet fever often proved fatal, particularly if the sufferer caught the disease when already at a low ebb both physically and mentally.

So now she sat in her kitchen watching the bread prove and keeping an eye on the clock whilst the oven reached heat and wondering what Stuart would have to tell her when he got home. For Stuart had applied for a job in Liverpool at last and it was a job after his own heart, furthermore. Deputy editor of a reputable evening paper, with the sort of responsibilities which he had been used to taking on in London. So today he had caught the milk train from Euston and would be in Lime Street – Nellie felt a great surge of envy – in good time for the interview.

Prejudiced though I am, Nellie thought now, getting up and putting the loaf tins on her kitchen table whilst she swung open the oven door a short way and prepared to face the blast of heat, I think my dear Stu stands a good chance. He's covered most of the work, he's a scouser born and bred and understands other scousers in a way an outsider would find impossible, and he's so bright and sensible . . . oh surely he'll get the job? Then we can go home at last!

He had said he might ring if he had time, but otherwise he would just jump on a train, and since she'd not heard it was either that they were going to inform the applicants by post or, worst and most unbearable of all, that he hadn't got it and would have to keep looking. Nellie sighed and slid the bread into the oven, closing the door with her usual excessive caution, though she had never flattened a loaf yet. She'd decided not to pester God with any more prayers or promises – she had popped into church every time she passed ever since Stuart heard he'd got an interview, for a few words with the Almighty – but she couldn't help herself having a little extra dig now.

If he gets it, God, he'll be givin' pleasure to so many people, she remarked in an offhand way, more as a chatty aside than a prayer as such. All them folk on the newspaper, my Stuart knows 'em all, he understands 'em ... if you've got any influence at all ...

She stopped short, horrified at herself. Either pray or don't, Nellie Gallagher, she told herself. Just don't hint He couldn't if He would! And then, since the loaves were safe in and Elizabeth would be at her nursery school for another couple of hours, she slid to her knees and said a few words of apology for her doubts, a few words of thanks for Elizabeth and Stuart, a reminder that Lilac was a good little soul and needed her family round her at this sad time ... and then she signed off, got to her feet and went to fetch the beeswax to polish the dining table and chairs.

Waxing away, her face pink with effort, Nellie began to go over in her head all the good reasons for returning to Liverpool, not just her own good reasons but Lilac's, too.

Lilac could see more of little Elizabeth, Nellie thought now, staring unseeingly at the table, gleaming like a dark lake beneath her ministrations. Nellie was still sufficiently besotted with her only child to believe that the mere sight of little Elizabeth would improve anyone's outlook on life. Why, the child adores her Auntie Lilac, having such affection must make a difference – and I could start to introduce her to young men . . .

Nellie had spent two weeks in Liverpool trying to help Lilac to pull herself round after the tragedy – though Lilac had been wonderful, full of courage and good sense – and had seen the Academy of Modern Dance in full swing. Had Lilac wanted to meet a nice young man, the dancing school offered unrivalled opportunities, but though unfailingly polite and as cheerful as was possible in the circumstances, no one could have failed to notice Lilac's total disinterest in the opposite sex. Clearly, finding Lilac another young man was going to be a formidable task and one which might never succeed. But reviving Lilac's interest in life – Nellie smiled at the mere thought of Elizabeth's smooth hair and wide, enquiring eyes – might just be possible when her little niece was present.

Having polished the dining table until she could see her face reflected in it, right down to a tiny spot on her nose, Nellie put away her duster and the beeswax and decided to treat herself to a little outing. She would fetch Elizabeth from nursery school and take a nice walk to Tooting Bec Common, where they would watch little boys sailing boats on the pond or large girls, in school uniform, walking across the grass, shouting, teasing.

I'll pack some sandwiches, Nellie thought, bustling through to the kitchen to check her bread, and a bottle of home-made lemonade, and we'll have a little picnic, Elizabeth loves a picnic. And just for a bit I won't think about the job, or worry about Lilac's state of mind, or fret about my baby being brought up away from home. And whilst I do our carry-out I can plan what to make Stuart for his tea, because he'll need feeding up, poor love, after the sort of day he's probably had!

In the morning the weather had been rainy, uncertain – typical April weather in fact. By the time Nellie set out though, the sun had decided to break through and the wind had dropped to a gentle breeze.

Elizabeth was, of course, last out of the gate. Nellie had often pondered on why it was that when she met Lilac out of school in the old days, Lilac had always trailed far behind the other kids; now here was her little Elizabeth doing just the same. But her daughter was with two or three others, all chattering and cheerful, surrounding the teacher who was young and pretty, clearly loving her job and her company, too.

Nellie saw Elizabeth scanning the waiting parents and nannies – for it was quite an expensive nursery school – without anxiety, though with some interest. Sometimes Nellie called for her daughter, sometimes another mother picked Elizabeth up when she called for her son, Simon. But today Simon had long gone so Elizabeth would realise that she was to be Mummy's sole companion this afternoon.

'I like that best,' Elizabeth had assured her solemnly on an earlier occasion, when Nellie had asked if she missed Simon. 'I have other children in school all day, I like it to be just you an' me.'

Nellie had been enormously pleased; now she waved as Elizabeth broke away from her teacher and came gambolling across the playground towards her.

'Mummy, mummy ... oh Mam, is that a picnic?' she squeaked, apparently guessing that a covered basket with a bottle sticking out of it indicated treat time. 'Oh, can we go to the common?'

'Would you like to?'

Nellie caught the enchanting child up in a tight embrace from which Elizabeth was slow to struggle free; she loved cuddling, could never get enough of it.

'Oh, yes, please! One day, when I'm bigger, I'll have a boat to sail on the pond, won't I? One day I'll be tall enough to swing on the swings without you to push, one day ...'

'One day you'll be pushing me on the swings,' Nellie said, setting Elizabeth carefully down on the pavement and straightening her short camelhair jacket and the grey skirt which she wore beneath it. It was a short skirt, but not so short as some of the mothers; my legs are too thin to show off me knees, Nellie protested when Stuart suggested she should try the really daring skirts. But it wasn't the main reason: short skirts were for girls, and Nellie was very conscious of herself as a woman.

'Did you bring me scooter?' Elizabeth said anxiously. 'Oh, I could scoot to the common in a minute ... in a second, very likely!'

'No, I didn't bring it, because you can't scoot on grass,' Nellie said. 'Besides, you don't want to be watching your scooter all the time we're eating our tea, do you?'

The handsome red scooter had pride of place in Elizabeth's affections right now, though she was passionately keen to own a tricycle. Simon had a tricycle and it meant that when his mummy took them to the park Simon was usually miles ahead of

324

them. Nellie, noting this fact with some concern, for even in a quiet place like Balham the traffic worried her, had privately decided that a tricycle would have to wait until Elizabeth was at least six.

'No-oo,' Elizabeth admitted. 'Sides, when I'm scootin' we can't talk much and I can't hold your hand.'

'True,' Nellie said, squeezing the small and probably grimy fingers securely clasped in her own. 'So let's step out; what shall we do first? The boating pond or the swings or our picnic?'

'Pond,' Elizabeth said decidedly. 'Then sarnies, then swings.'

Nellie wondered whether to correct the slang, then decided to leave it. Elizabeth isn't a little southerner, she's a little northerner, and if she sounds it so much the better, she thought defiantly. She and Stuart did their best to speak standard English, but in the comfort of their own home and each other's company they frequently lapsed a little.

It wasn't far from the nursery to the start of the common. They crossed the High Street, went under the railway bridge and there they were, though they still had quite a walk across the green grass before they reached the more interesting bits.

'Shall I tell you what we did in school today?' Elizabeth said presently, as they walked. 'We made sandpies in the sand-table first. Simon made a little sand-cake with the red mould and then he tried to eat it and Miss Millicent said it was dirty and Red-face said dogs widdled in sand and Miss Millicent said . . .'

'Darling, who's Red-face?' Nellie said patiently. She was endeavouring to stop her daughter from nicknaming, with very little success so far.

'Sara Boyle. She gets angry so quick, Mam, and

her face is often red. She hits the little ones and . . .'

'Yes, all right, only you should call her Sara, darling, because that's the name her mummy gave her. I hope you don't eat sand?'

'Only sometimes,' Elizabeth said sunnily. 'Not every day.'

Nellie tried to turn a snort of amusement into a cough. She blew her nose ostentatiously whilst Elizabeth continued to dance along beside her.

'Where was I, Mam, before you interrupted? Oh yeah, you said to call Sara Sara, only there's two Saras you know, Red-face and Sara, so I . . . poor Mummy, that's a really nasty cough!'

Nellie squeezed her daughter's small paw again.

'I love you, queen,' she said. 'Hey-up, here's the boating pond . . . and the old feller wi' the beard's sailing away already!'

The two of them leaned on the round concrete rim of the boating pond, watching the yachts – tall, elegant ones with painted hulls or gleaming woodwork, small, busy ones floating along, seizing as much of the fitful breeze as they could – and of course the owners, mainly small boys except for the elderly man with the nautical cap, the blazer and the white beard.

'I call him Cap'n,' Elizabeth whispered. 'Cap'n Whitebeard.'

Nellie turned away to hide another of her reprehensible giggles and got the feeling that she had just interrupted someone staring at her. It was an odd feeling, but unmistakable. Of the small group of people clustered around the pond on her right, one had been fixing her with a gaze . . . she glanced across, then away. A man, probably about her own age, had appeared to turn his eyes hastily back to the water, to where a small yacht was turning clumsily as its tatty sail suddenly picked up the wind and filled to a bulging cheek of plenty. He had a small, none-too-clean boy with him and he bent down and directed the child's gaze towards the small yacht.

'See 'er take the wind, Tommy? She's on'y small but she's cheeky . . . see the way she snatched the wind off of that big, white yacht?'

Tommy leaned over the parapet and beat the water with one hand. The small yacht, heading for him, hesitated as though in doubt over the advisability of its actions, then sailed stoically on. It came to harbour in the man's capable hands, then was taken out, dripping, and seized by the child.

'Awright, Uncle Joey,' the boy shouted shrilly. 'You stay 'ere, I'll go rahnd the uvver side, send 'er over to you!'

'Will do, me ole mate,' the man said. 'Orf you goes!'

As soon as the child had left him he turned to look at Nellie once more, and found her eyes already fixed on his. He coloured, then dropped his gaze to the water, then seemed to change his mind and looked straight across at her, grinning. He half-raised a hand in a salute, then began to stroll the short distance between them.

Nellie thought about moving away, then changed her mind. The man did look familiar, but she couldn't quite bring to mind where she had seen him. It was possible that it could have been in France, of course, when she had nursed during the war, but there was something about him . . . he had come, she was suddenly sure, from further back in her past, so she must have met him in Liverpool, because she had lived there all her life until going to France.

'Miss . . . oh cripes, if I 'aven't gorn and forgot your name, Miss,' the man said. 'Doncher remember me? Joey Prescott what found your little sister – if she was your sister – that time she ran away dahn the Wapping Dock in Liverpool? You 'ad a bruvver Charlie – that I *do* recall – an' 'is wife was 'avin' a baby. Your sister was called Lilac . . . Now that's not the sorta name a feller can forget!'

'Why, Joey Prescott!' Nellie exclaimed joyfully as light dawned. 'How could I have forgotten you, after what you did? I was so grateful, but we never exchanged addresses – and if you came to the Pool again you never looked us up.'

'War broke out soon afterwards,' Joey reminded her. 'My ship was torpedoed twice, I was lucky to escape wi' me life the second time. Well, if this ain't rich . . . 'ow about you an' the little lady joinin' me an' young Tommy 'ere for a nice cuppa? I'd be 'appy to treat you both to a bun, an all.'

Nellie laughed but shook her head regretfully.

'It's awful nice of you, Joey, but we've got our tea with us; Elizabeth was really looking forward to a picnic – Elizabeth's my daughter, by the way. I'm Nellie Gallagher now, not Nellie McDowell.'

'I see . . . yes, come to think, there was a sailor who glared at me that night – dark chap, curly 'air – you married 'im, did you?'

'Oh! No, that was . . . no, I didn't marry him, my husband was a war correspondent in France; now he works for the *London Evening Telegraph*. And Lilac was engaged, but . . .'

Joey Prescott whistled.

'Little Lilac, engaged! It don't seem possible, but then it don't seem possible that I'm out o' the Navy an' workin' for the Merchant line, fust mate on a coaster! I done the paperwork nights, an' got me ticket five year back.'

'Did you get fed up with the Navy?' Nellie asked. She watched Tommy, who was showing Elizabeth how to set the sails of his small yacht. Elizabeth was lying on the parapet on her tummy, small fingers deft on the tiny ropes, obeying Tommy's laconic instructions to the letter and completely absorbed, Nellie could tell.

'Fed up? Yeah, I guess I did. Wanted a bit o' stability in me life, wanted a wife, a family, that sort o' thing.'

'So you're married, too?' Nellie glanced down at Tommy. 'But the little boy said . . .'

Joey looked back towards the yachts and the water, at the sails filling and flattening as they caught and lost the breeze.

'I'm not married now, my wife died six years ago,' he said quietly. 'She'd just 'ad a baby – I lost 'em both.'

'Oh, Joey,' Nellie said softly. 'That's a dreadful thing. I am so sorry.'

'Oh, I'm awright now,' Joey said. 'Time takes the sting away, jest like they tells you it will. I was desperate for a bit, but . . . you learn to live wiv it.'

'Yes, but it's hard,' Nellie said. 'Lilac's fiancé was drowned at sea six months ago. She's still very unhappy.'

'The poor kid,' Joey said. 'Cor, an' to think I've been goin' up to Liverpool a couple of times a month this past year and never thought to try an' find the pair of you! Mind, I did just after the war, I went up and dahn the Scottie, popped into the Court . . . what was it called . . .'

'Coronation Court,' Nellie supplied, laughing. 'We moved out of there years ago. Now tell me, what are you doing on Tooting Bec Common in the middle of the week?'

'My ship's 'avin' a bit of work done,' Joey said. 'So I got me a few days free. I take it you're livin' in Tooting Bec?'

'Balham. Not far away.'

Joey nodded.

'I've got a room in Tooting, just for when I'm in the Smoke, but I'm savin' up for a place in the country somewhere. Then, when I retire, I'll 'ave somewhere nice to go. Is Lilac wiv you dahn 'ere? I'd like to meet the kid again.'

'No, she's still in Liverpool. She's a hotel receptionist during the day and she teaches dancing in the evenings. She's quite a little businesswoman . . . but so unhappy, Joey.'

Joey nodded, his expression sombre.

'Yeah, I know what she's goin' through. Wish I could 'elp . . . tell you what, give me the name of the 'otel and drop 'er a line, tell 'er I'll nip in for a chat next time I'm in the Pool.'

'That would be kind,' Nellie said. 'But why not come over to Balham, meet my Stuart and have an evening with us? We'd love it – Stuart would really like to meet you, we talked about you so much when Lilac was younger.'

'Well, I will,' Joey said. 'Fanks, Nellie! Tell Lilac I was askin' for 'er.' He turned to his small charge. 'Come on, old feller, time we got ourselves that cuppa.'

'Wait a minute, Joey; why don't you and Tommy share our picnic? I'm sure it'll stretch that far!'

'That would be grand,' Joey said. 'And then Tommy

and me, we'll walk you back across the park an' treat you to a cuppa an' a spiced bun at the Flora-Dora tea-rooms. And I'll write your address on something so we don't lose touch again.'

'That was a very nice man, that Mr Uncle Joey,' Elizabeth said to her mother as the two of them began the walk home. They had had their picnic, then their cup of tea and their spiced bun, and then they had waved goodbye to Joey and his small friend and set off. 'I liked him very much, Mam. He knows Auntie Lilac too, doesn't he?'

'Yes, though he hasn't met her since she was seven years old.' Nellie was struck by a sudden recollection. 'Elizabeth darling, do you remember Auntie Li telling you the story of when she ran away from the Culler? A kind sailor rescued her and took her home to Uncle Charlie's place and she saw Auntie Bess's new little baby – the baby that's your big cousin Henry now. Well, that sailor was Mr Prescott when he was in the Navy.'

'Then he *is* my uncle,' Elizabeth said joyfully. 'I told Tommy he was, only he wouldn't listen – boys!'

'He isn't really your uncle . . .' Nellie began cautiously, only to see her daughter shaking her head sadly.

'Oh, well, no, but a *relative*,' Elizabeth insisted. 'He's the nicest uncle I've got, and I don't have to call him Mr Thingummy after all! I just hope he tells Tommy! Tommy's just his landlady's son you know, not a real relative at all.'

'I thought you liked Tommy,' Nellie said. She was beginning to see a distinct similarity between her headstrong adopted sister and her small daughter and found the resemblance worrying. 'I thought you got on very well.'

'Yes, he's nice,' Elizabeth conceded, hopping along the pavement on one foot and swinging rather heavily on Nellie's hand. 'But even if he's nice that doesn't mean he can always be right, does it, Mam?'

'Well, no. But Joey isn't related to us at all, darling, he's just an old friend from long ago.'

'He's my uncle,' Elizabeth said in a tone which brooked no argument. 'My *unrelated* uncle. From long ago.'

Stuart was very late home indeed, but he came up the short path to the front door with such a light step and his key rattled so briefly in the lock that Nellie, who had been watching for him from their bedroom window, positively flew down the stairs and across the hall, arriving just as he entered the house, her face alight with anticipation.

'Well? Oh Stu, darling, you must be worn out! Elizabeth's in bed and asleep, your dinner's in the oven keeping warm – I did you a beef stew with suet dumplings because the longer it cooks the better it gets – and there's a lemon mousse for afterwards. Well, aren't you going to tell me what happened?'

'Guess,' Stuart said, smiling down at her. 'Just guess, Nellie Gallagher, who cared so little that she went off out this afternoon when I was frantically ringing to give her the news!'

'Oh Stu, darling! Oh, I waited until nursery school came out and then I picked the baby up and took her to Tooting Bec Common for a picnic and . . . you got it! You did, you did, and we'll be going home at last! Oh, aren't you the cleverest, the best . . .'

'Well, yes, I think I'm pretty damned good,' Stuart said with a conspicuous lack of modesty. 'There were eight of us – eight, sweetheart, imagine that – and every one a local man and most of 'em very nearly as experienced as me. One or two were the wrong side of forty, one was more or less my age, a couple younger, the rest late-thirties. I think we all interviewed quite well, but it was the fact that I'd done the nationals that told in my favour in the end I think.'

'That and your lovely, intelligent, trustableness,' Nellie said, hugging and laughing and kissing the side of his neck. 'Come and feast on beef stew an' dumplings, me lovely feller!'

'And what did you do with yourself today?' Stuart asked presently, when he had taken the first edge off his hunger, and sipped the wine which Nellie had anxiously bought, kept at room temperature and served in their best glasses. She had not dined either, preferring to wait for him, so they shared a pleasant candlelit dinner, with both of them glowing with achievement, though most of Nellie's glow was vicarious.

'Well, after you'd left at the crack of dawn, dearest, I sat down and wrote a nice long letter to Li. Then I got the babe up and got her breakfast. She was a little difficult, still cross because you'd not taken her to Liverpool with you, crosser when she found she'd have to wear her waterproof and her pixie hood because she says she can't skip in a waterproof . . . and she didn't like it at all when I said that was all right, since she wouldn't be taking her rope to nursery. It rained quite hard until nearly noon, you know, unless you were too busy to look outside.'

'I arrived like a drowned rat, but I was early so I

went straight to the gents and tidied meself,' Stuart admitted. 'We all had the sense to do that except for the snooty one who came from Crosby and travelled all the way by cab! He got wet running between the cab and the office and stayed like that until he dried off ... wouldn't crowd into the Gents with the rest of us – very infra dig! Go on though; what did you do next?'

'Oh, Stu, my life is so dull compared with yours! Well, I baked the bread for the week, and I prepared the vegetables for tonight, did the housework ... waited for the telephone to ring ...'

'We didn't know until three o'clock,' Stuart admitted. 'It was a series of interviews, and even when we knew I didn't have a chance to phone for an hour, they were taking me round from office to office, introducing me to people. It was fun, I enjoyed it. Everyone was dead friendly, honest!'

'Yes, well; it's home,' Nellie said. 'And then, as I told you, I picked Elizabeth up from nursery and walked to the common ...'

'I've got a ravishingly beautiful secretary called Iris,' Stuart said wickedly. 'Miss Holmes I'm supposed to call her, but I prefer Iris ... I bet she'll pander to my every whim.'

But if Stuart had expected an outburst of jealousy he was disappointed. Nellie's face lit up with a huge, beaming smile.

'Not the Iris Holmes I worked with in my last year in nursing! Can it be the same one? She's got deep blue eyes, set with a sooty finger they used to say, and black hair, lovely creamy skin ... oh Stu, is it really old Iris?'

'You're supposed to drag me off to bed to take my mind off the woman, not claim acquaintance,'

Stuart said, drinking the last of the wine in his glass and reaching for the bottle. 'What an annoying wench you are, Nellie me gal! But fancy you knowing Miss Holmes – it really is a small world, isn't it?'

'Liverpool is,' Nellie said contentedly. 'And it's our small world, Stu – won't it be wonderful to go back?'

They sat up until the early hours, talking. The salary was generous, a car would be provided, telephone and travel expenses paid. Stuart had asked about the availability of housing and was told that there was plenty available; they would be able to pick and choose a property at a price they could afford.

'I thought we'd buy, not rent, this time,' Stuart said as the two of them sat by the fireside, Nellie curled up on Stuart's lap gazing at the flames and no doubt seeing her city in the glowing embers. 'How about trying for something nice and neat on Hawarden Avenue, or Gresford Avenue come to that, in that area, anyway? It's near our old haunts, but you'd get the garden you're so set on and you'd be a sight nearer your Lilac than if we moved out of the city itself.'

'I wouldn't mind one of them big houses on The Boulevarde,' Nellie said wistfully. 'We could have our Lilac to live with us; not that it 'ud do, I know that. But I'd dearly like to have her under me eye until she comes to terms with losing Art.'

'That may take a lifetime, sweetheart,' Stuart said gently. 'And living with us wouldn't be the answer, I promise you that. Sometimes the happiness of people you love is nigh on unbearable.'

'But we wouldn't flaunt our happiness,' Nellie

said uncertainly. 'We'd be tactful, wouldn't we?'

'Nell, when our Elizabeth does something funny or clever, could you stop that great big grin spreading across your face? When I come in tired and you welcome me with a kiss and stories of your day, do I not relax, lean on you, show my love? To try to change, to hide our feelings, would ruin the best thing we've got, believe me.'

'All right. I agree then, that we can't ask her to share our home. But once we're back . . .'

'Oh come to bed, you little plotter! We'll talk about it over and over these next few weeks, I have no doubt. I'll give in my notice tomorrow and work my month, then we'll be off! I'm as excited as you, I promise you. There's a little pub near the offices . . . no, don't hit me, I'm to be allowed all sorts of indulgences because it is I, Stuart Gallagher, who got the job and will be bringing you triumphantly home!'

Towards the end of the month Stuart took a couple of days off which were owing to him, so that his small family might begin to plan their move, and on the first of these he offered to take Elizabeth to nursery so that Nellie might begin to get all her china washed, wrapped in newspaper and stacked neatly into the big tea-chests the removal company had lent them.

'Oh thanks, Stu,' Nellie said gratefully, lifting the delicate, rosy-petalled cups and saucers down from the dresser and carrying them over to the sink. 'It'll be a weight off my mind when these are packed away, because I expect there'll be a good deal of upheaval and they are so pretty and precious.'

So Stuart set off with his small daughter scooting

along beside him and chattering like a magpie all the way.

'Yesterday I told everyone in my class that I were going to move back to Liverpool and some of them ...' Elizabeth dug her toe into the pavement and scooted well ahead, then turned her head to shout. ' ... Some of them said horrid things!'

'Did they? What?'

'Well, Simon said could he have my scooter, which was unkind, wasn't it, Daddy? And Annabel said she would sit in my seat and Simon would love her best.'

'Stupid person!' Stuart said at once. 'You'll be taking all your things with you, naturally.'

'Will I? Oh, good,' Elizabeth said, clearly relieved of a secret worry. 'But not me friends, Daddy?'

'Well, no. But you'll make new friends, you see. Very easily and quickly, because Liverpool people are the friendliest people in the world.'

'Are they? Really? Friendlier than Londoners?'

'Oh yes, much friendlier,' Stuart said, thinking of journeys on the underground railway when no one spoke to anyone else except to complain if an elbow got them round the ear. 'Well you know Aunti Li, and Mummy, and me ... we're all friendly, aren't we?'

'Yes, and I are,' Elizabeth said. She had stopped her scooter so that Stuart could catch up but now she indicated it rather impatiently. 'Could you take my scooter now, Daddy, so we can talk? It's hard to talk and scoot, my puff runs out and my squeak starts.'

This frequently happened, so Stuart picked up the scooter and took his daughter's small hand in his. 'Righty-ho, sunshine,' he said breezily. 'Talk away.'

'Oh, thank you. Right. Well, I want to know whether that Uncle Joey Mummy and I met in the park is a really-truly uncle or just a pretend uncle. That Tommy – he wasn't Uncle Joey's real . . . well, Uncle Joey wasn't his real . . .'

'Hang on a minute, queen,' Stuart said, perplexed. 'I'm not following you. Which Uncle Joey? Which park? When?'

'Oh days an' days ago,' Elizabeth said in a rush, having given the matter some thought. 'On the day you went to Liverpool and lefted me behind.'

'Oh yes, Mummy said you'd gone to the common. And you met a man called Joey? Mummy didn't mention it.'

'I spec' she forgot. He said do you 'member me, and he said did you marry that chap you was with and Mummy said no she married you, an' who did Joey marry, and *he* said his were deaded an' he wasn't sad no longer.'

'Gosh, so Mummy knew him before she married me,' Stuart said, staring down at his small daughter. 'An old friend, then! What else did this old friend say?'

'Oh, he talked and talked, and Mummy talked and talked. And Tommy and me sailed his boat and we had ice-creams and little cakes and melonade which fizzed up our noses . . .'

'Lemonade, not melonade,' Stuart corrected automatically. 'Did Mummy say what his last name was?'

'Can't remember. But I know who he is . . . he rescued Lilac when she ran away . . . oh yes, he's a sailor.'

A sailor! A cold knot of apprehension began to tighten in Stuart's stomach. He was pretty sure that the father of Nellie's first child had been a sailor; if she'd met up with him again by chance, and he knew his Nellie too well to think she would plan such a thing, then no wonder she hadn't mentioned the fellow to him! She must have been hoping that the child would forget all about it too, never think about the bloke again, and nor she would have, had it not been for the double coincidence of his having a day off and Elizabeth's conversation turning to friendship and relatives.

'So what happened, love? What did Joey look like? Was he nice?'

'He was very nice,' Elizabeth said solemnly. 'Not as nice as you, but really nice. He had a brown face, light brown hair, blue, round eyes, he was same tall as you, trousers, shirt . . .'

'Yes, I know what you mean,' Stuart said, since Elizabeth was going puce with the effort of description. 'And he had a little boy, Tommy.'

'Yes, but he weren't Joey's, not really,' Elizabeth insisted. 'He was *my* uncle, not Tommy's.'

'I'll ask Mummy,' Stuart said soothingly. 'She'll tell me whether he was your uncle or not. But don't you have enough uncles, sweetheart? I'm afraid I can't provide any, but Mummy has several brothers. And you've scores of cousins.'

'Ye-es. But Joey's especially nice,' Elizabeth repeated with deep conviction. 'Oh, there's Simon . . . I'll go and tell him I'm taking me scooter to Liverpool with me . . . bye-bye, Daddy, see you later!'

Stuart waved until she and Simon had disappeared into the school, then turned his footsteps homeward with a heavy heart. He knew jealousy was a destructive and pointless emotion which could only harm him and those he loved. Why could he not believe Nellie when she said she had never truly loved another? Why was it so hard to be sensible, to ask outright about Joey just to set his fears at rest? He resolved to ask the moment he stepped through the front door, but knew he would not do it, knew it would fester within him until it became obvious from his attitude that something was wrong. Then Nellie would have to prise it out of him ... and no matter how harmless the explanation, there would always be that little, niggling doubt ...

But he was wrong this time.

He got back to the house and there was Nellie on the front step, talking to a man in a sports jacket and flannels. The fellow was tanned and fit looking; Stuart's heart began to bump. Could this possibly be the Joey his daughter had spoken of? And if so, just what was he doing on the doorstep, renewing acquaintance with his, Stuart Gallagher's, beloved wife?

Stuart could feel his hands forming fists, his temper beginning to build, as he flung open the gate and took the little path in a couple of swift strides.

'Nell? Who the devil ... ?'

'Stuart, you'll never guess who's come calling! Do you remember me telling you how Lilac ran away from the Culler when she was little, and was rescued by a seaman who took care of her for me? Well, it's him – Joey Prescott! We met on the common a couple of weeks ago, I came home full of it, only when you arrived back from Liverpool to say you'd got the job it just went clean out of me head!'

All the jealousy, all the fears, all the stupid, niggling doubts, disappeared. Stuart gripped the other man's hand and shook it heartily, a big smile forming.

'Well, Joey Prescott – it's like meeting a living legend, old feller, the times I've heard the women clacking on about how you saved our Lilac from a fate worse than death! Nell, love, what are you doing on the step – come in, Joey, come in . . . did Nell explain about me?'

'Talked about nothing else,' Joey said. 'I 'ear congratulations are in order? Though it's a bit late to congratulate you when you've been married 'alf-a-dozen years! I come over now because my ship's sailing in a few days so I thought I'd pop rahnd an' see whether Mrs Gallagher 'ad writ to Lilac abaht me callin' on 'er when I'm in Liverpool.'

Stuart led their guest through the house, hesitated outside the front room, then grinned at Joey and shook his head. 'No point in pretending we live in there; we live in the kitchen, and if I know Nell that's where we'll find the kettle singing away. But see that photo on the mantel? That's our Lilac, taken last year; quite a change since you saw her last, I daresay! You can see she's turned into a beautiful young woman. And now I'll just get the rum and some glasses, and we'll have a tot to celebrate this reunion.'

Joey stared hard at the photograph, then followed Stuart out of the sitting-room and into the firelit kitchen.

'That's a lovely picture of a lovely girl,' he said approvingly. 'This room's a treat, ain't it? You can tell Mrs Gallagher's a real 'omemaker. I 'aven't 'ad much 'ome life, so I loves a real kitchen.'

'You call her Nellie, and me Stuart, old fellow, and don't forget, we know all about you, me as well as the girls,' Stuart said, fetching glasses for the rum. 'They've told me about you over and over, believe me. You ran away from a London orphan asylum when you were twelve and went to sea. Nellie watched Lilac like a hawk when she hit twelve in case she had the

341

same idea, but she managed to leave the Culler in a more conventional fashion.'

'That's right; I lived in the Metropolitan Orphanage, to the east of Aldgate pump. We all 'ad brahn suits an' big boots, daily lectures on the importance of rememberin' we come from 'ardworkin' people – the deservin' poor rather than idle layabouts drinkin' their money away. No one told us where they got this money from, mind. No wonder I split!'

'Poor little boy,' Nellie said softly, beginning to make tea in the big, brown pot. 'Stu was a Culler boy – did you know that?'

'No . . . you never said, the other afternoon on the common. We was talking rather more abaht the past, though.'

'Here, a toast!' Stuart said. He handed Nellie a small drink and Joey a rather larger one. 'To absent friends – particularly our Lilac!'

They drank. 'And you really will visit our Lilac whilst you're in the Pool?' Stuart said.

Joey nodded. 'Oh aye; always intended to see 'er again one day. Mebbe I'll tek 'er on the ferry . . . I don't suppose Nellie said nothin' abaht it, but I lost my wife six years ago, so I know what young Lilac's goin' through.'

'No, she didn't,' Stuart admitted. 'I'm really sorry, old fellow.'

Joey sighed and raised his glass.

'She was a good gel, my Annie,' he said. 'But I've got some rare 'appy memories; they'll do me, for now.'

They didn't know how to tell Kitty. Matron, an awe-inspiring figure in a dress and apron so stiffly starched that they would have stood up quite unaided, said that someone who knew her well would be best, so Sister called Lilac into her office for a quiet word.

'Miss Larkin, we've had grave news of Kitty Drinkwater's family. I fear her mother and sister are both in hospital. Mrs Drinkwater isn't expected to live and the child, Betty is very ill indeed.'

'My goodness – what's happened?'

'They were taken to the David Lewis Hospital after they fell into some sort of a cellar . . . I'm not too clear on the details but I imagine the mother was the worse for drink. Apparently the cellar was full of something, coal dust, rubbish, I'm not sure what, which all but smothered the pair of them.'

'How did they struggle out?' Lilac asked. 'I suppose a cellar has stairs, though . . . or were they too injured to help themselves?'

'I imagine so, but fortunately a neighbour heard cries for help and managed to rescue them both, though not before considerable damage had been done.'

'What a dreadful story,' Lilac said with a shudder. 'I suppose Mrs Drinkwater must have fallen against the cellar door and brought the child down as she fell.'

'I don't think the cellar had a door; the health

visitor was shocked by the state of the house, and is strongly recommending to the authorities that the landlord must demolish the whole building, but that's no help to the Drinkwaters, of course. And in the meantime, what do you think? Should we tell Kitty?'

'I think,' Lilac said, 'that you had best start at the beginning, Sister, and tell me the whole story. Up to this moment all I knew was that you'd discovered Kitty's address and were sending someone round.'

'That's right. A health visitor went round, only to find the house deserted. Neighbours told her that as soon as Kitty was out of the way Sarah Drinkwater got herself up to the public house on the corner and began drinking again. The family next door heard the woman return home. Then they heard an argument, then a clatter followed by appalling screams which were suddenly cut off. Fortunately one of the older girls had visited the house and suspected what must have happened. She and the others managed to get a rope round the mother and hauled her out first, then realised that the child was still down there under . . . well, under the rubbish. They got her out, but they said she was blue . . .'

Lilac shuddered.

'Poor little soul. But she'd not developed the fever, at least.'

'Malnutrition had taken a sad toll of her health even before the accident, and now because of her breathing difficulties there is some doubt over her recovery,' Sister said. 'The mother is a big woman, her weight, crushing the child . . .'

Lilac shuddered again. 'Poor little kid. She wasn't fit before the accident, then?'

'No, indeed. Kitty is well-nourished so I'd guess that her time on that farm near Corwen stood her in good stead, but the other child was quite neglected. The health visitor spoke to the authorities and learned that two other children had been taken away from Mrs Drinkwater a couple of years ago, and that Kitty had taken two more little girls into the Father Berry Home only weeks before the accident, explaining that she could no longer feed and support them. It's very sad, but with unemployment affecting more and more people, and with slum housing conditions the way they are, I fear we can expect to see a good deal more disease and death amongst those forced to live in such places.'

'Yes, and the ones who go under are those who don't know where to go for help and have no idea of their entitlements,' Lilac said, trying not to let her emotions show in her voice. 'They're the ones who suffer. They hide away, sure they're in the wrong simply because they can't cope. There are good and caring parents seeing their children grow ill and weak . . .' her voice broke and she stopped abruptly.

'Ye-es, in many cases I would agree with you, but Mrs Drinkwater wasn't a good or caring parent,' Sister said firmly. 'She disliked Kitty and used to beat her; the child had a broken arm, cracked ribs . . .'

'What? She beat her children? I know it happens, but . . . how did you find out?' Lilac said. 'Did Kitty tell you?'

'Not exactly. But the signs are there for anyone to read – a self-set arm doesn't mend quite straight, one of the ribs had actually pierced the skin. It happened years ago, but we could see she'd been maltreated. So when she was more herself Nurse asked her how she broke her arm and so on and Kitty said frankly that her mother had done it when annoyed. And the neighbours said that Mrs Drinkwater gave the children almost nothing to eat and let them fend for themselves, though they seemed to think that Kitty had only lately returned to the house, which is no doubt the reason for her present good state of health.'

'What a wicked woman!' Lilac said, appalled. She thought she knew a good deal about life in the courts, but in Coronation Court there had been friendship and kindliness and a deep sense of loyalty as well as poverty. She remembered men fighting their wives and occasionally hitting their children, but not hitting to deliberately break bones. 'Kitty's well out of it, then.'

'I agree. If the woman was to recover . . . but I don't think that is likely to happen. And the family next door, though well-disposed to Kitty and the younger girl, have troubles of their own. One of the older girls and two of the children have taken scarlet fever and are being nursed on another ward here. But I mustn't digress; what I called you in to discuss was how much we should tell Kitty.'

'I'm inclined to think she should be told nothing, until their problems are resolved one way or the other,' Lilac said after a moment. 'There's no sense in worrying her needlessly. Should the subject arise, however, it may be necessary to tell her how things stand. In the meantime I'll visit the sisters at the Father Berry Home – I was in an orphan asylum myself a few years back, it wasn't all that bad, we were fed and clothed. Only . . . you like to know you aren't forgotten.'

'That's very good of you, Miss Larkin. You don't think perhaps Kitty may resent not having been told later, when she's better?'

'I think perhaps she can deal with resentment then more easily than she can deal with worry now,' Lilac said, again after thought. 'I may be wrong, but that's how I feel. She wouldn't be allowed to visit the other hospital, would she?'

'Indeed not.'

'Then there can be no harm in leaving her ignorant for a little longer.' She smiled at Sister and rose to her feet. 'If I may, I'll go along and have a quiet word with Kitty, tell her I'm off to the Berry Home, and then I'll catch a tram up there and tell the children that Kitty's improving fast. I won't mention their mother or the other girl unless one of the children asks outright, and I'll see how much I think Kitty can take.'

'I wouldn't want you to tell an untruth,' Sister said doubtfully. 'But I'm sure you'll manage to satisfy them that all is well without actually . . . thank you for your time, Miss Larkin. Perhaps we may have another chat later in the week.'

Lilac left Sister's office and went along to the ward. Kitty was sitting up in bed reading a book. She had chosen, or had had chosen for her, Lilac was not sure which, a book for very young children with very large print. Sensible, since she was still weak and lethargic and doubtless finding it difficult to focus – or concentrate – for long. She was following the adventures of a lively rag doll, but looked up and smiled as Lilac sat in the visitor's chair on the other side of the glass.

'Afternoon, Miss,' she said. Lilac could just catch the words. 'I'm ever so much better today – I 'ad an egg for me dinner!'

'Well done,' Lilac said, smiling. 'Would you like me to bring you some books when I come tomorrow? I'll choose more tales with big print, which will be easier for you until you're rather stronger.'

'They 'ave to stay on the fever ward, though,'

347

Kitty warned. 'You can't tek 'em 'ome with you . . . better leave it a while. Johnny, a friend of mine, 'e'd be shocked to 'ear they burns the books after a while.'

'It's to prevent the spread of infection, though,' Lilac said, 'so he mustn't be shocked. Kitty, my dear, I'm going to visit the Father Berry when I leave here and Sister tells me you've sisters in there. Would you like to send them a message?'

'You? Visit the Father Berry Home?'

'Yes, indeed. I was at the Culler Orphan Asylum myself for many years. My sister Nellie, too. If you'll give me your sisters' names . . .'

'Course. But I wish someone 'ud get a message to me sister Betty for me; she's at number 8 Paradise Court, off Burlington Street. I gits scared, 'cos me old woman can be 'ard to tek care of, an' Bet's only a bit of a kid really. You see, they'll be took care of in the Berry 'Ome, I know that; Mam an' Bet is on their own.'

'I'll get a message to her,' Lilac said steadily. 'I'll see it's passed to her even if I can't see her myself.'

'You would? Oh Miss . . . thanks,' Kitty said eagerly. 'You are real good.'

'It's no trouble, anyone would do the same. Now what do you want me to say?'

Kitty lay down her book and frowned at her white fingers on the cover.

'Say . . . Kitty's in 'ospickle but she'll be jest fine soon, an' back wi' Bet soon's she can. An' say I's awful sorry to 'ave left 'er in the lurch, an' is there anything she needs real bad,' Kitty said at last, all of a rush. 'An if they're mortal 'ungry, Miss, could you lend 'em a few coppers? I'll pay you back when I git outer 'ere, honest to God.'

'Don't worry about it any more. I'll see they're fed and as comfortable as they can be,' Lilac said. 'I bet you think they'd be better off in hospital, like you!'

'Well, they would be,' Kitty said frankly. 'I's shamed for you to see that 'ouse, Miss, but there's no 'elp for it.'

'Yes there is,' Lilac said. She leaned close to the glass, so that Kitty could hear her without possibility of a mistake. 'Kitty, your mother and Betty *are* both in hospital, getting the best possible care. After you were taken ill there was an accident. Betty was helping your mother upstairs and somehow they stumbled and ended up in the cellar. It was a nasty fall but they're being given every attention. They're in the David Lewis Northern Hospital.'

Kitty's furrowed brow cleared.

'Oh, thank Gawd,' she said fervently. 'Oh, Miss, you don't know 'ow you've relieved me mind! I 'ad visions of 'em starvin', the pair of 'em, like I thought about me dear ole Patch till you said you'd got 'er safe. I spec' me Mam were drunk an' they fell down the Drop ... it's a wonder they weren't smothered. Who gorrem out?'

'Your next door neighbours, whose name escapes me for the moment. Kitty, dear, if you would like me to do so I can go and visit your mother and Betty when I come back from the Home, and see how they are.'

'Oh Miss! Give Betty me love an' tell 'er to bear up ... tell 'er I'm gettin' well, an' she must, too.' She looked anxious for the first time since Lilac had broken the news. 'She will get better, won't she, Miss?'

'I see no reason why she shouldn't,' Lilac said stoutly. 'She's had a dreadful experience, but she's in good hands. Anyway, Kitty, I'd better be off because I'm on the evening shift at the Delamere so I've got quite a lot to get done this afternoon!'

Kitty agreed and waved her off and Lilac made

her way along the corridor and out into the fresh air.

It was not a nice day. It had started off with rain, light and drizzly, but now a yellowish fog hung over the city, with not a breath of wind to stir it. Lilac got a large silk handkerchief out of her coat pocket and looped it round her mouth and nose. It made breathing easier but it didn't do much for seeing. However, she found the small confectioner's shop she was looking for without much trouble, went in and bought a pound of toffee, and then walked a little further along to the tram stop. She didn't have long to wait before the tram she wanted inched to a stop beside her, but already by then the fog was penetrating her handkerchief and she was glad to climb aboard and sit down in the relative warmth. 'The Father Berry Home, on Shaw Street, please,' she said to the conductor when he came to collect her fare. 'When did this fog come down? I've been hospital visiting and when I went in it was just dampish.'

The conductor rattled her out a ticket and considered.

'Let me see ... sudden-like, it were,' he said. 'Must 'ave been an hour or more ago. Wind dropped away to nothing the way it does an' the fog began to pour in from the river. If it stays thick like this Gawd knows what time I'll git 'ome tonight.'

'Same for me,' Lilac said rather gloomily. She settled back in her seat as the conductor moved off down the tram. What a nuisance that she was committed to so much to-ing and fro-ing with the filthy yellow fog so thick! She knew from past experience that the trams got later and later, omnibuses simply ceased to run, people grew irritable and lost their way, and when darkness fell the traffic crawled, their headlamps unable to pierce the fog but merely lighting up the blanket so that seeing through it was even more impossible. Still, a promise was a promise, and she had made it clear that she would at least take a peep at the invalids in the David Lewis.

It took almost twice as long as usual to reach Shaw Street. Lilac hurried up it and along to the Home. She knocked, explained her errand, was admitted. She was a little surprised to be told by a friendly nun that she was not visiting two children, but four.

'Phyllis and Maureen have been here almost two years; they're a great support to their sisters,' the nun said. 'I daresay Kitty forgot that they were already with us when she asked you to visit. But come into the sitting room and I'll send the girls down to you.'

The four little girls who came into the superintendent's sitting room were not at all like Kitty to look at. They were all fair and blue-eyed, with round, rather blank faces. They had none of the sharpness of their elder sister, nor her ready smile, though when Lilac explained who she was, said that their mother had had a fall and was in hospital but that Kitty, also in hospital, was feeling much better and asking for them, and got out the toffee, divided into four small, brown bags by the kindly nun, smiles peeped for a moment.

'When I was your age I would have been mobbed for that toffee,' Lilac said as she handed it over. 'Have you got pockets?'

Four small heads nodded. Each child stuck a chunk of toffee in one cheek and the rest of each bag disappeared into the capacious pockets of their pinafores.

'I'll give Kitty your love,' Lilac said gently. 'And I'll come back and see you next week. When she's well enough she'll come herself, of course.'

The children watched, expressionless, as Lilac headed for the door. They did not ask about their mother, nor about Betty. Lilac was thinking them dull and unsympathetic when, just as she took hold of the handle, one of the children nudged the one next to her.

'Thanks, Miss,' the two of them said in chorus, and one added, 'Tell 'er we're awright, would you, Miss? Tell our Mam to get well an' all. An' tell our Kit as 'ow Eth's takin' care of the kids in 'ere.'

'I will,' Lilac said warmly, and made her way down Shaw Street and back to her tram stop, feeling that she had judged them rather too harshly. They looked stupid, they appeared indifferent, but that was what an institution did for you if you didn't exert your personality, and those poor little kids were probably still stunned by what had happened to them.

Outside, the fog caught at her throat and stung her eyes, making her reach into her pocket for the silk handkerchief. She fumbled in the narrow opening, but the handkerchief wasn't there. Cross with herself, for she remembered now that she had jammed it in carelessly when she climbed aboard the tram, she retraced her steps, but it wasn't in the street nor on the steps of the Father Berry Home.

Shrugging, Lilac turned back towards her tram stop. It was a nuisance, but she didn't need the handkerchief to get back to the Delamere safely, she could turn her coat collar up and keep her chin tucked down and she would still be able to visit the hospital and be back at the Delamere in plenty of time for her shift.

The trouble was, it was just not possible to get a tram on Shaw Street – or on Islington Square for that matter – which would take her straight to the

David Lewis Northern. She would have to change. And whichever way you looked at it, this was no weather to be hanging around at a tram stop whilst time ticked by and your shift got nearer and nearer.

Liverpool's pretty compact; if I go by tram as far as the Old Haymarket and change onto a Vauxhall Road one, then I can easily nip through to the hospital, do my visiting and then walk to Tythebarn Street, Lilac decided. Once she got in the general area of Exchange Station, in fact, the hotel and the hospital were quite close. But the fog was horribly thick and the tram, when it came, was the wrong one. Lilac squeezed herself aboard, wedged between two bad-tempered shawlies with enormous shopping baskets, and stood, peering out at the swirling yellow fog. She realised she was aboard the wrong vehicle when someone announced they were on Great George Street, so she pushed her way crossly out of the vehicle and waited for a tram going in the opposite direction.

She was lucky; a tram sailed up almost immediately and she climbed aboard, but the fog was getting thicker by the minute and to make matters worse the conductor was clearly new to this particular route, so whenever the tram slowed and stopped every passenger gave his or her opinion of their whereabouts.

'Dis is Renshaw Street – sure an' d'you t'ink I don't know me own social club? It's dat big buildin' . . .'

'Renshaw? And 'aven't I bin stoppin' off at Meece's o' Ranelagh Place to buy me taffy an' lickerish since I were a nipper; I can smell it, we're alongside Meece's.'

'Rubbidge, we're just agin de Regal cinema!'

'We come down Ranelagh Place minutes ago, dincher reckernise Lewis's? I reckon this must be Lime Street.'

'Nah, we'd 'a' smelt de trains ... we're well past de station; we'll be on St John's Lane be now.'

'Well, we ain't at the terminus yet,' the conductor said with a brave attempt at humour. 'Reckon we'll all know if we gets there!'

Various furious comments told him, in no uncertain terms, that if they found themselves at any terminus he could just take them all back where they belonged, so the conductor got off and consulted the driver as to their exact whereabouts. He then climbed back aboard again and gave them his driver's opinion.

'E can't see no more'n you can,' he said. 'Next crossroads, e'll stop an' I'll nip down, see if I can spot a road-name.'

So it was in this slow and unsatisfactory fashion that Lilac made the cross-city journey, eventually getting down at Exchange Station, hoping that it really was that station and not Lime Street, with her fellow passengers grumbling mightily as they were borne off into the increasing gloom.

Lilac, coat collar turned up, hands dug deep into her pockets, the moisture already beading her hair and her breath wetting the edge of her collar, checked that it really was Exchange Station, got her bearings and looked for the subway which would bring her out in St Paul's Square, within easy walking distance of the hospital.

The subway was horrid; usually it would have been crowded with people making their way from the station to the small streets which were crammed between the station itself and the docks, but tonight it was almost deserted. Lilac, still with her chin buried in her coat collar, passed a woman with a grizzling child, a tall man with a brightly striped muffler wound round his face, and a seaman with a kit-bag over one shoulder and a bulging paper carrier in his hand. The fog hadn't actually penetrated the subway but the walls ran with water and the smell and general aspect of the place was vaguely sinister. It struck Lilac for the first time that the subway could easily have been a sewer; all it lacked was rats.

However, she emerged into the fog again, crossed the road and began to walk up what she devoutly hoped was East Street. She knew it was when it crossed the railway lines; just here the lines massed, all of them meeting before plunging into the station, and she was able to walk alongside them, one hand on the bricks, until the road ended in a blank wall.

'Old Leeds Street,' Lilac reminded herself beneath her breath, turning left as she did so. She only had to follow the buildings now and she would be in Back Leeds Street which led directly into Leeds Street – not a lot of imagination had been used when naming streets in this area, she thought with an inward smile – which led, in its turn, to King Edward Street, where the hospital was situated.

The fog, if anything, was thicker down here, nearer the docks. But she found the hospital by keeping her wits about her and clinging to the wall, and was glad to enter the foyer, looking round affectionately at the familiar place, for it was here that her Aunt Ada had been cured of the flu, when Lilac had first met Stuart.

The woman behind the desk might have been the very one who had smiled so sweetly at them then, but this one, on being told of Lilac's errand, looked grave.

'I'd best call Sister,' she said. 'If you'd not mind waiting, Miss?' She indicated a hard chair set against the wall. 'I won't be more than five minutes.'

She was as good as her word and presently returned

with a ward sister rustling along behind her. 'Sister West, this is Miss Larkin, a friend of Kitty Drinkwater, who's in the Isolation Hospital. She's come to see Mrs Drinkwater and Betty, on behalf of the other girl.'

The ward sister did not smile, but she gave Lilac a direct and friendly look and held out her hand.

'How do you do, Miss Larkin? I'm afraid I've bad news for you. Mrs Drinkwater died earlier in the afternoon. Betty is sleeping; she's very weak. Would you like to come up to the ward?'

Lilac hesitated.

'I've never met . . .' she began, but Sister West shook her head.

'It's all right, the mother's body is already in the hospital mortuary. But the child . . . perhaps if you could tell her Kitty's well . . . the only time she speaks is to her sister, trying to explain how she came to let her mother leave the house, as though a bit of a thing like her could have prevented . . . but there . . . if you would follow me?'

Lilac followed. There seemed little else she could do.

The children's ward was a long one, and most of the beds were unoccupied at this time of the afternoon.

'Unless they're confined to bed they're having tea,' Sister explained in a low voice. 'Betty's in a side-ward. This one.'

She opened the door and went in; hesitantly, Lilac followed.

The child lay, so small and flat that she scarcely rippled the covers, neatly in the middle of the narrow white bed. Her skin was a strange, bluish-purple colour, her breathing ragged and stertorous. She was so thin, Lilac saw, that her bones seemed in danger of breaking through the skin and the hand lying on top of the covers was little better than a claw.

But Sister was bending over the bed.

'Betty, dear, a lady has come to see you – a lady who has been to see Kitty, too. Kitty knows all about your fall, she doesn't blame you in the least . . . but I'll let Miss Larkin have a word.'

She moved aside, then pulled a chair up to the bed. Lilac sat obediently down on it, and leaned nearer to the small, still figure. She glanced up at Sister, who nodded encouragingly.

'She can almost certainly hear,' she murmured. 'Do what you can, my dear.'

Lilac took the small, cold hand in hers and chafed it between her palms.

'Betty? Kitty's so sorry you're ill and says please get well, just as she's getting well, so you can be together again,' she murmured. 'She quite understands about the fall . . .'

The pale lips moved, the head stirred just a little on the pillow.

'It . . . were . . . the Drop, our Kit,' the child breathed. 'She were so strong an' 'eavy, there weren't nothin' I could do.'

'No, you did wharrever you could,' Lilac said at once. 'You did real good, our Bet, I couldn't 'ave done berrer meself.'

She didn't know what made her say it nor why she spoke with the thick accent she had used as a child, but Betty heaved a sigh which Lilac was almost sure was satisfaction. 'Oh, Kit, I loves you,' she said, her voice so faint that Lilac had to lean even closer to hear the words. 'But I does ache!'

The child took another deep breath, as though to say something more, then expelled the breath gently.

She did not breathe again.

357

When Lilac left the hospital an hour later she was in a very low state of mind. That poor little kid could never have made a full recovery, would always have been ailing, and her circumstances were such that she would have had to enter an institution. But even so . . .

A life snuffed out because of a selfish, drunken mother and an uncaring father, Lilac mourned as she stepped out once again into the thickness of the fog. If you're a foundling, like me, at least you aren't burdened by those who ought to support you but instead seem to do their best to undermine you and bring you low. Even if I'd not had Nellie's support I'd have been a good deal better off than the Drinkwater kids.

Art had been burdened by an uncaring father and a downright nasty mother, Lilac remembered, stepping out into the road once more, but he'd turned out lovely, had Art. Caring, strong and honest. As different from the other O'Briens as chalk from cheese. But despite her resolve to turn the loss of Art into something which would strengthen her and make her into a better person, it was still too new, too raw, to be anything but painful to think of him.

It would not always be thus, though. Nellie had assured her of this, said that one day Lilac would be able to remember Art with love and affection and enjoy the memories, as one would enjoy remembering a childhood long gone, or one's wedding day or first dance.

'Time really does heal,' Nellie had said in her soft voice, giving Lilac a strong and steady glance.. 'It'll

358

heal your hurt too, queen, I promise you, though it'll seem impossible for a good few months yet.'

And Lilac, remembering Nell's first love and the child she had borne, knew that the older girl spoke from experience and admired her more than ever, remembering her bravery at the time and her unfailing cheerfulness.

Presently, she realised she must have turned in the wrong direction when leaving the hospital, or perhaps she had unthinkingly left by a different entrance, for all of a sudden there was a change in the steady thickness of the fog, a feeling of space before her, and a sound she knew but could not immediately recognise, a soft slapping, chuckling, a gurgling ... Lilac stopped short and stared around her, considerably dismayed. It was water, that was what she could hear, so somewhere not too far away, unless she was much mistaken, was the edge of the dock! Darkness had fallen some time ago; she realised she had not so much as glanced at a clock during her time in the Northern Hospital, but now, when she looked up, she could not even see a glow above her. The fog was completely blanketing the street lamps, always presuming there were lit lamps near her, of course.

Standing still, with the fog beading her coat and hair with moisture, she realised that she could have turned a couple of times without realising it, and that the dock need not be directly in front of her but to the right, the left, or even behind. It was a horrid feeling, for the place seemed to be deserted and though Lilac could swim she did not much fancy her chances in the chill of the fog, especially when muffled in her coat and boots.

But she could not stand here for ever, waiting

for something to happen. She felt forward with her foot, found firm ground, stepped, felt forward again, stepped . . .

It would have taken a long time and she still might have ended up in the water, but she was saved by a commotion ahead, a little to her right. She could hear voices, a bumping sound, cheerful shouts: the dock was no longer deserted, she could even see a figure, dimly outlined, not more than a few feet from her.

Lilac started forward, beginning to smile.

'Oh, excuse me . . . I'm lost, I came out of the hospital and must have turned in the wrong direction . . . could you possibly guide me back to the road? I would be so obliged to you!'

They were sailors, still in uniform – deckhands, probably. Half-a-dozen of them. A couple of them looked at her incuriously, then shook their heads – could they be foreign, perhaps? But they were not, as they soon proved.

'Hello, chuck – lost, are ye? Right, folly us!'

One man took her right arm, another her left. They turned resolutely right, walking as though they could see through the fog, though Lilac, dragged bemusedly between them, could still see nothing.

A third man, slightly behind them, spoke in a thick country accent, his voice slurring a little.

'Thee's got a right shapely boom on thee, lass; Ah wouldn't mind an 'andful o' that!'

Best ignore it, Lilac was thinking, when the man gripping her right arm spoke sharply.

'Gerrout, Tam, finders keepers; Alf an' me 'as fust go.'

Lilac tried to tug herself free of the men, without success, so she began to struggle.

'Ay up, gairl, we'll pay ye all fair an' square,'

360

the man on her left said. 'We're jest ashore, see —
got plenty o' gelt. Ow much d'you charge? I reckon
it'll be five bob each, eh? Got a room?'

'No I have not,' Lilac said furiously. 'I told you I was
lost in the fog and lost I was! I'm not street-walking,
I'm a respectable woman!'

'You're a nice gairl — ain't they all?' the man on
her right said consolingly. 'But the money's good —
why, you'll tek 'ome fifteen shillin' jest from the t'ree
of us; can't be bad, eh?'

'You'll wake up in gaol after I've been to the police
. . .' Lilac began, then felt her captors veer abruptly
to the right. A narrow alley loomed, she could just
see the walls on either side. Oh God save me, she
thought as they dragged her, kicking vigorously and
telling them at the top of her voice that they were
making a mistake which they would suffer for, they
don't believe me, they're going to . . . to . . .

Desperation lent Lilac strength. She tore herself
out of the grasp of the two men, swerved to avoid
the third, and was away, running heedlessly now, no
longer fearing that she might plunge into the dock, no
longer fearing anything but pursuit and what the men
whose voices, shouting to her, were growing fainter
with every step she took, might do.

She was beginning to believe she had escaped,
that she really was free of them, when she heard
footsteps. A man's tread, she was sure of it. She
stopped short, staring blindly around her. She saw
ahead of her a tall building with golden light spilling
out of a doorway . . . she ran full out, her breath
sobbing in her throat, a hand pressed to a stitch in
her side, and just as she got close to that golden light,
just as she began to feel herself safe, she cannoned into
someone.

'Whoa, lass, whoa! You're in a hurry ... what's up, gel?'

A face loomed above her own. An intelligent face, the mouth curved into a slight, enquiring smile, the brows rising.

'Oh, oh, some men ... they're chasing me, they think ... they think ...' Lilac stuttered. 'Don't let them get me!'

'You poor gel ... come on, come into the 'otel, you'll be safe enough in there.'

The man pushed her gently in through the open doorway and Lilac, still trembling and with her legs beginning to feel as though they belonged to someone else, nearly fainted with shock and relief.

It was the Delamere! In her mad panic-stricken flight she had actually run to her destination!

She turned to the man standing beside her, a hand still on her arm.

'I'm very grateful,' she said awkwardly. 'I hadn't realised where I was ... I'd been hospital visiting and I got lost in the fog ...'

'You're soaked, you've been terrified, an' someone's nigh on tore the coat off your back,' the man remarked. 'Eh, your legs is black an' blue! Where's the receptionist, you need a clean-up before you goes on anywhere else.'

'I am the receptionist,' Lilac said with a watery giggle. 'I was on my way to work when those men attacked me. I expect I'm late, and Mrs Brierson probably thought as it was quiet she'd go down for her dinner. Thank you very much sir, for your help, but I'd better get behind the desk now and start work.'

'That you won't, ducks,' the man said decisively. He crossed the foyer in a couple of strides and banged the bell on the desk. 'You'll want to straighten up first

362

'... you're covered wiv mud an all, you know!'

Lilac, still trembling with reaction, glanced down at herself and had to fight back the tears. She was filthy, not just her coat but the dress beneath it as well, her stockings, her shoes ... and glancing in the mirror behind the desk she could see that she looked an absolute fright – her hair hung in wet witch-locks around a pale face on which scratches and a big blue bruise had appeared.

'You're right,' she mumbled. 'I'll have to sit down for a minute, too, before I can start work.'

One of the maids, coming to answer the bell, glanced across at Lilac and then stared.

'Oh, Miss ... what 'appened? I'll get Mrs Brierson at once, she'll see to you.'

The man got a chair from behind the counter and made Lilac sit down on it. Then he knelt and began to take her shoes off. It was quite a hard task since the shoes were thick with mud and Lilac's feet had been trampled on in the mêlée so that blood was caked round her torn stockings and black bruises were beginning to appear. As he worked he said conversationally: 'You're Lilac Larkin, ain't you? I reckernise you from your photograph.'

'Yes, I am. But ... but ...'

'I'm Joey Prescott; I met your sister Nellie down in Balham ... didn't she write?'

Lilac stared at him; yes, she recognised him now, he had changed scarcely at all, he even had his tiny little moustache, though she supposed he must look older – it had been fifteen years after all. She smiled at him, the colour beginning to creep back into her cheeks.

'Of course, she said you might come to Liverpool, but ... oh, Joey, isn't it strange? The first time we met you rescued me and now you've rescued me again! Thank you so much. I don't know what I'd have done if you'd not caught me – gone on running until I dropped, I imagine.'

'You poor kid,' Joey said. 'Ah, 'ere comes the marines!'

It was Mrs Brierson, looking very concerned.

'My dear Lilac, Ethel says . . . my goodness, you are in a state! Did you fall? Your poor little toes . . . you've been knocked down in the fog, everyone drives too fast these days, you're lucky to be alive!'

'It wasn't . . .' Joey began, but stopped at a warning glare from Lilac.

'I'm only cut and bruised, Mrs Brierson,' she said. 'If I can just have a hot wash . . . oh goodness, my clothes!'

'Exactly; you're in no state to sit behind the desk, my dear, even if I were to allow you to do so, which I most certainly shall not. Look, the hotel's half empty, I'll give you a room and lend you a nightgown so you can get a good night's sleep, and in the morning we'll hope the fog has cleared so you can go back to the flat. Only . . . are you sure I shouldn't call a doctor?'

Lilac laughed and stood up, albeit shakily.

'No, really, I'm just shaken up.' She turned to Joey. 'I'm so sorry, I should have introduced you; Mrs Brierson, this is an old friend of mine, Mr Prescott. Joey, my employer, Mrs Brierson.'

The two shook hands solemnly, then Joey cleared his throat.

'I was comin' to see Lilac, take 'er out for dinner,' he said rather awkwardly. 'But I'd like a room for a night or two, if you can manage that.'

'Aha, a customer! But it isn't fair, Joey, after you've brought me in here and helped me that you should

'. . .' Lilac began, to be shushed at once by her employer.

'Your friend's welcome to stay, dear. Special rates for friends and family, eh? Now Lilac, I'll give you Room seven because it's near the bathroom and you're going to need a good, hot bath. And Mr Prescott, Room twenty-two is free, that's on the third floor and next door to another bathroom.' She paused discreetly. 'Is it just the one night?'

'I'm not sure,' Joey said. 'Lilac might prefer me a bit further off!'

Lilac began to disclaim, but Mrs Brierson took her arm.

'Come along, my dear, you're in no state to stand here arguing! I'll get Eva to bring a tray of supper to your room presently, unless you'd rather put my thick dressing gown on and come down to the kitchen?'

'I'd like that; can Joey . . . Mr Prescott, I mean . . . come down as well?' Lilac asked. 'We've got rather a lot to talk about.'

Mrs Brierson gave Joey a quick, hard glance, then her face softened and she smiled.

'What an excellent idea; Mr Prescott, what do you think?'

'I'm more at 'ome in a kitchen than a posh dining room,' Joey admitted, returning the smile. 'Shall we say in 'alf an hour, give Lilac a chanst to get 'erself smartened up?'

'Half an hour it shall be; I'll warn the chef. Now off with you, Miss Larkin. I'll ring for George, he'll show Mr Prescott to Room twenty-two.'

Joey spent five nights at the hotel, and every spare moment with Lilac. When she was working he amused himself, walking Patch for miles along the docks, taking her on the overhead railway right out to Seaforth to run on the sands. Patch took to him at once, and revelled in the exercise after putting up with the very much shorter walks which were all Lilac could manage. When he wasn't walking the dog he looked round the shops and visited the museums and art galleries, informing Lilac with a grin that he had never known improving one's mind could be so pleasant.

On the second evening he went with her to the hospital and talked to Kitty, who was no longer infectious but very weak and lethargic still. The death of her mother and sister had put her back, there was no doubt of that, but Lilac could see that Joey was good for her. He made her laugh with anecdotes about Patch and his museum-visiting, he taught her how to tie various nautical knots, and he told her she was good company so he intended to visit her again. Having met Lilac's protégée, he then felt it incumbent upon him to buy her puzzle books, jigsaws and other amusements, and to invent games which could be played by someone propped up by pillows and with a short attention span. Kitty pulled a long face when he told her his ship sailed next day.

'Never mind, I'll be back in three or four weeks,' he said comfortably, when she turned her head into the pillow. 'You'll be out of 'ere by then, you can come and walk Patch wiv me – miles, we cover, ole Patchie an' me.'

As for Lilac, she found herself looking forward to her off-duty times with real enthusiasm, when Joey would buy her fish and chips and walk her along the docks, or take her riding the overhead railway so she could show her the big ships and explain about them, or just sit in a café drinking coffee and catching up with each other's lives.

And for the first time, Lilac found herself able to talk about Art without breaking down.

'It's because I've been in the same situation, so I knows 'ow it 'urts,' Joey said wisely, when Lilac commented on the way she felt. 'My Annie was a lovely gel, I wish you could 'ave met 'er, you'd 'ave got on a treat. But she's gorn and now I can look back on the good times and be glad I 'ad them, to remember 'er, see? I've made myself forget the bad times. She didn't want to die, see? She fought against it; them's the times you've gotta forget or you'd go mad.'

She understood. She told him, low-voiced, that she dared not let herself imagine Art's death, the pain was too bad. He nodded.

'Aye; thank God, littl'un, that you didn't 'ave to watch it. You just tell yourself it's over, the bad time, that your feller's at peace.'

She cried, then. Little, heart-tearing sobs, her head buried in his shoulder. And he was good, rocking her in his arms, telling her to cry out the pain, to let the tears bring her ease.

When the time came for him to leave he said he'd call in again, if she'd like him too.

Lilac nodded hard; to her own surprise she was too full to speak. He had been so good, he had helped her in a hundred different ways, yet he was almost a stranger . . . one meeting, fifteen years ago, and he had got closer to her than almost anyone else, save for Art and Nellie.

'He's lost a lover too,' Nellie said, when Lilac told her how she felt about Joey. 'He understands in a way most of us can't, even those of us who've . . . who've known sadness. He's coming back again, I hope?'

Lilac smiled and nodded. 'Yes, in about a month. I wouldn't be able to face Kitty otherwise. She says he reminds her of Johnny Moneymor, the boy who took her into Wales. There's no higher compliment than that!'

Chapter Fifteen

Kitty looked around her, at the bright summer day, at the clear blue sky above, even at the buildings opposite the Isolation Hospital, and thanked her stars that she was coming out of it on her own two feet, even though Lilac was insisting on hiring a taxi cab to get her home.

And not to Kitty's own home, either. She was to go to Lilac's flat as, Kitty supposed ruefully, she no longer had a home, not any more. After her mother's death there had been no one to pay the rent at the house in Paradise Court, and in any case the authorities had announced that it was to be demolished. That left her homeless . . . perhaps it had been that as much as her sudden loss which had brought about the relapse but, thinking about it now as she crossed the pavement on her shaky legs, with Lilac's warm hand on her elbow, Kitty suspected that it had been guilt.

When she had been told that Sary and Betty had both died her first feeling had been of the deepest and most dreadful guilt. Betty had managed before Kitty had come on the scene, that was what she kept thinking. Bet was only a kid and none too bright, but she had somehow kept what was left of their family together, she had even kept their mother alive despite her heavy drinking and the illness which hung over her as a result. Then along came Kitty, capable Kitty, and within a matter of months the kids were in a home and Sary and Betty were dead.

Kitty had stared at the ceiling for two days, ignoring what went on round her, waiting for death to smite her as she surely deserved to be smitten, wracked with grief for poor little Betty, who had tried so hard, who had actually loved the drunken hulk that was Sary Drinkwater.

It had taken Joey to point out the obvious – that they hadn't died of scarlet fever, brought home by Kitty, which was something to be thankful for. She could scarcely blame herself for contracting the disease, since she imagined she had caught it off Marigold, who had been in and out of the Isolation Hospital around the time that Kitty was at her worst. Marigold had recovered – Kitty was very glad of that – and was probably back at work already. Joey pointed out as well that it was because of Kitty's hard work and presence that Sary and Betty had lived as long as they had; it was only in her absence that they had been unable to keep going and had died.

'You stayed, 'orrible though that place was, an' did your best for 'em, when it would 'ave been easier to 'ave give 'em money and scarpered,' he said bluntly. 'You're a good gel, young Kitty, an' don't you forget it!'

It made Kitty feel a good deal better, though she did not blame herself unduly for Sary's death; it had been only a matter of time, she knew that. But Betty – ah, her sister was different. She had *earned* a life, Kitty thought confusedly from the depths of her weakness and guilt, but she had not lived to enjoy what she had earned. And that was wrong, wrong!

Then Joey told her about his Annie, how she'd contracted a horrible disease called meningitis which had killed her and their little baby. He told her of his deep feelings of guilt because he'd been at sea, had only returned in time to watch them die . . . Kitty had held his hand and cried, then, not for herself but for Joey's young wife and her own young sister, who had deserved better but who would not have dreamed of laying blame.

When Joey went the guilt and depression came back for a bit, but Lilac talked to her, restored a sense of perspective and a degree of self-esteem, reminding Kitty that she had other little sisters who would be proud and happy to spend time with her when she was out of hospital, reminding her – as if she needed reminding – that she had a debt to pay to Johnny, as well.

'He was a good pal to you, and though you never meant to leave him in the lurch, it happened,' she reminded Kitty. 'When you're well you'll have to get in touch with him, dear. Think how glad and grateful he'll be that you're alive and well, even if you never get that farm!'

But now Kitty crossed the pavement, her knees wobbling from the unaccustomed exertion, and stood on the kerb, breathing in the salt air with a blissful smile on her face. It was good to be out of doors again, good to be free of the hospital smells, disinfectant, doses, boiled cabbage. She smiled at Lilac, who was stepping into the road to hail a passing cab.

'Here's the cab; hop in, Kitty,' Lilac said cheerfully. 'We'll be home in a jiffy.'

Kitty got into the car and sank thankfully down on the soft leather seat.

'Phew, who'd ha' thought walkin' down a corridor and acrost a pavement could be so tirin'?' she gasped, leaning thankfully back against the cushions. 'I reckon I'll be good for nothin' for a coupla days, Miss.'

'That's all right; Patch will look after you,' Lilac said. 'I told her you were coming home today and she got so excited! She's a remarkably intelligent dog you know.'

'I does know,' Kitty said, contentedly watching the city go by through the side window. 'It's been ever so good of you to keep 'er for me, Miss, I won't forget it.'

'She's been good company; but now I'll have you, as well,' Lilac said. 'Isn't it odd, we exchanged a few remarks in a hat shop goodness knows how many years ago, yet even then I felt that you would be a friend, one day. And here we are, going to share a flat!'

'Only till I can gerrout and work,' Kitty said flatly. 'I've gorra get some money so's I can find Johnny and I can't let you do any more for me, Miss.'

'And if you persist in calling me "Miss" when you know very well my name is Lilac, I won't do anything at all for you,' Lilac said roundly. 'What's the matter, Kit? You called me Lilac in hospital without your tongue falling off!'

'Oh aye, but in there it were different,' Kitty said awkwardly. 'Oh Mi ... Lilac, I mean, look at me bloody legs!'

With boots on, and a short, full skirt, Kitty's thin little legs did indeed look pathetic, like a couple of pipe cleaners. Lilac patted her skinny knee consolingly.

'Yes, legs like a canary but a heart like ... like a lion,' she declared. 'Don't worry yourself, Kitty, you'll be strong and stout again in no time. And in a couple of days you can meet my sister Nell, because they'll be settled in their house by then, and she'll help me to feed you up and get you fit for this work you talk so much about.'

'I gorra work, for me own sake,' Kitty said, looking almost pleadingly up at the fair, smiling face so near her own. 'If I find Johnny an' 'e's awright wi'out me, I's still goin' back to the country, see? There's all sorts I can do there. But I'll need some cash, an' me full strength.'

'Good for you, then,' Lilac said. 'Just don't try to run before you can walk, there's a good girl. I'm going to enjoy taking care of you. Why, as soon as we get home you're going to have a proper dinner – roast beef, roast potatoes, cabbage – and then I'll pop you into bed with a nice cup of hot milk and some arrowroot biscuits and you can sleep off your exertions until morning.'

Kitty smiled, but inside herself she sighed. She did not know how to tell Lilac that she needed, above everything, to have a bit of independence after weeks and weeks of being babied and bullied and bossed by every ward maid and nurse at the hospital. She didn't want coddling, weak though she might be, she wanted the challenge of peeling her own spuds, boiling her own kettle, even shopping for her own milk and biscuits.

I were always better at lookin' after folks than bein' looked after, she thought rebelliously. 'I'll have to tell 'er, sooner or later, or I'll bust.

'Here we are, my dear,' Lilac said as the taxi cab pulled up alongside a large block of flats. 'Let me give you a hand – the driver will bring your bag up.'

Kitty's bag was full of the stuff which Lilac had brought her; nice things, pretty things, useful things. But not chosen by Kitty, nor paid for by her. I'll never stand it, Kitty thought desperately as Lilac insisted on helping her up every one of the twenty-four stairs to her flat. I'll go mad cooped up here, dependent agin, 'stead o' gerrin' out there an' copin' for meself.

Nevertheless, by the time they reached the flat she was glad to sit down and found herself quite unable to eat the excellent meal Lilac had cooked. But the welcome from Patch made up for her sudden weakness, for Patch was beside herself with joy. She tried to climb onto Kitty's lap and was gently pushed off, for Kitty was not used to such displays of affection and was very soon weeping, her arms round the dog's neck, her tears liberally bedewing Patch's thick neck-ruff. And Patch wriggled and whined and gave little yaps and licked and licked, her golden-brown eyes shining with devotion, her every movement proclaiming her love. Kitty found all her annoyance with Lilac for coddling her, all her guilt over Sary's and Betty's death, fading away to more manageable proportions. Patch loved her no matter what – and Patch reminded her more than anything else could have done that there really was another Kitty, another life, waiting out there for when she was well enough to go in search of it. So she would do just as Lilac said, get herself strong and fit once more. And then – ah then, she would find out what had happened about the farm, what had become of Johnny, if it took her the rest of her life!

Kitty had moved into the flat with Lilac at the end of May. It was nearing the end of June before she announced her intention of leaving, and then she did it not to Lilac, but to Nellie.

She had grown fond of Lilac's beloved sister and made a great fuss of little Elizabeth, but in fact she told Nellie her plans because it had struck her that Lilac's loving care was as much for Lilac's sake as it was for Kitty's own, and Nellie confirmed this.

'She lost her fiancé in a tragic accident at sea; they were to be married in a matter of weeks,' Nellie had explained. 'Stuart got the job in Liverpool soon afterwards, but Elizabeth and I couldn't leave the house in Balham until it was sold and then we had to find ourselves another house, organise the move and so on. Oddly enough, I thought I was coming home to take care of her, but Lilac's grown competent and self-reliant and doesn't need me the way she once did. In fact, my dear, it was you she needed – someone to take care of, to cherish. You've done her a great deal of good and if you feel that the time has come to act a little selfishly and move out, perhaps you'll be doing her even more good. There's a young man who seems fond of her . . .'

'Joey Prescott,' Kitty nodded. 'He's ever so kind but I don't know whether he's sweet on Lilac. She gets letters most weeks, he rings the hotel, but 'e 'asn't come up again yet. Joey said somethin' about a trip to New Brighton, but she said it were too soon.'

'New Brighton! That's where . . . she was right, it is too soon,' Nellie said decidedly. 'But Kitty, my dear, where will you go? You are very much stronger, you've got a good colour, you've fleshed up nicely, but jobs are hard to come by and both Lilac and I would hate to see you grow thin and pale again.'

'I said I'd git work first, but I won't, I'll go to the country,' Kitty said at once. 'Johnny an' me, we lost each other in Liverpool, but I know where he'll be, if he's able. It's a long story, but after I ran away from 'ome after I lost them trimmin's . . .'

She told Nellie the story and Nellie, making pastry on Lilac's kitchen table, looked doubtful.

'And you're hopeful that he found the witness

to the will and got the farm? My dear, of course it's possible, but if he had wouldn't he have tried to find you?'

'He would, of course,' Kitty agreed. 'But how? First I were in me mam's house in Paradise Court, the one place I swore I'd never go near no more, then I were in the Isolation 'Ospickle. I reckon he's give me up, but I ain't done for yet. Me and Patch 'ere, we know our way 'ome.'

'Tell Lilac, then,' Nellie advised. 'She'll help you, I know she will.'

Kitty could not explain, not even to Nellie, that she neither needed nor wanted help. In some part of her mind she believed that she would only find what she wanted alone, by her own efforts. So one overcast morning, when Lilac had gone happily off to the hotel, leaving Kitty to do the housework and cook a meal, she packed her bag, wrote her friend a note, and left. She and Patch trotted down the stairs, out of the front door and along the pavement without a single backward glance; their attention was fixed on what lay ahead – the grey ribbon of road which would wind slowly onwards until it reached the place they longed to be.

Footing it wasn't the fun it should have been with just the two of them and no Johnny, but even so, they enjoyed themselves. Once they were clear of the city Patch really perked up. She ran ahead, she loitered, she rushed into meadows and snuffled along river banks. But she kept an eye on Kitty and was at her side in an instant when someone approached.

The first night was spent in a garden shed, the pair of them curled up on a pile of old sacks. Kitty, who had spent the past months under a roof and sleeping between sheets in a proper bed, was surprised at how good it was to find herself a makeshift meal and sleep on sacking. No doubt it would pall after a night or two, but right now, it felt good. On the second day she got a job, of sorts. She passed a farm where they were haymaking and went into the field. Without a word she picked up a pitchfork and joined the line, turning the hay, whilst Patch disappeared and came back after an hour or so with a rabbit hanging limply from her mouth.

The farmer's wife let them share her midday meal and took the rabbit in exchange, she said, for allowing Kitty to sleep in the hayloft. And next morning, early, she invited Kitty in for a bite and asked if she would give a hand with the poultry before going on her way. She had a lot of poultry and wanted the sheds where they roosted cleared through so Kitty cleaned, disinfected, brushed, barrowed . . . and was fed again, and thanked, and sent on her way.

On the seventh day they had barely set out from their latest barn when they heard thunder grumbling and growling in the distance. The Welsh hills, for they were nearing their destination, were lit from time to time by flashes of lightning. But Kitty and Patch plodded on through the downpour, with their hearts set on reaching the farm. They got there just as the storm grumbled off into the distance and a pale and watery sun lit up the scene. Patch and Kitty, by common consent, reached the gate and just stood, staring. There was the house, its tiled roof steaming gently as the sun gilded it with long, golden rays. There was the barn, there were the haystacks, the sheep in the fields, their fleeces steaming too as the sunshine touched them with warmth. And behind, there were the humped shoulders of the Berwyn range, green with new bracken and gold with gorse, and the rowans and birches overhanging the pond, every leaf sparkling with raindrops.

'Ain't it just beautiful, Patch?' Kitty murmured, her hand on the dog's ruff. 'Oh, how'll I dust go up to the door? If that man answers the door ... oh, Patchie, I dussen't!'

But it was as though her body took over, since her hand reached out and swung the gate open, then latched it behind her. The two of them walked up the drive, Patch staying close, seeming to know by instinct that even on this familiar ground, Kitty needed her constant loving presence.

The front door was shut, of course. Country folk didn't use the front door. Kitty and Patch went round the back, seeing the familiar yard, the shippon, the byre.

A man was working in the byre, cleaning out after the day's milking. He was tall and strong, but he wasn't Elwyn Ap Thomas nor the poor half-wit who had worked for him. Kitty couldn't remember seeing him before and once more she hesitated. Johnny had been stringy and gangly, but very strong; was it likely that he would employ another young man to work for him? But it was possible – she had worked hard, perhaps Johnny could not manage alone? If he had the farm, that was, and she would never find out if she didn't move from this spot!

Resolutely, with a hand trembling on Patch's collar, she walked forward. The man came out of the byre, saw them and stopped short. Kitty stopped too, just for a minute. And then she was running, her arms held out, running and running, with her mouth stretching into a huge smile and words babbling from her lips, as wildly and foolishly as the words were babbling from his.

'Johnny! Oh Johnny, Johnny, Johnny! Oh, how I've missed you!'

And Johnny lifted her up and hugged her so hard that her babbling ended in a breathless squeak and then he put her down and hugged Patch and rocked the dog from side to side and called her his old love and his favourite dog. And then he put Patch down and grabbed Kitty again and held her tight, and the raindrops in her hair ran down and wet his checked shirt and she felt safe and comfortable in his arms.

'Oh Kit, I searched and searched, why didn't you come to the lodgings? I were late at the Shamrock but I went back two or three times over the next day or so around six . . . oh Kit, I've been desperate!'

'I left a message with the landlord,' Kitty said against his chest. 'I went back to the café, too. I were wi' me Mam and me sister, they was starvin', Johnny, and . . . oh, so ill and 'elpless. And then I got scarlet fever and they put me in the Isolation 'Ospickle, but I come as soon as I could.'

'Course you did, chuck . . . that bloody landlord though – I arst an' arst if 'e'd seen you . . . I lit out o' here at Christmas an' spent three days searchin'. Never thought to go up to the Court, though, seein' as you was so scared of meetin' your folk.'

'Oh Johnny, if only I'd ha' known! But I couldn't ha' left 'em, they wasn't fit to be left. In fact, I never did leave 'em. They died, Johnny.'

'Through no fault o' yourn, Kitty love,' Johnny said at once. 'That I do know. And ain't Patch fit an' 'ealthy? Oh, it's grand to see the pair of you, grand! Come in the 'ouse, I'll cook you a bite; I'm 'ungry an' all.'

They went into the kitchen. It looked neglected, dust lay thick, but the fire burned up bright and the pantry-cupboard was well stocked. Kitty's fingers itched to get going with a scrubbing brush, a duster, lots of hot soapy water, but it would have looked rude so she sat down and watched as Johnny joyfully fried bacon and eggs and made a pot of tea.

'Now . . . tell me about this place,' Kitty said when they were settled at the table with the food in front of them. 'What 'appened, exactly?'

'Well, I found John James O'Hare, but 'e was 'eadin' for the ferry, to go over to Birken'ead, so I 'ad to follow, acourse. That's why I weren't at the Shamrock by six. In fact, I lorst 'im, 'ad to spend the night prowlin' the area where 'e'd disappeared, but I picked 'im up again next mornin' and managed to 'ave a word. John James O'Hare's a real nice feller, queen. He'd got a week's leave from 'is ship but 'e agreed at once to come to Wrexham wi' me. We caught a bus, an' when we got to the lawyer's, guess what?'

'What?' Kitty said. Stuart had told her that any decent solicitor worth his salt would have had a copy of the will, but agreed that it might take force to shift the Ap Thomases, and also warned that if they had sold the farm on, it could be difficult to oust the new owners without a lengthy legal battle. But she would not have said any of this for the world, not with Johnny sitting opposite her, eyes shining, fair hair on end, proud of his story and longing to surprise her.

'They 'ad a copy of the will all along! If only we'd gone to 'em, Kitty, 'stead o' wastin' our time searchin' for that Jones boy! Still, it come out all right in the end.'

'You mean the Ap Thomases jest moved out?' Kitty said. 'Without a fight, even?'

'Well, it warn't quite so simple as that! But they was tryin' to sell it, see, so our solicitor – Mr Huw Hughes, Mr Hywel's son – said we'd 'ave 'em for fraudulently disposin' of ... I can't 'member the right words, but you know the kind 'o thing. They might not ha' budged for that, e'en so, but then the neighbours came.'

'The neighbours? Mr Dewi and Mrs Bron, you mean?'

'Aye, but not only them, Kit! The people you met in the market, the Morrises, the Evanses, the Llewellyns ... people what was kind to us, but I didn't think would ever *do* anything. They come up the road in a big crowd, wi' me in the middle, an' we walked right into the farmyard an' Mr Huw flung the back door open wide so' they 'ad to listen. An' the minister ... 'e fair thundered at ole Ap Thomas ... they all came. Kind o' shamed the Thomases into goin' ... Elwyn's missus wailed an' wept like a founting, said she'd 'ad no part in it, but it din't matter, they went. An' everyone 'elped me to move back in.'

'And you got the stock back?'

'Oh aye, Mr Huw made ole Elwyn cough up for the beasts. Bought stock at the Christmas market in Corwen ... you'll be pleased wi' them, our Kitty, they're prime! An' ever since, I been workin' as 'ard as I could, and a-prayin' you'd come back. Mrs Bronwen kep' sayin' you'd come, but it were a long time ... 'ere, 'ave some more bacon!'

'When you came to Liverpool, what did you do?' Kitty asked, accepting half-a-dozen rashers of crispy bacon. 'Where did you look?'

'I looked everywhere, then I put advertisements in the papers, wi' a box number, only there waren't no

381

replies. I don't suppose you read the papers much, eh?'

'Not much,' Kitty said, remembering those hungry, desperate days. 'No money to spare, see.'

'Aye, that's true. I stayed three days, then I 'ad to come back or we wouldn't 'ave 'ad a farm, but I were near out of me mind wi' worry. Only I 'ad a feelin' you'd not let me down. And 'ere you are, large as life an' twice as 'andsome!'

'Yes, 'ere I am,' Kitty agreed. 'I were lost without you, Johnny, an' that's the truth. If it 'adn't been for Patch I dunno what I'd ha' done.'

'Like me, you'd ha' soldiered on. Oh Kitty, love, it's blamed good to set eyes on your funny little face!' He leaned across the table, his eyes slowly travelling across her face. 'Ain't you growed pretty!' he said suddenly. 'And ain't you growed tall an' all, come to that! You're a big girl, our Kit.'

'You're a big feller yourself,' Kitty said contentedly. 'Not bad lookin', either.'

He grinned bashfully, then leaned back again and shovelled bacon into his mouth. 'When we split up we was a pair o' kids, but now . . . I reckon we oughter make this partnership official, don't you?'

'Dunno what you mean,' Kitty said suspiciously. 'Don't you trust me, Johnny Moneymor?'

'Course I do, but . . . aw hell, our Kit, you're not a kid and neither am I! If we stay 'ere, together, there'll be talk . . . don't you see what I'm gettin' at?'

'No,' Kitty said bluntly. 'Tell me.'

'We ain't brother an' sister; right?'

'Right. But no one round 'ere thinks we are, does they? We come clean wi' Mal ages ago.'

'That's right. So why don't we mek it official?'

'What the 'ell d'you mean?' Kitty said in an exasperated tone. She could feel her cheeks beginning to grow warm. 'Don't talk in riddles, Johnny.'

'Well, what I means is . . . no, that ain't quite . . . we oughter tie the knot, put our 'eads in the noose . . . dammit, our Kitty, we oughter git married!'

Kitty stared at him across the table. He was so tanned and fit, his hair sun-gilded, his eyes bright and clear – he could not possibly want to marry her, of course, he just wanted to set people straight.

'Git married?' she said faintly. 'You don't want to do that!'

Johnny got up from the table, crashing his chair onto the floor behind him. He came round and lifted her out of her own chair, so roughly that he knocked her knee on the table-edge, causing her to give a squeak of pain. Holding her tightly against his chest he spoke into her hair.

'Kitty, you don't know 'ow bloody mis'ruble I been, nor 'ow worried, nor 'ow pointless it all seemed without you! There weren't no fun in it, not jest for me . . . for two pins I'd ha' chucked it all up and teken to the road again! And I aren't agoin' to work 'ere an' see you go off an' marry some yokel like Eifion, just acos 'e's got more courage than what I 'ave. I – I *needs* you, queen, an' I 'opes you needs me.'

'Well, I does need you,' Kitty said. 'But we ain't in love, are we, Johnny?'

'Dunno. I jest likes you best of anyone.'

'Oh Johnny, that's just 'ow I feels,' Kitty said blissfully. 'I'd love to marry you, if you really want to marry me.'

'That's settled, then,' Johnny said. 'We'll get the Reverend to read the banns an' that. Mrs Bronwen will be pleased; she says ·we's made for each other.'

He stepped back a little from her and when she looked up at him he smiled, the old, dancing, mischievous smile that she loved so well and had missed so much. 'Close your eyes, Kit.'

Obediently, and wondering what was about to happen, Kitty closed her eyes. For a moment nothing whatsoever happened, and then she felt Johnny's lips gently fasten onto hers and they were kissing, and Kitty, who had never kissed anyone, found that she really liked it and could do it just right, or she supposed she must be doing it right since Johnny made a contented little mumble against her mouth and tightened his arms round her, squeezing her so hard that she felt she really ought to protest.

Only somehow, she was too busy – and happy – for a protest to make much sense.

Lilac was eating her breakfast, sitting in the spring sunshine with a cup of coffee and some toast and marmalade, when she heard the post plop through the letterbox.

She wasn't waiting for a letter, particularly, but curiosity drove her up from the table and into the hall. There were three letters, two personal ones, both handwritten, and an official one – a gas bill, she could tell. She returned to her meal, scanning the envelopes. One from Polly – that was nice – and the other was from Kitty. Kitty had written a couple of times in the months since she left, but the letters had been guarded, almost deliberately careful, as though she was keeping something from Lilac. Perhaps now she's going to tell me what it is, Lilac thought hopefully, slitting the envelope open with a buttery knife. She's such a dear little soul, I do want her to be happy, but I can't force her confidence if she's keeping something secret. I ought to go and visit her, her thoughts continued, but somehow I'm always so busy . . . and I don't know that Johnny Moneymor she's in partnership with . . .

She unfolded the letter. It was longer than usual, she saw with approval, and started off in a sprightly fashion.

Dear Lilac,

For a while now, Johnny and I have been talking about getting married. I expect you'll think we're too young, and don't know each other well enough, but when I got back here, Mrs Bronwen Jones, our neighbour from up the valley, said it weren't right us living in the same house, and I guess she knows better than most what's right, she's strong chapel is Mrs Bronwen.

I thought it would be best to do it right away, but you can't – did you know that Lilac? You have to have permission and that, if you isn't twenty-one – I'm sixteen acourse. So Mrs Bronwen said we oughter have a girl live in, and I got young Alwenna Evans from Corwen, she sleeps with me in Mal's big old brass bedstead and she helps with the housework so's Johnny and me can get on with the farm work.

But we can't stand it no longer, Johnny and me. We want it to be just us, just Johnny and Kitty, and Wenna's a nice kid but she don't like the country all that much, she misses living in a town and being with other girls her age. And there's feelings, Lilac, what I can't explain too good, but we both feel them, so we went and explained to the reverend and he agreed that feeling like we do, it were marriage or nothin, so we're

*going to do the ·deed and would like you to come to
the wedding, with your Nellie, your Stuart and your
Elizabeth, of course.*

*I wondered if you'd bring your Joey to the wedding,
Lilac? I'm mortal fond of Joey; everyone seems to like
him. But that's up to you of course. Wouldn't want
you to feel I was interfering.*

*I didn't say nothing before because I were ashamed
of wanting Johnny, I didn't think I ought, since we'd
not known each other for years, like some people do
when they wed. But we talked to the reverend and he
said it were natural, and that the only thing was I were
a bit young, only he said I knew me own mind – which
I does – and better to marry than burn, which sounds
very strange, but it was what he said.*

*Johnny reckons we've waited plenty long enough
– it's nine months since I came home to the farm
– so we won't wait no longer. The date is set for
14th April, so if you come down the day before, Lilac,
that'll be wonderful. You can stay here, all of you –
it's a big old house, lots of spare rooms – and after,
there's a dinner of course and then Eifion's going to
give an eye to the stock and we're having a honeymoon
in Llandudno, just a few days. Please say you'll come,
and please ask Nellie and the others for me, since there
won't be many guests, only local.*

*I hope you aren't cross at us getting wed, Lilac;
you'll always be me best friend, you were so good to
me, but Johnny's different. I want to spend the rest
of me life with him and that's the truth. Reckon I love
him.*

*With kind regards,
Your loving Kitty*

Lilac read the letter through once, then again. She chuckled several times, and then, to her horror, found she was crying. She mopped furiously at her eyes and chided herself; she wasn't losing Kitty, Kitty had never been hers to lose, the girl was clearly deeply in love with this Johnny Moneymor and though she was very young it was better, as the reverend said, to marry than to burn. And besides, working together on the farm as they did, anything other than marriage would be unnatural since they liked one another so well.

I'm twenty-three years old and I'm not getting married, Lilac found herself thinking as she put away her breakfast things and got ready to go round to Nellie's to show her the letter and pass on the wedding invitation. I was in love once, of course, deeply in love, but after I lost Art I simply stopped thinking about marriage.

Joey Prescott's intelligent, reliable face flickered into her mind. Joey wanted to marry again, she knew it, though he didn't talk about it much. They were good friends, she enjoyed his company, looked forward to his visits to the Pool but she never considered him a . . . a suitor. Kitty had only met him that one week, of course, and she'd liked him well enough to ask him to her wedding. But then she clearly thought that Joey meant more to her, Lilac, than he did. He was just a friend, just someone she could talk to, just a feller who came around every couple of months to take her out, have a laugh, talk over old times.

Lilac glanced out of the window, then chose her scarlet coat ·with the matching tam-o'-shanter. It was chilly, the March wind was whipping at the bare branches of the trees, so she might as well wrap up warm. She was off today since it was a Saturday –

Mrs Brierson usually tried to see that Lilac's weekends were free – so she could catch a tram up to Nellie's place and they could talk over the wedding there, with a whole day in front of them.

Lilac stuffed the letter into her pocket and picked up her scarlet wool bag, slinging it over one shoulder. A wedding! She hadn't been to many but the ones she had attended had always been fun. She would enjoy meeting Johnny and seeing dear little Kitty settling down happily . . . a honeymoon in Llandudno, that sounded nice, she must remember to ask Kitty when she replied to her letter whether she was having bridesmaids and if she would like Elizabeth to hand her a lucky horseshoe: the child had been disappointed once . . .

All the way to Nellie's house in Halkyn Avenue Lilac kept finding her annoying eyes filling up. It was the wind, she decided, only on the tram she could scarcely blame the wind. She remembered Joey's last visit, when he had invited her down to London, saying they'd make a weekend of it; how she had repulsed him, telling him that whilst she enjoyed his company she didn't intend to give people cause to gossip. He had been hurt, he had gone very quiet . . . but Joey was so good-natured, he'd been his usual happy self next day.

That had been five weeks ago though; he'd not been up to the Pool since. He'll come, he's probably waiting for better weather, Lilac told herself. After all, his ship's bound to come into the docks sooner or later, and then he'll come hammering on my door, with his big white grin and his steady gaze and his warm, safe hands.

He usually came once a month, regular as clock-work. She would just mention it to Nellie, see what her sister thought. As for asking him to Kitty's wedding, though, she couldn't possibly do that – that really would give him ideas!

When she reached the house Nellie was spring-cleaning. She had her hair swathed in a blue and white striped duster and a large paintbrush in one hand. She was, she explained, whiting the kitchen ceiling.

'Where's Stu?' Lilac asked suspiciously. 'And Elizabeth?'

'They've gone to Elizabeth's dance-class,' Nellie said serenely, climbing back on her stepladder. 'Put the kettle on, love, and we'll have a nice cup of tea when I've finished here.'

'How long will you be?' Lilac asked. She never did her own decorating, she used the man who kept the hotel in trim, but now, watching Nellie wielding the big, floppy brush on the ceiling, she itched to have a go. 'Is there anything I can do to help?'

'Would you like to have a go at keying up the surface of the old paint on the back door?' Nellie said diffident-ly. 'There's a bit of sandpaper . . . you just sort of make circles, then when I put the fresh paint on it'll stick.'

'Oh. Right,' Lilac said. 'Had I better wrap something round my hair, our Nell? You aren't half free with that whitewash!' She indicated the line of tiny white specks which had just appeared ·on the draining board.

Nellie laughed.

'Did I do that? Yes, perhaps you'd better cover up a bit. There's another duster in the drawer to the right of the sink, and you can borrow me old overall, it's hanging behind the door.'

Shortly, properly dressed and equipped with sand-paper to rub with and a feather duster to get rid of the debris, Lilac began on the door. She rubbed away industriously, whilst above her Nellie sloshed around with the whitewash, occasionally apologising as the spots flew through the air. By the time the kettle boiled both girls were absorbed, but Lilac left off for long enough to make the tea and then Nellie climbed reluctantly down from her stepladder and the two of them settled themselves at the kitchen table, Nellie sweeping off her duster and shaking her hair down as she did so.

'Whew, it's hot up by the ceiling,' she remarked. 'It don't half make your arm ache an' all.'

'And it makes you pale,' Lilac said with a giggle. 'Your face is white as a sheet, Nellie Gallagher!'

'I feel more scarlet than . . . oh, am I covered in whitewash?' Nellie said, standing up to peer at her reflection in the small mirror beside the sink. 'Gracious, me face is covered, I'd better fetch a flannel . . . only I'm going to have that cuppa first, I'm really dry.'

She sat down again and picked up her cup. Lilac waited until her sister had slaked her thirst, then fished Kitty's letter out of her pocket and spread it out on the table.

'Heard from Kitty this morning,' she said. 'She and Johnny are getting married, they want us all to go to the wedding. Have a read.'

'Getting married? Those children?' Nellie picked up the first page and scanned the neat lines of writing. 'Good gracious, so they are!'

'We'll go, won't we?' Lilac said, when Nellie lay the pages down again. 'I'm so fond of Kit, and you're the same. I'd hate to miss her big day.'

'I love a wedding,' Nellie agreed. 'Yes, we'd be happy to go. I daresay Stu will book us in at a hotel, rather than putting on poor Kitty when she's preparing for her wedding. What about Joey, queen? D'you think he'll come?'

Lilac picked up her cup and left her chair, walking over to the teapot where it stood on the draining board.

'I'm just pouring meself another cup,' she said. 'Joey? Oh, I wouldn't think he'd be interested, would you? He only met Kitty three or four times, when she was in hospital. Besides, he can't pick and choose where he goes, he has to fit his life ashore round his sailings.'

'Heard from him lately?' Nellie asked casually as Lilac, with her fresh cup of tea, returned to the table. 'It seems a while since he was in the Pool.'

'No, he's not written for a while. Nor visited, come to that,' Lilac said equally casually. 'I wonder if he's got as berth aboard a different vessel, one that doesn't touch the north-west, though I should have thought he'd write and let me ·know.'

'Oh, perhaps he's busy,' Nellie said. 'Want a biscuit, chuck? There's a bag of ginger nuts just inside the pantry door. Get 'em out whilst you're on your feet, would you?'

Lilac fetched the biscuits and sat down again with a thump. She opened the bag and fished out two biscuits, took a bite out of one and handed the other to Nellie.

'Lovely, my favourite,' she mumbled. 'Nell . . . is Joey cross with me?'

'Oh, Lilac love, you sound just like a little girl; I do love you! You come straight out with things sometimes . . . it's awful nice, that.'

Lilac put her biscuit down.

'He is cross, isn't he? Oh Nell, it's been nearly six

weeks . . . I miss him, really I do, but he wanted me to go down to London . . .'

The story poured out; how Joey had seemed to Lilac to be getting a bit possessive, had actually suggested she go down to London with him for a weekend. How she'd told him she didn't want people gossiping about her, how he'd gone a bit quiet, then seemed his usual sunny self. Only he'd not written since, nor visited, and she was worried, she wouldn't hurt him for the world . . .

'Have you written and told him so?' Nellie asked. 'But of course, you'll have done that.'

'No I haven't,' Lilac said at once. 'It was his turn to write to me, I couldn't write just out of the blue, it wasn't as if I'd said anything nasty, I only said what you'd have said . . . that I couldn't spend a weekend with him and cause talk.'

Nellie looked across the table at Lilac and raised her eyebrows, but she said nothing.

'Oh, Nell, don't look at me like that! You'd never . . . you wouldn't want me to risk my reputation . . . I mean think what people would say . . .'

The silence stretched. Lilac picked nervously at a patch of whitewash on the table.

'Nell? What's the matter?'

'Lilac, love, if Stu had asked me . . . whatever he'd asked me I'd have said yes, because I loved him so much. And I believe you're very fond of Joey.'

'Oh . . . fond! That's a bit different, surely, from wanting to chuck me cap over the windmill for him?'

'Perhaps it is; I'm not sure. Tell you what, flower, suppose I said if you had a choice, to – well, to sleep with Joey or never see him again, what would you choose?'

Lilac stared at the older girl.

392

'*Sleep* with him? I can't believe me ears, our Nell! Surely you wouldn't expect me to behave like that – you've brought me up to behave meself!'

'I hope I brought you up to be generous and loving – and to know your own heart as well as your own mind,' Nellie said gently. 'What would you do, Lilac love?'

Lilac got up from the table and carried her cup over to the sink. Without turning to face Nellie she said indistinctly, 'I dunno; it ain't a fair question, our Nell! I were going to marry ·Art, remember. I don't reckon Art 'ud think much of it if I . . . if Joey an' me . . .'

Tears were near. Nellie got up as well and took her cup to the sink, then put her arms round Lilac and gave her a hug.

'Perhaps it weren't a fair question, queen. But it made you think, and that's all I was trying to do. Now let's get on with this decoratin', or I shan't have made the dinner by the time Stu and the babe get home!'

Chapter Sixteen

Lilac stayed with the Gallaghers all day. She played with Elizabeth, helped Nellie to decorate the kitchen, walked round the garden with Stuart and admired his display of purple, white and gold crocuses, the snow-drops under the apple tree and the spears of daffodils and narcissi pushing up through the dark earth.

No one mentioned Joey, though the wedding was much discussed. Elizabeth, Nellie announced, would wear a primrose-coloured silk dress – it was bound to be warmer in a month – under her rust-coloured coat, just in case it wasn't. Nellie herself would have a new dress, to be worn under her own best coat – beech-leaf green – with a new hat, colour to be decided.

'What'll you wear, love?' Nellie asked her young sister, but Lilac just shrugged and said she'd prob-ably buy something new since it wasn't often she got invited to a wedding.

Nellie smiled and said if her help was needed there was nothing she liked better than a shopping trip and Lilac said with more enthusiasm than she'd yet shown that she would definitely get Nellie to go with her, because two heads were better than one when it came to choosing pretty clothes.

'I'll run you home, queen,' Stuart said when they'd had their tea and Lilac stood up to go. 'We'll all come, get some air.'

Nellie, however, declined the treat.

'You know I'd like to come,' she said with feigned

regret. 'But the place is such a mess and tomorrow's Sunday, I'd like to get it cleaned up before then. So I'll stay now, then we can go out for a ride in the country tomorrow afternoon.'

'Oh ... thanks Nellie, but I shan't be coming round tomorrow. I've ... I've been invited out ... just to dinner ... by one of the guests.'

'Well, that's nice,' Stuart said genially, shooting a quick, rather worried look at his wife. 'Umm, anyone we know?'

'No, I don't think ... it's a Mr Albert Evans, he's very nice, not married or anything,' Lilac said quickly. Her cheeks, Nellie noticed, had gone very pink. 'I've been out with him once or twice before, he comes over to Liverpool regularly, every few weeks. He's got a – a small business in Sir Thomas Street and another one in Manchester. Sorry I forgot to mention it before but it completely slipped my mind. I'll see you all next Saturday, if not before.'

'Right, love,' Nellie said cheerfully, kissing her sister's hot cheek. 'Have a lovely time with your friend.'

'He's not really my *friend*, just an acquaintance,' Lilac mumbled. 'You'll probably have far more fun driving out into the country, only I did promise . . .'

'It doesn't matter; I love you to have fun,' Nellie declared. She gave Lilac a friendly push. 'Go on, queen, Stu might let you get the car out of the garage and drive it as far as the gate if you hurry.'

Stuart, however, popped back a moment later, ostensibly to fetch a torch to light Lilac down the path. He grabbed one off the sideboard, then turned to Nellie.

'What's all this, then? I thought you said she was really fond of . . .'

395

'Shush! Talk later,' hissed Nellie. 'Go *on*, Stu, little Elizabeth has ears like a donkey. Drive carefully, I'll see you soon.'

Stuart, with a doubtful backward glance, left. Nellie waited until she heard the car cough into life, until she heard its engine disappearing down the road, then she took off her apron and walked through into the front hall.

The telephone stood on a small, round table, with a chair conveniently near. Nellie hesitated. Ever since Joey had come calling six weeks ago, in some distress, he had been ringing her whenever he was in port for a progress report. It was painfully clear that he was head over heels in love with Lilac, but he was very aware that Lilac was still telling herself she had buried her desire and ability to love a man in the grave with Art.

'I'm not gettin' any younger, Nellie,' Joey had said plaintively last time he had rung. 'I don't say I mind waitin', I'd wait for years, like, but 'ow do I know that at the end of the wait she won't turn to someone else? Someone not so patient wiv 'er?'

'Art nearly lost her through being impatient and trying to force her hand,' Nellie had said worriedly. 'Me and Stu are so fond of you both, Joey, that it would break our hearts if the same thing happened. Look, you're right to keep away from her, it's the only way to make her look at the situation. I believe she'll begin to miss you a bit, then she'll miss you badly, and by the time you come calling again, she'll see her feelings for what they are.'

'What are they?' Joey had asked. 'Damned if I know, gel!'

'They're stronger than she believes,' Nellie had replied. 'Strong enough to have her admitting how she feels when it's tell or lose you. Oh Joey, be patient, I'm sure it'll work out all right in the end.'

But now, standing by the telephone and gnawing her lower lip, Nellie wondered, for the first time, whether she was doing Joey a real disservice by advising him to stay away. She didn't believe Albert Evans existed, Lilac was a real little chatterbox as far as admirers were concerned, but she did believe that, if pushed, Lilac might jump in the wrong direction.

However, it was a week since Joey had last rung and if her calculations were right he should be back in London right now, in his lodging house. The house wasn't on the telephone, but she could ring the shipping office, see if she could get a message to him. On the other hand, sending a message seemed rather extreme. She could drop a line, ask him to telephone her.

She was moving away from the telephone when it rang, sharply, making her jump. She grabbed the receiver from its rest and held it to her ear. 'Liverpool 22212, Mrs Gallagher speaking.'

'Hello, Nell; it's me, Joey. Are you awright to talk?'

'Joey! I was standing right by the telephone, wondering how to get in touch with you . . . no, it's all right, there's nothing wrong, in fact I think it's rather good news. Kitty Drinkwater's getting married, and we've all been invited to the wedding – you as well. Lilac's worrying about you, Joey, and getting awful het-up. The wedding's on the fifteenth of April – any chance?'

'How important is it?' Joey's voice had lit with hope, Nellie could almost see the smile on his face. 'If I come, I mean.'

'I believe if you come to the wedding, you'll be able to suggest that the two of you set a date,' Nellie said.

'Her first reaction, I think, was that Kitty was much too young, which she is, of course. And I think it occurred to her that she was going to miss a lot by her determination not to marry . . . she's been very quiet all day.'

'An' you mentioned me?'

Nellie chuckled.

'I did. Joey, can you come to the wedding? It'll be in Corwen, North Wales.'

'I'll make a point of it,' Joey said. 'I'll come, no matter what 'appens, though I'm due a few days arahnd then. Tell you what, I'll drop Kitty a line but I won't say nothin' officially to you.'

'Lilac doesn't know you and I are in touch,' Nellie said. 'Better keep it that way.'

'Yes, acourse. Right, then. See you on the fifteenth!'

Nellie replaced the receiver slowly and walked back into the kitchen. Suppose she was wrong? Suppose the worst possible thing would be for Lilac to arrive at the wedding and find Joey there too? But it was no use worrying, she'd done it now. They would just have to wait and see.

Kitty woke and rolled over. Outside the window the sun shone, sending long golden beams through a gap in the curtains. Beside her, Patch stirred too, then stretched, sat up, and vigorously scratched her ear.

'I 'opes as 'ow you ain't got fleas, old gal,' Kitty said absently, tugging at the ruff round Patch's neck. 'We can't give you a bath today – we're gonna be too busy gettin' wed!'

The girl from Corwen, Alwenna, had not shared her bed, not last night. She had gone home, to prepare for the wedding. Kitty had told dear Mrs Bronwen that she wanted to spend her last night as a Drinkwater in her own bed, in her own room, and Mrs Bronwen, having given her a long steady look, had agreed it seemed sensible.

'After all, girl, if you'd ha' wanted to do wrong what need of a double bed when there's the whole farm at your disposal?' she said, with her usual practicality. 'I'll see to it that there's no talk. Not that they'd dare say a word against you, not wi' me an' mine to contend with!'

So Kitty rubbed Patch's ears absent-mindedly and was grateful for the sunshine and imagined Lilac, Nellie and the others in the hotel on the main street, waking to the country sounds of cocks crowing and cattle lowing instead of to the blast of ships' sirens and the constant noise of traffic.

In the next room she could hear Johnny whistling as he dressed and sloshed water about. She sat up and prepared to swing her legs out of bed, wondering whose turn it was to milk the cows but deciding she would get up anyway. There were bound to be a hundred tasks which needed their attention and the wedding was at two this afternoon. Then there was the wedding breakfast, and after that she and Johnny were going off for their short honeymoon in Llandudno.

'We'll wed in the afternoon so we can get the work done, then we can enjoy ourselves,' Johnny had said. 'Mrs Martha's bringin' the grub over in 'er wagon at about noon an' your posh friends will be arrivin' soon after. I like that Joey, mind. A feller after me own 'eart.'

'Yes, Joey's grand, and the others ain't no posher'n what we are,' Kitty had said, looking contentedly round the glowing farm kitchen. 'Oh Johnny, didn't

Joey love the farm? I can't wait for Lilac an' Nell to see this place, as well. I loves it, I does!'

Joey had arrived the day before yesterday. He had brought with him two presents, a green parrot which talked and a hand-embroidered tablecloth of such beauty and intricacy that even Johnny had been impressed. He had insisted that Joey stay with them rather than in town, once it had been revealed that Lilac didn't actually know Joey was coming.

'It's a surprise,' Joey said, looking rather hunted. 'I wanted to tell 'er, but Nellie said a surprise would be best.'

'Nellie knows Lilac better'n she knows 'erself,' Kitty had observed. 'Don't worry, Joey, it'll be awright.'

But right now the Day had arrived at last, their Day, and here was she, dreaming on the edge of the bed instead of getting up and getting going on the thousand and one things she had to do.

Kitty padded across the room and pulled back the curtains. Sunshine flooded in and through the open window wafted the familiar smells of a well-kept farm: hay, beasts; the tang of stables and byres came to her nostrils and over and above everything else the fresh country smell of meadow, brook and tree.

'You up, Kit? Don't forget, I'm milkin' this mornin', but you're cookin' us a decent breakfast. Joey's downstairs, tryin' to get the parrot to stop swearin' an' carryin' on.'

Johnny's voice came hollowly through the door. Kitty padded over and opened it. She grinned at him, then stood on tiptoe to give him a quick kiss.

'Mornin', Johnny! Glad Joey's makin' 'imself at 'ome. So this is it, eh?'

'That's right. Want me to put the kettle on as I go through? Then you can wash in 'ot water.'

'No, it's all right, I'll have a cat's lick an' a promise now, then fettle meself up good before the others arrive. I wonder what me sisters will make of this place, eh Johnny? I reckon they'll love it.'

'They can come an' stay next summer,' Johnny said magnanimously. 'Give us an 'and wi' the 'ay 'arvest. Do 'em good to 'ave fresh country air.'

'It would. I wish we could 'ave 'em 'ere all the time, but it ain't on; still, we're doin' okay. One of these days . . .'

'One of these days we'll 'ave kids of us own,' Johnny said practically. 'Your sisters will make their own way, chuck, same as you an' me.' He took her shoulders in his hands and swayed her towards him. 'Gi's a kiss, pretty Kitty.'

Kitty complied and for a moment they stood there, she in her worn cotton nightgown and Johnny in his homespun shirt, corduroys and socks, totally relaxed and at ease in each other's embrace. Then Johnny sighed, moved his mouth from hers, gave her one last squeeze and let her go.

'Best get on,' he advised. 'Us'll be sharin' the same bed in the 'otel tonight an' the big brass bedstead when we come 'ome, Kitty – we'll 'ave the rest of our lives for kissin' and cuddlin'.'

'Yes, I know. It's goin' to be grand, ain't it, Johnny?'

He nodded, smiling down at her.

'Aye, grand. Don't forget me breakfast, I's starvin' already and I ain't started the work yet!'

Lilac had spent the night in her hotel room alone, with the Gallaghers next door. She had dreamed about weddings, about loss, about sadness, and had woken with a heavy heart and dark-rimmed eyes. She had borrowed Nellie's scented talcum and tried to disguise the shadows, but without very much success – and what did it matter, anyway? She was only going to see country folk, no one she knew.

They were taken to church in the trap, Johnny having already left whilst Kitty, splendidly apparelled, waited nervously in the front room with Mr Dewi Jones, who was going to give her away. By the time they arrived the church was packed, but a pew had been reserved for them by a tall young man in a dark suit who saw them coming out of the corner of his eye and stood courteously to one side to let them slide past him to reach their seats.

Lilac went to pass him and stopped short.

'Joey! Oh Joey, it's so nice to see you, I wondered why you'd not been near us . . . are you all right?'

The surprise was total – she had refused to pass on the invitation in case he got ideas, but probably Kitty had written to him separately. And seeing him, dark-suited, handsome, smiling down at her as though they had never had a cross word – and they hadn't, really come to think – gladness was her principal emotion. She smiled up at him and took his hand in hers, and when he would have pulled it away she wouldn't let him . . . it was so very nice to see him again, such a marvellous surprise . . . she sneaked a glance at Nellie, next to her, but Nellie was finding her place in the Order of Service and showing little Elizabeth how to find the hymns and taking no notice of Lilac at all.

People were rustling behind her, turning. Lilac, too, turned. She could see Kitty's small sisters in the pew with some farmers from further up the valley and smiled at the four little blonde girls, giggling together

402

over an open hymn book, though she doubted whether the two smaller ones could actually read.

There was a commotion in the porch, then Kitty came floating up the aisle on Mr Jones's arm. She looked slender and beautiful, and a good deal older than her sixteen years. Her dress was white satin with lacy panels and a small, upstanding collar, and someone had arranged her hair with a coronet of flowers around it.

Lilac smiled at her and Kitty smiled back; a blissful smile, Lilac thought enviously. And then Kitty's eyes moved ahead once more and Lilac saw the expression in them soften and change as they fell on her bridegroom, his yellow hair slicked down, his dark suit immaculate, and his head turning, his eyes anxiously searching for Kitty.

Joey squeezed her hand. She looked up at him, enquiringly, and Joey leaned down towards her.

'Doesn't Kit look a picture? You can tell she's goin' to be so 'appy.'

Lilac nodded. She felt pretty happy herself, right now, but that was a transitory thing; Kitty's happiness, she suspected, would be a way of life, a permanency. Love was like that, you might be miserable on top, over some small or large thing, but you had the happiness beneath all right, just waiting to break through. When you had someone of your own, that was.

The bride and groom were at the altar now, about to make their vows. Kitty looked so different, Lilac thought. Slim and regal in her lace and satin even though the gown had been lent by Mrs Ada Morris from up the valley, with her bright, red-brown hair coiled up into a knot on her head and a wreath of tiny white flowers holding her veil in place, she would have graced any wedding in the land. No one would have recognised the starved little waif with her bare feet and filthy, oversized shirt in this beautiful, healthy young woman who kept glancing adoringly up into her groom's countenance. Even if she'd not known before, the wedding would have made it plain to Lilac that Kitty and Johnny were deeply in love.

'With this ring I thee wed; with my body I thee worship; and with all my worldly goods I thee endow.'

Johnny's voice, rich and deep and shorn of its usual accent for the occasion gave the words their full meaning and more. Lilac glanced at Joey and he was looking down at her, with such an expression in his eyes! She knew, at that moment, that Nellie had been right; if you loved a man you didn't worry about your reputation or the rights and wrongs of it, you just wanted to belong to him, to make him happy. And suddenly she knew that she loved Joey and wanted him as Kitty wanted Johnny. But how could she be so shallow, so fickle? She had loved and wanted Art, his death might never have come about had he not come home to be with her for a couple of days . . . how could she even think about loving someone else?

And then, as though the thought had triggered her memory, she found herself remembering in detail her dream of last night. Earlier it had just been a vague, confused recollection but now it all became clear.

She had been walking along the Scottie in the dream, with Art strolling beside her, he a lad again, she a lass. They were talking idly, of this and that, enjoying the sunny day and each other's company. And then, down the road towards them, came a young sailor with a rolling gait and a wickedly twinkling eye.

'Art . . . that's Joey Prescott, you know, the feller I told you about,' the young Lilac said excitedly. 'Oh, 'e's a nice feller – 'e rescued me, you know, when I run away from the Culler. I've gorra speak to 'im!'

She ran forwards and as she ran she grew up, so that by the time she reached Joey and held out her arms to him she was Lilac now, not Lilac then. And beside her was Art, grown up too, and he was smiling as well, smiling at Joey.

'Nice to meet you, Joey,' he said. 'You'll take care of 'er for me, won't you? She's a rare 'andful, but I wouldn't want 'er no different.'

The two men clasped hands and Art turned to her and she saw, in his dear, familiar face, the truth, just for one marvellous moment.

Art had always wanted the best for her and he wanted it still, wherever he was. He was no longer able to take care of her himself so he was handing the job on and doing it willingly.

She had turned to Art, wanting to thank him for her freedom, but instead she woke up, and outside her window the birds were singing and it was Kitty's wedding day and the dream had gone, leaving her bereft.

But now she had remembered, and all her stupid doubts and fears meant nothing. She felt as gay as the blackbird carolling away on the chestnut tree by the porch and as light as a puff of thistledown on a breezy day.

It was all right! She was doing the right thing, she knew she was. Art would be with her always, but not as a reproach for happiness or a spy for good behaviour. He would be, as he had always been, her friend.

The wedding march swelled out; Lilac looked at the faces of the young couple coming down the aisle, wreathed in smiles, and she felt hot tears rise to her eyes. But even as she mopped them carefully away with her small, scented handkerchief, even as she smiled mistily up at Joey and clutched his hand, she knew they were the right sort of tears: she was weeping, not for what might have been, but for joy.

'You awright, sweet'eart? Not upset 'cos I'm 'ere, when you didn't expect to see me?'

It was said in a whisper, but Lilac heard every word.

'Upset? Oh no, dearest Joey, I'm so happy and relieved, I can't tell you. And Joey?'

'What, Lilac?'

'I'm coming back with you when you go – to London, I mean. And I'm not going to let you leave me ever again.'

Joey squeezed her hand and then carried her fingers to his lips and kissed them.

'With my body, I thee honour,' he whispered. 'I love you, Lilac Larkin!'

A Selected List of Fiction Available from Mandarin

While every effort is made to keep prices low, it is sometimes necessary to increase prices at short notice. Mandarin Paperbacks reserves the right to show new retail prices on covers which may differ from those previously advertised in the text or elsewhere.

The prices shown below were correct at the time of going to press.

☐	7493 1045 6	**Body and Soul**	Marcelle Bernstein	£4.9
☐	7493 0494 4	**The Hour of the Angel**	Alexandra Connor	£3.9
☐	7493 0595 9	**Mask of Fortune**	Alexandra Connor	£3.9
☐	7493 1107 X	**The Well of Dreams**	Alexandra Connor	£3.9
☐	7493 0554 1	**People of this Parish**	Rosemary Ellerbeck	£4.9
☐	7493 0779 X	**The Future is Ours**	Margaret Graham	£4.9
☐	7493 0561 4	**A Fragment of Time**	Margaret Graham	£4.9
☐	7493 0500 2	**A Measure of Peace**	Margaret Graham	£4.9
☐	7493 1069 3	**Only the Wind is Free**	Margaret Graham	£4.9
☐	7493 0385 9	**The Barleyfield**	Sue Sully	£3.9
☐	7493 1066 9	**House of Birds**	Elizabeth Tettmar	£4.9

All these books are available at your bookshop or newsagent, or can be ordered direct from the address below. Just tick the titles you want and fill in the form below.

Cash Sales Department, PO Box 5, Rushden, Northants NN10 6YX.
Fax: 0933 410321 : Phone 0933 410511.

Please send cheque, payable to 'Reed Book Services Ltd.', or postal order for purchase price quoted and allow the following for postage and packing:

£1.00 for the first book, 50p for the second; **FREE POSTAGE AND PACKING FOR THREE BOOKS OR MORE PER ORDER.**

NAME (Block letters) ....

ADDRESS ....

....

☐ I enclose my remittance for ....

☐ I wish to pay by Access/Visa Card Number

Expiry Date

Signature ....

Please quote our reference: MAND